I0743951

DarkRise

THE ORIGIN PROPHECY

Copyright © 2022 M. A. Phipps & Rebecca Jaycox

WWW.BOOKISHDEN.COM

All rights reserved. No part of this publication may be reproduced, distributed, or transmitted in any form or by any means, including photocopying, recording, or other electronic or mechanical methods, without the prior written permission of the publisher, except in the case of brief quotations embodied in critical reviews and certain other noncommercial uses permitted by copyright law.

This book is a work of fiction. Names, characters, places, and incidents are either products of the author's imagination or are used fictitiously. Any resemblance to actual persons, living, dead or otherwise, events, or locales is entirely coincidental.

Cover and Interior design by We Got You Covered Book Design
WWW.WEGOTYOUCOVEREDBOOKDESIGN.COM

SHIRE-HILL PUBLICATIONS
UNITED KINGDOM

ISBN: 978-1-914483-13-4

THE ORIGIN PROPHECY

DarkRise

M.A. PHIPPS
REBECCA JAYCOX

SHIRE-HILL
PUBLICATIONS

light academies

The Serapeum
EGYPT
Gabriel

Mount Nebo
JORDAN
Remiel

Petra
JORDAN
Serathiel

Mount Sinai
EGYPT
Raphael

Sidon
LEBANON
Amenadiel

Mount Zion
ISRAEL
Uriel

Qumran
ISRAEL
Azrael

dark academies

Megiddo
ISRAEL
Lucifer

The Tower of Babel
IRAQ
Asmodeus

Sodom
ISRAEL
Leviathan

Gomorrah
ISRAEL
Belphegor

Ashkelon
ISRAEL
Beelzebub

Tyre
LEBANON
Mammon

Machaerus
JORDAN
Abaddon

*"The mind is its own place, and in itself can make
a Heaven of Hell, a Hell of Heaven."*

JOHN MILTON, *PARADISE LOST*

prologue

LUCIFER ONLY FELT RAGE like this once before. His eyes flash to his companion, her severe, stunning beauty still managing to undue him millennia later. The last time such all-consuming fury enveloped him was when Gabriel chose the Creator over him. When she chose servitude over love. When she rejected their relationship as if she had committed some crime, soiled herself by loving him, the Morningstar. While he burned the world to free himself of his golden shackles, she pledged herself to eternal bondage.

Although he hated her choice, it was hers to make. And if Lucifer valued anything, it was free will. The ability to choose his own fate. But this…

Anger spots his vision, and he blinks it away. By hiding Luna—his daughter, *their* daughter—from him, Gabriel stole his choice. She stole his free will. She stole the chance to know his only child.

Glaring, he watches her carefully walk around the stones of Adam's Calendar in South Africa. The site is more than seventy-five thousand years old, and power shivers around the old stones jutting from the ground, tingling his skin, but he doesn't feel what he's searching for. He can't hear his daughter's blood call to him. Such a sweet sound snatched away too soon. Pain pierces his heart.

Frustration pulling her lush mouth into a frown, Gabriel meets his eyes. "I can't feel anything. If they hid her, I don't think it's here."

Lucifer sneers. "You didn't know your own daughter was with you for months. I don't know if you could feel her, even if she were here," he scoffs, his voice a blade meant to cut.

The Archangel flinches, and he grins, happy his barb found its mark.

"I explained why I didn't feel her," she pushes out between clenched teeth.

Lucifer lifts a shoulder. "So you say, but as you've proven with your deception, I can't trust a word out of that beautiful lying mouth. And they call *me* the Father of Lies. I suppose that means you birthed them."

Gabriel snarls at him. "I told you I didn't know—you just refuse to listen."

His ire rises in his chest like a tidal wave, crashing into her. "Yes, just like you explained why you chose to hide my only child from me. Tell me, Messenger, did you think I'd let a prophecy touch one hair on her golden head? Did you believe I wouldn't protect her? You didn't even realize she'd been released from the prison you kept her in. Some mother you are. Did you plan to keep her in stasis for all eternity? Her potential guttering out like a flame in the wind?"

Her wings snap open, snowy white and large, and she resembles the bird of prey she is. "You could protect her?" Gabriel spits at him. "Like you protected her in Alexandria? You shine brightly, Morningstar, but you can't take on the Council. Even you're not that powerful."

His own wings release, a silky ebony lending menace to his tall form. "Perhaps if I'd known who she was earlier, I could've saved her. I had to come to grips with the fact that the bleeding creature in my arms was my daughter right before I was surrounded."

Derisive laughter fills the space between them. "You can protect her from the Creator? You think I hid her to be cruel… but she was all I had left of you and me. Something perfect and beautiful we created." Gabriel blinks, her orange-rimmed eyes shiny. Although he loathes to admit it, her tears still manage to hurt him. "And I couldn't take a chance with her. You might think me a selfish monster, but I loved her—*love* her—and I didn't know how to avoid the prophecy's fate for her. I didn't want her to become the Gray who tried to destroy the world… or the one fated to kill the Destroyer. Perhaps at the cost of her life. I just wanted her to live."

Confusion ripples through him. "What do you mean, the one fated to kill the Destroyer? I've never heard that part of the prophecy before." He eyes Gabriel, suspicion forming in his mind, which is only confirmed when she shifts her head, presenting her profile, a guilty flush spreading across her cheekbones. "They indeed named you wrongly, Messenger. What lies have you been spinning to us all these years?"

Her jaw clenches at his words, and when her gaze clashes with his, fury sparks there, matching his own. "We were divided when I discovered I was with child. I was alone, desperate, and after the prophecy was revealed to me, I knew I had to protect the child at all costs. She was not going to be the instrument of the prophecy. I wouldn't allow it."

Lucifer's heart clenches at her words, but a dark bitterness seeps into his soul. "You were never alone—you've never been alone. All you had to do was whisper my name, and I would have come to you."

One perfect dark brow arches. Doubt and disbelief spreads across Gabriel's face. "How can I believe that? You never forgave me for not choosing you—us. You avoid being in the same room with me unless you're forced, and yet, I'm supposed to believe that if I had called to you in my time of need, right after breaking your heart, you would have given up all your hurt and anger and answered me?" Her own laugh is bitter.

"If you would have changed your mind and returned to me, yes, I would have welcomed you with open arms. We would have plotted together to conceal our child…Luna."

"So, if I prostrated myself at your feet, begged for your forgiveness, and renounced the Creator and my beliefs, then you would've welcomed me back? That's what you really mean," Gabriel says, dark eyes hard like polished gemstones. "You need to be right. How noble of you, Morningstar."

"You're twisting my words," Lucifer growls. "Just like your precious Creator likes to twist the notions of love and duty."

Gabriel bares her teeth at him, wings flaring, and then she sags in on herself, drooping like a wilted flower. "This is pointless," she says, tears glistening once more. "Going over the past is pointless. We have to commit to the now. To saving our daughter. All our brethren will be hunting us once they realize the truth. I'm sure they're hunting us right now."

Lucifer's eyes dart away from her face, unable to watch her cry. Many of the angels and Fallen think of the Messenger as an ice queen, immovable and unemotional. But he knows better. The wall of ice she forms around herself is a facade she maintains in order to serve the Creator. In order to turn her back on Lucifer and hide their daughter. Rage glows inside him again, but he pushes it away. Gabriel is right, spitting past hurts at each other like hissing cats will not help Luna.

"They might not be hunting us now, but they will and soon. For all their faults, they're not stupid. They'll figure out our connection to Luna sooner or later, especially if they think hard enough about the past," he says, turning to face her once more.

A flush stains her face at his words, and she nods. He used to make her flush all over, her pale skin lighting up at his touch. Despite the fact that she's with him, she's so far away they might as well be on different continents. Their choices and actions created a gulf between them as wide as the Grand Canyon. But for Luna, they will have to find a way to bridge it.

A deep sigh escapes his chest. Lucifer feels weary down to his bones, the task ahead perhaps the most difficult he has ever faced. The most important. "You're right," he says. "We have to commit to the now and to rescuing our daughter. She's the most important thing on this Earth, and we can't allow her to be punished for being a product of love."

Gabriel's gaze snags his, and her eyes soften as they explore his face. "We'll get our daughter back, no matter the consequences or to what end."

Lucifer nods, determination lending him strength. Then he launches into the sky, and Gabriel follows.

one

CALEB

THE FORBIDDING CITADEL SITS on top of a large outcropping of rock at the base of steep mountains, appearing as ruins to the mortal eye. Alexander once conquered the adjacent city in what is now Afghanistan and has since overtaken the fortress, which was built by the last ruler of the Hotak dynasty—long after Alexander's time. Hundreds of years later, it still feels like a military fortress, lacking the modern amenities that I'm used to, like a toilet. Apparently, angels don't need to shit, but Nephilim still do. At least there's an underground spring we pump water from so bathing is doable. And Afghanistan isn't exactly a vacation spot. Neither was Iraq, but I felt more at ease at Babel than I do here. Not that humans pose much of a threat to me, but in this place, I'm not sure who is friend or foe.

I glare across the dais of the makeshift throne room where Alexander holds court. Four months, four goddamn months, and no sign of Luna. Sure, I'm allied with a powerful Gray angel, but I'm no closer to rescuing my Goldilocks. And Alexander keeps making excuses as to why we haven't come up with a solid plan to storm the proverbial castle and save her. I know we'll have to face both the Light and the Dark forces, but for Goldilocks, I'd take on the Creator.

My eyes narrow as I observe my grandfather's latest potential ally. She reminds me a bit of Ishtar in her regal bearing, but her skin is a dark umber, and her curly hair cascades down her back in black ringlets. Power radiates from her. More power than a Nephilim, even a first generation. I rack my brain, searching for her image in my mind, but I come up blank. I thought I knew all the angels and Fallen—the important ones anyway—but she is an enigma.

"Lilith," Alexander says, solving that mystery, and I gaze at the exiled Archdemon in shock.

The Council of Archangels and Archdemons in charge of the academies dismissed Lilith for reasons unknown—well, unknown by me. I'm sure all the Fallen know the story. They never speak of her—Adam's first wife. I mean, in the back of my mind, I realize she's been out in the world. But what the hell has she been doing? I'm kinda disturbed I never thought about it before. She's a Fallen with tons of power and probably pissed off at her former family. I guess Lucifer keeps tabs on her—or Gabriel—but the thought still makes a shiver of unease crawl up my spine.

Her full, scarlet lips twist into a coy smile. "Well, well, well,

Alexander. Empires have risen and fallen since we last met. Freedom suits you."

Alexander leans forward, resting his chin on his fist, his mismatched eyes roving over Lilith's petite, curvy frame. He finally lands on her face, and they stare at each other as the seconds tick away. They seem to be in their own personal battle for domination or for ferreting out secrets. They break the moment at the exact same time, as if some understanding has passed between them or some truce.

"Exile suits you," my grandfather shoots back with a sly smile. "Freedom has made you positively bloom, my beauty."

"I'm too old for flattery, and you're too young to know how to wield words to pander to my ego," Lilith says with a diamond-bright smile sharp enough to cut glass.

I cough to cover a laugh, but of course, with her supernatural senses, she hears me as does my grandfather. He glares while she wears a look of genuine amusement. I throw up my hands in surrender and apology.

"Who is this handsome young man?" Lilith purrs and goddammit if I don't blush at her suggestive tone, like she wants to use me as her boy toy. She'd break me.

Alexander huffs a laugh. "My grandson and the orchestrator of my escape," he says. "Caleb, meet the infamous Lilith."

"Should I bow?" I ask, unable to control my mouth. Ishtar enters the room, and I see her grin out of the corner of my eye. I inwardly cringe as I look at Lilith, avoiding my grandfather altogether. To my relief, her amusement remains, thank the Morningstar.

"You should crawl," the ex-Archdemon says sweetly. "But I'd hate to see such a pretty little Nephilim brought so low. And you *did* help Alexander escape, so that's worth quite a lot."

This time I can't stop my resentful glare as I focus on my grandfather. "Me and Luna," I say, and he stiffens in anger.

"Luna?" Lilith questions, arching a delicate brow.

I see Ishtar shaking her head behind Lilith, but I'm through with being cautious. "The other Gray, the real person who freed Alexander. Ishtar and I just helped. And now, we need to help her."

"Another Gray?" Lilith says, but her surprise doesn't seem genuine, though she has a look of shock painted on her face with as much skill as her eyeliner. I've dated around enough to recognize when women know how to wield an eye pencil like a weapon.

Rage simmers in Alexander's eyes, but he banks it. "Yes, another Gray. She'll make a great ally to us, Lilith. Under my tutelage, she'll help me finish what I started."

"If we ever rescue her from whatever prison she's in," I say bitterly.

"Caleb," my grandfather says, his voice deceptively soft, and the hair rises on the back of my neck in warning.

Grandfather or not, blood or not, I have no business pissing off Alexander the Great, terrifying badass. And he has no problem with punishing me, I'm certain, although I've managed to avoid it so far. I cut my gaze to Ishtar, and I can see the same anger reflected in her dark eyes. I'm sure my teacher is itching to get a whip and beat me with it for not keeping my mouth shut. I can almost feel the sting of the lash on my back. Wouldn't be the first time she's punished me for impertinence. But I'm tired of the bullshit, and I have a powerful Dark in front of me. I want my grandfather to explain to a potential ally why he's left his savior hanging out to dry.

"He's lovesick, Alexander," Ishtar says smoothly, stepping up to stand beside Lilith and giving her a knowing smile. The word *love* strikes me like a slap to the face. I've never told a girl I loved her before. The word is both disconcerting and freeing at the same time. I've never felt the way I do about Luna. "He can't help but be impatient."

My grandfather snorts. "Yes, I suppose he is. As I've told you before, Caleb, all in good time. I can't rescue Luna with so few allies. I'm outnumbered, but with the great Lilith on my side, we grow closer to freeing her." Alexander focuses on Lilith once more, eyebrow raised in question.

"You're too humble, Alexander. You don't need another Gray. You and the goddess of love and war are more than capable of inflicting damage. Look how well she used my information about your locale." Lilith inclines her head to Ishtar, who gives a shallow bow in response. Huh, well, that's how my teacher knew where Grandfather was hidden. "But that's not to say I don't want in on the fun. I have my own score to settle."

"While I do appreciate your attempt at flattery, the girl is vital to our mission, although gathering followers is more important than anything right now," Alexander says, waving a hand in dismissal of my Goldilocks's plight. I grit my teeth so hard my jaw aches. "The Council will have her locked somewhere hidden, much like they did me. When I rescue her, I want to kill as many of them as I can. I am through with games. This time I won't fail. The world will be mine."

"I admire your confidence, Alexander, but this Gray, this Luna, where does her lineage lie? Surely, you've questioned it. She's someone's dirty little secret," Lilith says and I frown. Luna isn't anyone's "dirty" anything, but the ex-Archdemon has a point. Who are Luna's parents?

When I thought Luna was just a Nephilim, it wasn't a total shock she didn't know who her parents were. Don't get me wrong, I thought it was shitty they abandoned her, but look at my pops. Nephilim being irresponsible dicks isn't exactly uncommon. But Goldilocks is an angel. And I know leaving her at an orphanage like she's the mistake of some shamed teenage heiress is no accident. This was very deliberate. What I can't figure out is why her parents were stupid enough to let her stay with the mortals. Her power was always bound to come out. Luna carries enormous guilt around, punishing herself for accidents she had zero control over, which her piece-of-shit parents are one hundred percent responsible for.

There are also Nephilim—and angels—who can scent out other bloodlines like hounds on the hunt. It's a rare gift but it exists. It's not a super popular gift, either, as my father hates it when people track his trail of sperm deposits across the world. Did I mention my dad is a bastard?

The Council will sniff out her bloodline soon enough. Then all hell really will break loose.

Alexander shrugs, indifferent. "Her family clearly abandoned her and deserve whatever punishment our brethren deem appropriate. I have little respect for parents who refuse to claim their get."

Lilith inclines her head and I mutter, "You must really love dear, old Dad."

Alexander turns to me, a vicious smile on his face. "Your father will be brought to heel soon enough, Caleb. His embarrassing womanizing and callous disregard for our blood will stop."

A genuine smile curves my lips despite my anger at the lack of action where Luna is concerned. "Couldn't happen to a nicer guy," I say and Ishtar chuckles.

"I'm sure you'll remind him it was his son who freed you, not your heir." Lilith's dark eyes shine with malice. She gifts me with another man-eating grin. "At least one of your line bred true."

I square my shoulders. "Yeah, I came through for the win. As did Luna," I say to my grandfather, and his face hardens until he resembles one of those marble statues the Greeks loved to carve of him.

"Don't test my gratitude, Grandson. I told you I would fetch Luna and I shall. To doubt my word is to call me a liar, an oath breaker. Is that what you accuse me of?" The quiet menace in his tone kicks my heart rate up until my pulse pounds in my ear.

"No, sir," I say, keeping my voice steady with effort and my head bent in submission to the warrior. This is a man who killed his way across a continent, and I know that, I do, but I'm so pissed about Luna that I keep forgetting when to keep my mouth shut. I'm no good to Luna maimed and out of commission.

A chilly silence blankets the room before Ishtar speaks again. "Alexander, Caleb is not only lovesick but loyal, as he was to finding and freeing you. His loyalty leads him astray in this moment, but it is still an admirable quality." My gaze flicks up to meet the Mesopotamian goddess's, and the warning blazing from her eyes is white hot.

I feel my grandfather's glare drill holes into my skin, and I resist my lizard brain telling me to run away screaming from the large predator waiting to rip me to shreds.

"Loyalty is important to me, Grandson, and I suppose I cannot fault you for your loyalty to your beautiful lover. I, too, had a lover once who was very dear to me, but I do not want you to push me again on this matter. Luna will join us when the time is right, you have my word," Alexander says, and I raise my head, meeting his eyes, which have thawed slightly.

"Yes, Grandfather," I murmur, and I wonder who this lover was, although I'm sure Gramps banged his way through the ancient world. "I apologize for my insolence."

Lilith clears her throat, drawing our attention. "While I mine allies in the Dark ranks, I'll see if there is any news of your Luna. I doubt the secret of another Gray can be kept for long."

Hope slowly fills me when Alexander stomps on it. "That is much appreciated, Lilith, but gathering allies is our first priority."

The cast-out Archdemon offers a noncommittal smile, and bitter anger grips me once more.

One thing is for certain: I can't wait around any longer for Alexander to get off his lofty ass and save Goldilocks. Wherever she is, it's not a five-star resort, and I'm sure the Archangels and Archdemons are torturing her. Bile rises up in my throat, and I feel sick as I imagine all the ways those ancient assholes could hurt my Luna. And while I don't have Alexander's or Ishtar's connections, there is one person who might help. I mean, I fully expect him to beat the shit out of me for helping Alexander, but he's a straight up badass.

It's time to go see Hammurabi.

two

LUNA

THE TRANSPARENT BARRIER BENEATH my fingertips is somehow both warm and cold, the glasslike substance a perfect representation of this bizarre in-between I find myself in. On the other side of the curved wall—my cage taking the form of a large egg, in which I begrudgingly play the part of the yoke—a white sea of nothingness stretches outward, the cloud-like blanket of air and mist as infinite and unending as my imprisonment.

No matter how many days pass—assuming they pass at all—this strange world never changes. Day is night, and night is day, and time has lost all meaning to me. How long has it been since I set Alexander free from his tomb? Since I learned the truth, not only about my parents, but about who I am?

About *what* I am.

My fingernails drum out a staccato rhythm on the barrier, keeping in perfect tempo with the slow metronome of my heart as I unfurl my wings out behind me. *Tap, tap, tap.* Fully extended, my wingtips touch the opposite wall, the silver feathers brushing against the glass in a way that makes me hyperaware of how claustrophobic this cell is. With less than ten square feet of space to exist and stretch my wings, I'm like a caged bird, and the urge to fly burns under my skin—a desperate itch to move and flap these new extensions of my body. Until I can, I'm not sure I'll be able to accept my true nature... regardless of the tangible proof of it attached to my back.

A shudder sweeps up my spine as I press my hand flat to the glass and then push away with a withering sigh. As I lower my arm, my gaze catches on the scar on my palm—the evidence of my role in Alexander's release a permanent mark on my skin, tainting me. Although the flesh has long since stitched back together, a gold line remains, as if the curse of the blood sacrifice mixed with my angel blood has resulted in some sort of magical Kintsugi. But there is nothing beautiful about this scar. Only the devastating and inescapable reminder of my foolish decisions.

Closing my eyes, I breathe in through my nose, drawing my wings back into my flesh just as I have hundreds of times before to pass the time in this place. I'm sure for an angel who's had centuries or longer of practice, this process is painless and easy. As natural as breathing. But for me, it's slow and agonizing as the feathers curl inward—perhaps because they've been confined for so long—sliding into the new slits in my skin above my shoulder blades, which seal over once the feathers vanish, leaving the flesh there unblemished—at least, as far as I can tell by touch. I don't enjoy this pain, but it gives me a much-needed release, as if everything I feel is bottling up inside me to near breaking point, and the pain is the only way to ease that pressure. To bleed out some of the poison filling me to the brim. It's also all I have—my only companion in the endless monotony of what's bound to be eternal confinement. Pain and the memories, which I am defenseless against as they rise again to consume me.

Despite the fact that he abandoned me to this fate, I'm struck by an overwhelming pity for Alexander now that I'm on the other side of the captivity he endured. In the grand scheme of eternity, I've only been stuck in this prison for a short time while he watched centuries and then millennia roll by in the darkness, alone. What memories was he forced to confront in the shadows?

What memories have yet to surface to torment me?

Gabriel's face flashes across my closed lids, and I grimace, biting back an onslaught of tears. Mixed emotions flood my chest, and it's all I can do not to laugh, or cry, or scream, or berate myself for my idiocy. How much of what I felt in her presence was because she was an Archangel and how much because she is my mother? Did she know who I was when Alaric brought me to the Serapeum? Did she recognize me at all? Or was I nothing but a stranger to her, just as she was to me?

And then there's my father. Lucifer. I still have difficulty wrapping my head around that revelation, but his voice in my ear when we met outside Alexander's tomb was as clear as his words were when he called me his daughter. Even if he hadn't said it aloud, I think I would've known from the song that raged in my heart the moment his citrine-rimmed eyes locked on mine. The blood that binds us knew who he was, and it told me without a single word he was family.

Another thought drifts to the front of my mind, one I've been battling with for nearly as long as I've been confined here. I don't know much about our world or what it means to be an angel—or hell, even a Nephilim—but I could sense that connection with Lucifer in my heart as clearly as I feel the air in my lungs. But I never once felt that connection with Gabriel. Her blood didn't sing to mine the way Lucifer's did, and yet, I know she's my mother. The Archangels and Archdemons—*the Council,* I correct myself, remembering how Alaric referred to them—stated plainly that her blood was the key to unlocking Alexander's tomb, which means I couldn't have set him free unless we were genetically related. Unless we were of the same ancestral line.

How else could I have liberated him unless she's my mother? I suppose I could be her granddaughter, but as far as I'm aware, Gabriel doesn't have any known children, which makes the likelihood of that possibility slim.

No, she's my mother, I tell myself. *She has to be.*

Still, doubt prickles my senses as this line of thought joins the flurry of others spiraling through my head, the cacophony of *hows* and *whys* bombarding me, never giving me a moment's rest—much like how I felt when Alexander's voice haunted my mind for all those weeks at school. It feels as if my brain is being dragged over hot coals, and my skull aches with the burden of every unanswered question.

Since the truth of my lineage was forced out into the open, I find myself dancing closer to the brink of madness than ever before, lured to that edge by the agonizing need to understand what I witnessed that day under the Serapeum—the almost tender exchange between the Archangel and Archdemon I now recognize as my mother and father.

For all her warnings about me and Caleb, was Gabriel forsaking the very laws the Lights and Darks have lived by since the Fall to be with Lucifer? A forbidden affair, like my forbidden friendship with Caleb? I might not know the Archangel well, but our interactions always left me with the impression she's far too pious to even consider breaking laws viewed as sacred by our kind. And she is one of the Faithful, loyal—even more so than her Light brethren—to the Creator.

So, where does her…relationship, whatever it may be… with Lucifer fit into the timeline between the Great Battle and now? I struggle to imagine them being able to hide such an illicit affair from the Council, especially one that resulted in a child, but the only other conclusion I keep reaching can't be possible…can it?

That their affair isn't recent at all, but from a time long before the divide was erected.

I rub a hand over my eyes and blow out a faltering breath, my sanity buckling under the monumental weight of that thought. The divide has been around since the Fall, so if Gabriel and Lucifer were together before then—if my conception didn't occur nearly two decades ago, like I previously thought, but back before the angels were separated by war—then that would make me several hundred thousand years old. Older even than Alexander, Alaric, and all my teachers at the Serapeum.

I go still at that realization, then quickly push it away, unable to face that notion at the moment or the inevitable identity crisis that would surely follow if I dared to look at it too closely. I shake my head. No, that can't be the case. I'm freaking out over nothing, surely. Angels and demons might look young, but they still age normally from birth until they reach the appearance of someone in their late twenties or early thirties. Their adulthood is eternal, not their youth, so clearly, I'm not like Gabriel or the others who have walked this earth since before the dawn of man. I'm still physically aging, and I can trace every year of my life back to when I was just five years old. So, there's just no way I've been around since the Fall. Angel or not, I know for a fact I'm only seventeen and not a single year older.

A groan rips through me as I once again find myself back at the beginning of a long line of questions that have been gnawing at me since I first woke up in this place. I try to shove them back, but there's one thought that lingers—that never leaves me alone and only sinks its claws deeper with every moment I spend caged. Despite my unrelenting uncertainty, despite not really understanding the full scale of what led to my imprisonment or what my future holds, nothing about my situation torments me as much as the constant sting of Caleb's abandonment. That's an ache I can't seem to shake no matter how many seconds pass in this timeless realm, perhaps because it isn't just abandonment I feel, but a deep, festering sense of loss. Loss of the first and only real friend I ever had—not an adult who felt responsible for me but a friend, someone on my level, who understood me in a way no one else could.

Loss of what I had allowed myself to dare to hope was something more.

I choke back a sob, refusing to give in to the tears blurring the edges of my vision or the lump swelling in my throat, which threatens to suffocate me. I need a distraction. I *need* the pain.

I need to forget, even if only for a moment.

To distance myself from the memory of Caleb's face, his voice, his mouth on mine, I force my wings out again, giving every fiber of my being over to the bone-crunching pain. As my lips part on a sigh, feeling the weight on my chest lift a little, I pace the cramped space of my cell just as I have countless times throughout the last however many months I've spent in this hell.

A chuckle escapes me as I pivot and glance at my reflection in the translucent barrier, the eyes of my mirror image glinting. Despite the changes I've noticed to my body since Alexander freed my wings—like the unexpected appearance of my aura, the silver threads dancing across my skin finally revealed—one thing has remained the same, that's carried over from my mortal life into the immortal. I see it behind my gaze now more than ever.

The broken mind that no amount of angel blood can ever fix.

No, this isn't hell, I realize as I drag the pewter feathers back underneath my aching skin, the cuts in my back flaming and raw, before pushing them out once again. This is the landscape of my festering madness.

And here I thought I knew what it was like to feel crazy.

"Hello, Luna."

A startled breath presses against the sides of my throat, and my wings fold around me like a security blanket as I whip around and slam my back into the curved wall, wincing at the searing pain radiating across the sore spots just below my shoulders. On the other side of the glass, a man with deep brown skin steps out of the mist, appraising me with severe, hooded eyes. A golden aura quivers along his skin, almost blinding in its intensity.

"You..." The word is heavy on my tongue. How long has it been since I last spoke aloud? "I recognize you," I whisper.

My memory flashes back to that day in Alexandria when Lucifer held me in his arms and faced off against twelve angry Archangels and Archdemons who all wanted to see my head on a spike. This man...he was one of them.

He was there.

The Archangel dips into a bow, his smile mocking. "My

name is Uriel, and I am the Archangel charged with overseeing the Light academy at Mount Zion."

My wings bristle, but I push them aside and behind me then force myself to take a step forward, presenting the illusion of courage, even though I feel anything but brave. "What do you want with me?"

A quiet laugh breaches the silence between us. "Come now, child. You are no fool. You know precisely why you're here."

"Because I opened Alexander's tomb?" I retort, hoping he won't hear the wobble in my voice. "Or because I'm a Gray?"

I remember something Caleb once said to me, about the Faithful and Fallen fearing those who straddle the line. Even if I hadn't set Alexander free, would they have imprisoned me anyway, just because I was born of both sides? Something in Uriel's stern expression says yes.

My hands curl into trembling fists. "You know what? Why don't you go ahead and do what you should've done to Alexander and just kill me already? If you're so afraid of what I am, then surely, you're better off with me gone."

Although I'm bluffing, there's a part of me—a large part, I'm terrified to realize—that means every word. I know what it's like to be confined against my will, and when Alaric took me away from the hospital, I vowed I would never allow myself to be locked up again. I'd rather be dead than spend the rest of my life in a cage, especially now that my life is endless and escape from this hell is only a dream.

"That…is not an option," Uriel says.

"Why?" Hysteria creeps into my tone as I spread my arms out, gesturing to the glass wall around me. "How is *this* any better?"

The Archangel makes a tsking sound with his tongue. "You are so new to the world, so young and naive. There is much you do not know, much you do not understand." His shadowed eyes sweep over the silver feathers adorning my wings, which vibrate at the feel of his piercing gaze and then draw close to my body again as if to shield me. Although I've gained some semblance of control over their movements, they mostly seem to have a mind of their own.

I open my mouth to challenge him further but silence devours my unspoken words. He's right. I am naive. And gullible. After all, I fell for the empty promises that resulted in my imprisonment. Alexander's promise to teach me control. Caleb's promise to take me to Babel. Faces I once trusted fill my thoughts when all I want is to wipe them away from my memory. To forget them all.

To abandon the pain.

My wings sag, the pinions brushing the cold floor of my cell. "What do you want with me?" I ask again, defeated.

Uriel clamps his hands behind his waist—the snowy white wings marking him as a Light Archangel tucked out of sight— and fixes me with the full force of his gaze. His brown eyes flash with intimidation.

"To talk," he answers simply.

"About?"

Despite the menacing way his aura ripples against his skin, I don't think he intends to hurt me. What else can he do to me that this long stretch of isolation hasn't already done?

"Let's start with the headmistress of the Serapeum," he suggests. "How did the Messenger hide you from us? Was she involved with your plan to free the Conqueror?"

Conqueror? I suddenly remember Gabriel saying that same word through the haze of pain that seized me that day under the Serapeum. *He must be referring to Alexander.*

I narrow my eyes on Uriel's face, his expression stony. The lack of emotion in his gaze unnerves me almost as much as the mention of Gabriel, the mere passing thought of her like lead in my stomach. Her face forms in my head again, but I shove it away. I don't want to talk about her. I don't even want to think about her right now. I haven't fully processed how I feel about what's happened to me—about the likelihood of her being my mother—and the last thing I want is for the Council to somehow weaponize those feelings against me.

My lips pinch at the corners. "I have nothing to say to you about *her.*"

"Interesting." Uriel raises a hand and traces a circle around his mouth with his thumb and forefinger before pressing his fingertips together at the point of his chin. "She said the very same thing about you…right before she disappeared."

His lips peel back into a predatory grin when my eyes spring wide in surprise.

Disappeared? The way he said that word twists my gut, making me fear he means something else altogether.

The last time I saw Gabriel, in the underground corridor leading to Alexander's tomb, she was bleeding out on the stone floor from a wound that would've killed any human. Hell, it probably would've killed a Nephilim. But Gabriel is neither. She's an angel, and the Morningstar assured me she would be fine. She survived. I know she did.

She had to.

My mind races, wandering down an even darker path. What if, after the Archangels and Archdemons imprisoned me, they went back for Gabriel and punished her for her part in creating another Gray? What if all this anger I've been holding onto and building during these numberless days…what if it goes unexpressed and I never see her again?

What if I lose my mother after only just finding out who she is?

A sharp, biting laugh echoes around me, like a crack of thunder in the silence. "Have I piqued your interest yet?" Uriel asks. "You must have so many questions. Questions I may be able to provide insight to…if you answer mine first."

My feathers twitch at his words. I do have questions, but I'm not sure he'd be able to answer them. Or if it's even smart to ask them at all. I might be naive but I'm not dumb enough to believe the Archangel won't lie or manipulate any conversation we have just to get me to talk. If Alaric didn't trust the Council, I shouldn't either.

Uriel takes a step toward me, and I shrink away from his imposing figure despite the thick glass separating us, letting out a stifled moan when my back once again hits the smooth surface of the wall behind me. I couldn't put any more distance between us even if I wanted to.

My heart hammers against my ribcage, my breaths coming short. Although I'm terrified of Uriel, the fear consuming me is basic and human, animalistic, even—the same genuine terror someone might experience if they were being hunted or stalked by a serial killer. I take comfort in that for the simple reason I don't seem to feel the same innate desire to please him as I did in Gabriel's presence. Whatever allegiance I felt with her hasn't passed on to the other Archangels, which means I still hold some power in this situation, even if it doesn't seem like it.

Even if I *feel* powerless.

But how to use it? I don't know, and it's impossible to think with the Archangel glaring at me. So, I do the only thing I can think of. I clamp my lips shut, refusing to speak. If answers are what the Council wants from me so badly, they'll be the thing I deprive them of until I know how to turn those answers to my advantage.

Or, at least, until I know whatever I say won't carry dire consequences.

Uriel lets out a sigh, disappointment dragging his thick

brows into a vee. "Clearly, these past four months have done little to convince you of your reality here. Perhaps I will return in a few years and see how you feel about conversing with me then. Or perhaps a century in isolation will be enough to loosen your tongue."

Panic rips through me, tearing through my wavering composure like paper. Four *months*? I've been here that long already?

The same length of time I spent at the Serapeum.

The irony of that realization would make me laugh if I wasn't on the verge of a complete mental break. The months I've spent here have felt like a lifetime, and yet, I can't imagine years or even a century trapped in this place. How did Alexander survive thousands of years of this torture with his mind intact? I'm not strong enough for that. Any longer and I have little doubt I will tumble over the edge into oblivion.

Shock grips my tongue, even as I urge myself to speak—to ignore any misgivings I have and just give the Archangel what he wants. But my terror is paralyzing, and I can't find the words.

Mistaking my silence for rebellion, Uriel turns and storms off into the mist with a derisive snort, the white blanket of fog shifting around his legs in billowing wafts that make it appear as if the fog is rising like a mouth opening to swallow him whole. As the berth between us widens and he begins to fade into the barren landscape, my self-preservation instincts kick in, unlocking my lips, and I shout out into the abyss.

"Wait!"

I can't do it. I can't stand the idea of being abandoned again—of being left in this place for a second longer, even if the alternative is prostrating myself before the Council and telling Uriel whatever it is he wants to know. What information could I really give them that they don't already possess anyway? Maybe if I cooperate, they'll realize I'm not a threat and let me go.

That…or put me out of my misery.

The mist falls away, and the Archangel shifts to face me again, a sly smile warping the defined contours of his mouth. "Are you ready to answer my questions?"

I nod despite myself. *Just answer his questions and he might let you go.* I repeat this thought like a chant, though there isn't a single part of me that believes it. Still, I cling to that hope like a lifeline. After all, I'm nothing like Alexander. I might've been tricked into letting him go, but I never tried to conquer anything. We might both be Grays, but that's where the similarities end. I don't deserve this. I might be dangerous but I'm not a danger to our world—not intentionally. I don't want to burn anything. I just want to be free.

We aren't the same.

"Where is Alexander?" Uriel asks.

I blink at him in confusion. "I don't—" An incredulous laugh slips out, interrupting my words, and I shake my head, eyes wide as I gape at the Archangel in disbelief. At his disgruntled look, I clear my throat before posing a counter question, once again gesturing to the glass egg around me. "How am I supposed to know that?"

A glower darkens Uriel's face. "Gabriel said he was speaking to you for weeks before his escape, and you were the one who set him free, were you not? It's not beyond the realm of reason to assume you would know where the Conqueror is or, at least, where he intended to flee."

I recoil again at the mention of my mother, at knowing she talked about me to the Council. That she told them about Alexander but treated me like I was crazy when I went to her for help about the strange voice I was hearing. "I'm sorry, did you fail to notice that he left me behind?" I hiss back, unable to keep the sharp edge from my tone.

Uriel scoffs. "As did your friend, the Dark transfer from Babel. Caleb, was it?"

My jaw goes slack at his words. How does he know about Caleb? Alexander fled with him and Ishtar before the Council arrived at the open tomb. At the scene of my crime. The crime for which I'm being punished. It didn't even occur to me until now that they might be hunting him, too, or that he might be on their radar. Does this mean Caleb is in danger?

Where is he right now?

My heart buckles in my chest, and suddenly, the anger and heartbreak that consume me whenever I think of him are displaced by an overriding worry. Caleb left me here. I should *hate* him. And yet—

Uriel chuckles once under his breath, as if he's aware of my inner turmoil. "Ah, yes, the Messenger told us all about the boy when we questioned her before her unfortunate disappearance. She pleaded your case quite passionately and said it was the Dark transfer who had convinced you to unleash Alexander."

That's a lie! I try to scream, but the growing fury rocking my body makes it impossible to push the protest from my lips. Gabriel saw us both under the school that day but pinned the full weight of blame on Caleb without any evidence that he was the instigator. I could've been the one leading the charge but because she believed me to be a Light—one of her own kind— and never approved of our friendship, it's no wonder she would automatically blame him. Hell, she was trying to warn me away from him when I was still at the Serapeum. She's been trying to paint him as the villain and me as the unsuspecting victim from the beginning.

Isn't he, though? the voice of doubt taunts me. *He lied to you and then left you to rot in this cage.*

No, I bite back. *He told me the truth. He told me about Alexander, and I chose to help him because we trusted each other. Because we were friends.*

And because of that, regardless of the deep wound in my heart—regardless of the lingering sense of betrayal eating away at my sanity every second I spend here—I have to believe he wouldn't have left me on purpose. Not unless he had no other choice.

Because that hope, however faint and eroded, is all I have left to hold onto.

I bite my lip when Uriel tilts his head, his eyes crawling over my face with keen examination. He's looking for a reaction—a slip in my features that will tell him something I refuse to say with words. But…how much am I really willing to reveal to the Council?

What is the price for my cooperation?

Swallowing, I cast my eyes on the floor so they don't expose my pain to the angel. "I have nothing to say about him, either," I mutter.

Uriel offers a noncommittal grunt, but I can sense his impatience bleeding through. "Then what of the Morningstar? Will you refuse to speak of him, too?"

My chest tightens. Does Uriel know the truth about Lucifer? Does he know the Morningstar is my father, or was that another one of Gabriel's well-guarded secrets?

Slowly, I lift my gaze to the Archangel's. "I don't know anything about Lucifer. That day at the Serapeum…that was the first time we met."

Uriel's unblinking stare burns invisible scorch marks into my skin. "And yet, he defended you almost to the point of losing his wings. It's very curious."

I steel myself, trying my best to hide the increasing tremor in my voice. "I don't know anything," I say again. "Haven't you heard? I'm just an ignorant orphan. I didn't even know angels existed a year ago." Then, with more force, I add, "Maybe you should've done a better job questioning Gabriel. I guarantee she knows a lot more than I do."

Uriel juts out his lower jaw then lets out a harsh, barking laugh. "You are quite amusing, aren't you?" He walks slowly back and forth in front of my cage now, and with his wings out of sight, he looks almost human. "I've given you no reason to trust me, I know this. But remember, you are not the one we're after, Luna. The sooner you help us understand the chain of events that led to Alexander's release, the sooner you can go free. Isn't that what you want?"

Just answer his questions and he might let you go, I repeat to myself, but this time, my panic is dulled, and I only feel repulsed by that thought. I can't bring myself to do it—to be the inflicter of such a betrayal, even against someone who betrayed me first. The guilt would eat me alive and the madness would pick at what remains of my bones.

Besides, common sense tells me there's no way the Council would ever really let me go, especially with Alexander on the loose. Especially if my fellow Gray is as dangerous as I'm beginning to suspect and it's my fault he's walking free. Even if unleashing him wasn't enough reason to imprison me, then the Council's fear of those who aren't easily defined by the divide would be. My existence as a Gray will always make me a threat.

No, I'm never going free, and by talking, all I would be doing is sentencing yet another person to the Council's wrath.

Still, I can't ignore how tempted I am by his words. After seventeen years of never fitting in, of never being able to go anywhere without my troubled past following in pursuit… freedom is all I want. A chance to escape everything and finally start over.

Like I was supposed to do with Caleb.

Squashing that thought before it makes me do something I regret, I force a scowl onto my face, directing it at Uriel, who bows his shaved head, his broad shoulders shrugging with indifference. "Very well," he relents. "But believe me when I tell you that eternal confinement is not the worst fate that will befall you should you choose to walk the path of silence. There are far more unpleasant things to endure than isolation."

My blood runs cold at the cryptic warning behind Uriel's words, but I say nothing as he pivots and struts away from my cage for a second time, suppressing the urge to call out again. As the mist rises to shroud his body, his eyes flick over his shoulder.

"Beware the horrors of your own mind. The unchecked thoughts of your unhinging sanity will be your worst enemy here. Not me."

He then fades into the landscape without looking back.

three

CALEB

PALE SUNLIGHT BREAKS THROUGH the overcast sky, warding off the chill and rain of a London spring day. It's practically hot now. Typical London. You go through four seasons in one afternoon. Although I love the city, I'm shocked to find this is where Hammurabi said to meet. I wait outside a sushi bar on Portobello Road, the brick above me painted with a bright mural, and scents of spice waft from the Thai restaurant on the second floor. My stomach rumbles. Living in an ancient, abandoned citadel has not exactly provided culinary delights, and London offers a mosaic of cuisine begging to be sampled.

I lean against the exterior wall, keeping watch on the bustling street before me. It's market day, and the swell of people press against me. My eyes narrow as I focus, my vision as sharp as a raptor's. I don't want Hammurabi sneaking up on me. I sent one of my little clay figures through the shadows last night to give a message to my teacher. Although he agreed to a meeting,

I don't know how pissed he is with me. I lied to him and freed my grandfather, which goes against all the strict rules he follows with a rigid devotion. Hammurabi and his laws. He might stab me—a discreet knife slipped under my ribs—and I'll die on this beautiful, happy street as the crowd swallows me whole.

But instead of a stealthy approach, the former Babylonian king plods down the street at a leisurely pace. His wide shoulders create a path before him, and he looks unusually relaxed, stopping here and there to look at the merchandise displayed on the sidewalks. I blink. Good lord, did he actually just sniff a *candle*? He offers the woman behind the table a devastating smile and she practically purrs. Well, shit. Does Hammurabi come here to get laid? I shake my head, trying to wrap my mind around this new side to my stern, scary teacher.

That all-too-familiar wariness rises within me as his dark gaze clashes with mine, and his eyes harden to ice chips. The woman's smile falters as she observes his sudden arctic expression. Then his attention flicks back to her, and he turns on the charm, leaving her blushing. He pays for the candle and whispers something in her ear and she preens. Damn, hail to the king. Hammurabi's got game. All warmth melts from him as he walks toward me, and the sick feeling of dread returns.

Sweat beads around my hairline at my teacher's pissed-off expression. If he could shoot icicles out of his eyeballs, he would. Which begs the question, can angels do that? I suppress inappropriate laughter at the image of Gabriel shooting ice out of her ass. Get it together, Caleb.

I give Hammurabi a wary nod, afraid even a simple "hi" will enrage him more. He stands in front of me, and the crowd breaks around him like he's a large stone in rushing water. A delicate paper bag is fisted in his big hand, which somehow doesn't detract from his badass image. He glowers at me for a long moment, and I lift my chin. Never show your fear to predators.

"Caleb, do you realize what you have done?" he finally growls.

I repress a flinch, but my own anger rises.

"Rescued my grandfather from eternal imprisonment? The rest of you seemed willing to let him rot there," I bite back. "He's my blood. He's also an angel! Something everyone conveniently kept from me. A *Gray* angel." Fury rides me hard as I think about how everyone lied to me. I have no idea if Hammurabi even knows what a Gray is, but if he does, the deception from the Darks runs deep.

The Babylonian king doesn't even blink at the word "Gray," confirming my suspicions, as his expression grows stormy. "Yes, he's your blood, but did you ever question why I'd be willing to let him rot?"

"Because being both of the Dark and the Light messes with your strict world order?" I snarl. "Because his existence breaks your precious rules?" I know arguing with him is not going to help me rescue Luna, but I'm too angry to keep my mouth shut. Yeah, Gramps isn't perfect, and he wants to rule the world, but being entombed for all time doesn't seem fair.

And let's face it, probably wasn't good for Alexander's sanity. I also carry an enormous boulder of guilt around that my actions caused Goldilocks to be taken, and I might have unleashed a dangerous threat onto the world.

Hammurabi steps closer, his rage an almost living thing coiling around him. "Do you think me that petty, Caleb? That I would condone the imprisonment of Alexander the Great because he was a *Gray*? You don't suppose it had anything to do with his desire to master the Earth and all its inhabitants? Or do you support his plans to subvert the free will of humanity?"

Guilt oozes into my stomach, making me sick. "Grandfather likes humanity," I protest weakly. "He just doesn't want us to hide anymore. He wants to stop the chaos."

Hammurabi snorts. "Oh, young one, what is it that you children say? That's total bullshit. Yes, Alexander loves humanity. I won't deny it, but his love does not give him permission to be king of all. It does not give him permission to start a war that will kill millions."

I shake my head in denial. I know my grandfather doesn't want to kill millions of humans. He has no trouble taking out Nephilim and angels but he genuinely loves mortals.

Hammurabi's voice gentles. "Caleb, what do you think will happen to the mortals when Alexander wages his war against the Council? The earth will tremble and run red with blood. He won't target humans, but they will be collateral damage. It's unavoidable. Alexander is not the victim or the hero in this scenario. He is the villain of the piece."

The picture he paints makes my queasiness worse. "If he's the villain, you've all made him one. I doubt you were accepting of him being a Gray," I accuse.

He releases a long sigh. "Walk with me, child." He turns on his heel, and I follow him down the sidewalk. His stride is sure and confident, as if he's taken this path hundreds of times before. He probably has. He's older than dirt.

We take a left down a side street and stop at a…donut shop. There isn't an inch of fat on the warrior king, so I wouldn't have guessed he has a sweet tooth. Then again, we're Nephilim, so the normal human fallacies don't apply to us. He orders some donuts at the window and hands me one with a maple glaze.

"Um, I know you're angry with me, so why the treat?" I say as I take a big bite of the sweet pastry. Bacon and maple explode in my mouth and I sigh. Finally, food that tastes good.

He takes a bite of his own donut, studying me for a moment before walking again. I keep up with his long stride easily, although my anxiety ratchets up. Usually when people give you comfort food, they're about to tell you they crashed your car or slept with your girlfriend.

"I am very angry with you, but I also know that Ishtar was behind this as well. I'm sure she had a hand in convincing you to help your grandfather, and I know how convincing she can be," Hammurabi says, cutting me a side glance.

"She's a huge fan of Gramps," I admit around a mouthful of

donut. As we get farther from Portobello Road, the crowded sidewalks thin.

His grin is grim. "Yes, she always was. She hates hiding what she really is." He gives a bitter laugh. "She hates rules, too. She does love power, though. She longs to be a goddess in truth."

I snort, nodding. That she does. I think she misses being a queen, misses being worshipped. "She played the family angle. I don't know my dad, so…I wanted to know *him*. He's freakin' Alexander the Great and my grandfather. She didn't have to push me hard," I admit, shame creeping in.

Hammurabi is quiet for a moment. His black eyes are grave as he studies me, reluctance written on his face, and then he sighs. "I understand the need to find your blood, especially because your father is the worst sort of bastard. And you couldn't possibly know about the prophecy. It's not something the Archdemons or Archangels want shared. Only a few Nephilim know about it."

"Prophecy?" I demand, my feet slowing. "You mean the one I overheard the Council talking about when I snuck my little toy warrior into Gabriel's office? The one they were pissing themselves over?"

For a moment, admiration shines on my teacher's face. "You infiltrated Gabriel's office? Clever boy." He shakes his head. "The prophecy decrees that a Gray will destroy the world and wage war on Heaven and Earth," Hammurabi says. "And Alexander certainly was—and is—bent on that."

I roll my eyes. "Why are these prophecies all about the end of the world?" I scoff.

"Alexander almost succeeded in conquering the known world before," Hammurabi points out. "And he killed an Archangel."

Shock ripples through me. "What?" I ask. I mean, I know he wants to kill them in revenge, but I had no idea he took one out before he was entombed. "*Who?*"

"Michael."

I reel back on my heels. I had no idea Michael was dead. No one ever talks about it. And I'm not a Light, so I've never given the Archangel much thought. It's not like he shows up at Archdemon reunions, passing out cookies and judgment. I get why no one talks about it either. Most Nephilim believe Alexander was a first generation, certainly not an angel. If it got out that he'd killed an Archangel, there would be lots of explaining to do.

Realization kicks me in the face, and I curse myself for being so stupid. "Did he use the dagger you gave me?"

Hammurabi nods. "Yes, he did. The dagger belongs to your family, and only your bloodline can wield it. Alexander didn't always know he was a Gray, Caleb. He grew up as a pampered prince, self-assured in his power in the mortal world, and believing he was a Dark Nephilim. Once he discovered what he really was—a Gray angel—he felt betrayed. The dagger was from the Fall, belonging to one of his parents, but I have no idea how he managed to find it. What I do know is he felt he was the only one to set the world back to right, being both of the Dark and the Light. And there lies the issue. Your grandfather truly believes he's the chosen one. People like that are dangerous, so righteous in their convictions they're blind to their tyranny. I'm a Dark Nephilim, Caleb. Free will means everything to me."

His words eat their way into my conscience like worms through rotting food and I flinch, studying the cracks in the sidewalk. I know Grandfather wants to rule the world, and I doubt the Creator is happy about that. Still, I feel sorry for Alexander if fate had decided his path before he ever got a chance to not be defined by some prophecy.

"There's another Gray angel," I blurt, and Hammurabi's square jaw drops. Wow, I've actually managed to stun the king. I frown as another realization smacks me in the face. I recall the conversation I overheard with Gabriel and the other Archangels and Archdemons, how they kept Alexander's true identity a secret. "Hang on, how do *you* know Alexander is a Gray angel when Ishtar didn't realize what he was until she saw his wings? How was that kept a secret? I mean, you all were there back in the day."

Hammurabi's brows draw down into a sharp vee. He gives me a long, hard stare, which I meet without faltering. "I altered her memory," he admits. "I'm not proud of it but it was necessary."

"Wait a minute. I thought only Archangels or Archdemons could wipe our memories, not other Nephilim. You can break into our minds, but you can't alter them completely like you can with humans," I protest, my world order once more upended.

His smile is sharp enough to cut. "That's mostly true. I'm the only known Nephilim with that talent. Asmodeus charged me with burying the fact that Alexander was an angel. Considering the role he played in human history, removing all knowledge of him would've created too many complications, and seeing as there are far fewer Nephilim than humans, the Council settled on altering our minds over the alternative. Asmodeus felt it was the only way. She didn't want to lose Ishtar, and if Ishtar remembered what the Great truly was, she'd have started a rebellion much sooner than she did." Bitterness radiates from him. "It was Asmodeus's hope that the goddess would let Alexander go. A foolish hope as I feared. Ishtar never forgot your grandfather. Time only nursed her determination. You think she would have learned her lesson from the first rebellion."

"Why are you telling me this?" I demand. "I helped Ishtar. Why trust me not to run and tell her you screwed with her mind?"

"Because you just told me there's another Gray," Hammurabi answers calmly. "You came to me, which means your loyalty is torn, and I'm assuming this other Gray is the reason."

Heat creeps into my cheeks. Would I have abandoned my grandfather and his megalomaniac need to conquer if it weren't for Luna? "I met a girl at the academy. Luna. She'd recently been brought there, but she was around my age, and she didn't seem to understand that as a Light, she should hate me. The other Lights treated her like shit. We became…friends. And weird stuff kept happening to her—she had Dark and Light traits. Then Alexander started speaking to her, leading her to him. She could see Enochian. I…with Ishtar…used her to help me free Alexander." Those words scrape my throat as shame fills me. My Goldilocks is probably entombed somewhere and it's my fault. "I didn't want to use her like that, and I only went along with it because Ishtar promised to get Luna out with us. But Gabriel showed up and I…I stabbed her with the dagger. Alexander grabbed me and Ishtar, and the last time I saw Luna, she was screaming on the ground with wings coming out of her back. *Gray* wings."

The confession tastes sour in my mouth. I feel stupid for putting my trust in Ishtar and Alexander. Don't get me wrong, I wanted my grandfather free, but not for the price I paid. Not at the expense of Goldilocks. That dull ache in my chest that never seems to go away sharpens.

The corners of Hammurabi's mouth pull down. "We imprisoned Alexander so we could suspend the prophecy. There was never supposed to be another Gray. I honestly don't know how there is one."

"Well, there is," I growl, "and you'd better go ask Asmodeus about it. Gabriel took Luna somewhere, I know it, and I'm sure Asmodeus knows where. It's the one damn time everyone takes the sticks out of their asses and works together."

"Your Gray could possibly be the one the prophecy refers

to, and in that case, it's better that she is sealed away from the world," he argues, and I want to strangle him.

"I refuse to believe Luna is the Gray in the prophecy, Hammurabi. She's sweet and gentle, and she certainly doesn't want to take over the world. We have to help her. She doesn't deserve to be thrown in a hole and left there. She's an innocent girl who's been lied to her entire life."

A troubled expression crosses the former king's face. "She's not a girl, Caleb, she's an angel. A Gray angel. She's dangerous." He holds up a hand to stall my immediate angry protests. "I'm not saying your Luna is deliberately dangerous or has ill intentions, but that she might accidentally hurt others as she comes into her powers. Being of both factions, we still don't even know what Grays are capable of."

"That doesn't mean she deserves to be imprisoned or punished for sins she hasn't even committed!" I shout, catching the attention of people passing by on the sidewalk. Shit, I forgot we were in the middle of busy London for a minute.

"Keep your voice down," Hammurabi hisses. "I don't enjoy altering human minds. It's obvious you care for Luna deeply, but don't let your feelings blind you, Caleb."

I grind out through gritted teeth, "I'm not. Luna is a kind, caring person who doesn't deserve any of this. She belongs with me—with the Darks. We're supposed to be the open-minded ones, aren't we? We're about free will, so shouldn't Luna be allowed to choose a side before she's condemned for nothing more than being born different?"

The Babylonian king studies me then sighs. "I'm not condemning her for being different, but anyone untrained with that much power is dangerous. I will speak to Asmodeus, boy, but I can't promise anything. She fears Grays. They all do."

"Please," I beg, feeling helpless and hopeless as the proverbial clock keeps ticking. I keep picturing Luna, alone and feeling betrayed. Hating me. "Tell her Luna is different. Please, I need her help. And yours."

"I will do my best, Caleb," Hammurabi says, backing away from me. "Now, I suggest you get back before Ishtar misses you. I'll be in touch."

I watch him walk away, my heart heavy. What will I do if Asmodeus won't help?

four

LUNA

A GASP PARTS MY lips as my eyes snap open, consciousness slamming into my mind like a brick wall. My arms shake beneath me as I slowly push up from the floor, my vision foggy and glazed as I search for whatever it was that startled me awake. I could've sworn I heard somebody calling my name, but…the other side of the glass is deserted.

Like always, I'm alone in this place.

Heaving a tired breath, I prop myself upright against the transparent wall, ignoring the ache in my back when the bare skin of my shoulder blades touches the barrier. My fingers reach for the shredded remains of my T-shirt as it begins to slip down my arms, carefully sliding the sleeves back into position. I'm not sure what disgusts me more—that I'm still donning the same torn outfit I was wearing the day these wings sprouted out of my back or that the Archangels and Archdemons keeping me here haven't had the decency to at least provide me with a fresh change of clothes. Maybe when you get to be that old, manners and hospitality no longer matter.

Then again, I'm a captive here, not a guest. I highly doubt Uriel or any of his cohorts give a damn about my comfort.

A hoarse laugh rumbles deep in my chest. Of course, they don't care. If they did, they wouldn't be treating me like some prisoner of war, depriving me of food and water or access to facilities to bathe and relieve myself…not that I ever need to do the latter. Since that day under the Serapeum, certain bodily functions have ceased being necessary. I've been trapped in this cage for four months and I haven't eaten so much as a crumb. I *could* eat but my survival doesn't seem to depend on it anymore. Hell, maybe it never did. I can remember instances of food being withheld as punishment during some of my stricter foster placements but I never felt the desperation they expected of me when it was finally offered again. I always passed that lack of appetite off as fear, but now, I'm beginning to question if it was always because of this. Because of what I am.

Still, there's a hollowness in my stomach that seems to expand the longer I go without, and I can't help wondering if angels *can* starve—if maybe it just takes a lot longer than it would for a mortal. Centuries, even, if Uriel's threats about my captivity hold any weight.

Then again, Alexander was imprisoned for thousands of years and he didn't die of starvation. If anything, I imagine the Council is using that growing discomfort against me as a way of encouraging my submission, hoping it will eventually make me crack. And maybe it will. Maybe the sensations accosting me will only get worse until spilling my secrets to them will feel like the sweetest form of relief if doing so means a potential escape from such torment. Or maybe what I'm feeling is all in my head, and any malaise is merely a result of my own degrading mind.

Since the Archangel's visit, the air has felt thinner, making me dizzy, like there's a sudden lack of oxygen in the cramped space of the egg. My senses were already dulled, my powers unreachable—no doubt suppressed by whatever magic created my prison—but now, my helplessness is amplified. It reminds me of the countless days I spent locked in that padded room in the hospital, my head muddled by claustrophobia and a building anxiety as the hours passed in an interminable blur. If I close my eyes, I can almost imagine myself back there again, and what truly terrifies me is that I'm not sure if I crave that or not. If believing I'm mortal and crazy again is preferable to whatever unknown fate awaits me here.

Shaking that thought away, I raise my arms and stretch until my shoulder joints pop. Angel or not, my body is accustomed to seventeen years of human habit, and although I also don't seem to need to sleep anymore to function or survive, I long for it. I lose my days to it. What else is there for me to do? If anything, I'm relieved I'm still capable of it. It's a much-needed interruption to the monotony of this lonely existence. And in sleep, instead of the nightmares I expect, I have the refuge of dreams—sweet imaginings of Caleb that are a knife to my waking heart but, in unconsciousness, form a safe haven from the questions pressing at the back of every thought and breath. Questions about what I am and about how I could've gone nearly two decades without knowing the truth. If I've always been an angel since birth, then why did my wings and these other new changes to my body only become apparent when Alexander touched me? What did he mean when he said he was giving me my freedom?

Once again, I hear those strange words Alexander whispered in my ear—Enochian, I'm guessing, given the lilting similarities to the words Ishtar taught me to open his tomb.

Tomb… My mind catches on that word, and a broken laugh parts my lips as I glance at the rounded wall of my cage. My own eternal crypt.

When I think of freedom, this is the opposite of what I envision.

Scowling, I hug my legs to my chest, already fed up with the endless barrage of questions nagging at my thoughts. It's only a matter of time until my frustrating ignorance becomes too much to bear and then, with answers still far out of reach, I'll drift away from it all and into the welcome embrace of sleep. In those moments, more than anything, I dream about the fresh start I should've had at Babel with Caleb, despite having no idea what that would've looked like, and regardless of the pain that image stirs in my heart. My imagination runs wild, dreaming up grand halls and long, winding corridors and Caleb always at my side. And happiness. Pure, unbridled happiness.

But those feelings never last, because once I wake up, the truth of my situation smashes them to pieces, until all I'm left with is a large void in my chest and the taunting realization that I'm all alone. There can be no fresh start because, as consciousness always reminds me, Caleb left me behind.

Everyone always leaves me behind.

"Luna."

I spring forward onto my knees and whip around at the whispered sound of my name, my racing heart jumping up into my throat as panic conspires to choke me. It takes a moment for my gaze to focus on the figure emerging from the milky white mist, my eyes bolting wide the moment the newcomer's features slide into focus, crisp and clear. Disbelief forms a name on my lips as the Archangel steps free of the last wisps of fog.

It can't be—

"Gabriel?" I breathe.

I rub at my eyes, unable to accept what I'm seeing. The last time Gabriel and I were in the same room, the Archdemons were threatening to torture her for keeping my existence a secret. The last time we were together, I was certain we were both going to die.

Granted, some time has passed since that day, but still, I'm shocked to see her here, looking the perfect picture of health—the opposite of how she appeared in the moments before I was

taken away to be punished for my part in Alexander's release…
and for being a Gray. Her ebony hair is straight and sleek, just
like I remember, and the planes of her cheekbones are sculpted
and sharp, like the edge of a knife, showing how deadly she
really is behind that fair angelic exterior. But although her
dewy skin glows, tendrils of shadow writhe over her skin,
contradicting what I know of her aura.

Purple and black shadows instead of the golden hues of a
Light.

I falter back a step, my pulse picking up speed. This isn't
right. Gabriel isn't a Dark. Her aura should be bright—
blindingly so. Not like this.

Before I can make sense of the change or the sudden fear
gripping me, she rushes forward, pressing a long-fingered hand
to the glass. "Thank the Creator. I don't have much time."

Relief and doubt sweep through me, warring with each other
for dominance. On the one hand, part of me is elated to see her
again—not because I'm certain she's my mother but because
she's *alive*. Because now I can let go of the guilt that would
have swallowed me had she actually died. But on the other—
the side where I retain some sense of logic past my growing
derangement—I can't ignore the suspicious timing of her
appearance or the bewildering fact that she's here at all. How
long ago was it that Uriel questioned me about my relationship
with the headmistress of the Serapeum? How long ago did he
claim she disappeared from their grasp? How is she here, right

in front of me now, without alerting my captors to her presence?

This isn't right, I repeat to myself as a darker realization begins to sink in. Only the Faithful and Fallen who imprisoned me know about this place. So, how is it that Gabriel knew where to find me unless she's working with them? *For* them?

Whose side is she really on?

Yours, a voice inside me insists, but I refuse its invasion into my thoughts, unable to believe such a lie. If she was on my side, she wouldn't have abandoned me to suffer the human world in ignorance of what I am. If she was on my side, she wouldn't have let the Council imprison me for being an unwilling result of *her* transgressions. If she was on my side, she wouldn't be here at all, no doubt to serve as my interrogator.

If she was on my side, she would have loved me and accepted me the way a mother should.

"I…" I hesitate, swallowing a little too loudly. Despite the thick, transparent wall between us, I'm certain she must've heard it with her keen senses. My fear grows, encasing me like a shroud. Can she also sense my suspicion of her? "Uriel said you disappeared," I mutter before forcing out, "How are you here?"

Her hand slips away from the glass as a somber frown pulls at the edges of her mouth. "They found me. I'm imprisoned in this place, just like you. They're only allowing me to speak with you because I said I could convince you to tell them the truth."

My entire body stiffens at her words. They're *allowing* her to speak with me? As if Gabriel, the feared headmistress of the Serapeum and Messenger of the Creator Himself, has ever sought anyone's approval to do anything.

An incredulous laugh rises up in my throat. No…I believe Gabriel is a prisoner about as much as I believe she's actually here to help me.

I examine her for a long moment, my eyes trailing across the unnerving undulations of the inky whips of darkness outlining her body. Was I wrong to assume all Darks are defined by shadow and all Lights by glowing golden wisps? The only person I ever dared to ask about auras had no idea they even exist, so I'm alone in my minimal understanding of them. Maybe I was too quick in my assumptions and there's a deeper psychological aspect to them. Maybe what I'm seeing now is the real Gabriel and her aura has changed in my eyes to reflect that, the darkness of her heart revealed. If so, if auras are really just a reflection of how I view those with angel blood, then that would explain why I see what looks like shards of glass floating along my skin, my own unearthed aura a mirror image of my fractured soul and mind. It's just like the one I saw around Alexander, who suffered the same persecution and isolation I've fallen victim to. Is that because we're both Grays or because we're both damaged? Or both? Maybe, the truth is, we have more in common than I've allowed myself to admit.

My fingers curl into fists, my nails biting into my palms to keep from ripping my skin off my body, my increasing vexation like an itch I can't scratch, unbearable and maddening. None of this makes any damn sense. If auras reflect a person's soul, then why did I see darkness when I looked at Caleb?

The answer stabs me like a knife to the heart.

Because part of me always knew he'd betray me. That he'd eventually leave me, too.

Swallowing the rising sob in my throat, I force myself to focus on Gabriel. On what she said. On why she's here.

"They're only allowing me to speak with you because I said I could convince you to tell them the truth."

The truth. I nearly scoff at the thought.

"Luna?" Gabriel prods, and I realize I've been silent too long.

I clear my throat. "Why would you say that?" I ask, fighting to keep my tone calm. "I already told Uriel I don't know anything."

Like I told Uriel, if the Council wants answers, they should get them from Gabriel. After all, she's the one who hid my birth—my very forbidden existence—from them, from the rest of the world, and from, I assume, the Creator. She lied to them. She lied to *me*.

If anyone has anything more to hide, it's her.

Anger is a raging river in my veins, but as I examine the sharp planes of Gabriel's severe countenance, another face abruptly springs to mind. Yet another person she lied to.

My lips tighten as I picture my father. I recall the pain in those vibrant blue eyes the moment he realized who I was— when our blood sang to each other, revealing a long hidden truth. Since that day, I must've replayed that memory more than a thousand times, analyzing it from every possible angle. At first, I wondered if he was equally at fault for my pain, for the horrors I suffered through all because I didn't know what I was. But with time, my doubt has withered, leaving only the bitter truth and more questions.

Lucifer…he had no idea I existed. If he had, would he have wanted me? Or would he have buried my existence the same way my mother did?

I stare at the stunning creature before me, wondering what drove her to abandon her child. Was it fear of the Creator, or was it shame that kept us apart? Maybe she just didn't want anyone to know she's a hypocrite.

"You must know something. Please," she presses, her voice uncharacteristically tender. Pleading. So unlike the cold Archangel I know. "The Council have said they'll tear off my wings for my part in Alexander's release."

What part? I'm tempted to ask before wincing at the mental image of wings torn from flesh. Before I was reborn, my own wings unleashed, I wouldn't have been able to imagine that pain. Now, having experienced the crack of bones shifting and feathers protruding from my skin, I can envision the agony all too clearly. It's a pain I don't want to imagine, let alone ever experience firsthand.

Gabriel raises a hand to the barrier between us again, her fingertips turning milk-white where they press against the glass, leaving behind tiny impressions. She bats her thick lashes, blinking tears from her eyes, and yet, everything about her expression seems false.

"Luna…I need you to tell them what happened down to the most minute detail. You need to reveal where the Conqueror is and end this. It's the only way to save us both."

My heart tugs, but it isn't the obedient terror I normally feel in the Archangel's presence. Strangely, I don't feel that at all, though my realization of that is buried under the weight of all my other conflicting emotions. My wings tear free of the restraints of my skin and whip upward, pulling me to my feet, and this time, I barely notice the burn consuming me. In this moment, all I'm aware of is anger.

"I don't know where Alexander is!" I screech, my self-control slipping. "What part of 'he left me behind' is everyone here not understanding? Besides, you saw what happened with your own two eyes. I can't tell them anything you haven't already."

"Luna—"

"No," I cut her off, my tone scathing. I've waited seventeen years to meet my mother, and the disappointment flooding my body is worse than if I'd never known her at all. "You don't get to ask for my help. I came to you, and you pushed me away, remember? I warned you Alexander was leading me to him, and you did *nothing*. Oh, wait, that's right." I sneer, remembering the conversation I overheard in her office. "You told Alaric to 'assess my mental state' and determine if I was going to be a problem. Mom of the year, everybody."

Her soft gaze brightens with surprise—the change so fleeting it's already passed before I've even fully registered it. In the blink of an eye, her expression turns molten, her features darkening with warning. "So, you'll do nothing?" she growls. "You'll let your own mother suffer?"

"What about *my* suffering?" I practically scream. "I spent my whole life in foster care being tossed from one home to another like a stray dog nobody wanted. Did you know that? Did you know I was committed to a psychiatric hospital because everyone thought I was too dangerous to be around normal people? You must have—I know Alaric told you—so where were you when *I* needed help? Where were you when I needed a mother?" I shake my head, biting back the tears scalding my eyes. "You know, if this situation is anyone's fault, it's yours. You were too busy focusing on my friendship with Caleb to listen to what I was trying to tell you. Seriously, why did you even bother inviting him to your school if you have such a problem with Darks?"

As these words leave my lips, something occurs to me. Gabriel was fine—at least, in appearance—with Caleb being a student at the Serapeum until he began spending time with me. Until he began influencing my behavior, my powers. And then it hits me: Caleb was never the problem, not really. It wasn't our friendship that she didn't like...

It was what our friendship reminded her of.

"Oh, I get it. You didn't like me spending so much time with

Caleb because it reminded you of what you had with my father."

Her hawk-like gaze sharpens, her eyes narrowing on my face. "What do you know of your father?"

I startle at her accusatory tone. Despite being my mother, her blood never once sang to mine, not like my father's did. Maybe that's why she thinks I don't know the truth. Maybe she assumed our connection would be as damaged as the one I have with her.

I shrug, refusing to waste any more energy on this pointless conversation. If she isn't here to help me, then I'd prefer she leave me condemned to my eternal solitude. "Nothing. Just like I know nothing about you because you've both been absent my whole life."

Her face reddens. "You must know something about him. *Speak*," she commands, that single word uncomfortably abrasive.

My pulse quickens at the sudden shift in her demeanor, her normally straight back hunched and her beautiful face contorted with a terrifying fury I can't comprehend. The shadows lapping over her skin have gone rigid, like a den of cobras preparing to strike.

Gone is the pleading woman from only a few moments ago.

The change sucks the moisture from my mouth, leaving my tongue brittle. Swallowing past the dryness, I give a slight shake of my head. "O-Other than what I learned about him in history class?" I stammer, unable to keep the fear from my voice. "Not really. How would I?"

"You know your father's identity?" she presses.

The weight of my surprise tugs my mouth open, and I stare at the Archangel, dumbfounded by her hostility and this peculiar line of questioning when it's obvious I know the truth. Maybe her injury that day was far worse than I thought. Can angels suffer from amnesia? Why else would she be so shocked I know who my father is when she was there to witness our meeting?

Or maybe her reaction isn't about me at all. Maybe she's just struggling to accept that the full extent of this secret she's held onto for thousands of years is finally out in the open.

"Why does that surprise you so much?" I ask. "You were there when we met. Or did the blood loss from your wound damage your memory?"

The frustration stretching across her face fades with the same speed as drawing a breath, returning her reddening skin to its normal alabaster complexion. As she straightens her back, resuming a rigid, imposing posture that resembles the Archangel I know, her pupils dilate, her eyes widening with comprehension. "Your father is the Morningstar," she breathes, as if confirming something she suspected but didn't know for sure.

Furrowing my brow, I take a careful step forward, my wings wrapping around my frail body, as if to protect me from a potential attack. Dread spreads under my skin like a rash.

"You say that like you didn't already know," I whisper.

As Gabriel meets my gaze once again, I see something strange in the depths of her eyes. The writhing darkness spreads over her skin, and it dawns on me that this woman, this unrecognizable creature, isn't here to help me…

"Beware the horrors of your own mind. The unchecked thoughts of your unhinging sanity will be your worst enemy here. Not me."

Because she isn't my mother.

"You don't," I realize, my voice a barely-there breath as Uriel's warning comes back to haunt me, "because you're not really her." *Because you're not really here.*

The misty shroud coating the empty landscape rises up in a wave and smashes into the walls of the egg, engulfing my surroundings. I spin around in a blind panic, but no matter which way I look, I can only see white, and no matter how hard I strain my ears, I can only hear the thundering sound of my own terror.

Slamming my hands over my ears, I sink down to the ground, curl into a ball, and rock back and forth, waiting for the fog to settle and the chaos of my mind to ease. When it does, I'm unsurprised to find I'm alone again, trapped in my own private world, like always.

And the hallucination—the projection of the Archangel concocted by my broken mind—has vanished.

five

CALEB

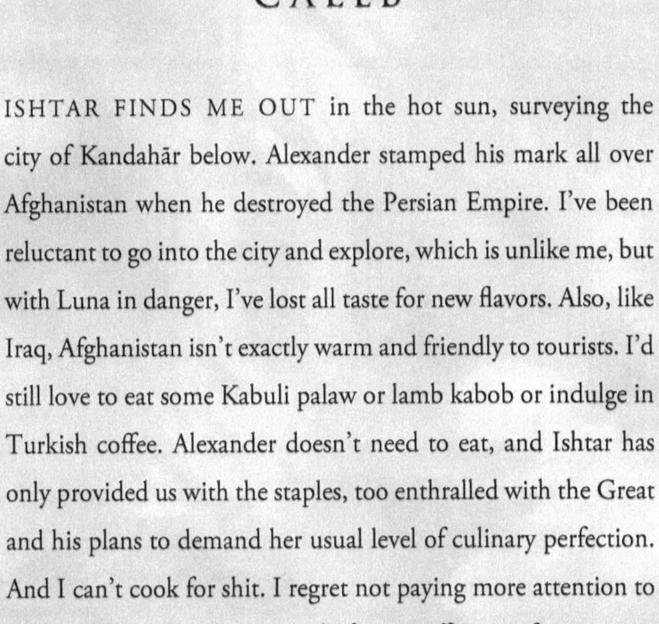

ISHTAR FINDS ME OUT in the hot sun, surveying the city of Kandahār below. Alexander stamped his mark all over Afghanistan when he destroyed the Persian Empire. I've been reluctant to go into the city and explore, which is unlike me, but with Luna in danger, I've lost all taste for new flavors. Also, like Iraq, Afghanistan isn't exactly warm and friendly to tourists. I'd still love to eat some Kabuli palaw or lamb kabob or indulge in Turkish coffee. Alexander doesn't need to eat, and Ishtar has only provided us with the staples, too enthralled with the Great and his plans to demand her usual level of culinary perfection. And I can't cook for shit. I regret not paying more attention to Mom's delicious dishes instead of just stuffing my face.

The scent of cardamom and sugar hits my nose, and I glance over at the former goddess to see her holding a small plate filled with Gosh-e fil, traditional fried pastries. My stomach rumbles, but I look at my teacher with suspicion.

"What are those for? I haven't been a good boy lately," I say tartly, crossing my arms over my chest. Being rude to Ishtar isn't the smartest move I could make but I'm pissed. I haven't heard back from Hammurabi, and I'm sick of waiting around and twiddling my dick for Alexander to find Luna.

"No, you haven't. Come now, lovely boy, pouting doesn't become you. Eat these delicious treats before I shove them down your throat," Ishtar answers, her voice dripping with venom and honey.

I reach for one and take a big bite. Damn, they are good. "Thanks," I say after I swallow. "What's up?"

"Must something be 'up'?" she asks, popping a pastry into her mouth and chewing. I raise a brow at her, and she chuckles. "Alexander wants you in the receiving room. He expects more Nephilim today, and he wants you with him to observe. If you are to take your place in this war, you need to learn strategy."

I almost choke on my second bite. "My place in this war?"

It's her turn to arch an incredulous brow. "What did you think your role here was, Caleb? Did you think you'd simply free Alexander and be the pampered prince, waiting around for your Luna to be brought back to you on a silver platter?"

I don't know which of her words pisses me off more. I used to like and admire Ishtar, no matter how much of a hard-ass she was, but now I begin to feel hate encroach, replacing some of the love and respect I have for my teacher. I'm not a "pampered" anything and never have been. My dad abandoned my mom, and we had a regular, middle-class existence until the Nephilim came for me. My teachers like me because I'm talented and work hard, and I'm popular with the Darks because I treat people well. Honey always traps more flies than vinegar, and I can be as sweet as fuck.

But my blinding rage toward my teacher—a woman I used to have the highest respect for—is from hearing Luna's name tumble from her ruby lips in such a derisive, dismissive way. Like Luna was just a convenient tool to get what she wanted, and she won't be bothered to take her out of the drawer again until she wants to hammer something. Luna is an angel, for the Morningstar's sake. She shouldn't be treated lightly. Hammurabi got one thing right: no one knows what Luna is capable of. Not even Alexander.

Oh, and I sure as shit didn't sign up for any war, especially one I'm not on board with. I feel like the biggest idiot on the planet, so obsessed with freeing Gramps, I glossed over what that actually meant. I was so focused on the injustice of it all, of the utter unfairness of chaining an immortal creature—not that I knew that about him at the time—for all eternity, that I never thought much of the fact that said immortal being was going to be enraged and want revenge. That's just first class dumbassery.

I take a deep breath, trying to calm down and not choke on my fury. Part of me wants to throw Asmodeus's betrayal in her face to hurt her, but I know better than to show that hand. Even if it would give me immense pleasure. "Despite having a famous gramps, pampered isn't a state I'm familiar with, and you know it. And I don't know exactly how helpful I'll be in a war, as I haven't even graduated yet from the academy. I'm only eighteen, not exactly a hardened warrior like you."

Ishtar's smile is sly. "Well, then you'll just learn to be one, like the good little student I know you to be. Run along now, the Great's patience has limits, and you do try him so." She waves a hand at me, shooing me along like a bothersome fly.

I clench my teeth, wanting to punch her in her smug, beautiful face. Normally, I'd feel guilty about wanting to hit a woman, but considering she could and *would* take my head, I don't feel so bad. Giving her a tight nod, I start to walk toward the citadel.

"Don't disappoint me, Caleb. I always had such high hopes for you," she calls after me, and I still for a moment. The sugar-coated threat in her voice is clear. She wants me to fall in line and be an obedient servant of Alexander just like she is.

I force a smile on my face and say over my shoulder, "I aim to please."

She inclines her head. "See that you do."

I wonder if Alexander has asked her to keep an eye on me or if she's determined that I don't embarrass her or threaten their mission. Despite the fact that Ishtar is genuinely fond of me, she'd choose Alexander over me in a heartbeat. She's no true ally of mine unless I swallow the Kool-Aid and jump on Team World Domination. I haven't exactly been comfortable here, with Grandfather and Ishtar and their growing list of soldiers, but I haven't felt unsafe before. Until now.

Crossing under a stone arch, I enter the citadel, momentarily shaded from the bright sun as I make my way into the large courtyard. The ancient building still only houses the three of us, but I have no doubt it will be brimming with Nephilim soon. They pop in and out of the Shadow Road, gathering intel for Alexander. I pass a pale woman with ebony hair, her skin moon bright in the sun, and she gives me a respectful nod. I give her an uneasy nod in return, Ishtar's barbed words "pampered prince" echoing in my mind. She got the pampered part wrong, but maybe the prince part wasn't too far off. With the current absence of dear, old Dad, I guess I am next in line to the proverbial throne—at least until Gramps brings my father to heel. I'm heir not by might, but by blood. That sick pool of dread that never dries up in my stomach sloshes around.

I walk through the courtyard and make my way into the receiving hall, an enormous, cool chamber boasting a few of the treasures Alexander collected when he sacked the city of Persepolis, like a colossal stone bull's head that rests behind his makeshift throne. I don't know how he managed to haul it here when he was campaigning, but it sends a clear message of power and authority. Of, *whatever you have, I can take.*

Alexander focuses on me, his mismatched eyes hooded and unreadable. I can't help but think back to Hammurabi's words about the prophecy and Luna. It's been damn difficult to play ignorant these past two weeks. I take my place next to him, surprised to find the room empty.

"Grandfather," I say, inclining my head in deference, keeping my expression carefully blank. I don't want him to know how badly I want to be anywhere but here. "Ishtar said you wanted me."

"We are going to meet a special guest today, Grandson," he says, a cold smile cutting across his face.

"I hope it's Luna," I reply, unable to help myself. I bite my tongue until I taste copper when I see his eyes fill with rage.

An invisible force bats my face, and my knees hit stone. I wipe my fingers under my nose, and they come away glistening with blood. Shit that hurt. I earned that. Me and my stupid mouth. I'm actually shocked Gramps was so restrained.

Alexander's voice is low, deadly. "Caleb, I thought all that was settled, and you trusted me to retrieve Luna when I decided the time was right."

I lift my chin, meeting his hard eyes and swallow my fear. Alexander won't respect me if I cower, and he'll think it unworthy of a member of his bloodline. "I do trust you, sir. I apologize for my impertinence. It won't happen again." My tone is humble, my gaze direct and reflecting what I hope can pass for sincerity.

His stare feels like a physical weight pressing down on me. Hell, he's an angel, so maybe he can give weight to his dirty looks. And I know that he basically gave me a slap on the wrist, a warning shot across the bow. My nose is already knitting itself together.

"I do not enjoy hurting you, Caleb, but I will if I must. Discipline is necessary, especially in young ones," my grandfather says, and I wince at the disappointment in his voice, which is ludicrous.

I'm mad as hell at him, but some part of me still wants to please him, still wants my grandfather—Alexander the freakin' Great—to be proud of me. I don't like to acknowledge it often, and most of the time I bury it, but man, I have daddy issues, and it's screwing with my head.

"I'm sorry. I know you only want what's best for me," I say, which I know is a lie. He only wants what's best for him.

He tilts his head, his eyes softer as they regard me. "You may not believe this, but I do only want what is best for you, all that this wonderful world has to offer, especially when I set it to right once more."

A chill washes over me at his words. Eager to change the subject, I say, "So, who is this special guest?"

A wolfish grin crosses his lips. "We are going to go see them now."

My eyebrows reach for my hairline. "You're leaving—I mean, we're leaving?"

Alexander has only invited select Dark Nephilim and Fallen here, as the entire Council is out to get him. Those are fourteen badasses not to be fucked with. Grandfather is not exactly jonesing to go out in the world and get caught again, content to bide his time and build his army. Well, content isn't exactly the right word. He's pretty damn twitchy to get the conquering on, but he's a patient man. He's been planning his revenge for literally thousands of years.

Alexander rises and flicks his hand at me, fingers curling. I follow him into a corner the light doesn't reach. I step into the shadows, unsure of our destination, and the secretive smile Alexander wears doesn't make me feel better. I'm tired of secrets and surprises. The path we travel is familiar, but I can't quite place it.

We come out of the Shadow Road into a dimly lit cavernous chamber filled with seemingly endless tall columns, regally marching in perfect rows, reflected in the shallow water they sprout from. The vaulted ceiling and marble columns in the Ionic and Corinthian styles tell me exactly where I am. I even know where to find the Medusa column base.

The Basilica Cistern in Istanbul is usually full of tourists, but today it is eerily empty. I've been to this ancient city loads of times, but I don't generally make it a habit to pop out of the shadows in a heavily visited attraction, though this one happens to be one of my favorites. Why is it empty? Alexander has been hiding out, so he hasn't had time to mentally manipulate an entire tourist office.

I take a deep breath of the musty air and glance around, my vision unaffected by the poor lighting. "How'd you manage to get everyone to stay away? Or is this Ishtar's doing?"

Alexander shoots me an amused look. "It's closed today. Ishtar did not do anything untoward, much to her chagrin."

Well, shit, don't I feel like an idiot. I also wonder what sort of tricks an Ishtar without restraints is getting up to, but my plate is piled to the ceiling, and I can't dish any more problems on it right now.

I look around. We're all alone, no arrogant, deadly goddess in sight. "Where *is* Ishtar?" I just left her not fifteen minutes ago.

As soon as the words leave my mouth, light spills down from above, pooling on the staircase leading out of the cistern. I catch a glimpse of Ishtar's inky hair as she latches onto a tall figure. The door slams shut behind the two of them, and she's whirled around and pressed against the door. Well, we've got a show—now all we need is dinner. The real question is, who's the surprise guest?

As the make-out session grows more heated, I glance at my grandfather, hoping he'll clear his throat or shoot lightning out of his fingertips or something. Watching Ishtar get laid is at the very bottom of my to-do list today. Just as I contemplate drowning myself in the shallow water below, Ishtar breaks away and leads the man downstairs toward where we wait as still as the columns behind us. I arch my brows, shocked, but I really shouldn't be. There in all his holier-than-thou, hypocritical, Light glory is Gilgamesh.

Alexander's wings flare out, the snap of feathers and muscle obscenely loud in the quiet. Gilgamesh startles, his eyes round as he takes in Alexander the Great, and little ol' me, Caleb the adequate, but possibly great if given enough time. I'm great at stepping into major shit I can't seem to get out of, that's for sure.

Gilgamesh's head swivels toward Ishtar, and I see the anger and betrayal flashing on his face like a neon sign in the dark. The shock at my grandfather's wings. I guess the Council managed to keep the fact that Ishtar is a turncoat under tight wraps. At least from the Lights. The Dark rumor mill has been rumbling along.

"Welcome, Gilgamesh, King of Uruk and hero of old," Alexander says, his commanding voice swallowing the emptiness of the enormous cistern and filling it with an unmistakable authority.

Gilgamesh whips back around to face my grandfather, his golden skin ashen. Fear reflects in his eyes. He shakes his head, as if he can't quite figure out what he's seeing, but is resigned to it at the same time.

I forget sometimes that Gilgamesh and Ishtar are older than Alexander. Hell, they're older than dirt, more like primordial slime, but they ain't angels. And while they did rule Mesopotamia for quite some time, they never achieved what Alexander did. They didn't dare.

Ishtar takes Gilgamesh's hand, but he yanks it away. "How could you?" he snarls.

"She could because I asked it of her," Alexander answers for the former goddess, his tone making it clear that he has the greater claim on Ishtar. That *he* has her loyalty.

Gilgamesh bristles but brushes past his lover and descends the final steps to stand before us. "What do you want of me, Conqueror? I thought you were dead. Too bad you didn't remain that way." He stares at the silvery wings on display and shakes his head again. "I forgot what you were…" His laugh drips bitterness. "I suppose I didn't forget, did I?"

Ishtar's voice is equally bitter as she steps up beside Gilgamesh. "No, they didn't want us to remember, my love. Best we forget the Council's dangerous little secret lest we forget our place, forever apart and divided."

"They prefer you divided. You're much less powerful that way," Alexander points out. "I'm a glaring beacon of rebellion, of freedom. Real freedom, not the carefully constructed facade of liberation the Darks present, and certainly not the freedom the Lights try to sell you with the myth of Ascension and the promise of your precious wings. I am a product of both the Dark and the Light, blessed with the abilities of both and none of the preconceived prejudices."

Gilgamesh frowns as he spares me a quick glance. "Caleb, what in the Creator's name are you doing here?"

My smile is all teeth. "What in the Creator's name are *you* doing here, G? I thought you didn't sully yourself with demons." I hear Ishtar's indrawn breath as guilt fills Gilgamesh's face.

Alexander's eyes flick to me for a brief moment before he

sneers at Gilgamesh. "The Creator has nothing to do with my grandson. Caleb is no concern of yours. Like Ishtar, he belongs to me. And unlike your fickle Creator, I take care of what is mine. I do not make idle promises I never plan to fulfill just to keep my flock in line like brainless sheep for my own vanity."

A dark flush stains Gilgamesh's cheekbones. Direct hit. Ouch, Gramps just sunk your battleship.

"Ascension is real," he growls. "As is my loyalty to the Creator. I will not succumb to your poison."

I roll my eyes so hard I think I sprain them. The Lights and their pipe dream Ascension.

"Am I poison, King of Uruk?" Ishtar hisses, fingers clenched into fists at her side. "When you make love to me, do you enjoy my sweet sting?"

"Isn't that supposed to be your line?" I say to Gilgamesh then wince as I shoot my grandfather a panicked look, fully expecting to bleed again. I just really can't deal with any more talk of Ishtar's sex life, or I will stick my head in the water. Instead, an amused grin flashes across Alexander's face before he quickly suppresses it.

Gilgamesh glares at me, his jaw so hard you could crack concrete on it. "You should know better than to be here, to be a part of this, Caleb," he squeezes out between clenched teeth. "Despite our philosophical differences, I thought highly of you."

"You mean for a Dark, for a *demon*, I was okay?" I say, my own bitterness leaking out. Everyone at the Serapeum other than Luna treated me like a pile of dog shit they had stepped in. Even the teachers could barely conceal their disdain for me under a thin veneer of politeness.

Ishtar's boo shakes his head. "That's not what I meant." He shoots Ishtar a disdainful look of his own. "Obviously, I don't dislike all Darks, despite their deceptive and self-destructive tendencies."

Ishtar bares her teeth at her lover and takes a step toward him, and I expect an epic battle of the sexes when an invisible force pushes between the two of them, shoving them apart. Hard. Gilgamesh smacks into the metal guard railing with a crunch, and Ishtar skids across the concrete floor, her knees bloodied under her flirty skirt. Alexander pins his second-in-command with a quelling look of disappointment, and she visibly cowers. Wow, that's the first time I've ever seen my proud teacher anything less than brimming with unapologetic arrogance. It doesn't last long. Within seconds, she's back on her feet like a Jack-in-the-box, the wounds on her knees already sealing over. Gilgamesh clutches his ribs but straightens with a grunt.

"I expect such rash behavior from my grandson, goddess of love and war. Not from you." Alexander chides her in such a gentle, fatherly voice, it has to grate on her. He *is* like a thousand years younger than her. He then turns his stern eyes to Gilgamesh. "And you should stop punishing Ishtar for being in love with her just because you're too cowardly to stand up to Gabriel and your other Light brethren."

Damn, Gramps is handing asses out today.

Throwing back her shoulders and swinging her glossy black hair behind her, Ishtar once more looks like the regal badass she's known to be. "Forgive me, Conqueror. When it comes to matters of the heart, I suppose we're all only children."

I glower at her for the dig she throws my way. Pot meet kettle.

"That was unnecessary," Gilgamesh says, "but not surprising that you would choose to control your followers with violence."

Alexander's smile is chilling. "Oh, King, when I choose to get violent, you'll know it. You're a Nephilim and an elite warrior. The little swat I gave you barely slowed you down. The two of you could have easily destroyed this precious piece of history with your foolishness. Such behavior is unbecoming in a hero like yourself. I won't allow either of you to damage such beauty." He throws a hand out, emphasizing the stunning columns surrounding us. "Humans make such wondrous things, though they have gone astray for some time and need a gentle hand to be put on the right path again."

His words bring the queasiness in my stomach back in full force, and Gilgamesh stares at my grandfather in horror. "What do you mean, humans need a gentle hand? What are you planning?"

Alexander folds his wings neatly behind him. "What has your Creator done for humanity lately? Look at them. Look at the Earth. While the Creator makes you abide stringent rules by telling lies, He lets his greatest creation run amok, destroying the planet and each other. Such chaos, civilization hanging on by a ragged thread that is fraying more as we speak. I will not stand by and watch the mortals I love destroy each other. Heaven is not our home, Gilgamesh. Earth is. We were meant to rule it. To help the mortals flourish and achieve greatness. As a being born of the Dark and the Light, *I* was meant to rule it. I'm the only one who can."

Hammurabi's words echo through my mind like a gong. Gramps has one big, raging Messiah complex. Oh, and what about Goldilocks? You know, the other Gray who threatens Alexander's special snowflake status. Wouldn't that mean *she's* meant to rule as well? Alexander doesn't seem like the sharing sort, but I have no doubt he's not above using Luna to get what he wants. Is he going to claim she's his true heir? If he hadn't been rotting in an underground tomb for millennia, I'd have a real fear Luna and I are related, but I know that's impossible, so he's got to come up with some explanation when she surfaces. And by the Morningstar, she will surface. I have to make that happen or die trying.

Gilgamesh sneers. "If you're meant to rule, wouldn't I just be exchanging one master for another? Instead of endless servitude toward the Creator, am I to come to you on my knees and pledge fealty to you so you can use me in your war? And if we win and you take your throne, what spoils could you possibly bestow upon me that are worth more than my wings?"

Alexander's laugh is cruel. "Anything on this Earth is worth more than your wings. If the Creator desired to reward you with Ascension, he would've done it millennia ago." Then he says in a much kinder voice, "Release this illusion, throw off your chains, and be free, Gilgamesh. I neither want a slave, nor a servant. I want a warrior with a true heart who cares for these mortals as I do. A warrior who knows this divide must be bridged for the good of the world."

I mull my grandfather's words over in my head as I shoot a discreet look at Ishtar. I know Alexander loves her, values her, but I don't think he believes she's his equal. Though he might not refer to her as a servant, she serves, whether she likes it or not. Whether she'll admit it or not. Not that I don't believe Gramps will reward her if he does conquer the world. I'm sure she'll get a nice little fiefdom where she can rule as she sees fit. And as much as I love her, that thought isn't a comforting one. Ishtar needs checks and balances.

Gilgamesh twists his mouth into a scowl but studies Alexander for a moment. Shit, he can't really be thinking about switching sides, can he? Not with that permanent stick up his ass.

"I will admit the divide is…burdensome." His eyes dart to Ishtar, and despite the fact I know he's furious with her, his face slightly softens. "But our goals are so different, our natures so at odds, I don't know how you can bridge that chasm." Gilgamesh glances at me. "Even the way we teach history to our young ones isn't the same. They've been bred to despise each other. Caleb knows this."

I shrug a shoulder, uncomfortable. "I don't know if I was *bred* to hate the Lights," I protest, and Gilgamesh gives me a withering look. I blow out a sigh. "Fine, I wasn't taught to love them, either. But honestly, if any of them had ever been nice to me—other than Luna—I would've been nice back."

Maybe. Okay, I was a dick to Luna at first because I thought she was playing some cruel joke on me, but I apologized and got over myself. But Gilgamesh has a legit point. We are taught that Lights despise us, thinking they're better, but we all have to get along for the sake of the world. Before Luna, I probably wouldn't have pissed on a Light if they were on fire.

Gilgamesh snorts, clearly not buying it, but he admits, "Luna is different, but only because she came to us late." I wonder why he doesn't react to Luna being missing for almost five months. What excuse did the Council make up for her absence?

Alexander frowns, and I know he wants to take the focus off Luna and fast, which only makes unease blow up in my stomach. It's not that I don't think my grandfather won't use Luna for his world-domination plot—he will—but how long does he plan on letting her rot in the meantime? And how is he going to fit another Gray into the narrative he's weaving like a true bullshit artist? I might get both legs broken if I reveal the fact that Luna is a Gray to Gilgamesh, so I decide to be smart for once and shut up.

"Remember the age you flourished in, Gilgamesh? The Bronze Age?" Alexander asks, and I stare at him, surprised by the change in subject. "What do historians call it now, the empires and cities that ruled then—the Club of Great Powers? The first attempt at globalization, when Egypt was in full bloom and Babylon was a jewel of learning and culture. When trade and language and prosperity flourished. When different kingdoms depended on one another in an intricate system."

Gilgamesh gives him a puzzled look. "Yes, I'm intimately acquainted with that time period."

Alexander's smile is calculating. "Doesn't this time period remind you of that glorious age before its collapse into darkness?"

Startling, Gilgamesh sends Ishtar a questioning look, but she simply shrugs. "You know it does if you search your soul."

"Caleb," my grandfather says, demanding my attention. I focus on him, unsure of what exactly is happening. "Let us have a history lesson, shall we?"

I give a slow nod, hoping this somehow doesn't end up with me bloody again. I straighten up like a good little show Poodle.

"What brought about the collapse of the Bronze Age, Caleb?" Alexander asks, watching Gilgamesh.

"Um, let me think." Thank the Morningstar they drill ancient history into our heads at Babel. I hold up a hand and tick off a finger. "Climate change. Natural disasters," I say, ticking off another finger. "Internal rebellions, political instability, and invasions…" All my fingers are down, and I see his point. Well, shit.

So does Gilgamesh. "Yes, the similarities are striking," he admits, glancing at Ishtar again.

Her smile is feline. "Indeed. The humans are pushing themselves into another dark age, only this time with their advancements in technology, it might be permanent. They've already caused a mass extinction with their selfish behavior."

"If I don't step in," Alexander says. "If *we* don't step in." His face is grave as he regards Gilgamesh. Grave and kingly. "You know I speak the truth, dear friend. And you know you were destined for more than just hiding in the shadows. You're half mortal. Will you ignore their silent cries and leave them to their fate? Will you ignore their pleas when you know you could aid them?"

My heart sinks as the last of Gilgamesh's indignation falls from his face. He looks at Alexander with a thoughtful expression. A minute ticks by and then another. And when he opens his mouth, I know he's drunk the Kool-Aid.

"I loved my mortal father," he says, his expression mournful. "He taught me everything about being a warrior, a king. I watched him die, his body shriveling like worn papyrus folding in on itself. I was only allowed so many years to rule, to be a hero. My place was with the Lights—so I was repeatedly reminded. I've always…regretted it. What could I have accomplished if I hadn't been forced to fade away like my father?"

Ishtar steps closer to him but doesn't touch him. "Great things, my love. And you can still achieve great things."

Alexander lets his wings flare out in a casual display of power, and Gilgamesh traces the pewter feathers with his eyes. "Greatness is in our blood," my grandfather says. "We must stop denying it. Join us, Gilgamesh, and save humanity and build a perfect, new world."

A sudden fervor flares in Gilgamesh's eyes, making him look like a zealot, and I know we're up shit creek without a paddle. Although it hurts like hell to admit it, blood or not, I don't belong with my grandfather. I don't believe in this war. I just want Luna back and Alexander stopped before he decimates half the planet. But everyone here punches above my weight class, and I have to get to Hammurabi again. I need all the help I can get to save Luna and humanity.

six

LUNA

I PACE BACK AND forth, clipping my thumbnail between my chattering teeth. In all the time I've been trapped in this place, I've never felt more on the brink of losing touch with my sanity than I do at this moment. Time drags, indiscernible and gnawing, each second bleeding into the next and yet never moving at all. Sleep evades me now as my conversation with Gabriel replays in my head in a constant loop, tormenting me with questions, which pile onto the many mysteries already plaguing my thoughts. But it wasn't real. *She* wasn't real.

And I fear I have truly lost my mind.

I drag my hands through my sweaty hair, my nails scraping over my scalp, my feet following the same path they have for the last however many minutes, hours, days, or weeks it's been since my encounter with the imagined manifestation of my mother. With every passing moment, the similarities between this place and the padded room at the hospital grow stronger,

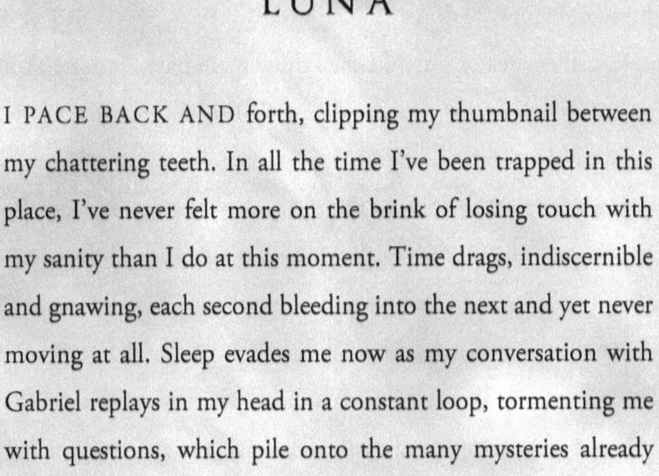

clearer, until I begin to wonder if they aren't actually the same place. If Gabriel wasn't real, then maybe none of this is. Maybe I've been in that claustrophobic room this whole time, trapped in a world of my own creation. A world where there was some explanation for why I am the way I am. A world where I could have a taste of the relationships I've always desired and then have them torn away because it's what I deserve.

A world where I can continue to punish myself for every horrible thing I've done.

I push my wings out and then draw them back into my skin again, clenching my teeth at the pain. This searing, raw agony certainly *feels* real…

I waver, torn between the idea that this is all actually happening and I will be imprisoned forever and the only slightly more palatable thought that everything I've experienced these past months was an elaborate delusion and I've finally completed my descent into madness. Neither option makes me feel any better, and both wear my already frail mental state thin. So, I force myself to consider the third option—the option that threatens to rip my splintered heart into two pieces, severing the few flimsy threads holding the remnants together. If the Gabriel I encountered here wasn't a fabrication of my unhinging mind, then it seems the Council has grown tired of imprisoning me without something to show for their efforts. It means my own mother is willing to work with the people harming me just to save herself.

No. No, it *couldn't* have been her. The realization I witnessed spreading over her face is razor sharp in my mind as I recall our last moments together. *"Your father is the Morningstar,"* she said, her voice laced with a surprise that continues to baffle me. She didn't know about my father. But how could that be if Gabriel is my mother?

Unless she isn't, the voice of doubt murmurs. *Unless there's some other reason you were able to open Alexander's tomb.*

Or maybe you're just trying to make me second-guess everything I think I know, I counter.

A venomous growl burns my airways, and I suppress the growing urge to scream. I don't even know what's true anymore. I'm certain Lucifer is my father—I felt the truth of our connection in my blood. But Gabriel...her blood never spoke to mine. All I ever experienced in her presence was a crippling sense of forced loyalty. A loyalty I didn't feel when I saw her here, much to my bewilderment. Of course, that could boil down to our degrading relationship and the fact I no longer *want* to please her or, the more likely reason, because it wasn't really her. That what I saw was all in my head.

A low laugh breaches my lips. Even if I did know anything about Alexander, I'm not sure the Council would be wise to believe a word I say. I can't discern what's real and what's not, and doubt is my ever-present companion, confusing my memories and making me question everything I thought I knew about my life and this world. There is only one thing I know with absolute certainty. Real or not, Alexander left me behind. Caleb left me behind, just like everyone in my life always has. Because—

"I am nothing," I whisper.

"Except a Gray," a ringing voice chimes in.

An exhalation punches from my lungs as I spin around, my unfocused gaze searching for the source of this new interruption to my otherwise solitary existence. I half-expect to see Uriel there, ready to once again attempt to prod me for information I don't have. Instead—

My eyes blow wide.

"Hello again, Daughter," Lucifer says soothingly. His golden hair shines like the morning sun, and dark tendrils lick over his skin in greeting, his aura the same as the last time I saw it, bringing me a momentary sense of comfort and ease until I notice the absence of sound between us. Where I expect to hear that familiar call, that ethereal melodic hum in my blood, there is nothing.

Only inexplicable silence.

"You—" The word sticks in my throat, distorted by the threat of tears, and it takes every logical thought I still possess to remind myself this is a lie. Just like Gabriel, this isn't real. *He* isn't real. "You aren't really him. You're just in my head."

If he was here, wouldn't I feel him? The one and only time we met, our blood announced its connection in an enchanting melody, the vibrations of which I felt right down to my marrow, like strings plucked on a harp made of my tendons and bones. Now that we're together again, wouldn't his blood sing to mine like it did then? Or does such a connection only occur once—upon initial meeting—never to be heard again? If so, maybe that's why I never felt Gabriel. If it *is* a singular, one-time event, then her blood would've sung to mine when I was born—too new to the world to retain any recollection of that moment. Or of her when our paths eventually crossed again.

A flicker of indecision crosses the Morningstar's face, the luminescent golden curls crowning his head bobbing slightly when he lifts his chin. "I assure you I am as physically present as you are."

"No." I shake my head. "She wasn't real and neither are you. You're a figment created to torment me, just like Gabriel."

Because if he *is* here, that means he betrayed me, too, and I'm not sure I can handle that.

He did hand you over to the Council, that small voice in the back of my head reminds me.

"Gabriel?" Lucifer sputters her name as if he hasn't heard it spoken aloud in centuries. "Dear child, the Messenger is not here. I'm afraid no one among the Fallen or Faithful alike has any inkling where she is."

So, it wasn't her. As that realization sinks in, I find myself torn between relief and bitter disappointment—relief that my own mother didn't turn on me like I feared and disappointment that she didn't even try to come for me. That she fled the

Council at the first opportunity. That she saved herself and didn't look back. And why would she? She didn't want me when I was born. She has no reason to want me now, especially after what I did.

If the Council went to such extreme lengths to secure Alexander, what chaos have I unleashed on the world by freeing him? I never allowed this thought to fully form before now, too much of a coward to take responsibility for my actions and face my own culpability. But now, it hangs on every breath I draw, gripping my conscience with guilt.

Heart racing, I stare up at Lucifer, trying my best not to quiver under his scrutiny. The cold-edged detachment in every word he utters is mirrored in those brilliant blue eyes, which pin me in place, paralyzing my body. This is nothing like how he spoke to me at the Serapeum, the tenderness in his voice supplanted now by what could almost be mistaken for disdain. But for whom? For me? Or for Gabriel?

The answer doesn't seem to matter, and as my belief that he's just another hallucination begins to weaken, I can't help spitting out, "Messenger? Is that how you refer to a woman you once loved?" *Or at least liked enough to sleep with,* I refrain from adding. "The woman you share a child with?"

But as these words leave me, doubt encroaches again, and I wonder if I'm wrong about everything. If Gabriel isn't my mother at all.

But Lucifer doesn't deny my accusation, cementing what I've

suspected since the Council put the thought in my head. That despite the missing blood song between us, Gabriel really is my mother. Instead, he lets out a stony laugh. "How little you understand about our world."

I balk at his callous tone and take a reflexive step backward, pressing my back to the glass wall behind me. Is this really the same person who held me in his arms and promised to find me again? He wears my father's face but the cruelty I find in his features is unrecognizable.

This isn't real. He isn't real, I remind myself, but at the same moment, that nagging voice of doubt purrs in my ear, *He didn't need to find you because he always knew exactly where you were.*

Nausea twists my stomach in knots. Lucifer is on the Council—I gathered as much from the interaction I witnessed between him and the Archangels and other Archdemons who were present that day under the school. But could he be working *with* them, like I worried Gabriel was?

Did he help them put me in this cage?

Chest heaving, I watch, panic swelling in my ribcage, as the Morningstar folds his hands behind his waist. "Gabriel went against no one for my sake, that much I know. After the Fall, we went our separate ways. The Fallen took our desired places on Earth, enjoying the freedoms we yearned for and went to war over while the Faithful remained by the Creator's side, always his dutiful servants. Gabriel more so than the others."

A breath catches in my throat, and my pulse skitters under

my skin as that daunting revelation I keep coming back to presses at the edge of my thoughts again, screaming for me to finally accept it. If what I'm hearing right now is true, that would mean my parents conceived me before the Fall. Before the angels' war. A war my father started.

Confusion scratches at the scattering pieces of my mind. *That can't be right,* I assure myself, repeating the excuse I've always countered this idea with every other time it's surfaced since I was imprisoned. *I'm seventeen. Only seventeen.* The vivid memory of my terrible childhood solidifies that certainty, so either Lucifer is lying and he and Gabriel were consorting long after the divide was established, or she found some way to…what? Delay my birth? I guess anything is possible when you can wield magic, but surely someone—Faithful, Fallen, or Nephilim—would've noticed a pregnant Archangel. The alternative is that I'm wrong about everything and she didn't give birth to me seventeen years ago. In which case…when the hell was I born? Why am I not older if I am actually *older*?

And if I was conceived before the divide was erected, before the Lights and Darks took on the form of their choice during the Fall, then why am I a Gray? Before free will transformed the Fallen into Darks, wouldn't all the angels have been Lights, reflecting their pure allegiance to the Creator? Or were they something else altogether? Hell, maybe they weren't even that different to Grays, the irony of which is far from lost on me given my current predicament.

The thought of Grays steers my mind in another direction, down a path I've never wandered before. Was Gabriel the reason Lucifer defied the Creator? If so, the hypocrisy she displayed in regards to my friendship with Caleb makes perfect sense. Considering which side Gabriel chose in the Great Battle, it's no wonder she didn't approve of us mixing. Maybe she didn't only see her past with Lucifer reflected in our budding relationship, but feared history itself would be repeated in some destructive, sweeping way, and she'd be helpless to stop it.

If Alexander is as dangerous as I'm beginning to think, then I suppose she was right to worry. After all, it was our friendship that led to his freedom.

Shaking off that thought, I stare hard at…my father? Or yet another hallucination wearing his face, just like the one of my mother? He stares at me like a hawk watching a mouse, waiting for the perfect moment to strike—or in this case, for me to break the lengthy silence. The appraising way he looks at me reminds me of the doctors I encountered at the hospital, of the psychiatrist I was forced to speak with on a near daily basis to try to get to the bottom of my unforgivable actions. Of the crimes which landed me in there to begin with. There's a sense of perception and curiosity behind his gaze but little else. Certainly none of the warmth I glimpsed in those startling blue depths when we met.

"If you had known—" The words tumble out of me of their own volition, my desperation for validation—for the parental love I've been deprived of since birth—like fingers tightening around my throat. I flinch, wincing at the crack in my voice before clearing it, but I can't seem to bring myself to finish the thought. *If you had known about me, would you have abandoned me, too?*

He considers me for a moment, his brow pinching then easing again as understanding takes shape in his eyes. "If I had known," he growls, flattening his palm to the glass, "do you believe I would've allowed you to be an orphan? I would've claimed you, and you would've stood at my side as you truly are—not a half-mortal child but an angel worthy of deference. Luna Morningstar, my daughter and the heir to my legacy."

Luna Morningstar...

Strange, that in all the time I've been here—however long that's been, given the way time seems to work in this dimension—I've never once thought of myself with that moniker. Even knowing who my parents are, I've never seen myself as anyone other than this broken, only partially-filled shell of a person, still human in so many ways. I was empty before I met Caleb, and I was only just beginning to grow accustomed to life as a Nephilim before the revelation of my real heritage was dropped onto my head like a bomb. How could I have ever considered my identity as a Morningstar when I can barely embrace myself as an angel?

"But I'm a Gray," I protest, recoiling from his words despite how much I wish them to be true. "My very existence is sacrilege in the eyes of your kind."

Lucifer scoffs. "The Fallen are more forgiving of what our kind would deem forbidden transgressions than our Faithful brethren. We don't take kindly to orders from others, one of many differences between the Lights and the Darks."

This comment triggers a memory—when Caleb told me he'd take me back to Babel with him once I helped him free his grandfather. I remember contemplating how that would work, but he seemed so certain of the Darks, that they would accept me as one of their own without hesitation, regardless of my Light blood. Now, I can't help wondering if he was blinded by his own acceptance of me and by his fear of losing the friendship we both held onto so tightly. After witnessing what I did in Alexandria—the debate among the Council over my part in Alexander's escape—I can see now what would have really awaited once the truth of what I am got out. It didn't matter what Caleb said. He's just a Nephilim while far more powerful figures dictate our every move and fate.

To them, a prison is the only place I belong.

Unease tightens in my stomach like an overwound coil. "And now?" I manage, the words a mere whisper.

"I would've claimed you, and you would've stood at my side…"

Is there any hope for such a thing to still happen?

His gaze softens. "That depends on what you do next."

Sweat breaks out across my skin, and my heart thunders in my ears in anticipation of what he'll say—of what inevitable demand he'll make of me on behalf of the Council. Because that's what this is: a negotiation. I see that clearly now.

"Luna." The golden-rimmed azure of his irises seems to sparkle as he leans in, bringing his face so close to the glass I can make out every detail of his features with ease. Every sharp plane. Every speck of light in his eyes. "How long have you known?"

Fear is a lump in my throat, suffocating me. *Known?* "Known what?" I rasp.

"Your parentage," he answers, almost barking the words. "When did the Messenger reveal the truth to you, Daughter? Just how long have the two of you known and been conspiring against the rest of our kind?"

Shock tears the air from my lungs. Conspiring? Is that really what the Council believes happened? Does Lucifer really think I'm capable of such a thing?

Why wouldn't he? that voice of doubt retorts. *He doesn't know you…and you don't know him.*

You're right, I realize, gaping at my father, my eyes darting between each of his, noting the lack of affection I glimpsed the day we met. Could this really be the same man who tried to stand between me and the Archangels and Archdemons he considered his brothers and sisters? The same man who once started a war over a desire for free will and, after what I witnessed between him and Gabriel when he came to her aid under the Serapeum, perhaps even over the freedom to love? *I don't know him at all.*

"The Council is willing to be merciful," he continues, but his voice barely penetrates the distress rooting me in place. "Tell me this and you can go free."

"I-I didn't," I stammer, fumbling over my protest. "I had no idea who either of you were to me until that day. Gabriel… she had nothing to do with what happened." He snorts, unconvinced, and I snap, "This isn't some conspiracy. Gabriel told me next to nothing in the few months I knew her. I don't think she knew who I was, either. Suspected it, maybe, but if she did know, she never said anything. Not to me, at least. And we certainly never worked together to free Alexander or *conspire* against the rest of our kind."

Lucifer's irises darken to a startling black, like shadows melting through a thick sheet of ice. "You expect me to believe that you did not recognize your own mother? That her blood fails to call out to yours or yours to hers? That is not possible."

He doesn't comment on the lack of our own bond song, perhaps hoping I won't notice it's missing or I'm too ignorant of our species to question the change. But I do notice, and his words are enough to answer one of the many mysteries pestering me, finally giving me clarity on at least one matter.

"You mean," I begin, my own voice a tremulous whisper now, "like how yours is supposed to be calling to mine?"

His eyes flash. "Your prison nullifies such magic, so I am not surprised you do not hear the call of my blood. You may not feel it, Daughter, but I assure you, *I* do."

Despite the vehemence of his tone—the forced conviction I sense behind every syllable—the subtle way his lips twitch at the corners is all the confirmation I need. He's lying. He doesn't feel the song between us because it isn't there. Because this isn't happening.

Because he isn't here.

"You're lying. This isn't real. *You* aren't real."

"I already told you—"

"The last thing you said to me..." I hesitate, my breath hanging on the knife's edge of the question that will confirm my suspicions once and for all. "Back at the Serapeum. What was it?"

"I..." He pauses, clearing his throat, then shakes his head. "I cannot recall."

Because you aren't him.

As if reading my thoughts, the hallucination masquerading as my father pulls his hand away from the glass, leaving behind a fogged, opaque impression. Then, with an exasperated sigh, he shutters his eyes and takes several steps away from my cage, the mist shrouding his body until all trace of his black clothes and golden hair is lost in a rising sea of white. When the fog settles once more, as expected, all I find where he stood before is empty air.

My wings tense around me as I inch toward the wall where the imprint of his hand remains, printed into the glass like a scorch mark. Holding my breath, I press my fingertips against the ghostly stain of his, remembering the last words my real father said to me before the Council brought me here to inflict their punishment.

"I will find you again, Daughter. I promise."

"No," I murmur, my wings going slack as the imprint fades and I slump to my knees, my body suddenly weak. My hand falls away from the glass, limp at my side, as a tear drips down my cheek. "You won't."

seven

CALEB

THE SHADOW ROAD DIRECTLY into Babel is well-traveled, so I have to find a path that's less obvious. More human, like playing tourist as I stare at the ruins of Babylon, the Tower of Babel standing out like a beacon. My aviators beat back the glaring sun as does the baseball cap with a Yankees logo shadowing my sunglasses. My vanity protests at the cap and the fact that it makes me look blatantly American, which should be suspicious to any local paying attention. Not many American civilians flock to Iraq these days for vacation. However, my mom is Iranian, so I guess I don't look too out of place. Who am I kidding? I have Westerner stamped all over me. Ugh, fuck hats, my locks need to roam free. I might be one of the few dudes on the planet who feels that way.

Out of patience and fucks to give, I sent my little clay golem to pester Hammurabi, who agreed to meet me out here and then take me to see Asmodeus, which makes me twitchy. I'm not quite sure I can trust the Archdemon. With stopping Alexander, sure, but with Luna? My gut roils, but I'm out of options.

"Nice hat," a deep voice drawls behind me.

I whip around from my inspection of Ishtar's gate to find Hammurabi watching me with an amused expression. I should've recognized that baritone, but I'm on edge and jumpier than a virgin on prom night. Not that I know what that's like. Nephilim don't do prom, and I lost my virginity at the tender age of fourteen.

I touch the brim of my cap in mock salute, my shaggy hair clinging to my damp skin. "They're not just for Americans anymore," I protest.

"Of course not. I have a closet full of them," the Babylonian king shoots back.

I snort despite my tension. The thought of Hammurabi wearing a cap with a sports logo is so ridiculous I want to laugh aloud. The king has modernized, but judging by the length of his beard, not that much.

His face darkens, like an eclipse over the sun, wiping away his humor. "You've risked much, Caleb, to come here. I have no news of your Luna."

Well, that sucks. I take a deep breath. "We'll get to that in a minute. Shit just hit the fan," I say.

One black brow arches. "Young one, 'shit hit the fan,' as you so charmingly put it the moment you helped release Alexander into the world," Hammurabi growls.

I resist the urge to flinch, squaring my shoulders. "Yeah, yeah, I suck. We've been over this, okay? Let's focus on the here and now. I need Asmodeus's help, and I have info she needs about Alexander."

Hammurabi gives me an assessing look, his dark eyes slicing into me like a scalpel trying to cut to my true intentions. "You've chosen to leave your grandfather then?"

I ignore the bitter concoction brewing in my gut as I willingly turn my back on my blood. Yeah, I've chosen a side. Luna's. I have to get her back. And Armageddon isn't my idea of a good time. Mortals will die, mortals like Mom. I can't let that happen.

"Yes," I say, knowing once I meet with Asmodeus and convince her to help me, there's no turning back. I *can't* go back to the citadel. Alexander will know I betrayed him, and he'll send Ishtar on the hunt if I step one foot in Afghanistan. I try not to piss my pants at the thought of the goddess of love and war coming for me.

A look of pride spreads on Hammurabi's face, making me feel reassured about my decision. He's trained me well. He and Ishtar. I can handle my shit.

"Come, Caleb, let's get you inside before someone recognizes you," he says, touching my arm and pulling me into a shadow and right into Asmodeus's office.

It's a neat trick—one I would've used if I knew how. Students aren't exactly privy to the direct route leading to our headmistress's office. And to be honest, Asmodeus, like all the Archdemons and Archangels, is intimidating as hell. Earth-shattering power sheathed within a stunningly beautiful shell. I was always on her radar for being top of my class, and that's all I wanted to be on her radar for. Definitely not for breaking Alexander the Great out of his prison and helping to start a war, with her best friend, no less.

I focus on Asmodeus, my nerves prickling in fear and anticipation. The Archdemon sits on a settee that looks like it belongs in a swords-and-sandals epic. The delicate legs are gilded with golden lion heads carved into the wood in the Babylonian fashion. Her red hair holds none of the orange notes from a fire. It's the color of garnets, gleaming and otherworldly. Cat-green eyes lined with citrine stare at me, uncomfortably blank. I can't get a read on her, and I flick my gaze away first, acknowledging her dominance.

"Caleb," she greets me in her smoky voice, the light rasp making the hairs on the back of my neck stand at attention. "You've been a very naughty boy." The words are light but devoid of humor.

I swallow, my throat suddenly dry. I say the only thing I can. "I'm sorry... I didn't fully understand the situation. He's my grandfather—my blood—and I—" I clamp my mouth shut. Asmodeus isn't interested in my babbling reasons. I broke the Conqueror out of prison, and no excuse in the world will make up for that.

But she surprises me by saying, "Yes, I understand the pull of blood, especially for you." Her words make me feel raw, like my daddy issues are on display for her to dissect. "And I know how persuasive Ishtar can be." Those last words are hissed, like a spitting cat with its back arched and fangs bared.

Glancing back up, I meet her eyes. They are no longer cold and blank, the bright green reflecting anger and bitter disappointment. I've been so busy with Gramps and trying to find out where the hell Luna is that I haven't given much thought to how betrayed Asmodeus must feel by Ishtar. They're besties, for the Morningstar's sake. To stab an Archdemon in the back is no small feat. Ishtar better hope Alexander can protect her from Asmodeus or that she never runs into the Archdemon on the Shadow Road.

"Ishtar talks a good game, and I probably never would have gone after Grandfather if she hadn't suggested it," I admit, but I can't totally throw my mentor under the bus. "But in the end, I wanted it just as badly as she did. He's Alexander the fucking Great. It wasn't that hard to convince me."

No, she didn't have to persuade me too much to go to the Serapeum, but to involve Luna... That was the hard sell and she managed, to my lasting regret. My mouth tightens and I look away.

As if Asmodeus reads my thoughts, she asks, "And the girl? The Gray?" Her voice lingers on the last word.

"Luna is innocent in all this," I say, voice hard. "She didn't know what she was really getting into, and I...I should have never asked her to help me."

A sudden thought hits me. I've been so busy trying to get myself out of the quicksand of shit I willingly jumped into that I've missed the obvious. If I had never gotten Luna involved with this madness, would she have ever found out she was an angel? And a Gray, at that. I seriously doubt it. The parents who abandoned her didn't seem too concerned about her celestial status. And they were complete dumbasses, too. Letting an *angel* out in the world, believing they were human. Of course, Luna dished out some accidental damage, and of course, she feels horrible for it. I'd like to use my special angel-killing knife and take a pound of flesh from her mom and dad for what they put her through.

Asmodeus arches a perfect brow. "How long did you know she was a Gray?"

Startled, I glance at Hammurabi. I explained all this to him already, and I know he passed it on to his boss. "For a hot second. I didn't even know Grays existed." I don't mention that Luna could see the Enochian under the Serapeum when I couldn't and that should have made my Spidey-senses tingle. "I didn't know she was an angel until Grandfather brought her wings out. Shit, I didn't know *Alexander* was an angel, either." I nod to the Babylonian king, standing at attention at the Archdemon's side, face wiped clean of emotion. "I've told him all this already."

Asmodeus frowns, and the temperature noticeably drops a few degrees. I suppress a shiver. "And you'll tell me. Everything. *Now.*"

I spill my guts again, this time adding on details about Gramps's plan, pausing before I say, "Lilith is on board and so is…Gilgamesh."

Asmodeus's eyebrows reach for the sky, and shock erases all that stoicism on Hammurabi's face. "Because of Ishtar," Asmodeus says, and it's not a question.

"That's part of it," I say. "But he honestly believes in Grandfather's mission statement. He resents being forced into retirement and watching his golden age be destroyed. He thinks history is repeating itself, and Alexander can save us all."

Asmodeus's eyes flick up to Hammurabi. "A true believer."

"That's dangerous," Hammurabi answers. "If one Light falls, then—"

"Others are sure to follow," she says, her eyes pinning me in place. "And you, Caleb? Are you a true believer?"

I take a deep breath, knowing that after what I say next, I won't ever be welcome at family holidays again. "No, I'm not. If Alexander starts a war, millions of mortals will die in the crossfire. The Earth as we know it will be destroyed. We can't let that happen."

Her bright green eyes study me. "And the girl? Luna?"

My chest tightens. No way am I abandoning Luna. I'll go at it on my own if I have to. "She's innocent in all this. I don't care if she's a Gray. That's not her fault. She's a good person. I won't let the Council do to Luna what you did to Alexander. She's not like him, and if you plan on keeping her locked away, I will switch sides again. Yeah, Gramps wants to use her, but at least she'll be free."

I know challenging an Archdemon and Hammurabi is a stupid move, but I can't help it. If they don't kill me or lock me up, I'll go running back to Gramps and beg him on hands and knees to free Luna, feeding him lies that I can convince her to help win his war. Anything to save her if Asmodeus won't help me.

"You'd aid the Great in conquering the world just to free the girl?" Asmodeus asks and Hammurabi scowls.

I glare at her. "She's an angel," I hiss. "Your equal. I'd lie, cheat, and kill to right this wrong. And I'm ashamed as a Dark that you would strip someone of freedom just because of what they are. You of all people should be on her side!" The last words echo around the stone walls of her office, and I flinch. Screaming at her will only get me killed. But I'm so tired of this hypocritical bullshit from my Dark brethren.

The silence stretches between us, and I glance at Asmodeus, wanting to face my beating head on. To my shock, she wears a pleased grin, as if I've passed some test. Hammurabi looks as confused as I feel, his fists clenched at his side.

"Stand down, King," she says, placing a delicate hand on his muscular forearm. He might look stronger, but I know her pretty hand could snap him like a twig. "I, too, have an interest in Luna. I do not wish to entomb her as we did Alexander—"

"But the prophecy—" Hammurabi begins.

"Alexander is the Gray in the prophecy, King. I feel it in my very bones. Luna won't be a part of it unless we allow it, unless we allow Alexander to capture her before we do. And can we trust what the Messenger told us about the prophecy?" She purses her lips, glancing at me and Hammurabi and I frown, wondering why she wouldn't trust Gabriel's word.

"Two Grays are very dangerous. We barely survived one," Hammurabi argues, and I bristle at his unforgiving tone.

Asmodeus goes icy again, and my breath clouds in front of me. "Did we create Alexander with our fear of the prophecy? Shall we do the same to Luna? We have an opportunity here to right so many wrongs, Hammurabi. She can be the bridge to unite us, not the wall to divide us, like the Conqueror."

I raise a hand. "To be fair, Gramps wants the divide gone, too."

Asmodeus's eyes narrow to slits. "Oh, yes, he does. He also wants to subjugate us all to his rule when that divide falls, because he knows best." She gives a disdainful snort. "And he criticizes the Creator for being overbearing and arrogant. He thinks it's his right to rule us."

I shrug, conceding her point. "So if you don't want to imprison Luna, you'll help me?" Hope begins to fill my chest. Asmodeus actually has the power to get me to Goldilocks.

Then I frown. "Don't get me wrong, I'm grateful to have you on my side, but aren't you on Team Council? Didn't you help put Luna away? Why the sudden change of heart? What's in it for you?"

Asmodeus regards me for a moment, as if choosing her words carefully. "I understand why you'd be suspicious, but my intentions are good. I'm doing a favor for a friend. I want to see Luna reunited with her parents."

My eyes round. I guess that means the Archdemon knows who Luna's parents are, but I wonder how that's possible if Goldilocks being a Gray is such a big no-no. I hear a soft rap on the door, and I jerk my head around so fast I almost give myself whiplash. Fear tightens my chest as I wonder if Asmodeus has been sweet-talking me while alerting the Council.

"Ah, the cavalry has arrived," the Archdemon says, her smile saucy. Hammurabi scowls, and she pats his arm as if she's reassuring a child, not a nearly four-thousand-year-old badass. "None of that, King, all will be well. We need Luna. Enter," she commands.

A tall stranger walks into the room. He's Nephilim, that I'm sure of, and a powerful one at that. He's also a…Light. What the actual fuck? Cool, collected Hammurabi snarls at the man, who just returns a serene smile to the pissy king. Calmness radiates from his amber eyes, and his angular features are perfectly relaxed, as if he enters Dark strongholds on a regular basis. He turns his gaze on me, and instantly I feel my tension seep from my muscles.

Suspicion grips me as I stare at the Light. I don't appreciate this manufactured calm, and I bare my teeth at him.

"Caleb," Asmodeus snaps, and I tear my gaze away from the stranger to focus on her. "That's no way to treat a guest, especially one who wants to aid you. Alaric, thank you for coming."

I arch a disbelieving eyebrow. Alaric stares at me with those knowing eyes, searching for something.

"You must be Alexander's grandson," he says. "You smell like him."

I reel back, blinking.

Asmodeus smiles. "Alaric tracks down Nephilim for Gabriel. He's a regular bloodhound for our Light colleagues." The last words hold a shade of malice.

Okay, so we're on the same side but not friends. "Why would you help me?" I demand, knowing I'm likely to get a slap down from Asmodeus, but to my shock, Hammurabi jumps rank and says, "I'd like to know the same thing."

Frost bites my hand and I shudder, looking down at fingers gone blue with cold. My skin looks dead. Hammurabi isn't much better off, but he still glares defiantly at Asmodeus.

Alaric's lilting voice cuts in, "Don't punish them on my account. It's really not necessary."

I can't place his accent, which means he's old. Really old.

Asmodeus smirks at him. "Dear Alaric, it's not just for you. I despise bad manners, and guest rites must be upheld."

I can no longer feel my right arm, and I don't have the time or fortitude to get into a pissing contest with Asmodeus.

"I'm sorry I was a dick," I say to Alaric. He shoots me an amused grin.

"I apologize, son of Michael," Hammurabi says, suspicion heavy on his face. "It's been an age since you've associated with Darks."

Whoa, this guy is *Michael's* son? As in the Archangel Alexander killed? He must hate my grandfather. Then again, I wouldn't blink an eye if my pops gave up the ghost.

"I'm never as far away as you think," Alaric answers, and there's this weird tension that passes through the three of them that I don't understand. Does Alaric have his memories back now, too? Did someone on the Light side do a wipe like Hammurabi did? "None of that matters now. Luna is what I've come for."

I can't keep my trap shut. "Why?" I ask again, my tone more subdued so I get to keep my fingers. "I'm not trying to be an asshole, but what's your interest in my Goldilocks?" I give an inward groan at my slip. Yeah, they all know I have the hots for Luna, but revealing her nickname exposes a depth of vulnerability I'm certainly not comfortable with.

Alaric's lips curve. "Goldilocks? Fitting. Luna is special and damaged, and she doesn't deserve to be burdened with the Council's fear of the prophecy. She didn't come into our world with prejudices. She's truly a bridge between us. Look at the two of you, at your relationship. It gives me some hope. I won't allow the Council to do to her what was done to Alexander."

He speaks Gramps's name with an underlying emotion that isn't hatred. There's affection there despite what Alexander did to Michael. Is it brotherly affection or…something else? I can't tell.

"So, you're okay with Gramps wanting to conquer the world?" I ask.

Alaric frowns. "No, I'm not, but I'm not entirely sure he wasn't pushed into the prophecy by the Council, either."

Asmodeus has the grace to look slightly guilty, but I'm not so sure Alaric is right. I've seen exactly what my grandfather wants. Unification, but with him ruling all. Did the Council force him into it? That I can't say. I wasn't there thousands of years ago, but I don't know if that thirst for power, that absolute conviction that you were meant to rule is something you're pushed into.

Anyway, I can't be bothered with all that ancient history now. I have to save Luna, and I have a powerful Archdemon and Nephilim on my side. And a reluctant Hammurabi. I'm not a dumbass. We may be a band of merry misfits, but these misfits pack a serious punch.

"Let's go get my girl then," I say to Alaric and he grins.

eight

LUNA

MY EYES TRAIL ACROSS the milky haze flooding the expanse on the other side of the glass, my lids drooping, threatening sleep—an escape I once longed for but which ceases to bring peace now, every moment burdened with the same images plaguing my waking thoughts. Days, maybe even weeks, have passed since the encounter with my phantom father. The impostor wearing Lucifer's face is so vivid in my head I can practically see him before me, his presence haunting me like a ghost.

Uriel was right. The Council isn't the real danger in this place—my mind is. I'm unraveling. I don't know what's true and what's not, and every second I spend trapped in this hell makes me question the veracity of every event I experienced since that day Alaric brought me to the Serapeum.

Assuming they even happened at all.

I'm going insane. I realize that now—or, maybe, I'm already

there. If I doubted my sanity before my imprisonment, then my recent encounters with the imagined manifestations of my parents have made it clear that my mind is not only unstable, but damaged beyond repair.

No, that taunting voice in the back of my skull chides me. *Not damaged. Broken.*

Broken… This isn't the first time I've thought of myself this way, like a porcelain doll with cracked skin, tossed into some dusty corner of an attic, abandoned by its owner. The forgotten remnant of someone else's mistake. Surely, that's what Gabriel must have seen me as—why else would she have given me up? Why else would her blood refuse to call out and sing the song declaring me family?

I recall what Lucifer said about how he would've proudly claimed me as his daughter, as a Morningstar, had he known I existed. But those were the words of an apparition, and although the real Lucifer's blood called to mine when we met in the tunnels beneath my school, I can't be certain he would share these false sentiments now—that he would see me as anything other than undeniable proof of a forbidden liaison. For all I know, what he said in my ear right before surrendering me to the Council were empty words. A fleeting consolation to ease the burden of his own guilt as a failed parent and, in that moment, protector.

A demented giggle surges up from my throat. Once again, I consider the possibility that everything I remember—Alaric, my time at the Serapeum, even Caleb—are figments of my imagination, but now, instead of picturing myself back in the hospital, I wonder if I've always been stuck in this place, trapped for being the product of a union this prejudiced world disagrees with.

What if nothing I know is real at all, and I've actually spent my whole life here, alone?

I hug my legs close to my chest and tuck my wings around my body until I'm huddled into a ball, rocking back and forth, suppressing another deranged fit of laughter.

"Nothing is real... Nothing is real..."

"My, my, my," a melodic voice croons behind me. "What has become of you in such a short time, my young savior? Captivity does not become you."

My arms loosen, unlocking my legs, my wings flaring out as I scramble around on the floor and press myself against the wall farthest from this new intruder. A tall, lithe man with mismatched eyes stares back at me through my transparent cage, a curious smile pulling at his full lips.

"A-Alexander?" I stammer before sinking my teeth into the tip of my tongue. This is just another delusion. It has to be.

He arches an elegantly curved brow. "You seem surprised to see me."

I gape at the towering angel, taking him in fully for what seems like the first time, considering the last time we met, our introduction was cut short by my foray into unimaginable pain.

My initial impression of him pales in comparison to what I see now. His hair, which nearly swept the floor before, has been cut into the same hairstyle he donned in the memory he showed me of him and Alaric, his complexion glowing and clean of the grime millennia of imprisonment had caked onto his skin. His eyes, one brown, one blue follow me with a grim amusement, but they fail to hold my focus, my own eyes tracing the outline of his body, registering the distinct shadows of his aura.

My chest deflates with a sigh as I note the inky black threads. I might have only stood before him for a moment, but I saw his aura, and it was nothing like this. It was silver and angry, like shards of glass. Now, it's wrong, just like Gabriel's was.

Why does my mind keep warping this detail?

"No, I'm not," I mutter. "Because you're not really here."

He nods, as if my doubt doesn't surprise him. "I remember this well." At my questioning look, he touches two fingers to the side of his head. "The hallucinations. Madness lingers close to the surface when one is confined in solitude for too long. You forget, I was imprisoned by the Council for thousands of years. Lunacy was my constant companion."

I say nothing at first, willing the hallucination to disappear, to leave me to my solitude. I don't want to talk to him. I don't want to encourage the madness he speaks of or feed it. I just want him to go away.

But, like with Lucifer and Gabriel—like with the psychiatrist I was forced to speak with every day at the hospital—I know

Alexander won't simply go away because I desire it. The delusion won't end until I participate in this pointless charade born from the twisted depths of my thoughts. Until I respond to whatever hold this place has on my mind.

None of this will end until I give in.

Fatigue grips my senses as I reluctantly cave under Alexander's pressing stare. "You seemed sane enough when I opened your tomb."

"Did I?" His wide mouth splits into a smile, and he saunters closer, skirting around the arcing wall of glass until he's standing just beside where I sit, unable to move from my spot on the floor. Squatting down to my level, he lowers his voice. "Well, I assure you, it was not without effort. But then, I had something to fight for in the darkness, to hold me afloat in the tempestuous tides. Such mental anchors help keep us tied to our sanity." He appraises me, rubbing a hand over his well-defined chin. "I wonder, do you intend to fight, too, my young savior? Or will you submit to the chaos breaking your mind?" When I don't speak, he narrows his eyes and scoffs. "Will you allow your light to be dimmed by self-pity?"

I blanch at his words. Is that what I'm doing? Wallowing in destructive despair? I struggle to see my current state of mind as something as simplistic as that. After all, I've experienced exile and the worst kind of betrayal. The anger and heartache eating away at me are more than justified.

"I'm not a Light," I bite back, finally distancing myself from everyone at the Serapeum who treated me like a monster and from the Light angels who chose to imprison me here. I'm not a Light.

But you're not a Dark, either, that voice in the back of my head reminds me.

Caleb's face appears in my thoughts, triggering a suffocating pain that spears my chest. Once, I would've given anything to be like him, but if everything between us was fake and he used me—if I really was just a tool to him, a means to the end of freeing his grandfather—then I can safely say the Darks aren't any better than the Lights. Everyone on both sides has their own agenda while I'm trapped in the middle, drowning.

I shake my head. "I'm like you. I'm a Gray."

Alexander unleashes a barking laugh and pushes to his feet, his eyes fixing me with a patronizing look that reminds me far too much of Gabriel. "And what are Grays but celestial beings composed of both the Light and the Dark? We threaten them, Luna. We jeopardize their precarious truce. That is why they fear us and condemn us to cages. But I can free you." He gestures calmly to the foggy expanse. "I can spirit you away from this prison, and together, we can build a new world. A world where the divide no longer exists. A world where we can rule as the superior beings we are."

His words give me pause. Is that what we are? Is that why the Council insists on keeping me locked here, in this impenetrable egg where my powers are muted and my senses are dulled? Am I here not because I helped free Alexander, but because they want to see all Grays subjugated?

"Join me, Luna," Alexander continues, his deep timbre taking on a slight pleading edge. "Let us gather our strength and challenge the rule of the self-righteous who lord over us. Or…" He pauses, shrugging broad shoulders that seem capable of holding the weight of the endeavor he speaks of. "Stand against me and perish when the world is engulfed by the flames of war."

"Why—" My throat is scratchy, the word barely a breath above silent. Swallowing, I carefully push onto my feet, keeping one hand on the wall for support, and for a long moment, I stare at him as question after question presses at the inside of my skull. Although he can't give me answers I don't already have, I can't stop myself from asking, "Why are those the only options? Why does the world have to burn for the divide to be broken? Why are the Lights and Darks so afraid of each other? Of *us*?"

Alexander lets loose a menacing chuckle that raises the hair on my neck and arms. "They do not fear each other. They fear the Creator. But together, we can bring Him to heel."

A shiver of terror ripples over my feathers. Are these really Alexander's intentions? Or just what I expect from the man who left me to rot in captivity?

"You… You want to take on the Creator?"

He preens at my question, grinning. "To create a new world order, those in power must be overthrown and any threats to our unification destroyed. Let the Creator keep His Heaven. I wish to rule over Earth, to build my kingdom in these mortal lands where our true calling lies. Now is the time for the Lights and Darks to choose a side—to decide which of our two lands will be their Eden. My way, with the reign of the Grays, is the future. Only on Earth can we all truly thrive."

I try to envision it—a world where the divide is gone and the Grays are in power—but all I see is a life where I'm alone, like I've always been. As far as I know, Alexander and I are the only Grays in existence. Maybe we're the only ones who have *ever* existed. So, if we were to rule over this world torn between Dark and Light, what would that mean for those who fall distinctly on one side or another? Is he looking for angels and Nephilim to join his fight?

Or is he looking for people to rule over?

My chest tightens as Caleb's face floods my thoughts again. Despite the pain eating away at my heart, I can't stomach the thought of him being subservient to anyone, least of all to me. The Darks believe in free will above all. How long before they grow tired of Alexander pushing his dominant views onto them? How long before they become his new targets in the war I sense looming before us?

"And what of your grandson?" I blurt out, the words escaping in a rush, as if I have no control of my lips. "Where does he fit into this new world order?"

Confusion mars Alexander's brow. "My grandson?"

His piercing eyes press me for an explanation, but I

instinctively snap my mouth shut, my pulse pounding along the underside of my skin as I'm overcome by a deep, crippling sense of dread that I've said something very wrong—just like I felt with Gabriel when she asked about my father.

I tremble when Alexander takes a step toward me.

"I see," he murmurs, the darkness lapping over his skin thrashing in a frenzy of black and purple blurs. "You mean the transfer from Babel." A low chuckle swells in the space between us. "It seems Asmodeus has some explaining to do."

Asmodeus? The headmistress of Babel?

His words confound me. Didn't Alexander notice his connection to Caleb when they met, just like I recognized Lucifer as my father? Didn't their blood sing to each other in that moment the way the Morningstar's blood sang to mine?

If not, then what the hell does that mean? And what does Asmodeus have to do with any of this? Is she working with Alexander? Ishtar was, so it's not too far-fetched to think the Archdemon in charge of Caleb's school would be involved, too. If she is, it would certainly explain how Caleb managed to snag the transfer opportunity, not that many Darks were up for the challenge—assuming what he told me about that was true.

I think back to the day of Alexander's release, recalling the accusatory faces of the Archangels and Archdemons, who all looked at me like I was the enemy. If Asmodeus is secretly aiding Alexander, then it would seem Gabriel isn't the only one in the Council living a double life behind everyone's back.

Who else is keeping secrets?

And what explosive effect will those secrets have on our lives?

I shake my head. *Stop it. You're panicking over nothing. This isn't real,* I tell myself for what feels like the thousandth time. And yet, no matter how many times I repeat these words, I can never seem to convince myself of it.

I shake my head again, more fervently this time. *This can't be real, Luna. Stop listening to him.* This place is guarded by the Council. How would Alexander have even gotten here, wherever here is, without alerting them all to his presence?

Slamming my hands over my ears, I shrink into the floor and clamp my eyes shut.

This isn't real. This isn't real.

Movement on the other side of the glass wrenches my eyes open, and doubt festers under my skin when Alexander turns on his heel and sets off into the mist without so much as a word and without looking back. Despite my firm belief that he's just an illusion, despite the fact that I *want* him to go, I lurch forward until my hands and chest collide with the glass, my movements driven by a single thought: *What if he isn't?*

What if Alexander is really here and by leaving, he takes my only chance of escape with him?

"Where are you going?" I shriek.

He stills, then turns to face me again, offering me a bored scowl. "Your hesitation leads me to believe you aren't ready to join me, and I cannot very well set you free if there's any chance you may stand in the way of my mission. It would seem your imprisonment serves everyone equally well at the present moment."

What about the freedom you promised me? But when I try to scream those words, he cuts me off with a mocking laugh.

"Besides, you have bestowed us with a wonderful gift—a lead to help us hunt down the Great." As he speaks, the whips of shadow slithering over his skin vibrate with unmistakable pleasure.

A strangled breath parts my lips. "I…" *I don't understand.* But as those words cross my mind, it dawns on me that I do understand. I understand very well. I've been tricked—fooled into believing my mind was the enemy when, all along, the real threat was always the Council.

Uriel lied—lulled me into a false sense of paranoia and terror. And by doing so, by believing this was all in my head, I finally gave the Council something it wanted.

No. I choke back a sob, unwilling to believe I could be so naive. So stupid. That I could fall into his trap so easily, like prey walking willingly into a predator's den. *This isn't real. None of this is real. This is just another hallucination.*

A lump lodges in my throat, disbelief gripping my windpipe, which tightens as I force out the only question I can manage in my panic. "Aren't you Alexander?" I breathe, hoping with every fiber of my being he'll prove me wrong and say yes.

The angel bares his teeth in a sinister smile, more Cheshire Cat than human, letting his guise slip for the briefest of moments. Blood red eyes glare back into mine.

"Now, that is the real question, isn't it?"

nine

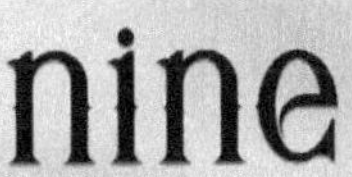

CALEB

ASMODEUS MOVES US FROM her office to a large room I've never seen before deep within the bowels of Babel. Nothing modern has touched this place. Torches provide the only light, casting the room in writhing shadows. It's a creepy and fitting place to plan a jailbreak. I sit at the large table that dominates the room. Made from obsidian, the ebony surface reflects the firelight, adding to the dark mood of the chamber. If the circumstances weren't so dire, I might have a laugh at how cliché it all is.

But my focus is on Alaric and the newcomer murmuring to Asmodeus. A Dark. She popped in from the Shadow Road a few minutes ago, her rich brown skin glowing in the firelight. She's tall and willowy, and she seems vaguely familiar, but I can't place her. She feels like a first generation, her power like a live wire, but I can't tell how old she is.

Alaric gives her a welcoming smile that she returns while

Hammurabi remains sullen. I feel like I've stepped into a bizarre reality no one bothered to tell me about. How is it that Alaric—a *Light*—is so friendly with all these Darks? I was convinced only Luna was open-minded about the divide.

"Nzingha, this is Caleb, the Great's grandson," Alaric says, gesturing to me with a sweeping hand.

I flip through the files of first generations in my brain. Ah, okay. Now, I know who she is. She was the Queen of the Ambundu kingdoms of Ndongo and Matamba. She's not nearly as old as Hammurabi or Alaric, though she's still an antique. She raises an eyebrow as she looks me over, but I don't wither under her hard stare.

"Gramps has a lot of grandkids, Alaric. I'm just the one who got manipulated," I say, grinning at Nzingha, whose eyes flash with surprise.

"Ah, yes, your useless father likes to seed all the gardens, doesn't he?" Alaric says. "Then leaves before the harvest."

I blink. Huh, I guess *everyone* knows my dad's an asshole. "That's a nice way to put it," I say.

"Too nice," Nzingha says, snorting. Well, I guess she's not a fan, either.

"I was trying to be tactful in the presence of the child," Alaric says, winking at me.

I shrug. "Don't worry about me. I haven't needed a security blanket in a long time. I'm a big boy. I can tie my own shoelaces and everything."

Nzingha smiles at me. "Well, you must have your mother's sense of humor." Her eyes snap to Asmodeus. "I'm sure Alexander will bring…" Her lips purse, and her gaze flits to me for a moment. "Your grandfather will teach your father his place soon enough."

I suppress a growl. Enough about that dick. "I'm sure Gramps will find out he's a waste of space before long. But I don't care about him. I care about Luna."

To my utter shock, Hammurabi nods. "Yes, let's focus on someone actually worth our time. The Gray."

I glare at him. "Yes, *Luna*." He scowls at me, and I resist the urge to give him the middle finger. Reckless I am, stupid I am not.

Asmodeus clasps her hands in front of her. "Yes, children, let's get on with it. Time is wasting. Alaric, tell us what you know."

Alaric taps the side of his nose. "As you so charmingly put it before, Asmodeus, I can sniff out Nephilim and more importantly, bloodlines. I always knew there was something special about Luna and I was right."

"You always knew she was a Gray?" I demand, stunned.

He shakes his head. "No, but there was always something that didn't quite add up about Luna's upbringing and the fact we somehow failed to catch wind of her when her powers first began manifesting. Not to mention her scent was strangely dull for someone with celestial blood. Then during my last encounter with her and Gabriel…well, let's just say things became clearer."

I jerk back at the implication, and Hammurabi's mouth drops open, the normally stoic king looking as shell-shocked as I feel. "Um, are you saying—"

Nzingha laughs, but the sound holds no humor. "I'm shocked she'd be stupid enough to do something like this. Not the perfect Messenger."

My eyes swing back and forth between everyone. Asmodeus doesn't seem the least bit surprised, and the other three—now that Hammurabi has recovered—seem resigned to the fact. But I have to make sure.

"You're saying stick-up-her-ass Gabriel is *Luna's* mother?" I can't wrap my head around it. Gabriel is so cold she's glacial. I can't imagine her getting down and dirty with anyone, least of all a Dark. Holy shit, Gabriel fucked a *Dark*.

And that brings up the million-dollar question: Who is Luna's father? And why didn't Gabriel acknowledge her own daughter? Why did she let Luna think she was crazy? Why did she allow the Council to take her? Hot rage sweeps through me so fast I feel dizzy. She's Luna's *mother* for the Morningstar's sake. How could she have just abandoned Luna like that?

Alaric's eyebrows rise at my words. "Yes, she is."

"She's an Archangel, Caleb, give her the respect she's due," Asmodeus says, and I gape at her.

I see red, clenching my fists, and bang them on the table. "That bitch abandoned Luna and let her think she was crazy this whole time, even at the Serapeum. She let the Council take her! Her own daughter."

My father might be a shit, but my mother loves me with the fierceness of a lioness. I can't believe Gabriel of all angels let her daughter loose on the world, knowing what the consequences could be.

"Punish me if you like, but parents who abandon their kids don't deserve my respect, even if they're an Archangel," I spit out.

I don't care if they think my fury stems from my daddy issues. Oh, and where the hell is Luna's daddy? Images of all the Fallen swim through my mind, but I can't match any with my Goldilocks. Wait, that's not true. The conversation in Gabriel's office when I sent my clay golem to spy claws at me. Some weird remark about Lucifer. *Lucifer.* He shines like the sun and so does Luna. By the Creator, it's so obvious if I really think about it. Gabriel is there, too, in the striking beauty of Luna's face, but her coloring, her glow is all the Morningstar.

My mouth drops open as I stare at the others.

Asmodeus gives me a nod, eyes full of pride. "Go on, Caleb," she commands. "Say it."

"Lucifer is Luna's father," I whisper, shaking my head as if that will make it less true or help me make sense of it.

"Lucifer with *Gabriel*?" Nzingha hisses. "I didn't think anyone could thaw the ice queen."

"For once we're in agreement," Hammurabi says.

I ignore them, thinking. When did Lucifer and Gabriel get it on? I mean, I now understand how tight-lipped the Council are about their dirty deeds, but that is one hell of a dirty deed to cover up.

Asmodeus turns to Alaric. "Babel students are the brightest of all the academies, Dark or Light, especially Light. Your precious Nephilim couldn't find their way out of a paper bag. Too busy worrying about their wings to see the bigger picture."

I resist the urge to roll my eyes at the Archdemon's pettiness. Even now, even here, she can't resist getting a dig in. We're all doomed.

To my surprise, Alaric just grins. "Yes, our students seem to operate with blinders the majority of the time," he admits.

"I always did like that about you," Hammurabi says to Alaric. "You recognize your weaknesses."

I wave an impatient hand, suddenly feeling like the adult in the room. "Yeah, yeah, we're better than you, blah, blah. Alaric, how did this happen?"

Alaric chuckles. "Caleb, I'm sure you can figure out *how* it happened."

"Yeah, they got naked, got it. But they're the Morningstar and the Messenger! That's not supposed to happen. And Luna is only seventeen, so how did they manage to keep their affair a secret? Was it hate sex? I can't..." I shake my head again.

"Luna is much older than seventeen, Caleb," Asmodeus says gently. "Well, in a way."

What the hell does that mean?

"Lucifer hasn't been with Gabriel since the Fall. I know this. He avoids her like, well, the plague," Asmodeus explains. "He still carries the wounds of what happened between them, festering away. So that means Luna would have been conceived—"

"Before the Fall," Nzingha says, glancing at the Archdemon and then at Alaric, mouth slightly agape. She shakes her head. "But if that's the case, the girl hasn't been out and about this whole time, or we would've known it. Gabriel must have hidden her somehow."

Alaric nods. "Yes, I believe so. For all intents and purposes, she's a seventeen-year-old girl, but if what Asmodeus says is true—and I have no cause to doubt her—Gabriel must have given birth around the time of the Fall. It's the only thing that makes sense."

Hysteria bubbles through me. Does it? Nothing about this situation makes sense. Thank the Creator I'm sitting down, or my ass would hit the floor. "Since the *Fall*? Where has she been this whole time? That means she's older than Alexander. Than most of *you*. So why doesn't she look older, like you all?"

"That I don't know," Alaric says. "I followed Gabriel to Easter Island just before you released Alexander." He gives me a knowing look, and I go cold with guilt. "She had acted somewhat strangely during a conversation we had about Luna, and when I caught her scent leaving the Serapeum, I knew something was wrong. I assume she was checking on Luna's original birth place, and when she found it empty, she rushed back."

Asmodeus frowns. "Luna has been on Easter Island this entire time? Well, minus seventeen years. But how?" Her cat-green eyes widen. "Ah, the statues. Of course."

Confused, I glance at Alaric, who nods. "Yes, wards, but they're no longer working."

"Someone broke the Messenger's wards to release her daughter," Hammurabi says. "Someone who had to know where the Gray—Luna—was kept." The king looks at Asmodeus.

"I assure you I didn't know. I only suspected Gabriel was hiding a child from Lucifer, but I never had proof," the Archdemon says.

"Who else would have suspected Gabriel was pregnant?" Nzingha asks, dark eyes thoughtful.

Asmodeus flashes a cruel smile. "Lilith and the Messenger were always close." Her voice drips with malice.

Well, the hits keep on coming. Lilith's meeting with Alexander plays through my mind, and I wonder again what she did for Lucifer to ban her. Well, I guess not just Lucifer, the whole Council. And does the Morningstar banging Gabriel count as a betrayal, too?

"The traitor?" Hammurabi growls.

Alaric sighs. "Perhaps she wasn't a traitor, or at least she didn't think she was. Two Grays does rather skew the prophecy, doesn't it?"

I hate being the most ignorant person in the room, but there's so much history between these players, so much subtext and bullshit, that I'm constantly behind. "What does that mean?" I demand, not bothering to hide my irritation.

Alaric turns solemn eyes on me. "Lilith backed Alexander."

Oh. Damn. I guess that explains her cozying up to Gramps. "Okay, but why? Because she knew about Luna?"

Asmodeus forms a steeple with the tips of her fingers, resting her chin on them. "It's a possibility. She may know more than all of us as well. Gabriel would have confided in her."

I hold up my hands. "Okay, but I don't get it. Were Lucifer and Gabriel a one-night stand? Why hide Luna from him? Just because of the prophecy?"

Asmodeus gives me a pitying look. "Much like you and your Luna, Lucifer and Gabriel were in love." I go cold then hot at hearing the L word again. I'm not quite ready to face it yet. And if I do, it won't be in front of an audience. Just Goldilocks. "He went to war for the right to love her, and she chose the Creator in the end."

Well, at this point, my jaw is going to be permanently stuck to the floor. Poor Lucifer. To have the woman you love, the woman you've risked everything for, run back to the Creator with her tail between her legs must be a straight up kick to the nuts. No wonder he didn't show up that night when Gabriel called the meeting. He probably can't stand to be on the same continent as her, let alone in the same room.

I rub my temples, willing my brain not to implode. "So Gabriel rejects Lucifer, the Fallen are kicked out of Heaven, and she finds out she's knocked up. At that point, I guess she can't go to Lucifer."

A bitter laugh escapes Asmodeus. "Of course, she could have, the arrogant fool. He would have taken care of the child if she wouldn't have. He loved her. He loves her still, more's the pity."

"She believed she couldn't go to him anyway," Alaric says softly. "They're together now, so maybe they can finally work on all their issues. For the good of their child at least."

Asmodeus's lips curve into a venomous smile. "I'm sure they'll put aside millennia of heartbreak for the good of their child now that Gabriel has toppled off her pedestal of moral superiority in such a spectacular fashion."

"Not Gabriel's biggest fan?" I say to Asmodeus and she sneers.

"The Morningstar deserved better," she says, and the room goes icy for a brief moment, my breath clouding in front of me.

"Revisiting ancient history isn't helping us," Alaric says gently.

"Speak for yourself," I retort, happy to finally have a peek behind the curtain, and oh, what a peek it is. "And it's not like it's not relevant." My poor Goldilocks. When we find her, she's got one hell of a shock coming her way. I also know she'll be incredibly hurt Gabriel was her mother this whole time and never said anything to her. Wait a minute. "Alaric, you said Gabriel went to Easter Island to see if Luna was still there? If

Luna is her kid, wouldn't she have recognized her immediately?"

Nzingha looks to Asmodeus. "She cloaked her, even from herself," she ventures and the Archdemon nods.

"Yes, I believe she concealed her from all, hiding the call of her blood. She did it so well she didn't even know her own daughter was in her presence. After all her deception and lies, she wasn't able to save Luna in the end. I'd toast her downfall if I didn't know how her betrayal will sting Lucifer," Asmodeus says.

"Like a scorpion," Hammurabi adds. "Lucifer has no other children."

"Luna is the true innocent in all this," Alaric says, and I can't believe I'm thinking it, but I actually like this Light. "And whether they're fighting like hissing cats—or what did you say Caleb, having hate sex?—we need Lucifer and Gabriel to help protect her."

"You had no luck finding them?" Asmodeus asks, drumming her fingers on the obsidian table.

"They're moving too quickly, and we can't wait around. You know Luna's location," Alaric says. "You called to *me*."

That still surprises the hell out of me, and I can't figure Alaric out. He's a decent guy. I wince at myself, my prejudices hitting me in the face. It might take more than Luna to heal this divide.

Asmodeus twists her full lips as her hard gaze weighs over each of us. "You're here because I trust you," she begins, and I slant a glance at Hammurabi. He might not be on board, but I can't see him running to the Council to tattle, either. "We have to stop the Conqueror, and in order to do that, Luna must be free. She cannot be allowed to fall into his hands." Her bright green eyes land on me. "And whether he's delaying fetching her or not, Alexander is no fool. He's a military strategist who will use every tool at his disposal. We've underestimated the Great before and we cannot again."

It's a pretty speech, but it doesn't exactly reveal where Luna is.

Asmodeus takes a deep breath, and I notice a slight tremor ripples through her frame. She doesn't like betraying the Council, I realize. She believes she's in the right, but it still doesn't sit well with her. I want to beat the table with my fists, but like the other three, I keep my mouth shut and let the Archdemon take her sweet time. Not like I can force her to hurry anyway.

"Luna is suspended in a pocket reality between the Shadow and Blessed Roads. Each member of the Council—with the obvious exception of Gabriel and Lucifer—used our essence to create her prison. Brute strength can't break it, and as we learned with our mistake with Alexander, blood can't break it, either. Only the Council together can unravel what we've woven," Asmodeus explains, face grim. Her shimmering eyes focus on Alaric. "I was hoping you could find Gabriel and Lucifer. As members of the Council, maybe they could combine their strengths and create a weak point in our defenses. As we both have Darks and Lights in our party, I can tell you how to travel there, but although you'll be able to interact with Luna, you won't be able to free her."

"So, this has all been a waste of time?" I cry, and this time, I do pound my fists on the table. I glare at Asmodeus. "Why bring us together if you can't do anything?"

Hammurabi is in my face in two seconds flat. "Don't speak to your mistress like that, child," he hisses, hand fisted in my shirt. His eyes brim with fury, and I want to smash my forehead into his nose so bad I can taste it. And yeah, it will feel fantastic for a few seconds, and then I'll get my ass beat.

I swallow down my bitter words and lower my eyes, giving the Archdemon a deferential nod. "Sorry... I'm..." I can't finish the sentence, too disappointed and pissed for a decent apology, so I just stare at the ridiculous table.

Asmodeus's voice is shockingly gentle. "I understand your frustration, Caleb. Alaric will find Lucifer and Gabriel soon, and then we will save Luna. You have my word."

I look up, my gaze clashing with Alaric's and that damn Calm washes over me. It still pisses me off, but this time, I just let him do his thing. He's putting his dick on the line, too, helping an Archdemon and me find Luna.

"It will take me some time, but I'll find them," Alaric reassures me, and I drag a smile out from somewhere and paste it on.

"Come along, Caleb," Asmodeus says, rising on liquid joints. "I'll show you where you're to stay this evening."

Nzingha strides to the door. "I'll keep my ear to the ground. Perhaps Mammon will feel particularly chatty about Gabriel and Lucifer."

"One can only hope," Alaric says, following her out the chamber.

I go to follow Asmodeus when Hammurabi stops in her path. The Archdemon cocks her head, sizing up the king, and I release an irritated sigh. I swear if he starts bitching to us about saving Luna, I will smash his face in, even though I know he'll get back up again and break my spine.

Hammurabi places a finger to his lips and gestures behind him. Asmodeus nods and suddenly it feels like we're under water.

"What is it you wish to share, King?" Asmodeus says, flipping lustrous red strands over her shoulder. Her voice has a weird echo to it, and I know she's ensured we're not overheard by Alaric or Nzingha.

"I may know of a way to save Luna without the Morningstar and the Messenger," Hammurabi says and nods toward me.

The fuck? If I knew how to save Luna, I wouldn't be here in the dungeon of doom. I'd be out saving her.

"The dagger," Hammurabi reminds me and I blink. Oh, Gramps's knife.

"The dagger?" Asmodeus's brows rise. "*Alexander's* dagger?" she snarls, and I shiver at the sudden arctic temperature. "*Caleb* has it?"

The Babylonian king squares his shoulders. "Yes, I wasn't going to allow him to go to the Serapeum like a lamb to the slaughter. He needed to protect himself. He's the only one who can wield it. Besides Alexander, of course. And his bastard father, wherever he is—and I suppose all his children who are out there."

Asmodeus's icy rage terrifies me, but in the blink of an eye, she has herself under control, which is even scarier. She turns those predator-green eyes toward me, and I want to shrink in on myself and disappear. "Gabriel was wounded, and I assumed it was from Alexander, but it was you, sweet child." Her flinty gaze finds Hammurabi. "We'll speak of this later, King, but I have to admit this changes things."

Hope floats to the surface again, and I tentatively ask, "It does?"

An unholy grin lights her face. "Yes, it changes the game."

ten

LUNA

TERROR CLAWS AT MY flesh, cutting deep, until the fear rushing through me seems to bleed from my pores. I've been at the brink of insanity so many times—thought I was already there—lost myself in what I was sure were the tumultuous waters of delirium, and yet…nothing has ever felt like this. This nagging in my brain, this constant questioning if I can trust what I'm seeing and hearing… I thought I knew what it was like to have my mind play tricks on me, but never have I experienced this infuriating sensation of uncertainty, not even at the Serapeum when I was truly convinced I was crazy.

Crazy… I choke out a laugh. If that's what I am now, then what I was before was the opposite. Even with Alexander's voice in my head, I was more sane during those handful of months in Alexandria than I am at this moment.

Now, when everything and everyone I see is a lie.

Nothing I've encountered in this place has been real.

Gabriel. Lucifer. Alexander. But they weren't hallucinations like I thought. They were manifestations created with the sole purpose to strip me of the secrets I didn't even realize I kept. Secrets like the identity of my father. Secrets like why Caleb helped me free Alexander.

A shudder rips through me at the memory of those unsettling vermilion eyes staring back into mine, the intensity of the Fallen's gaze seeming to tear back my skin and bones and see into the deepest parts of my soul. It was a Dark posing as my parents and Alexander—I realize that now. Hell, I should've realized it the moment I noticed Gabriel's aura was wrong. But I didn't and as a result, I have become the one thing I never wanted to be.

A betrayer.

Agony lances my heart, and I wince as my interrogator's words flood my ears. *"You have bestowed us with a wonderful gift—a lead to help us hunt down the Great."*

My insides curdle as horror spreads through me, sluggish and deliberate, taking its time to undo me. The Archangels and Archdemons playing the role of my captors were missing a vital piece of the puzzle, and I just unwittingly handed it to them. They must have suspected there was something else linking me to Alexander aside from our shared legacy as Grays. Why else would I, a girl with limited prior knowledge of our world, have set him free unless someone else was pulling my strings? Someone like the Great's grandson and heir.

Someone who could potentially be used to draw the Gray

out of hiding.

Tears prick at my eyes, but I swipe them away. Caleb's too smart for that. He wouldn't be stupid enough to let anyone use him, not the way I have. Besides, he's likely off-grid with Alexander, and to find one, they would need the other. So long as they stay out of sight, he'll be safe.

Unless—

I press my palms to the curved wall of glass, bowing my head as a nauseating fear twists my stomach. *This is why they're keeping me alive.* Not because I'm a Gray, but because they know, heartbreak or not, Caleb means something to me…and they're hoping he'll be foolish enough to come here. To try to rescue me.

They aren't afraid of me, I realize. I'm just the bait needed to catch a much larger fish.

A hysterical laugh escapes me. It doesn't matter. Caleb won't come. He left me here. He doesn't care—

But if he does? that voice of doubt dares to ask.

My growing terror pulls me down to my knees.

"Then I hope he stays away," I breathe, my voice cracking.

Although the thought sends a rush of pain to my chest, I find myself hoping that what Caleb admitted he felt for me at the Serapeum was a lie. A ploy to gain my trust and turn me into his pawn—a tool to be disposed of once I fulfilled my intended purpose. Because if that's all I was to him, he'll have no reason to come back for me. And if he doesn't come back for me, he'll stay safe. Whether he played me or not, I don't want him caught up in this. I want him to stay far, far away where the Council can never lay a finger on him…

Even if that means I remain here forever.

"Stay away," I whisper again as scalding hot tears stream down my cheeks.

The hours pass in a fitful daze. I'm not sure how many crawl by uncounted—maybe it's even been days since the impostor wearing Alexander's face pried the knowledge of Caleb's identity from my lips. Like always, time eludes me in this place, and all I can do in my cage is wait.

Wait and see if Caleb comes for me like I fear my captors are hoping.

The soft patter of footsteps behind me has me launching to my feet, my body tense as I spin on my heel, my heart racing, my senses on high alert. As the footsteps draw closer, the fog of mist parts, and a familiar face emerges from the haze.

"Hello again, Luna," Uriel says, dipping into a bow, the Archangel's brown skin radiant against the colorless mist. He straightens, tapping a finger to his chin as a knowing smile darkens his gaze. "It's a pity, the upbringing you've had. A misplaced nobody who was bound to live life as a mortal, hidden among humans who would only ever view her as a threat. As something they could not understand." Knitting his hands behind his back, he looks me up and down with a sort of restrained curiosity that raises the hair on the back of my neck. Or maybe what I'm sensing is distaste. It's impossible to tell which. "But you are not no one, and you are certainly not mortal," he continues, "although the threat part remains to be seen. The certain grasp we had on the truth has crumbled with the revelation of your mother."

Uriel scoffs, disregarding the surprise on my face. "Gabriel, the Messenger, bearer of the Creator's words," he spits, his brusque tone lethal. "Who is to say she told us the whole truth pertaining to the Gray destined to destroy our kind and our world? Your very existence begs the question. Perhaps you, forbidden child of the Dark and the Light, are the real bringer of our demise." He shakes his head, tsking under his breath. "And we have your parents to thank for that. Their sins and lies have been exposed as has your true identity."

The Archangel pauses, glancing over his shoulder as another figure emerges from the mist. I gape open-mouthed at the familiar countenance of my father, but the blue eyes I expect to find are gone, replaced by a searing gaze the color of blood.

"You—"

The impostor's face splits into a monstrous grin. "Luna Morningstar," he hisses.

As these words leave his lips, my father's features shift and change until a vaguely recognizable hulking beast of a man stands in his place, glowering at me. His shoulders are broad and his hair is ashy, clipped close to his skull in a buzz cut. Dark blond brows sit like stagnant caterpillars on his furrowed brow.

I recognize him, having seen him among the other Archangels and Archdemons the day I freed Alexander. At the time, I hadn't noticed the color of his eyes, too consumed by terror and pain. Now, those blood-red irises haunt me.

Uriel claps his hands in delight. "Ah, but where are my manners? Luna, this is Mammon, headmaster of the academy at Tyre. As I'm sure you've realized, Mammon is an Archdemon with a rather splendid talent. Crude modernisms would refer to him as a shape-shifter. But what Mammon is capable of is so much more complex, for his gift affects the very subconscious of his victims, drawing out truths even they weren't aware they were hiding by using the manifestations of their own minds against them. Of course, I can tell from your stunned expression that you've already discerned that."

I swallow past the growing lump in my throat, staring daggers at the Archdemon responsible for messing with my head.

"I knew it," I manage after a long, tense moment. "I wasn't really—"

"Losing your mind?" Uriel quips. "'Going crazy,' as the children today say?" He chuckles. "Quite the opposite, actually. If anything, you've shown remarkable resilience to the effects of this ethereal plane."

Ethereal plane? My eyes dart from side to side, taking in my surroundings with renewed interest. *Just where exactly is this place? I always assumed it was somewhere on Earth, masked by magic to suit the Council's means, not that unlike Alexander's tomb beneath the Serapeum, guarded by wards only a Gray could pass through and a lock only Gabriel's blood could break.* But now, as the mist—the tendrils almost sentient in their movements—laps against the side of the egg, I'm not so sure where I am. *The only thing I do know is this purgatory surely isn't Heaven.*

If anything, it's Hell.

I flinch away from the transparent wall as Uriel closes the distance between, pressing a long-fingered, elegant hand to the glass. "Despite your involvement in the crimes for which you are being held, I do not believe you are like Alexander. Just as I do not believe you are the Gray, the harbinger of our doom, that the Messenger spoke of."

I go rigid at his words despite their undertone of sincerity. *Something about this exchange isn't right. They want something*—I can tell by the predatory way Mammon keeps staring at me—*but what, exactly? What else could they possibly want from me?*

What else do I even have to give them?

As if reading my thoughts, Uriel leans forward, bringing his tall frame in line with my own until he's crouching and we're eye to eye. "Given the calamity Alexander has already wrought once and intends to unleash upon us again, it's clear what part he has to play. For that reason, I am here to make you a deal."

"A deal?" I echo. "What kind of deal?"

Mammon steps forward, his face a stern mask of contempt. "Tell us, daughter of Lucifer…what role will you play in the coming war?"

My wings bristle. "You tell me. I'm the one locked in a cage."

Uriel waves a dismissive hand. "A precaution. Perhaps you are unaware of the Conqueror's past—as I believe you must have been to knowingly partake in freeing him from confinement—but thousands of years ago, he nearly subjugated the known human world. Had he succeeded, I assure you, he would not have been content merely ruling over the humans. The destruction of our very kind was at stake. And with the emergence of another Gray, we could not afford to make the same mistake twice. It is not personal—"

I let out a barking laugh. Everything about this whole situation feels personal.

"*But*," Uriel continues, his glare piercing, "despite your lineage, you do not seem to possess the same thirst for power as your Gray brethren. Am I wrong in assuming this?"

I deflate as all the anger rushes out of my body, replaced by a sadness so intense and enduring that I struggle to breathe past its grip on my chest. My voice is thick as I force out the words. "I never wanted any of this. You're the ones who dragged me into this world. I only wanted—"

"To protect the boy," the Archangel interrupts, nodding

solemnly. "Caleb, was it? If that still rings true, then you may be interested in hearing what I have to say."

"We know the transfer from Babel is of the Great's blood," Mammon says, his tone cutting, like a knife to my throat.

Because you tricked me, I nearly say, but instead, I flatten my hands to the glass, screaming out, "Caleb is innocent! He doesn't even know his grandfather. He thought he was helping him. Helping me! *I'm* the one who wanted to find Alexander because—" I hesitate, unsure if I should say anything more. How much of my complicity will help my case?

And how much will harm it?

"Because?" Mammon presses.

I swallow, shifting my focus away from those penetrating crimson eyes. Instead, I look at Uriel. Of the two, he seems more lenient. More…merciful.

"Because he said he could help me control it."

"Control what?" he asks, looking genuinely perplexed.

"*This,*" I mutter, gesturing to all of me, signifying that I am the real problem here, not Caleb. "What I am."

Uriel's mouth twitches, and a glimpse of sympathy shines out from his steely, unfaltering gaze like the first glimpse of sunlight breaking through storm clouds.

"Control is not your problem, child," he says gently, his voice almost kind. "You were bound. You could not have mastered your innate gifts anymore than you could have unleashed your wings. Now that the bind is removed, you are free from such…

instability. Although," he adds after a pause, "as I'm sure you've realized by now, your powers are of little use in that cage, assuming you can call upon them at all."

Bind? Confusion sends a chill rushing through me. What is he saying? That the Dark side of me was locked away behind some kind of invisible door? But if that's true, then—

"When Alexander touched me…"

Uriel nods. "He removed the bind. Although we're not entirely sure how."

I shake my head, struggling to comprehend what he's saying. "But if my Dark half was bound, then how come I could use Dark abilities back at the Serapeum? Why has my fire always been red?"

The Archangel shrugs, seemingly unconcerned. "Perhaps the bind was failing. A binding spell requires the caster to be of the same descending side as the one receiving the bind. In your case, you are of both the Light and the Dark. Whoever bound your powers bound only your Dark half, leaving the Light side fully intact. Doing so left you unbalanced—and incapable of the control you so craved from Alexander—which brings me back to the point."

My eyes narrow. "Which is what?"

"Caleb," Uriel clarifies. "We know he fled with Alexander. Tell us where and you will be freed from this cage. You need not endure millennia in isolation and darkness—"

He goes silent mid-sentence, but I can hear his unspoken

words hanging heavy in the air between us. *Just like Alexander.*

Terror envelops me, my voice barely a whisper. "I don't know where." *And even if I did, I wouldn't tell you.*

Mammon expels a threatening growl, baring his teeth. "Why do you insist on protecting this boy when he so readily left you behind to rot? Such half-breed traitors are beneath our kind."

I snap my gaze in the Archdemon's direction, once again taking in those ominous eyes, but this time, I don't look away. His face is harsh and cruel—not at all like the masks of my parents and Alexander he wore so convincingly to trick me. He reminds me vaguely of the orderlies at the hospital—always looking down on me. Always viewing me as broken.

And to think, Mammon is responsible for the lives of however many young Nephilim at Tyre. Nephilim, who he just referred to as half-breeds who are "beneath our kind."

My upper lip peels back in disgust. "I would rather be like him than be anything like either of you. Angels. Demons. You think you're superior to Nephilim, to humans. But you're just as misguided and immoral as anyone else on this planet."

Uriel sneers. His patience with me seems to be waning. "Your loyalty is admirable but misplaced. If you will not be swayed by the temptation of freedom, then consider this. Our greatest error in judgment from the first time Alexander tried to seize power was not disposing of his supporters upon his imprisonment. We showed them mercy, believing calamity had been avoided. But, like with our imprisonment of the Conqueror, we will not make the same mistake again."

All the air seems to seep out of the egg, and I can practically feel the color drain from my face. "What are you—"

"*Anyone,*" the Archangel booms, his voice overpowering mine, "Light or Dark, be they angel, demon, or Nephilim, found supporting the Great will meet a swift end. There will be no second chances. Not even for those you deem supposedly innocent."

My entire body trembles and my heart races, pounding in my ears, dampening the volume of Uriel's every word. I try to swallow, but my tongue is sandpaper.

"*But,*" he continues, staring at me intently, "if you do as we ask, you have my word, the boy will be spared. He, and he alone, will be granted clemency…but only if you tell us where we can find him. The alternative will not be pleasant, I assure you."

The threat is clear on his face, and I know without having to ask what that alternative is. It's the entire reason I'm still alive, what I've been dreading since Mammon deceived me with Alexander's face, and then let his mask slip, revealing those menacing eyes. If I don't tell them where Caleb is, they'll use me as bait to draw him out. And if that happens, there will be no mercy.

If that happens, they'll kill him.

"I don't know where he is," I grind out through clenched teeth, biting back tears.

"Foolish, stubborn child!" Mammon roars, swiping a hand

through the mist. "We extend an olive branch but still you refuse? You're just like your unrepentant mother."

"Finally. Something she and I have in common," I croak.

"A war is coming, daughter of the Morningstar," Uriel growls, "and we will prevail, just as we did all those thousands of years ago, the first time the Conqueror waged his war. You may choose not to help us now, but we will find the boy regardless, make no mistake about that. When we do, I will take great joy in personally presenting you with his head. When that time comes and you stare into his cold, dead eyes, it will dawn on you that we gave you the chance to save him…and you chose not to take it."

My wings flare out to the sides, my vision going white, as an all-consuming rage overwhelms me, blinding my senses, which in this moment, are no longer dulled but sharpened, honing in on my target. I step back and then hurl myself forward repeatedly, slamming my fists into the glass with all the strength and force I can muster. "If you touch him, I'll kill you. I'll *kill* you!" I scream.

It's only when Uriel laughs under his breath that I cease my assault. Drawing in a shaking breath, I follow his gaze, noting how the wall of the egg has cracked beneath my touch. A sudden hope sparks within me, but it's quickly diminished when the glass begins to heal, the fissures fading until all evidence of my outburst is gone.

Smirking, he turns and disappears into the mist, Mammon

following closely at his heels.

"I don't believe you will," Uriel calls over his shoulder.

The Archangel's departing words ring in my ears as an unexpected night falls across my surroundings, trapping me in the same darkness and foreboding silence he once offered to spare me from. An offer I refused. Now, I will live in this darkness forever, just like Alexander before me.

Sobs wrack my chest as I collapse to the ground, and the shadows inch closer to my cage. As they pass through the glass and crawl over my skin—the touch of the gloom icy cold—I let out a choked whimper, crying out for the only person in this whole world who ever really mattered to me.

"Caleb…"

His face in my mind is the last thing I see when everything around me goes black.

eleven

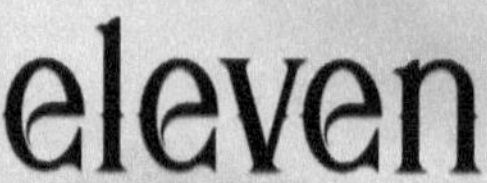

CALEB

I LACE UP MY boots and try not to vomit over the worn-in black leather. Alexander's dagger rests against my back in the hidden sheath Ishtar gave me, rendering it invisible to everyone else. I guess my teacher has contributed to saving Luna after all.

Standing, my eyes rove over our party of three—well, four, counting me. We're back in the creepy conspiracy room, all in black, which seems like overkill, but what else are you going to wear when breaking into a supernatural prison and defying Archangels and Archdemons? This has to work. Luna has been in that place for months, and it's my fault she's in there. She's strong but fragile, and I can imagine all the things they're doing to break her. Fuck Ishtar. Fuck Gramps. Fuck all the promises I wasn't able to keep to Goldilocks.

I'm very aware of the consequences if we get caught. The rest of them might get off with hard labor or imprisonment, but as the Great's grandson, I know I'll get the chopping block.

Or definitely tortured for information and then discarded like garbage after the Council has gotten everything they can from me. But I don't care. Luna's worth it. I glance over at Asmodeus, clad in a ridiculous green dress that matches her eyes, as she's not part of our humble rescue squad. She gives me a small nod, and I tilt my head in acknowledgment.

I'm to keep my mouth shut about the dagger until the last minute. All the weapons from the Fall were supposed to be confiscated and tucked away, out of the hands of mere Nephilim, or from angels and Fallen for that matter. No more killing of the Creator's children. Somehow, before his imprisonment, Alexander got a hold of this family heirloom. I don't think he knows who his parents are, but I'm hella curious about that and how he got this blade.

Although Asmodeus says she trusts everyone in the party, clearly she doesn't. Or she doesn't want Nzingha or Alaric poaching the knife. They couldn't wield it—only Alexander's bloodline can—but they could take it off me and bury it somewhere, never to be seen again. It does help that the sheath makes the blade invisible. That's how I got the jump on Gabriel. The thought of cutting into the Archangel still makes me sick despite her being an all-time terrible mother to Luna.

Shaking my head, I force myself to concentrate on my current shitshow. So, two days after our last meeting, Asmodeus called the others back to Babel and fed them some bullshit story on how to open the prison while Hammurabi and I know the real plan. Get into the weird, ethereal plane where Luna is being held and cut that cage wide open.

This plan has to work. The thought of actually getting there and seeing Goldilocks only to leave her shreds me. If I think about it too long, I really will boot my breakfast everywhere. Determination squares my shoulders, and I wait, restless, for us to get on with it already.

"Return directly here. I don't care if you run into the Morningstar himself, Luna is to be brought to me. I can shield her for a time while the Council runs around, searching for traitors. Or Alexander, which is what I'm going to lead them to believe," Asmodeus purrs, smiling.

Hammurabi gives Asmodeus a bow. "As you wish. Come Caleb, Nzingha."

The king steps into the deep shadows and disappears. Nzingha follows but I hesitate, pausing on Alaric. He can't travel with us, as no Lights are allowed on the Shadow Road. It's the sunny, Blessed Road for him.

If he chooses a time to screw us over, this would be it. He nods at me, his face solemn, and he doesn't exude that irritating Calm that rubs me the wrong way. I nod back and step into the shadows.

The Shadow Road greets me, an endless expanse of smeared gray and black, like looking through a soot-filled window. The Road is tricky, all the markers look the same, and it's cold as hell. You need to know where to go, but I don't know what to look for now.

We're traveling to a place in-between, where Darks and Lights both have access simultaneously. Other than Earth, of course. My eyes land on Nzingha. She works for Mammon the same way Ishtar used to work for Asmodeus, teaching students combat and the art of persuasion—or how to break into minds.

The Council can't be there all the time, and though they've created a prison with their essence, they don't want Gramps or his allies finding Luna. Mammon and Uriel are in charge of prison security, each having trusted first generation Nephilim on a rotation, and guess who just happens to be one of Mammon's badasses of choice? Nzingha.

We're sneaking in on her watch. As the Blessed and Shadow Roads spit everyone out at the same spot in the prison, there is only one guard stationed there at a time, so Asmodeus didn't need to pull a Light ally out of her ass somehow to let Alaric in. This also draws suspicion away from her because she's not providing any Nephilim to guard Luna.

Even though Nzingha is Mammon's girl, she's awfully tight with Asmodeus. That might make me suspicious but look at Ishtar, loyal to Alexander after all this time. I thought she'd never betray Asmodeus. Then again, I never thought Lights could be chummy with Darks or Lucifer and Gabriel could stand being near each other, let alone have a kid.

The cold penetrates my bones and I shiver. We've been walking for a while, and this is an unfamiliar path. I navigate the

Shadow Road like a pro, but I'm lost right now. Hammurabi and Nzingha slow, and I stop behind them. Raising a brow, I look around, not seeing a marker. But then a slithery sensation creeps over me, and my shiver turns to a shudder. Revulsion fills me, and I want to step back.

Nzingha steps forward and then I spot it, like a weird overlap in reality. It resembles wallpaper that's been poorly pieced together with one layer spread on top of the other. She touches it with an elegant hand and disappears, sucked inside.

My guts knot, and I glance at Hammurabi. His face is grave, lips pressed into a hard line.

"Don't reveal your hand until the last," he commands.

"You don't trust them?"

"I trust no one but my mistress, and even in that, I have been disappointed," he says, his voice bitter.

I suppress an irritated groan. He's still pissed Asmodeus didn't confide in him about there being another Gray, but after Ishtar, what did he expect? Nodding, I say, "I understand. I want Luna free, and I don't have time to get into a wrestling match with those two over the shiny toy."

The king grips my arm, and I flinch at the sudden violence of it. "Having the means to kill an immortal being is nothing to be flippant over."

I rip my arm free of his grasp. "I know that," I growl. "We each have our own way of dealing with stress. You're a rigid asshole, and I'm a facetious dick. We all have roles to play."

His scowl is fierce, but I stalk past him and reach for the marker. I'm sucked into an even bleaker space than the Shadow Road, nothing but roiling blackness and ghostly mist. I roll my eyes. The Council sure has a flare for dramatics. Then I realize Goldilocks has been alone in the dark for who knows how long and nausea overcomes me again. Nausea and rage.

As my eyes adjust to their usual feline sharpness, I spot Nzingha waiting, lines of impatience creasing her brow. Hammurabi pops behind me and Alaric appears from the left. I guess Asmodeus is great at giving directions as the Light made it here without help.

Alaric's expression is troubled as his gaze takes in the oppressive atmosphere. It's cold here, too. An invasive chill worms its way against my skin. But maybe Luna being an angel, she doesn't feel the cold anymore. I hope. She thought she was mortal for years so she felt mortal pains. And that pisses me off more. Gabriel is a real piece of work.

"I hope we haven't come too late," Alaric murmurs to himself, and I whirl on him.

"Why do you say that?" I demand, voice guttural with anger and fear.

"You know why," he murmurs. "I'm the one who found her."

My eyes dart away, shame flushing through me. He found her in a mental ward, isolated and alone. Luna doesn't like talking about her time in the hospital, so it's no wonder she's never been chatty about Alaric. And I help put her in this desolate prison. I want to go on a full berserker rage. I want to weep in a way I haven't since I was five and found out what a piece of shit my father is. But I do neither and just say, "She'll need us both then."

Alaric's eyes widen, and I hear Hammurabi's snort of disbelief. I know what I said is shocking. A Dark admitting they need the help of a Light. Luna would be proud.

Alaric gives me a warm smile. "Luna was right to have chosen you as her friend."

My answering smile is bitter. "I'm responsible for landing her here. Some friend I turned out to be."

"You're here now, aren't you?" Alaric says. "You chose friendship over power."

Again, there's a hint of something, a layer beneath the surface of his words that I can't see and don't understand.

Nzingha bites out, "Let's cut through the emotional drivel and carry on with it, shall we? We must make haste."

I scowl at her but nod. Alaric gives her a cool look of reproach but follows her without protest farther into the mist. Hammurabi and I walk together, the weight of my dagger pushing against my skin.

This place creeps me out. Though it feels like I'm on solid ground, this dimension lacks the density of Earth or even the Shadow Road. I glance at my feet. They're shrouded in pearly haze. Hell, I have no idea what I'm walking on.

With each step, my nerves wind tighter and tighter until I

feel like there's a noose around my neck. My heartbeat kicks at my chest. In a few moments, I'll see Luna. What am I going to say to her? How can I atone for what I've done?

Suddenly, a shape hovers in the darkness in front of us. Inky blackness rests inside, and I can only make out the curves of the enclosure due to the white fog. They aren't even allowing her a light.

My eyes trace the curves of Luna's prison, and to my surprise, it resembles an egg. A giant egg. Nzingha stops in front of it, holding out a palm. Bright purple light floats above her hand like a ball of grape jelly.

The egg is an ironic choice. Ra, the sun god, was said to have been born from a cosmic egg. I'll cut Luna from her shell, and she'll emerge like the golden goddess she is.

The interior of the shell illuminates as we approach and I gasp. Luna lies on the floor, curled in a ball, her magnificent wings spread around her. Despite her frail appearance, her wings are glossy. The pewter feathers shimmer in the light. Luna lifts her head, meeting my eyes, and I take an involuntary step back.

Luna confessed to me once about how she thought she was losing her mind, succumbing to the madness stalking her since she was a child. I assured her she wasn't crazy—Alexander messed with her head. And before, well, her powers were repressed. Of course, there were going to be mishaps. But now...

Those beautiful hazel eyes latch onto mine, shadows swirling in their depths. She looks surprisingly mortal, as if immortality hasn't set in. And she's enraged. Pushing herself to her feet, her wings flare out, smacking against the curved wall of the egg. She bares her teeth at me and I flinch.

I knew she'd be pissed but I'm no coward. Swallowing, I square my shoulders and step up to the glass. Well, it isn't glass, and up close, it looks like tiny diamonds are studded throughout. I place a hand on the slick surface.

"I'm here to get you out, Goldilocks," I say quietly. "I'm so sorry I couldn't come sooner. I'm so sorry I got you into this mess." My throat feels raw, and I have to blink a few times to see clearly.

Luna strides toward me, mouth twisted in a snarl. Looking up at me, her fist strikes the glass where my face is. My head snaps back on reflex, but soon, I focus on her again.

"Luna," I plead. "You can beat the shit out of me when I get you out of here, I promise. Just step back so I can free you."

Her laugh carries a tinge of insanity, and terror soaks my skin in cold sweat. They've broken her.

I've broken her.

"You've come to get me out?" She cackles and then sobers so quickly it chills me. "You're not real."

I reel back, stunned. "I'm real, Luna, I promise. Baby, step back from the glass and let me help you." I hear the desperation in my own voice, and I hope she hears it, too.

Luna stays put, golden hair limp around her beautiful face. "You won't trick me again, Mammon. You're not Caleb. I keep telling you I don't know anything!" Her voice rises, and she screams the last words, striking the wall again. Spider web fissures spread over her prison's surface, and I hear Nzingha gasp. Then the glass—or whatever the hell it is—knits back together.

Alaric steps up beside me, and Luna stares at him, her eyes wild, almost feral. She shakes her head over and over again, and I want so badly to reach out and comfort her it hurts.

"Luna," Alaric says, his voice as gentle as a summer breeze. Calm radiates from him, dosing me, and my heart rate slows. Can his Calm reach through Luna's prison? Does it even work on an angel? "Caleb is real. We're all real, I promise you." He gestures to Hammurabi and Nzingha behind us. "We're here to help you. You don't belong in there."

"No, no…this doesn't make sense. There's only ever been one of you before," she whispers, rocking back and forth. "I don't know you." Her gaze darts to Hammurabi and Nzingha. "I don't know anything. Why can't you believe me?"

"Why doesn't she think we're real?" I ask Alaric, panic gripping my chest like a vise.

"Mammon can change his shape," Hammurabi offers. "It seems like he's used his gift on the Gray. Luna," he says after I glower at him.

"Shit," I say, staring at Luna. "Goldilocks, listen to me, I'm real. Remember, I saved you from those asshole Lights when they tried to hurt you? Gave them nightmares for days."

"I took you out of the hospital and to the Serapeum," Alaric says. "We rode on the plane to Alexandria together."

Luna's mouth twists into an angry grimace. "Mammon could have found Caleb and tortured him for information," she counters. "And finding out who took me to the Serapeum is easy. That doesn't mean you're real."

"I was your first kiss," I say, once again splaying my hands on the glass. I mean, she never said so, but I'm pretty sure that's a safe assumption. "I helped you unlock your Dark powers. I promised to take you to Babel with me, but then it all got fucked up. I'm so sorry for that, Goldilocks. Please believe me."

She hisses at me. "Don't you dare call me that, Mammon. Only Caleb can call me that. What have you done to him?" She sobs, and I feel like I just took a spear to the heart.

Nzingha steps up beside me. "We have no time for this. Get her out now or leave."

I bare my teeth at her. "I'm not leaving her," I grit out. "If you're so afraid, run along back to your master."

Nzingha lunges for me, but Hammurabi's hand shoots out, grabbing her arm and shoving her back. "We don't have time for this either, Queen. Asmodeus will be displeased if we return without the girl."

Nzingha raises her chin, her face a mask of ice. "If we are caught, Asmodeus's displeasure will be the least of our concerns."

Luna wails, and I whirl back to face her. Her fists and wings collide with the glass like a hammer, and a large boom sounds as fissures spread across the egg again like cracks on a frozen lake.

Cold fear once again grips me.

"Have you considered how dangerous she'll be once we release her? She's clearly unstable."

I hear Nzingha's voice over my shoulder, and I fight the urge to punch her in the face, but her words do hold some weight. Luna could kill us all if we let her out, but that gruesome possibility won't stop me from freeing her. I promised her a better life, and I'll keep that promise. Even if it kills me.

"Luna," Alaric says patiently, "even Mammon cannot be four people at once. Think past the fog, find that kernel of yourself that recognizes truth. Even Gabriel doesn't know how close we are."

At the sound of the Messenger's name, Luna's head snaps up. "You mean my mother? The one who abandoned me? I thought we've been over this. Will you bring up the Morningstar next?"

So, Luna knows about her parents, and the Council has been torturing her with that intel. Usually, I'm good with my place in life. I've never wanted to Ascend like those Lights, chumps pretending to be good while waiting for wings that'll never sprout. But in this moment, I want to be an angel so badly I'd trade my soul for wings. That way I could take my dagger and my newfound power and hunt down all those on the Council and carve them up for what they've done to Luna.

Alaric and I share a look, and I know what he's thinking. Luna has finally become the dangerous creature she's always been afraid she was. And it's not even her fault. It's due to months of isolation and mental torment. Things I'm responsible for.

"We have to get her out now," I urge, throwing a glance over my shoulder at Hammurabi. His face is troubled but he nods. He'll follow Asmodeus's orders.

"Let's hope we can control her," Nzingha says. "King, Asmodeus gave you her essence. Break the binding."

Hammurabi levels her with a flat, hard-ass stare. "Child, you don't give me orders," he says, and her face darkens with rage.

For fuck's sake, even Darks can't get along. And no one has time to pander to someone else's delicate ego.

Alaric steps between them. "Enough of this. We're wasting precious time."

A cackle sounds behind me and I pivot. Luna stares at us with mad eyes, shaking her head. "Maybe you're not here, Mammon. Maybe all of you are delusions I've made up." The clouds lift from her eyes for a moment as she focuses on Hammurabi and Nzingha. "But I don't know why I'd hallucinate you," she mutters. "I don't even know who you are."

"Goldilocks," I try again, and she growls at me. "You're not delusional. We're really here, and I'll prove it to you."

She gives me a heartbreaking smile, tears wetting her cheeks. "They told me they'd kill you if I didn't cooperate. If I just told them where Alexander was, they'd spare you. But I don't know, do I? So you must be dead." Her voice breaks on the last word, and her chest heaves on a great, body-wracking sob.

Hate swells in my heart for Mammon and whoever else has

been screwing with her mind. I'm even pissed at Asmodeus despite her putting this little rescue squad together. Could she have done more to help Luna somehow?

The dagger clears the sheath before I fully comprehend what I'm doing. Someone gasps behind me, but I don't slow down to see who it is. I stab the curved surface of the egg, giving the handle a vicious twist. I expect resistance, to struggle, something, but the blade slices through the essence of immortals like a scalpel through muscle. I drag the knife down, over, up, and across, cutting a large rectangle that's slightly uneven. Satisfaction flares in me after I sheath the knife and wedge my fingers under the rectangle, pick it up, and hurl it with all my strength. I watch as it goes sailing into the mist.

I never hear it land.

My eyes snag on Luna once more and stay. Taking a deep breath, I step inside her prison. She gazes up at me, her lashes spiked from the weight of her tears. Her brows arch in shock, and she shakes her head again, as if trying to make sense of what she's seeing. I know she can kill me. I know I should be afraid, but as I reach for her and pull her into my arms, I find I don't care if she does. Relief at finally having her near shudders through me, and I breathe in her scent, like sunshine and the sea. Her hair is silken under my cheek. I'm so happy to hold her again that at first I don't notice her entire body going rigid.

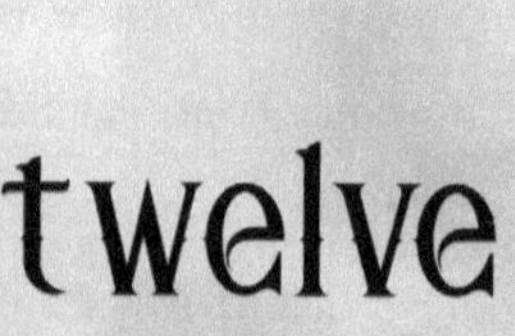

twelve

LUNA

THIS ISN'T REAL. THIS isn't real. This isn't real. This isn't real—

My heart jackhammers against my ribcage, my senses muddled, like wires crossing, as sensations and smells—both new and familiar—assault me, driving me even closer to the edge. I note the stagnant air of my cage, slightly fresher now from the large hole in the glass. Faces stare at me from beyond the wall of my prison, but all I'm aware of is the warmth of the arms wrapped around me and the intoxicating aroma wafting into my nose, which screams out a single word in my head.

Home.

I clamp my eyes shut, shuddering against my tormentor—the mask he wears now so much crueler and realistic than any other I've been forced to witness.

But this isn't real. It can't be real.

And yet—

I hold my breath. Why would Mammon cut through the wall of my cage just to prove this is all another delusion? He's already demonstrated how easily he can get inside my head and pluck out the small details I've clung to even in my darkest moments. Caleb's nickname for me. His scent—a heady aroma I can never quite place. Mammon could emulate these things with ease, that much I'm certain about.

But this…

I tense in his arms, torn between revulsion and a fleeting ember of hope. If Uriel and the others wanted to fully unhinge me, they've stumbled upon the right method to do it. Killing Caleb in front of me would've been a mercy compared to the false relief tearing through my body. Because this isn't real. It *can't* be. I'm alone, just like I've always been. These aren't Caleb's arms around me. That isn't Alaric staring at us with shock and loving concern in his eyes—

I pause, my gaze catching on the Nephilim's face. His *face*.

Which glows with the familiar golden sheen of his aura.

Of all Mammon's mind tricks, this one element of all angels and Nephilim is the one detail he overlooked. The auras were always Dark, which worked for the impersonation of my father—and for Caleb, if the arms around me are a lie. But for Gabriel and Alexander…the auras were wrong. So, shouldn't Alaric's aura be wrong, too? Unless…

My breath hitches, my knees buckling slightly, as the illusion wearing Caleb's face hugs me closer, and I allow myself to entertain the foolish belief that what he's been saying these past few moments is real. That *he* is real, and the Nephilim holding me in his arms is the Caleb I know and love.

My best friend, come to save me from this hell.

I pull back just enough to look into his eyes, the dark swirling pools brimming with remorse and threatening to pull me into their depths and drown me. I exhale, a rising sob in my throat making me stammer. "Y…You…"

"It's me, Goldilocks," he whispers, cupping my face. His breath is hot on my cheeks as he leans in even closer. "I'm here. What do I need to do to prove it to you?"

Prove it to me? I shake my head. *I don't know.* "I—"

His lips are on mine before I can get the whole thought out, his mouth swallowing my startled gasp. I go rigid for a moment before melting against his firm chest when his hands snake around to the back of my neck, a shiver rippling through my body at the feel of his fingers trailing over my skin. They weave up through my hair, each touch desperate and hungry as if, he too, is trying to assure himself that I'm real. He holds me to him, deepening the kiss, every caress a silent vow that he'll take however long is necessary to prove that he's not just another memory torn from my mind and used against me as a weapon. He kisses me, embraces me, as if we have all the time in the world. As if every moment we spend here isn't hurling us closer to him being discovered.

That thought sobers me, and I find myself breaking the kiss, much to my dismay. And his. A frown downturns his lips, which part to protest, but I shake my head again. "Caleb—"

Brow furrowing, he brushes his thumb across my lower lip. "Hey, what's that look for? Did you really think I wouldn't come back for you?"

My throat tightens as the hysteria I've been biting back finally bubbles to the surface. "You shouldn't have. If they find you here—"

"Yes." My eyes dart past Caleb's shoulder to the stern woman standing behind him in the mist. "If they find us here, we are done for," she hisses. Her face darkens, her gaze fixating on Caleb's, which seems to harden in response to her words. "So, if you are quite finished with your dramatic reunion, we really should make a move. Oh, and little Dark?" she adds, her tone snide. "Once we escape, assuming we do, you *will* tell us where you found that dagger."

Caleb's upper lip curls back at the patronizing nickname. "It's really none of your business, is it?" he counters. He moves to my side, shifting his arm protectively around my waist. "The knife did the trick. We got Luna out—"

The woman steps forward, her gleaming teeth bared. The glowing ball of light in her hand trembles, and the mist parts around her feet, as if in fear of her fury. "Such weapons were said to have all been accounted for—"

"Or destroyed," Alaric mutters softly. His expression is distant. Contemplative.

The fourth member of their party—a towering, radiant presence despite the black and deep purple tendrils of darkness surrounding him—brushes the woman aside, planting himself firmly between her and Caleb to safeguard the younger Nephilim from her. "This is neither the time nor the place for such a discussion," he growls.

Shaken free from whatever thoughts had gripped him, Alaric nods in agreement. "He's right. We're wasting time. Save the questions for later."

Everyone looks at me then, and Caleb nudges me gently, pressing his side against mine. His fingers tickle my hip where they touch me. "Come on, Goldilocks," he murmurs, offering me a small, lopsided smile that might be the most beautiful thing I've ever seen. "Freedom awaits."

He steps through the rectangular hole in the glass and urges me forward, but I pause at the brink, frozen in place by the inexplicable hesitation sweeping through me. Could it really be so simple? By stepping out of this egg, will I really be free?

Caleb repositions himself in front of me, taking both my hands in his. The broken edge of the egg separates us. "I know you're scared, baby, but I'm here. I'll never leave you again. Never," he promises.

Never. That word repeats in my head like the toll of a clock bell chiming midnight. Our eyes meet, and the subtle nod he gives me is the only encouragement I need. Real or not, hallucination or not, trick or not, I just want us to be together.

I don't want to be alone anymore.

I stumble forward, stepping over the cracked lip of the egg, my grasp tightening around Caleb's fingers to steady me. My feathers shiver as I tuck my wings close to my back, and I sense the immediate change in the atmosphere around me once I'm fully clear of the glass. The air is somehow sweeter outside my cage, the white mist saccharine on my tongue, like spun sugar. And yet, even with the calming scent, out here in the vast open, the threat of the Council feels more immediate. Despite some hazy semblance of ground beneath my feet, this plane extends outward in all directions with no apparent end in sight. Without the safety of a physical barrier to shield us from an attack, our enemy could literally get the drop on us from any direction.

The others who arrived with Caleb watch my every movement with guarded apprehension, more frightened and wary of me—the unpredictable, insane Gray angel—than they are of Uriel or any of the other Archangels and Archdemons on the Council, the real threat to us escaping this place in one piece. The only one besides Caleb not looking at me like I'm a ticking time bomb is Alaric.

My heart clenches at the sight of him, and although I'm still not entirely convinced any of this is real, I long to tell this man who has been the only father figure I've ever known how happy and relieved I am to see him.

Instead, I blurt out the only words I can think of. "You're here."

Alaric's handsome face splits into a smile, and he steps forward, tousling my hair. "Of course, I am. Coming for you was never a question."

Tears flood my eyes as a dozen conflicting emotions strike me at once. My hands, which tremble at my sides, jerk forward as if they have a will of their own, my chest colliding hard with Alaric's as my arms wrap around his torso in a hug that would break any normal man's back. For a long, silent moment, he holds me, one hand gently stroking my hair and the other hovering against my exposed upper back, careful to avoid the roots of my wings. He doesn't rush me, even though every second I waste like this only puts them all in further danger.

The sudden manifestation of Uriel's face in my mind is like a sharp slap to my cheek. Drawing in a shaking breath, I release Alaric, sniffling as I wipe my nose with the back of my hand.

"Okay," I say, glancing at Caleb again. "I'm ready to go."

"Finally," the woman huffs, clicking her tongue.

Caleb shoots her a scathing look before grinning at me. When our eyes meet, the annoyance in his gaze instantly softens. "As beautiful as you look with those wings, Goldilocks, they're a bit too conspicuous. Do you know how to hide them?"

My cheeks flush at his words, and I nod. I don't dare say anything, afraid of what my voice might reveal with the audience observing our every exchange. Instead, I purse my lips, grimacing, as I focus on the feathers nearest my back. To my surprise, this time when I draw them back under my skin, the agony I've grown so accustomed to experiencing is almost nonexistent, as if being freed from my prison has removed whatever block—physical or mental—was preventing the broken flesh from healing. Although sensitive still, the pain is gone, making me wonder if it was always in my head—a negative psychological impact of my inability to accept and embrace what I really am. Whatever the reason, one by one, the feathers slip under my skin until the weight sitting at my shoulder blades has eased, my wings now phantom limbs. Instead of an angel, I once again resemble a human or Nephilim.

An uncontrollable shiver rocks me to my bones at the touch of the chilly air on my skin—a mortal habit I can't seem to shake since the cold doesn't seem to afflict me the same way it used to when I thought I possessed human blood. Still, I cross my arms, holding my torn T-shirt in place.

"Here," Caleb says. He peels off his black T-shirt, revealing his muscular, deeply tanned torso, before nodding to the tattered remains of my own shirt, split in the back from where my wings tore through the fabric when they first emerged. "I think you need this more than I do."

"Oh, for Lucifer's sake." The woman rolls her eyes.

As Caleb hands me his shirt, my eyes linger on the defined planes of his abs, a blush sweeping up the full length of my body, heating me right down to my core. His lips quirk into a smirk when I quickly glance away.

Turning my back to the others, I drop my shredded T-shirt

to the mist-covered ground and pull the replacement over my head. Once I'm covered, I turn to face Caleb, who takes my hand in his, smiling broadly. I don't think I've ever seen him look so happy to see me before, and it warms the dark place in my chest that's grown like a black hole the few months I've been here, constantly on the brink of swallowing me whole.

"Let's go," he urges, tugging me forward.

Alaric and the other two Nephilim—whose names still elude me—form a protective vee around us like a flock of geese…if geese were all-powerful and possessed angel blood. I stumble along beside Caleb, clinging tightly to his arm, attempting to reassure myself this is happening. That Caleb is really here with me and, within a matter of moments, I'll finally be free of the prison I was certain I would never escape.

As we advance through the eerie shroud of mist, the silence is almost tangible, feeding my unease. Alaric walks directly in front of us, frequently peering back at me with an unreadable, focused expression. Every time our eyes meet, a sense of calm floods my body, pushing my fear back behind a wall in my head. In those fleeting moments, the oppressive weight pressing down on my chest lifts the tiniest bit, and I can breathe thanks to Alaric's gift, even if it's not as potent as it was when I thought I was mortal. The feel of Caleb's fingers squeezing mine settles me even further.

"We're nearly there," he whispers, just loud enough for me to hear.

"Where is this place?" Caleb meets my questioning gaze, and I can see in his eyes he knows what I'm really asking. *Where the hell is the exit?*

"In a space between the Shadow and Blessed Roads. We'll use them to get out."

Trepidation tears a fresh hole in my chest as my eyes dart toward Alaric and hang there. As a Gray, born from both the Light and Dark, I can probably travel either route. But what about him? "But Lights can't use the Shadow Road."

"Alaric's a big boy. He'll be fine," Caleb assures me. Noting the disgruntled frown twisting my lips, he adds, "Don't worry. He got here on his own, and he'll get out again the same way. He'll meet us back at Babel."

Babel. A thrill rushes through me at the thought of this mysterious place I've spent so many months fantasizing about, usually in my worst moments when the threat of insanity was closest. It had seemed like such a pipe dream—this notion of being with Caleb at a place where our friendship would actually be accepted—but now, that dream is just an arm's reach away. I'm almost afraid to believe it.

"And once we're there…what happens then?" I press, although part of me is terrified of the answer.

"Quiet," the female Nephilim snaps, the ball of purple light in her hand vibrating as she turns in place, scanning the unending blackness, predatory eyes alert. Caleb exchanges a worried glance with the regal Dark Nephilim to our right while I find my own gaze drawn to Alaric. His eyes latch on mine, and the faint caress of Calm he's been throwing back at me abruptly ceases, as if some unseen force has wedged itself between us.

"Luna—" he begins, but whatever he was going to say is interrupted by a sharp, grating cackle erupting from the silence behind us. Caleb and I whip around toward the sound, but my vision is blurry in my panic. It takes a moment for me to make out the tall figure standing before us in the mist, the broken egg looming in the distance behind him.

"Going somewhere?" Mammon asks, those blood-red eyes gleaming.

Raw, oppressive terror spreads through me, and I stumble backward, mouth agape, staring at the one person responsible for my rapid mental descent. My eyes flick left and right, but no other Archangels or Archdemons appear. Probably because they don't see the need. One full-blooded angel against four Nephilim, no matter how old or powerful, is no contest. The angel will always win.

Except, broken or not, I'm an angel, too. And I want nothing more than to make Mammon pay for toying with my head.

I clench my jaw, my hands balling into tight fists. Beside me, Caleb is tensed for a fight, his fingers hovering by his waist, within reach of the knife he used to cut me out of my cage, although I can't see where he put it.

Mammon steps toward us, clicking his tongue. "Your betrayal wounds me, Nzingha. And here I had such high hopes for you."

I glance at the female Nephilim, who bristles at his words.

Mammon's eyes shift to the intimidating Nephilim a few feet to Caleb's left. "And you as well, Hammurabi? Now, this is surprising, indeed. What about this mere whelp of a girl could have convinced someone as morally led as you to betray your own kind?"

"My reasons are my own," the Nephilim—Hammurabi—answers in a powerful voice. "Perhaps I am not the one whose convictions have been swayed."

Mammon cocks a thick eyebrow. "Such condescension from one so young."

Young? I stare at the ancient Nephilim, his billowing aura emanating age and wisdom. Even if I didn't recognize his name from the history class I took at my last human school, I would know he was old just by looking at him. Then again, to an angel who was there at the Fall, I suppose we must all seem like children, ignorant of the millennia of life and experience they have over us.

Years, which have clearly clouded their judgment.

Once again, the question of my own birth and age scratches at the back of my brain. If I ever see my mother again, I'll get that answer out of her, one way or another.

The Archdemon takes another step forward, radiating danger and power.

Caleb roughly shoves me behind him. "Go with Alaric. Take

the Blessed Road and get out of here."

The panic gripping my chest squeezes tighter. "No! Not without you—"

A sad smile hitches up the sides of his mouth, but he makes it a point not to meet my gaze. "I failed you once, Luna. I promised myself I wouldn't fail you again."

"Caleb—"

"Alaric!" he calls over my objections.

A gentle hand grabs my arm, tugging me back, and that familiar Calm dulls my growing alarm, stronger this time with the direct contact of Alaric's hand on my skin. The sensation courses through my body like a drug.

"No," I try to protest, feeling drowsy.

Caleb glances at me before looking at Alaric. "Go."

The meaningful gleam in his eyes tells me this arrangement was planned—a plan B, so to speak, in the likely event we were ambushed. In my peripheral vision, I see Alaric nodding.

I struggle against the arms wrapping around me, but it's so hard to fight against the onslaught of Calm on my senses, like a flood of water filling my lungs. I know Alaric's only trying to help, just as I know Caleb is only trying to protect me, but I can't keep being this person, this victim—this damsel in distress, always in need of saving. I'm not helpless. I'm an *angel*.

And I refuse to leave Caleb behind to die.

Fighting the Calm, I watch in horror as Mammon sprints forward, his vermilion eyes flashing to mine and his lips peeling back into a ferocious smile, revealing perfect white teeth that remind me of fangs. In the blink of an eye, the Archdemon is gone, his features morphing until his real face is hidden behind the mask of yet another person I recognize. They're identical in every way; if Caleb wasn't already standing in front of me, I wouldn't be able to tell them apart.

Caleb pulls his knife free of its sheath, and time and space ripple around the blade as it takes physical shape, the edge of the metal catching a glint of light despite the enclosing darkness. He rushes at Mammon, whose smile only deepens at the challenge. He is a predator closing in on his prey, and his sights are set on Caleb despite the larger threat of the two older Nephilim flanking him.

Hammurabi extends his arm, but Mammon catches him by the fist and swings the Nephilim to the side, flinging him into the mist like a Frisbee. Nzingha comes in from the right, but he dodges her blows with practiced ease, anticipating her every move. To the Archdemon, she and Hammurabi are playthings.

A strangled scream rips from my throat. I don't want to be a helpless bystander. I want to join the fight. I focus on Caleb, and determination is my antidote as I feel the effects of the Calm fading, its hold on my senses loosening ever so slightly. Drawing in a steadying breath, I wrench free of Alaric's arms.

"Luna, we need to go," he begs, grabbing my wrist. The desperation in his voice hurts my heart. I know he's only trying to protect me, and I know how much he and the others sacrificed to come here. But it's because of that sacrifice I can't leave them behind to die.

I can't leave Caleb behind to die.

I snatch my arm away. "I won't abandon Caleb."

My blood runs cold at the grunt piercing the silence, and I swing around, dread filling me at the sight of the two Calebs, locked in heated battle now the other Nephilim are out of the way. One holds the other by the neck, and despite their identical features, I know with a single glance who is who.

Caleb claws at Mammon's hands where they flex then tighten around his throat, and the Archdemon smiles, like a child playing with his food before eating it. The knife Caleb was holding—his only real defense against the Archdemon, I'd wager, based on Nzingha's earlier reaction—is nowhere to be seen.

Fear and anger swell within me, adding to that burning fire of mania that has consumed me so fully these last few months. Before I wanted to push the madness away, but now, as I watch Caleb writhe in Mammon's grasp, I welcome the flames of my wrath and fury, letting them devour me whole. They lick over my skin, setting my entire body ablaze, and as they take hold, I recall all those times I felt a similar sensation of power and was too scared or ignorant to know how to use it. But I'm not the same girl I was when Alaric first brought me to the Serapeum. I'm no longer meek Luna, the orphan girl.

I am Luna Morningstar.

And now, I'm beginning to understand what I am capable of.

thirteen

CALEB

MY EVIL TWIN—OR Mammon, the piece of shit—grips my throat, and I gasp as my air supply dwindles. Even though my vision starts to get fuzzy, I know he's not using a quarter of his strength. He's playing with me like a house cat plays with a mouse, taking pleasure in flexing his claws. My dagger clattered somewhere at my feet, but the thick mist makes it hard to keep track of, and soon, I won't be able to see it anyway. Soon, I'll be dead. Regret over a thousand things I'll never get to do floods through me, but above that swims the beautiful face of Luna. Alaric will get her to safety. I'll finally keep my promise.

Before darkness can consume me, the pressure around my throat releases, and I'm suddenly blinded by a flash of crimson light, bright and hot. So hot. Searing pain eats up my right torso and arm, and I smell flesh cooking. I hit the ground hard, the mist blanketing me, obscuring me from view.

I hate this place. But the blinding pain tells me I'm not dead, and that means I still have a chance to make it out of here alive. Flames dance in front of me, penetrating the blackness, and I raise my head to see Mammon engulfed in fire, his face contorted in a scream. I glance down at my arm and see blistering, blackening flesh. My eyes find Luna, who hasn't left with Alaric, but whose hands and arms blaze brightly, like she's a righteous angel of death, come to deal out judgment.

Fuck, I just got the backlash of her power, but Mammon got the full brunt. I feel my skin healing itself, and I'm just a Nephilim. Mammon will get his shit together soon, and then he'll come for Luna with serious payback in mind. And while I'm impressed that she's let go with some damn good accuracy, she doesn't have the battle experience the Archdemon does. She might be as powerful as him, but she doesn't know how to wield it yet. I start sweeping my hands against the ground in a frantic search for my knife.

The fire begins to dim around Mammon, reduced to a halo instead of an all-consuming inferno. Hatred swells in his ruby-red eyes as he stares at Luna. He takes a step forward, but she doesn't shrink back, standing her ground. Shit, shit, shit. I can't let him hurt my Goldilocks or lock her up again. Where is that goddamn knife? My fingers scrape uselessly across the ground.

"Little girl, I shall punish you for that," Mammon says, grinning. He resembles a demented clown, with his half-melted skin and macabre smile.

Luna blanches, but then I see red flush her cheekbones.

Flames burst from her once more. She's pissed off beyond reason. Mammon's grin grows at her rage, showing teeth, shockingly white against his burnt skin. I feel power gather around him, like electricity before a storm. Desperation seizes my chest as I look for the dagger.

Out of the mist, a freight train known as Hammurabi tackles Mammon from the right while Alaric dives for his legs from the left. They all roll to the ground in a flurry of limbs and blows. Mammon kicks Alaric off him, sending him sailing into the mist, but the Babylonian king lands some wicked hits before Mammon finally gains control and snaps his head back with a punch before pile-driving my teacher into the ground. Hammurabi disappears within the heavy white vapor. But it doesn't matter. My teacher's attack served its purpose. My fingers close around the hilt of the dagger, and triumph fills me as the Archdemon focuses on Luna once more, we lowly Nephilim forgotten.

My eyes narrow in on the wings he presents to me, still smoking, but knitting themselves back together, feathers filling in the raw patches. My smile is vicious. Like Ishtar once said to me, why go for the kill when you can go for the pain? Rolling to my feet, I sprint silently toward the Archdemon. I leap in the air just as he starts to turn, sensing the danger, but it's too late.

The blade swings down, and savage satisfaction fills me as the dagger cuts through muscle and sinew like a hot knife through butter. I land in a crouch and watch as Mammon's severed wing is swallowed by the fog. He roars, the enraged sound blasting my eardrums. Hammurabi grabs me and swipes Luna, and all three of us run toward the marker that will take us to the Shadow Road. I hope Alaric makes it to the Blessed Road where Mammon can't follow.

Fire sprouts on Luna's skin again and Hammurabi hisses, "Get control of yourself, child." He points ahead of us. "There it is!" He flings all of us at the marker just as a bolt of electricity slams into Luna, shooting us into the Road like a bullet.

Goldilocks drops, convulsing, and I kneel by her side. "Baby, are you okay?" My worried hands roam over her body.

"Boy, she's an *angel*. She'll heal. Throw her over your shoulder and run," Hammurabi orders. "Mammon comes."

Fear ripples up my spine, but I ignore him, my imploring gaze on Luna. "Goldilocks?" I prod. She looks up at me, big hazel eyes blinking. I stroke the smooth skin of her cheek.

Sitting up, she shakes her head. "I'm fine. It just hurts, but I'm…" Surprise shines on her face. "I really am fine," she says in astonishment. She notices my burnt arm and side, and she raises trembling fingers to my injury, not quite touching it. Tears pool in her eyes. "Oh, Caleb, I'm so sorry. I didn't mean to—I shouldn't have—"

Wrapping my fingers around her hand, I touch my forehead to hers. "You should have. He had it coming. And I'm fine, too. Already healing." It still hurts like a bitch, but the pain is dulling, and I'll be fully healed in a few minutes.

Hammurabi grips Luna's arm and hauls her to her feet, taking me with her. "Of course, you're fine," he growls. "Let's keep it that way, shall we?"

I swivel around. "Where's Nzingha?"

Shaking his head, Hammurabi says, "I don't know, but she's on her own now. She's not my responsibility. You two are. Now *move*."

Although Luna is an angel and outranks Hammurabi, the command in the Babylonian king's voice straightens her spine. I obey as well, even though I don't like the fact we're leaving one of our people behind. Nzingha is a pain in the ass, but she did put her life on the line to help. Then I see Mammon's head and shoulders pop through into the Shadow Road, and I decide Nzingha is a big girl and can fend for herself.

Hammurabi runs, his figure a blur, and we follow, my hand in Luna's. Her grip is fierce, and I sense her terror. The iciness of the Road whips at my face. Hammurabi reaches for a marker, and I drag Luna after him. We pop up in the Alhambra in the twilight of the gardens. The fresh scent of flowers and fruit trees invade my senses along with the cool trickle of water running through marble canals. I spot orange and pomegranate trees, as well as jasmine and lavender plants. I've never been to another place on Earth that smells as good as this, other than the Hanging Gardens. Luna's eyes round as she takes in the breathtaking beauty surrounding her, lingering on the Moorish architecture. The almost lacy clusters of stone that form intricate patterns catch the eye and hold it in the budding moonlight.

"Stop gawking," Hammurabi says to her, and I glare at him, but Mammon appears a moment later, and my heart thunders as Hammurabi pulls us into the shadows once more.

The next time we emerge is in Chinatown in San Francisco, and it's daylight bright. Luna squeezes my hand, blinking. We're in a dank alley running along a row of restaurants that stink of garlic and freshly gutted fish. Goldilocks's nose wrinkles, and she looks so damn adorable that I kiss her, nipping her lower lip and smiling at her pink cheeks.

"Do you want to die, child?" Hammurabi says, cuffing the back of my head. Hard. "Back in the shadows."

The charcoal-gray Shadow Road swallows us once more, and we zigzag our way across the globe. I only catch a glimpse of Mammon twice, once in Machu Picchu and once in Hong Kong. Worry gnaws at me that he'll follow us to Babel or that he's letting us run around like a dog chasing its tail while he's decided to lay in wait and ambush us at the academy. But I don't really know if he suspects Asmodeus or if he thinks Hammurabi has sided with Alexander. If Nzingha can turn against him, maybe it'll be easier to believe that Hammurabi betrayed Asmodeus, too. I mean, I'm sure Mammon knows just how persuasive my grandfather can be.

Finally, we emerge into the Hanging Gardens, the comforting scents of citrus trees and flowers washing over me. I didn't realize how much I've missed Babel. It's just as much my home as my mom's apartment in New York City. But I am surprised Hammurabi dropped us so close to the academy. I'm about to call him out on it when he whisks us away again, yanking us into the same creepy room down in Babel's subterranean level.

Asmodeus sits at the head of the table with all the regality of a queen. Alaric paces beside her, thank the Morningstar, and to my shock, Nzingha stands to her left, spine rigid. I thought she'd go AWOL for a while, but then again, Asmodeus does offer some protection from Mammon's wrath. It is a little weird, though, that she doesn't have a scratch on her, considering she betrayed her boss. Mammon should have been gunning for her hardest of all. Yet, she's the only one who escaped the Archdemon unscathed, having missed most of the battle.

Alaric stops moving the moment he sees us, a profound look of relief passing over his face when his eyes meet Luna's. She gives him a warm smile, and I would be jealous, but I get a total dad vibe when he looks at her. Her smile dies when she meets Asmodeus's calculating green eyes. Luna curves into my side, and I slide an arm around her waist.

"Well done, King," Asmodeus says fondly. She tosses her red hair, focusing on me. "And well done, Caleb. Babel truly molds the most outstanding students. Even when half naked, they manage a rescue."

I flush at her salacious grin, but I can't deny I like seeing my shirt on Luna. It'll smell like her now. She'll smell like me.

Asmodeus's eyes meet Luna's. "You must be Luna, the

Morningstar's daughter. You resemble him, child."

That draws a shy smile from Luna. "Do you really think so?" she asks, as if seeking affirmation from someone who knows her father well. My heart swells with tenderness for her. Yeah, my dad sucks, but I had my mom. She had no one. I tuck her even closer to me, so happy to have her near me again.

"Yes," Hammurabi says gruffly. "You do, but I can see your mother, too, if I look closely."

"I admit that I can't," Nzingha says, "but it might be because I dislike your mother."

Luna stiffens, but says, voice all jagged edges, "I guess we have something in common."

This draws a laugh from Asmodeus. "Aren't you delightful?"

"You mean for a Gray?" Luna says, anger clouding her face, and I'm proud of her spunk. "Did you help put me in that place?" Her accusation rings out, harsh and cutting.

I flinch, looking at Asmodeus. The Archdemon tilts her head, sizing Luna up, and it hits me once again that Luna isn't a Nephilim like me. She's an angel. She could seriously hurt Asmodeus, but the Archdemon doesn't suffer disrespect. She's also used to being on the top of the food chain, and even though Luna *is* an angel, she hasn't fought in wars like the mistress of Babel. Asmodeus won't look at her as an equal.

"I did," Asmodeus says, and frost coats every surface of the room. "And you should be glad of it, because if I'd refused to participate, I would've been hunted like your parents and in no position to give you aid. You would have rotted there until the Conqueror decided to use you. You're new to the world—*my* world. You've yet to learn to play the game. Righteous indignation about the unfairness of it all rarely keeps you alive. I do regret you've suffered, as I would hate any child of Lucifer's to suffer, but I came for you as soon as I could. All the pieces needed to fall into place."

Luna is quiet, digesting Asmodeus's words. She looks up at me, placing a few inches between us. "Why didn't Alexander come for me? Why bother to remove the bind at all if he was just going to abandon me?"

If she ripped my heart out of my chest, she couldn't hurt me more as I hear her unspoken question: Why didn't *I* come sooner? "I tried to convince him, Luna. I tried to tell him we had to get you out immediately, but he wouldn't listen. And I knew if I pushed him too far..." I hope she hears the sorrow and desperation in my voice, the fear. "I had to see if I could get some allies on my side so I could come for you. Gramps is too busy building an army. Oh, he would've gotten you out— when it was strategic for him. He's not who...I wanted him to be." Shame burns through me, and I don't want to reveal any more of myself to the rapt audience around me. When Luna and I are alone, I'll tell her more. How the father figure I always wanted turned out to be a selfish asshole like my real dad.

Alaric watches me, a frown pulling at his mouth, a faraway look in his eyes. Hammurabi's face reflects rare sympathy, and I glance away, taking in Luna's expression. There's no condemnation written across her skin, just an exhaustion, a weariness she wears like a heavy blanket she can't shed. Maybe she's tired of people failing her. Relief pours through me as she clutches at my hand once more. I squeeze back, wanting so badly to kiss her but leashing myself. I've given our audience enough of a show.

"People are rarely who you want them to be," Asmodeus tells me kindly. Her expression hardens. "Let's put the family squabbles aside and focus on more immediate concerns. Now that the Council knows exactly who helped Luna escape, they'll be hunting you. I can't allow you to stay at Babel."

fourteen

LUNA

MY HEART PLUMMETS INTO my feet as my resurfacing terror surges up my throat like vomit. Just like when I thought I was human, even now, no place will keep or accept me. I'm a curse on this world, bringing chaos and danger wherever I go. Here at Babel, I thought I would finally find a place I belong but, like always, I was wrong. I can't stay here. It isn't safe—not for me, but for them.

Because I'm not safe.

That thought is a wrecking ball to my chest, and my legs go limp as the air seems to rip from the room. Each inhalation is a desperate gasp as I claw at my throat, no longer able to breathe.

"Luna!"

Alaric's voice reaches me from somewhere in the distance and strong arms catch me before I hit the floor. I glance up through my blurring vision to find Caleb looking down at me, his body rigid, and those molten eyes rounded and wild. "Hey, it's okay. I'm here, Goldilocks. I got you. Just breathe."

But as much as I try to heed his words, I can't. My lungs might as well not exist.

Do angels even need oxygen?

A choked, crazed laugh escapes me at the fleeting notion. I must truly seem mad to the others.

"Alaric," Caleb bites out. His tone is pleading, but I struggle to process why through the hysteria overwhelming me.

My lips part on another broken inhale, the room around me spinning as the world tilts on its axis. But then, the returning lunacy drifts away, pushed back by a sense of serenity that mutes my panic and sends my body into a state of forced relaxation. Gradually, my airways open up, and I draw in a breath, gasping as I drag air into my lungs.

Calm, I realize as I slowly regain control of my senses. Although every other time I've hated Alaric using his gifts to subdue me, in this moment, I'm thankful for it. I can think clearly now. Sanity actually seems within reach.

Cradling me, Caleb lets out a ragged sigh before redirecting his attention toward the headmistress of Babel. His piercing eyes stare daggers at her. "I'm sorry, am I huffing glue, or did you just say we can't stay here?"

Asmodeus's unblinking gaze hardens on him. "You were discovered aiding Luna in her escape. The Council knows who you are, who *each* of you are," she amends, glancing at every face in the room in turn. "You knew what you were signing up for. You knew this was a possibility."

"Not five seconds after getting her back!" Caleb shouts, fury emanating from his body like heat.

Hammurabi steps forward and plants a firm hand on Caleb's shoulder. "There will be repercussions for any who defy the Council, boy. You know this. Asmodeus cannot continue to help us if she is exposed—"

Asmodeus holds up her hand to silence the Nephilim then turns her focus back to Caleb, who props me upright against his warm side. Despite the fuming glare he throws her way, her own expression softens, and behind her intimidating exterior, I catch a glimpse of the Archdemon's fondness for him. "You are so young to this world, and your mortality makes you brash and reckless. As much as I admire your spirit and desire to intervene in unjust crimes against our kind, I do not have the luxury to do the same. You might not like it, but I will not cut off my nose to spite my face. If my part in this is discovered by the Council, I will be cast out, and you will be without the help of a powerful ally." She lowers her voice, her eyes hooded and sad. "Believe me when I say an eternity is a very long time to spend in exile."

She and Caleb exchange a knowing look, and he seems to understand something I don't because he mutters, "Like Lilith."

Lilith?

Asmodeus nods. "She made her choice and look what happened. I cannot afford to be impulsive, and I will not abandon my students for the sake of claiming some moral higher ground. I know where my allegiance lies and so do those who need to know it."

"So, what is the plan then?" Alaric asks.

He stands to my left, tall and lithe, leaning against the stone wall with his arms crossed over his chest, his clean-pressed linen shirt wrinkle-free, as if we didn't just escape a supernatural prison by the skin of our teeth. His expression is grave, and although he exudes that poised air of composure I've come to expect from him, the flustered, squirming movements of his aura make me realize he's anything but. The faint sheen of sweat on his forehead also indicates a strain he's trying hard to hide.

The Archdemon waves her hand impassively toward the door. "You require protection, which, regrettably, I cannot give. But there are others who can."

Her sharp, calculating eyes meet mine, and I grasp her meaning at once. "You mean my parents."

Across the room, Hammurabi scoffs. "Even with the Messenger and Morningstar by their sides, the children are still outnumbered, and need I remind everyone, they are just that: *children*. This is a battle that cannot be won through sheer force of will."

With a devilish grin, Asmodeus cuts her gaze to the regal Nephilim's. "Which is why you'll be accompanying the *children* until we have a plan. Gabriel and Lucifer cannot do this alone, and they will need me on the inside to keep you all informed of the Council's movements."

This seems to catch Hammurabi off guard, and I suspect he's not someone who surprises easily. His Dark aura quivers in the silence as he stares at the Archdemon.

Asmodeus arches an eyebrow. "Is that a problem?"

Composing himself, the Nephilim places a hand on his chest, over his heart. "No, Headmistress. Besides, it must fall on someone to keep young Caleb out of trouble."

"Um, need I remind you I'm the badass who cut off Mammon's wing?" Caleb protests, earning a shocked glance from the Archdemon, who clearly wasn't aware of that yet.

A shadow crosses her face as she shoots a terrifying glare at Nzingha. "If that is true, Mammon will be out for blood. We may all be in far more danger than we thought."

Nzingha says nothing, and I peer around the room at the others, confused. "Won't it just grow back?" I recall when I set those students on fire back in Alexandria. They healed quickly enough, and they were just Nephilim. Surely, an angel would heal even faster.

Caleb frowns. "Do you remember the library at the Serapeum? The museum tucked away at the back?"

I nod, remembering the rows of glass cases with clarity. Especially the display of moths where I first heard Alexander's voice.

"The weapons stored there were all from the Fall. The reason so many angels and demons died during the Great Battle was because those weapons were designed to maim and kill those with celestial blood…" He trails off, pulling the knife he used to cut me free of my egg from a hidden sheath, holding it up for everyone to see. Even crusted with Mammon's dried blood, I can make out the symbols etched into its blade. They're Enochian—not that unlike the writing we found outside Alexander's tomb.

As I stare at the length of steel, I'm reminded of Nzingha's surprise and ire at seeing Caleb with the dagger. In the moments after he freed me from my prison, that was all she seemed focused on.

"So, this knife can kill angels?" A new kind of fear sinks into my mind, and instinctively, I shrink away from the dagger and out of Caleb's grasp, even though I know he would never turn such a weapon against me. I stumble across the room toward Alaric, putting distance between us.

Caleb's skin pales at my reaction, and he quickly shoves the dagger back into his belt. "Yes, but—"

"Wait," I interrupt as a memory takes shape, and I see my mother curled up on the ground beneath the Serapeum, clutching her bleeding side with one hand and reaching for me with the other. "How long have you had this weapon?"

Caleb averts his gaze, red-hot shame flushing his skin. In his silence, I find my answer.

"You stabbed Gabriel," I realize.

He bites down on his lower lip, risking a glance at me. "I didn't know she was your mom," he says weakly.

Inching forward, I return to Caleb's side, taking his hand in mine, and his eyes widen with surprise as I say, "I'm just trying to understand. Does this mean she didn't heal?"

Relief washes over his face, but it's Alaric who speaks. "A flesh wound would've healed with time. By now, your mother should be back to normal."

"But Mammon?" I hedge.

Asmodeus scoffs. "Cutting off an entire appendage is quite different. We are not lizards, child. We do not regrow our tails when they fall off."

I scowl at her patronizing tone. "Well, how am I supposed to know?" I fling my free hand in the air, frustration leaching into my words. "This is all insane."

And that's coming from someone who is actually crazy.

"Mammon's wing will heal at the site of the wound, though he will be marked by the loss and will forever be flightless now. Losing one's ability to fly is a fate worse than death for an angel." Asmodeus stares off into the distance, as if contemplating the horror of such an existence.

A tremor runs over my back and I shiver. Having lived so long without wings, would I feel their loss as greatly as someone like Asmodeus?

"Lilith seemed to be coping just fine," Caleb muses.

The Archdemon lets out a sharp, scornful laugh. "There's a reason no one has seen Lilith since Alexander's last conquest for power."

"So, why emerge now? If she's so fucking depressed about

losing her wings, why team up with my grandfather?"

"Why, indeed…" Asmodeus scratches her chin. "Lilith's motivations for supporting Alexander were always a mystery to the Council. I think that is a question best saved for the Messenger. She and Lilith were always close, even after the Fall."

Caleb snorts. "It's hard to imagine Gabriel with a bestie."

The conversation dims to a background hum as my thoughts take a turn in another direction. If my mother was close with this Lilith as Asmodeus claims, would she know about the circumstances surrounding my birth? Perhaps she's the only one who does.

Nzingha huffs loudly, shaking me out of my thoughts. "We are getting off track. What is the plan moving forward?"

Asmodeus looks around the room, meeting each of our questioning gazes. "I can mask your presence here for two days but no more. Any longer and we risk being discovered, and that's assuming Mammon doesn't come here sooner, sniffing around like the dog he is. In the meantime, I will try to throw the Council off your trail."

"And where do we go after that?" I press, my voice wavering. *If we can't stay here, where else can we go?*

"That is not for me to decide, and the fewer who are aware of your whereabouts, the better." Asmodeus pushes her chair back, the wooden legs scraping across the stone floor as she stands. "But you cannot do this alone. Angel or not, you are vulnerable. All the more reason to find Gabriel and Lucifer quickly. They will protect you, wherever you go, from those who wish to do you harm."

"Yeah, and then what?" Caleb growls through clenched teeth. "We just go on the run forever?"

"Not forever," the Archdemon counters. Her eyes shift to mine. "I am not Lucifer's only ally, but we need time to prepare. Your parents can buy us that time."

"And how are we supposed to find them?" All eyes swing to Hammurabi. "No one has seen them in months."

Alaric nods, his expression grim. "I tracked them for weeks, but they're avoiding the Roads. They're traveling everywhere by air, and I'm not able to follow that way."

"You don't need to." Asmodeus crosses the room to Alaric and grabs his hand, turning his arm and tugging up his crisp shirt sleeve until his wrist is exposed. "This will allow you to commune with the Morningstar. Not verbally—the connection is more of an echo—but it will be enough to lead you to his location or call him to yours. Find him, agree on a safe place for the interim, and get back here before two days have passed." She places her other hand over the skin at his wrist, and when she pulls it away, a small circular Enochian symbol is visible, a white marking branded into his flesh. "I know you could track him down with that nose of yours, but this will make the hunt quicker."

Alaric gapes at Asmodeus, shock and disbelief evident in his gaze as he snaps his startled eyes up from his freshly tattooed wrist to meet hers. "Nephilim are never granted the sigils."

A sly grin stretches across the Archdemon's face. "I suppose there's a first time for everything."

We all watch the exchange in stunned awe, but no one comments on the enormity of this moment or dares to protest against the Archdemon's decision—that not only is a Nephilim receiving an honor it seems is only reserved for angels, but that a Light is receiving such a gift from a Dark. Maybe everyone is just too afraid to question Asmodeus.

My chest tightens at this unabashed display of respect, and for the first time in months, I feel renewed resolve that the divide doesn't have to be permanent. That it can be bridged, paving the way for a future where Caleb and I can be together despite everything.

I look over at him, feeling my cheeks heat, watching him closely, willing him to meet my gaze. But his focus is pinned firmly on his headmistress, those beautiful brown eyes alight with rage.

"Wait a minute, you've had the angel equivalent of the Bat Signal this whole time and what? Just chose not to use it?"

"Don't be dense, boy," Hammurabi chides. "It is common knowledge our mistress is...*close* with the Morningstar. The Council likely assumes she would be the first person he'd run to for aid."

"Not to mention, the sigils are traceable, our magic identifiable," Asmodeus says. "Were Alaric to be caught by the Council, they would immediately know I was the one who bestowed it upon him. But we no longer have the luxury of time, so"—a coy grin shapes her lips as her eyes snap to Alaric's—"do try not to get caught."

Beside me, Caleb attempts to protest, but Asmodeus clicks her tongue, silencing him.

"As for why I didn't contact the Morningstar directly after he fled with the Messenger…" She arches a brow, the warning—and reminder of the danger we face—clear in her emerald gaze. "Like you, they are fugitives. We needed to maintain that separation so no one would question my loyalty to the Council. It was a risk we could not afford, especially if I was to help release his only child from her prison. Hence why I helped lock you away in the first place."

She casts a meaningful glance at me, and Caleb flushes, clenching his jaw so tightly I swear I hear the muscles pop.

I peer at each of the somber faces around me, frowning. I feel so out of the loop—it's like everyone is speaking a foreign language, and I'm only picking up bits and pieces of what they're saying.

My frown deepens when Alaric crosses the room toward me, purpose behind every step. He meets my gaze, his own expression morose.

"You're leaving again," I push out before he can say it.

"I have to, for your sake." He places a hand on my cheek and offers me a gentle smile, a fatherly fondness in his gaze I've never seen from anyone else in my life. "But I *will* be back. This time, with your parents in tow."

Caleb, seeming to sense my unease, slides his arm around my waist again. "Be careful." He extends his right hand, which Alaric takes without hesitation. "And thank you. For helping me get Luna back."

His smile falters. "Our world is a cruel and prejudiced place. I only hope I can help shape a future where the two of you can be happy. And free," he adds so softly I barely hear it.

Although he keeps his composed mask in place, behind his words, I hear everything he isn't saying. I sense the regret he must feel over his own past, even if he refuses to voice it aloud.

And in this moment, as I glimpse the sadness welling in his amber eyes, I know he's thinking of Alexander.

fifteen

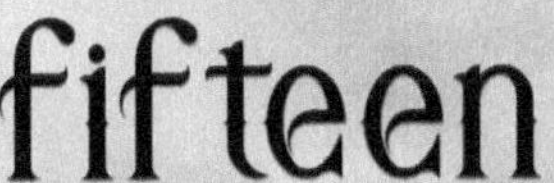

CALEB

"CALEB, A WORD BEFORE I go?" Alaric says, startling me.

I glance between him and Luna. What does he want to say to me that she can't hear? "Um, sure." I look to Asmodeus, silently asking for help.

"I'll show Luna where you'll be staying. You can catch up when you're finished," the Archdemon says, amusement shining in her green eyes.

Luna shoots me a panicked look, clearly uncomfortable with being alone with Asmodeus. Hammurabi and Nzingha stroll out of the room, and I guess they know where they plan to hide away for the next two days. Lucky them.

Alaric smiles at Luna. "I promise I won't keep him more than a minute."

Asmodeus sweeps from the room, and a reluctant Luna trudges after her, glancing over her shoulder at me one last time.

I face Alaric, waving an impatient hand. "I don't want to leave the two of them alone longer than I have to, so spill," I say.

The Light Nephilim nods. "Luna has been traumatized," he begins, and I resist rolling my eyes and yelling, "Duh!" at him. "I need you to help ground her now. Adrenaline is keeping her afloat for the moment, but she can't afford to be overwhelmed by her emotions or fall into some catatonic state once it wears off. She needs her wits about her if she's to survive what is coming."

That quickly sobers me. "How do you suggest I do that? I'm not a shrink. I don't want to fuck things up even more by saying the wrong thing. And I know she's upset with me." I wince as those last words escape my lips. It took me months to get her out of that cell, and she found out I stabbed her mother. We got a lot of issues to work out, and I don't want to accidentally push her over the edge.

"Caleb, Luna cares for you a great deal. If you're honest with her, I'm confident she'll understand. I think she'll also appreciate your candor. It will feel like she's gained some control over her life because she will have more information about what has been happening. She needs that control. Keeping her in the dark will only make things worse. Tell her everything. Beg for absolution. She'll grant it. Of that I'm certain." He squeezes my shoulder and I nod.

"I'll do my best," I promise, even though queasiness settles into the pit of my stomach. I hope that when my guts are spilled and laid out before her, she does decide to forgive me. Her kisses and acceptance of my touch give me hope, though.

I can't totally repulse her if she seems to need to touch me as much as I need to touch her.

"I never had a doubt," Alaric replies. "Be well, Caleb. Oh, before I forget." He hands me a scrap of paper with a number on it. "My cell."

I snort, taking the paper. "Thanks. Good luck finding the Morningstar," I say then add grudgingly, "and the Messenger."

Alaric taps his wrist. "I won't need luck."

He strides out the door and I follow. I spot Asmodeus and Luna ahead, Asmodeus keeping a snail's pace, bless her. Alaric disappears onto the Blessed Road, and I trot ahead until I pull up next to Luna.

"Did I miss anything interesting?" I quip, winking at Goldilocks, whose relief shines like a beacon on her face.

"Only minutes of uncomfortable silence," Asmodeus says, rolling her eyes, and I smother a laugh.

"You're the charming one," Luna tells me. "I'm the crazy one."

My humor fades. "You're not crazy. And Asmodeus makes everyone uncomfortable." My mistress scowls over her shoulder at me. "What? You do."

"Children," she mutters under her breath and even Luna smiles.

"Where are you taking us?" I ask, eyes trailing over my surroundings. I hoped she'd be leading us up, but we continue to snake down twisted hallways. It's like there's another Babel beneath Babel, but I don't like living like some worm burrowing underground. "Why can't we stay in the academy if you're masking us?"

"I'm not taking any chances," Asmodeus says. "Remain here until Alaric returns with word of Luna's parents or until Hammurabi or I give you permission to leave. You're safer here, as few know of Babel's secrets."

"You mean they don't know you rent out the basement to film horror movies?" I ask, and a giggle escapes Luna. An actual giggle. My chest inflates with ridiculous pride that I caused that sound.

The mistress of Babel arches a haughty brow at me, throwing me serious shade over a creamy shoulder. "Your mouth will get you in trouble one day, child."

"I turned my back on Alexander the Great, broke Luna out of angel prison, and cut off Mammon's wing. I think I'm already ass deep in trouble," I point out as we stop before an oval door made of thick wood with iron hinges.

Asmodeus's face darkens with foreboding. "Alexander will be disappointed in you, but you're blood, and while he might dole out painful punishment, he has need of you because eventually he will come for Luna. It is Mammon that is your true worry now."

I shiver. I don't regret taking his wing after what he did to Luna, but I'm smart enough to know I just made a huge enemy—one who will want to take my head and drink the blood from my skull.

Swinging the door open, Asmodeus ushers us inside. The room is blessedly lit by electricity. There's a large, four-poster bed made of heavy wood that dominates the room. There's no other furniture, and I see a door to the side that I hope leads to a bathroom with a shower. The room carries a faint musty smell but looks clean. I wonder why these rooms exist and if Ishtar ever took Gilgamesh down here for one of their secret banging sessions. My eyes flick to the bed again. Ugh, best to scrub those thoughts from my brain.

"It's not that I'm shy," I begin, brushing a hand down my shirtless front, "but I would like some clean clothes. I left some in my room." I don't add that Mammon's blood stains my skin in rusty streaks. And I want to clean the burnt flakes of dead flesh off me, too. "Please tell me there's running water down here."

"I want to shower," Luna says almost desperately, and I know she wants to strip her body of all memories of her imprisonment.

"Yes, there's a bathroom, and I'll bring clothes to both of you, along with some food," Asmodeus says. "I'll return shortly."

She steps out and shuts the door firmly behind her, leaving behind a strained silence.

I offer Luna a lopsided grin. "Take the first shower. You need it more than me."

Her hazel eyes crawl over my torso, that faint flush I love so much pinking her cheeks. "You've healed?" she whispers.

I glance down at myself, stretching out an arm. "Under this

grime is brand-spanking new skin," I assure her. When that worried frown pulls her lips down, I cup her face and tilt it toward me. "I'm fine, Goldilocks. It was worth getting a little cooked to see you go full badass."

"I was badass?" she says, eyes locking on mine.

"Hell yeah, you were," I reply then nudge her gently toward the bathroom door. "Go. We'll talk after we're done cleaning up."

She hesitates for a moment, staring at me, as if she's soaking me in because I might disappear at any moment. "You'll be here when I'm done?"

Her doubt is like a gut punch, but I remind myself she's just spent nearly half a year in a prison cell, so she's allowed to feel all the feels. If she wants to doubt me, well, I can't really blame her.

"I'm not going anywhere, baby," I say, and she nods at me, turning and making her way to the bathroom.

True to her word, Asmodeus returned with a fresh white T-shirt and jeans for me, along with some clothes for Luna, and delicious *biryani* resting on a silver tray on the bed. The scent of lamb and spices makes my mouth water. Fully dressed and clean, Luna and I devour the food. She gives a small moan, and my skin gets uncomfortably tight. Asmodeus brought her a black, long-sleeve tee that is completely split open in the back and tied with strings at the nape of her neck. Her lack of a bra doesn't help cool me down, but no matter how much I'd like to touch her right now, to celebrate that she's actually here with me, she needs time and space.

Then like a moron, I realize the back is open for her wings. Her beautiful pewter wings. I put my plate on the floor so as not to mess up the fancy navy duvet shot through with silver thread. I guess Asmodeus figures if she's going to hide fugitives down here, she'll do it with style.

Alaric said to ground Luna in reality, and the best way to do it is to talk about what happened, even if I'd rather have metal tacks driven under my fingernails. I can't bear to see her disappointment in me.

Luna watches me and pushes her own empty plate aside. Her eyebrows raise as I take a deep breath, squaring my shoulders. "Caleb?" she asks, her voice painfully cautious, as if I'm about to drop another bomb on her.

"We should talk about what happened, Luna," I say, reaching out and clasping her hand.

Her face shutters. "I don't want to talk about what happened to me in there." She means that elegant, terrible egg they caged her in. The fear in her voice is palpable, and I want to cut off Mammon's wing again in retribution. Once wasn't enough.

I simply shake my head. "No, not about that, but about Alexander, about what happened at the Serapeum. I want you to know—I *need* you to know—I didn't leave you behind. Alexander took me away from you. I begged him to take you, but he didn't listen. I would never, *ever* have left you of my own free will. You have to believe me."

Her dark gold eyelashes lift, her gaze probing mine. "Did you know Alexander was an angel? Is that why you have that knife?"

I give a violent shake of my head. "No, no, I didn't know. I swear to you. Ishtar didn't know, either. Hammurabi did something to her memories—to all the Nephilims' memories—so they would forget what Grandfather really was. I always thought I was just an exceptionally badass third generation. I didn't know I was that close to my angelic bloodline."

"And the knife?" she repeats, and I know she's thinking about me stabbing her mother.

"Hammurabi gave it to me, to protect myself in case shit went bad at the Serapeum," I explain. "Luna, I would never have attacked Gabriel if I knew she was your mom. I'm so sorry." But a secret part of me thinks she deserves it for abandoning Luna.

Her mouth twists in thought. "Yes, you would've, to save your grandfather. I'm beginning to understand how important blood is to angels and Nephilim. And it's not like…it's not like I really know her. She abandoned me." Her voice catches, the last words passing out through trembling lips. She squeezes my hand so hard it actually hurts. I squeeze back, letting her know I'm here for her.

Taking another deep breath, I confess, "I don't think you get why freeing Alexander was so important to me. I had my mom, you know that, and she's amazing, but my dad..." I clench my teeth, releasing her hand so I don't accidentally crush it. Then again, Goldilocks is Wonder Woman, so can I crush her hand? "He's a piece of shit who just makes little Nephilim and doesn't take care of them. I have all these brothers and sisters out there, and I don't know who they are. All this *family*. I'll never know—"

Luna raises a hand. "But your blood sings to each other—it's right here." She balls up her hand and places a fist over her heart. "I felt it when I looked at Lucifer, that beautiful knowing."

My laugh sounds like a rusty knife. "Yeah, Daddy dearest made a deal with the Archdemons to mask our blood from each other so we wouldn't come looking for him, doling out payback for being such a bastard."

Surprise cuts across her features. "Do you think that's what Gabriel did to me? I never felt..." She trails off.

I frown. I never really thought about it like that. "Yeah, I guess she must have." I shake my head at her mother's treachery. "So, you see, I wanted to free Alexander so badly because— well, he *is* Alexander the Great—and I just wanted...a dad. Some connection to my angelic heritage." A humorless chuckle escapes my lips. "Fuck, I sound like I'm a five-year-old crying for his daddy."

Slender fingers grip my jaw as Goldilocks forces me to meet

her eyes. "There's nothing childish about wanting a family," she chides and I flush, kicking myself for inadvertently saying the wrong thing to her, especially when a family is the thing she's wanted most in the world. "There's nothing wrong with wanting a father."

I turn my face and kiss her fingers, my eyes catching on the golden scar on her palm. I didn't think angels *could* scar but there it is, as clear as day, and I hate myself even more for dragging her into this mess. For asking her to free my grandfather, her flesh forever marked by my lapse in judgment.

She blushes, releasing me, and I sigh. "I know, I just feel stupid. I wanted it so badly that I ended up hurting you in the process, and I can't forgive myself for that," I tell her, and she drops my gaze, staring at her lap. "And he wasn't who I wanted him to be. I begged him to keep his promise, to come back for you, and he told me he would when the time was right, but he was too busy building an army. Too busy dreaming of ruling Earth. And the more I kept pushing… Let's just say if I pushed him too far, things wouldn't have ended well for me."

Luna looks up at me then, eyes rounded with shock. "You think he would've killed you?"

I shake my head. "No, I'm his blood, but he would have made an example of me to bring me in line. And if I was hurt badly enough, it would've taken even longer for me to find you. So in the end, I left him and came to Hammurabi for help. Gramps had big plans for me, too, from what Ishtar said.

Wanted me to fight in his war." I snort. "That's a hard pass."

"You turned your back on your grandfather for me? Your family?" Luna says in a quiet voice, hazel eyes stunned.

"Of course, I did," I say, bringing my face close to hers. "Luna, I made a promise to you, and I was going to keep it no matter what."

"Even if I cost you your grandfather?" she presses, and I hate the uncertainty in her eyes.

"You didn't cost me anything. Even if Alexander had brought you with us, we wouldn't have stayed. You don't want millions of humans to die in his war anymore than I do."

She jerks back at that. "Millions of humans will die?"

"My grandfather genuinely loves mortals, I'll give him that, but once he goes to war, who do you think will be the collateral damage? And he did want you by his side—he still does. I think part of the reason he left you in there was so that when he did finally rescue you, you'd be so grateful you'd fall in line with his plans."

A glint of that madness I spotted when we found her enters her eyes. "I would've been so broken I would've been useless to him. And he played me, preyed on my worst fears... He..." She shakes her head and gives me a piercing look. "Did you— did you play me, too, Caleb? To free Alexander?"

My heart drops right to my feet and shatters. I've been wondering when she would ask this. The dread has been like a fist encasing my heart, waiting for the right moment to squeeze.

Shame tightens my throat, and I have to clear it. That simple sound makes her face wilt like a dying flower. "I never played you, not like you think," I confess, my heart drumming so loudly in my ears I can barely hear my voice. "I've always cared about you, even when I thought I shouldn't. And the closer we got, the harder it was for me to think of you as a way to get to my grandfather. You were my friend—*are* my friend. I was caught between you and family and this horrible wrong I thought had been done to Alexander. When I met with Ishtar, I wanted to leave you out of it…but she reminded me where my loyalties belonged. That you don't turn your back on blood." I can't hide the fury in my voice at Ishtar, at myself. "But I made sure she swore to take you with us, that you'd be safe at Babel. That was the only way I agreed to keep you involved. I swear, Goldilocks, I had no idea how it was going to go down. And I've been trying to get back to you every day since you were left behind. You can't know how sorry I am, how much I regret getting you into this shit with me."

Tears brighten her eyes as she stares at me for a long moment, mulling over my confession and apology. Her next words will give me absolution or damn me, but to my surprise, she says, "Did you come after me just because you felt guilty? Did you kiss me out of some weird obligation?"

This girl knows how to deal out a gut punch. "Of course, I feel guilty, Luna. Jesus, you've been tortured by those monsters, and *I'm* responsible for it. But that's not why I came for you.

You have to know how I feel about you. I sure as shit have never kissed you out of obligation." I push into her space, cupping her face. "I kiss you because you're gorgeous and sweet, and I like how it feels." To prove my point, I seal my lips over hers. After a few moments, I deepen the kiss until we both break away, gasping for air.

She looks a little dazed but manages to say, "How *do* you feel about me?"

Luna is going to make me spell it out, but I owe her that. She's insecure about me, about everything, her world in total chaos right now. I want to settle her with the truth. The truth is just damn hard to say because I've never told a woman this before, other than my mom, and that hardly counts.

I touch my nose to hers, taking a deep breath and inhaling her scent. Then I ease away to look into her eyes. The words are like a boulder on my chest, hard to lift. When they escape me, she'll know she has the power to gut me and leave me bleeding. She already has that power.

"I love you, Goldilocks," I say, my voice rougher than I intended. "I'm *in* love with you." Tears puddle in her eyes and fall, and I kiss them away, tasting salt. I can't stand to see her cry. "Hey, I wasn't trying to make you cry," I whisper, gathering her to my chest.

She buries her face against me, hands clinging to my back. She sobs harder, and I feel it down to my soul. "No one has ever said that to me before." Her words cause me to stiffen in anger, and she looks up at me, big eyes afraid again, vulnerable, as if she's said the wrong thing.

"I'm not mad at you, baby," I say. "I'm mad at everyone in your life who should have been telling you they love you. Gabriel has a lot to answer for." I can't keep the venom from my voice, and she flinches. "I'm sorry. I know she's your mom."

Her fingers trace my lips, and I resist the urge to bite them, letting her talk. "It's okay. I don't know how to feel about her. I have so many questions…" Luna's eyes search mine. "I don't think it's your fault, what the Council did to me." She gives me a shy kiss when I open my mouth to protest. "People you trusted manipulated you. People you care about, who you thought cared about you. That must have been hard to say no to, especially because Alexander is your family."

"That's partly true, but I still shouldn't have gotten you involved," I say, shaking my head. "I should have told Ishtar to fuck off."

A doubtful chuckle escapes her. "Do you think she would've let you do that?"

"No," I admit. "Most of the time, I think she believes she's a goddess in truth. And she's obsessed with Alexander. She's a true believer."

"What does she believe Alexander can do? For her, I mean?"

"As a Gray angel, she thinks he can heal the divide, bring everyone together. That he was meant to rule here on Earth. That he's the only one who can do that."

A frown mars her smooth brow. "But what about me? I'm a Gray."

A wry smile touches my lips. "Exactly. You're a Gray. Doesn't make him such a special snowflake, now does it?"

Luna laughs. "Well, from the sounds of it, there are only two of us, and he *is* Alexander the Great, so that does make him kind of special."

"Yeah, but he's selling himself as the Messiah or some shit. I don't know how he was going to explain you to everyone, but I bet he was going to claim you as family somehow. Like you were a long lost princess come home."

Her arms slide from my side, and her hands find mine, lacing our fingers. "That would've been awkward with us kissing. Don't you think?"

Her cheeky grin is so unexpected, as is her joke, that I guffaw, almost choking. My ribcage feels ten times lighter, like I could float to the ceiling, even if I don't have wings. Speaking of wings…

I rise from the bed, my hands slipping from Luna's, and her eyebrows shoot up in question. I circle around her, and she twists her neck to look at me. My hand hovers over her smooth back, and I tilt my head, waiting for permission. She nods, curiosity lighting her face. My fingers make contact with her warm skin, and I know it sounds cliché as hell, but a jolt of electricity travels up the pads of my fingertips. She shivers.

"May I see them?" I ask, not bothering with a more detailed

explanation. She knows.

That endearing shyness sweeps over her, and I think she's going to refuse, but wings start to sprout from her shoulder blades like spring flowers. Awed, I step back, giving her room. Moments later, large wings curve around her, feathers spilling across the bed, their sheen almost metallic. I suck in a deep breath, wanting to touch them so badly I have to ball my hands into fists.

But I don't touch without consent. I'm not that kind of guy.

"They're beautiful, Goldilocks," I tell her, throat suddenly dry, yearning raw in my voice. I'm embarrassed by how much I want to brush my fingers along those pearly feathers, but I can't hide it. I don't want to. Luna needs to know she holds power in our relationship, too.

Her gaze snags mine. I notice she has a gold sheen to her irises that wasn't there before, as if releasing her wings brought out the full angel. She takes in a deep breath. "Do you want to—"

"Yes," I say, eagerness filling the words, and she gives a breathless laugh. I sink my fingers into the velvety feathers near her shoulder and she sucks in air, her back bowing. I snatch my hand back, horrified. "Did I hurt you?" I ask, worried eyes running over her wings.

"No," she chokes out, her face scarlet, chest heaving. "They hurt when I was in that cage, but now..." She swallows loudly. "They're sensitive and..." Her chin drops to her chest, as if she's too embarrassed to look at me.

Oh. *Oh*. Well, that's interesting. I've never touched anyone's wings before. It's not like Asmodeus or Alexander went around offering, and now I know why.

Goldilocks peeks up at me. "You can…you can touch them again."

Damn, everything below my belt grows uncomfortably tight. I smooth a palm over her wings again, and her little gasp heats my whole body. I pull my hand away, my own breathing uneven.

The sexy, slumberous look in her eyes almost undoes me. "Why did you stop?"

Why indeed? Oh yeah, because I'm a good guy, and good guys don't let their dicks rule them. "Because it's been a long day, and you need to rest." When she starts to protest, I say, "And I know it's your decision, but I'm making this decision for me. I don't ever want you to look at me with regret. I would love to hold you, though, while we sleep. Is that okay?" I sit next to her and she nods, her wings retracting. I fall back on the bed, tugging her with me, until her head rests on my chest.

And I savor this rare, perfect moment.

sixteen

LUNA

I LIE STILL NEXT to Caleb, relishing the calming repetition of his breaths on the back of my neck and the delicious heat of his body pressed against mine, his hand splayed across my stomach, holding me close, as if he's afraid to put space between us. As if he's afraid to let me go.

I know that fear all too well; I'm consumed by it. Except in my case, that terror revolves around sleep. If I dare to close my eyes for even a second, will I wake to find this is all only a dream? Will I end up back in the prison the Council constructed to keep me captive—trapped forever in that confining glass egg like an immortal baby bird? If so, then those beautiful words Caleb spoke to me earlier, words I never thought I'd hear someone say to me...

"I love you, Goldilocks."

If this is only a dream, then none of that was real.

Tears prick at the corners of my eyes at the thought, and I

wipe them away with the heel of my hand, stifling the sob in my throat. This—being at Babel with Caleb, however fleeting—is so unreal to me, and I can't escape the constant fear nagging at the back of my brain that this is all an illusion. Another way for Mammon to get inside my head.

I flip over, snuggling closer to Caleb, tucking my head under his chin and pressing my face against the warmth of his chest, needing to breathe in the smell of him. To prove to myself this is actually happening—that he's here and I'm in his arms, and we're together again as we should be. His hand, which was previously on my stomach, now presses flat against the small of my back, and I flush at the feel of his fingers on my bare skin, a shudder creeping up my spine. The shirt Asmodeus gave me leaves little to the imagination, but I understand the need for it, even if it leaves me feeling exposed and reminds me far too much of how I was clothed all those months trapped in the Council's cage. Until I've acclimated to having wings, I'll have to dress sensibly. The last thing I need is to accidentally tear through a shirt in a moment of wavering composure and flash everyone around me. I'm sure nobody wants to see that.

Except, maybe Caleb, a snarky voice says from somewhere in the back of my head.

My cheeks burn with the intensity of a thousand suns, and my fingers grip Caleb's arm as an aching need surges through my body, my wings trembling under my skin with the sudden urge to rip free of my flesh. Great. Even as an angel, I clearly have trouble controlling my hormones.

"What's wrong?"

Gasping, I pull away slightly and glance up at Caleb, who peers at me with half-open eyes hazy with sleep. His voice is a husky purr in my ears.

I swallow as the heat threatens to devour me whole. "Can't sleep," I whisper.

Smirking, he grazes my cheek with his knuckles. "Why so flushed, Goldilocks? You weren't having any untoward thoughts about me just now, were you?"

The warmth in my blood reaches boiling point, and I bolt upright at the same moment my wings spring free of my back, unable to hold them in any longer. Caleb gapes at me, his eyes widening as realization sinks in, and he begins to laugh. Mortified, I cover my face with my hands, wishing I could find a rock to bury myself under.

"Hey, none of that." The mattress shifts as he sits up beside me, and I jolt when his hands wrap around my wrists and gently pull my hands away from my face. When our eyes meet, a noticeable shiver rolls through me. Even better. I've gone from unstable horny teenager to vibrating Chihuahua.

If I was capable of dying, I would.

"This is so embarrassing," I mutter, averting my eyes.

Caleb grips my chin and turns my face, forcing me to look at him. "You never have to be embarrassed with me, Goldilocks. Besides, you aren't the only one having untoward thoughts."

He clears his throat as my eyes dip down, and suddenly, our breaths seem deafening in the silence of the room. A room we're very much alone in. Licking my lips, I brush my fingertips across his right cheek, and his gaze seems to glow as he takes me in, his own arms curling around my back and pulling me close until our chests are touching. When his hand grazes my wing, an unbidden gasp slips from my lips, and he flashes a roguish grin.

Leaning in, he croons in my ear, "Careful now, Goldilocks. You keep making sounds like that and I won't be able to control myself."

A squeak of a laugh escapes me. Between us, he isn't the one who needs to worry about losing control.

As if to prove my lack of willpower, I thread my fingers in his disheveled hair without thought and yank his face down to mine, devouring his lips. His arms tense around me, and I sense his own hunger as he reciprocates my advance, his thumb tugging on my chin, coaxing me to part my lips and let him inside. As his tongue sweeps over mine, I melt in his embrace.

He leans me back onto the mattress, my pewter wings spread out behind me like a blanket of feathers, and as he trails biting kisses along my neck and collarbone, his fingers tickle over the most sensitive parts of my new appendages.

I finally understand why none of the angels or Fallen tend to keep their wings on display—and why Alaric laughed at me when I asked about Gabriel's shortly after I met her. There's something so personal about having wings, and when they're out in the open, I feel somewhat naked. Like they're meant for me and only me.

And now, also for Caleb.

A low growl rumbles in my chest at his teasing, and he chuckles, leaning in to kiss me again. But just as his lips are about to touch mine, a thunderous sound in the distance has him pulling away, his breath hitching and eyes suddenly wild like a hunted rabbit's. Sitting back, he snaps his gaze toward the closed door.

"What is that?" I ask, sitting up beside him. When he doesn't answer, I place a hand on his bicep. "Caleb?"

"War horns," he says absentmindedly.

I can practically hear him straining to listen, and I follow his wide-eyed stare when the two-tone sound is repeated a moment later. The floor shakes as it reverberates through the space.

"War horns?" I repeat, hoping he'll elaborate.

His focus doesn't shift from the door when he answers. "The horns are to Babel what the bells are to the Serapeum. They use them to signal day-to-day things like the end of class, but..." He trails off, and the hair on the back of my neck stands on end at the thought of what he isn't saying.

"But what?" My voice is a whisper, the words gritty like sand in my mouth.

Finally, Caleb meets my questioning gaze, and the unease in his eyes nearly undoes me. "I—"

A sharp knocking on the door makes us both jump. Before I

can get another word out, Caleb leaps off the bed while I fist my hands in the bed sheets, unable to move—crippled by fear and still flustered from the last few minutes. Caleb throws open the door to a disgruntled Hammurabi. The Babylonian king's tall frame fills the doorway, and the black and indigo tendrils of his aura ripple with agitated alarm as he peers past Caleb into the unlit room, meeting my gaze.

"We need to leave." His voice is a commanding snarl. Turning his glare on Caleb, he adds, "Grab the girl and let's go."

My upper lip curls back into a grimace as scenes from the past seventeen years replay through my head like some sort of masochistic slideshow. How many times have I been referred to this way, like I'm not even present or allowed to be involved with any decisions concerning my own life? How many times have I been spoken to like I'm not even a person worthy of consideration?

The heat and lust I reveled in only moments ago melt away, swallowed by a blinding, white-hot anger that blackens the edges of my vision. Scowling, I grind out, "The girl can hear you."

Hammurabi and Caleb both gape at me, blinking like fools, clearly taken aback by my tone and the way I spit each word through clenched teeth. Rolling my eyes, I draw in a deep breath then exhale, searching for some semblance of calm within myself—assuming there is any part of me that hasn't been infected by the chaos I always feel scratching at my thoughts. Dragging in one more steadying breath for good measure, I retract my wings and rise from the bed.

"Caleb, what the hell's going on?" I manage, once the anger has dissipated.

He thrusts one finger in the air when the war horns blare for a third time, their rumbling shout ominous. "You hear that? The horns only make that sound—that *specific* call—when an Archdemon is visiting Babel. It's an announcement of sorts so we can all be prepared to act like the star pupils Babel has shaped us into." He lowers his gaze to the floor, his eyes vacant, as that fear I glimpsed before returns to his face. "But last I checked, Archdemons don't make house calls for a friendly chat in the middle of the night."

Hammurabi glowers at me. "Whoever has come, they will be here for you."

Apprehension sharper and more powerful than anything I've ever felt before sends an uncomfortable tingle up my spine. "They…as in the Council? They're here?" The ancient Nephilim's silence is all the confirmation I need.

Caleb runs a hand through his hair, the ebony strands still messy with sleep, his lower lip jutting out in annoyance as he blows out a vexed breath through his nose. "How the fuck—" He sneers, swallowing whatever he was going to say, before flashing a quick look in my direction, his expression written with so many unspoken thoughts I can't even begin to fathom what he's thinking. Shaking his head, he snaps his focus back to his teacher. "I thought Asmodeus masked us." I don't miss the accusation in his tone.

Hammurabi cocks a warning eyebrow. "She did, but that protection means little if those she's hiding us from know where we are. If I had to guess, we have a snake in our midst."

Caleb scoffs. "You mean someone sold us out."

The intimidating Nephilim seems to grow three sizes bigger as he puffs out his broad chest, crossing his arms. "It does not matter how they came upon the information. What matters is that the Council has breached these walls, and if we don't flee now, with our hides still intact, they will sniff us out. Then all of our efforts to get this far and save the girl will have been for naught."

Flee? We were supposed to have more time. We can't leave now. Where can we even go? Where on this planet is safe for us?

"And go where, exactly?" I ask, unable to keep the panic from creeping into each word. "What about Alaric? My parents? We can't leave without them—"

Silence swallows my voice, and the tears resurface as everything I've been bottling up threatens to explode out of me in a cataclysmic wave. We can't go yet, not when I'm so close to finally meeting my parents. Well, technically, I've already met them, but I didn't know who they were at the time. Meeting them now would be different—a moment I've been waiting for all my life. So, we can't leave now.

We can't.

"Hammurabi..." The way Caleb utters his teacher's name

sends pinpricks of icy fear along my skin. "What about Asmodeus?"

The Nephilim's face is an unreadable mask. He might as well be made of stone. "It was my mistress's command that I keep you both safe, and that is what I intend to do." His eyes, two black voids in the darkness, flick to mine. "If the Council has truly infiltrated Babel, then they will know of the role she played in your liberation—"

"Not to mention the whole harboring fugitives thing," Caleb grumbles. "I doubt the Council would look too kindly on that."

Hammurabi deflates, showing a rare glimpse of emotion on his otherwise stern face. "Indeed. Asmodeus likely sounded the horns to warn us and give us enough time to get out. There is little any of us can do for her now except honor her wishes… and survive."

Survive. That's all I've done for seventeen years. I'm tired of just surviving. I want to live. I want to be happy. I want to be free of this nightmare.

Free… My stomach drops as a sudden thought hits me.

"What if it's a trap?" The horror of such a notion is like a hand wrapping around my throat, and the more I think about it, the more I'm certain I'm right. "What if they're trying to spook us? To make us run so they can corner us in the Shadow Road? I was a captive of the Council long enough to know how much they like head games, and after Mammon—"

"They'll be watching the entry points around the school, of

that I have no doubt," Hammurabi says over me with a grim nod, stroking his beard in contemplation. "If we enter the Shadow Road from here, the Council will surely know it."

The silence that follows is suffocating, like a thick, choking smoke permeating my lungs. I can barely breathe past it, and I know I must be hyperventilating because Caleb's hands are on my face, my hair, my back, constantly stroking me, trying to calm me down. I blink up at him through the watery film coating my eyes, and the expression I find there—the acceptance, the defeat—shreds my soul into two.

"Luna, listen to me," he says, gripping both my hands in his and holding them firmly between us. Swallowing, he frowns down at our entwined fingers. "You could go the Light way. Use their Road. Even if they're watching it, they might not expect you to actually use it, especially if we draw their attention away. If we distract them, you can escape—"

I yank my hands free of his, unable to believe what I'm hearing. "No!" I shriek, not caring how unbalanced or hysterical I sound. "If we run, we run *together*. I don't want to be separated again."

The tears flow freely now, and I crumple to the floor, my fingers clutching at my head as that unhinged darkness inside me rises like a tidal wave, ready to finally drown me.

Caleb squats beside me and pulls me into the comforting warmth of his arms. "Okay, Goldilocks," he murmurs into my hair. "Message received. We won't be. I'll stay with you no matter what."

Do you promise? I try to ask him, but I can't find the words.

Caleb plants a kiss on the top of my head, and his soothing baritone vibrates through me when he says, "Hammurabi, what are our options?"

The older Nephilim—who remains by the door, peeking out into the hallway every few moments, checking for any sign of our pursuers—doesn't look at us when he replies, "Escape on foot. Put enough distance between us and Babel so that when we do enter the Road, they won't see us. Then we move and get out again as quickly as possible."

With one hand on my back and the other around my waist, Caleb stands, helping me to my feet. He offers me a reassuring smile then exchanges a knowing look with his teacher. "Is Hilla far enough?"

The Babylonian king shrugs. "I guess we'll find out."

We make our way through the web of underground passages beneath Babel, taking extreme care as we tiptoe through the dank gloom, every movement precise and exaggerated, like we're trapped in an episode of *Scooby Doo*. Caleb never leaves my side, his hand a permanent fixture around mine.

He casts frequent glances at me before finally leaning in, his mouth tickling my ear. "It's going to be okay," he breathes so softly even I struggle to hear it with my enhanced hearing. "I won't let anyone take you again."

I offer him a small smile, even though the expression is forced. As much as I want to believe him, he's only one Nephilim up against eleven celestial beings of unmatched power. He wouldn't stand a chance against them in a fight. They'd break his bones and shred him like a paper doll just for trying. Even Hammurabi, who is a first generation and seasoned warrior, would be overpowered by a full-blooded angel.

Trepidation clenches my stomach, my thoughts growing darker. The sooner we get out of Babel and away from immediate danger, the better. Even if doing so means I might not see Alaric or my parents again.

I think of them now, picturing each of their faces in turn. As much as I want to see my parents—to speak to them, to understand the circumstances surrounding my birth—the person I'm most concerned about is Alaric. He sacrificed so much for me, risking exile or worse, by crossing the divide and working with Darks to break me out of my prison. If he's caught, I can only imagine what the Council will do to him. And to Asmodeus for giving him a sigil.

Be safe, I pray, holding onto the thought of his face. *Until we see each other again.*

Hammurabi hooks a right down a narrow passage, which, at first glance, appears to be a dead end. I'm about to ask if we're lost when he proceeds to walk into the brick, passing through the hard surface as if even the laws of physics can't compete with the Nephilim's power. Caleb follows without hesitation, tugging me along behind him like a distracted puppy being guided by its owner. As we step through the mirage, the air shifts, distorting like rippling water, before settling into the gardens we initially stepped out of the Shadow Road into last night.

The scent of citrus trees clings to my nose as I turn, taking in the broken wall we stepped out of among the ruins standing outside Babel. I place a hand on the stone, the texture rough beneath my fingertips. Clearly, that was a one-way exit. I resist the urge to roll my eyes. What is it with angels and their glamors? Nothing is ever as it appears.

Hammurabi pauses at the brink of the gardens, his head on a swivel as he scans the shadows with narrowed eyes that gleam in the darkness. I follow his gaze, my angel vision sharp in the cover of night. Even though I see nothing, goosebumps pimple my skin, and I shiver despite the warmth in the air. The gardens are quiet.

Too quiet.

Fear is a symphony drumming along the underside of my skin as Caleb's hold on my hand tightens. I can sense his growing alarm as clearly as I feel my own, and I know we're thinking the same thing. Something is coming.

We both whip around at the abrupt crunching of sand as Hammurabi throws himself in front of us like a shield, but in the split-second before he blocked her from view, I caught a glimpse of our pursuer's face. It's burned into my retinas, along with the sting of her betrayal.

Nzingha.

I shake my head. I don't understand. She helped free me, so why turn on us now?

I sidestep Hammurabi, needing to see her again—to know for sure we've been double-crossed by one of our own. By someone Caleb and Asmodeus trusted to help them. Her lips twitch when our eyes clash, her skin burnished sienna in the dim light of the cloud-obscured moon.

Hammurabi lets out a dismissive snort. "It seems our snake has finally slithered out of hiding. Asmodeus was wrong to put her trust in you, Queen."

"Asmodeus was a fool for thinking she could defy the will of the Council," Nzingha bites back.

Beside me, Caleb tenses, his face contorted into an expression of fury. "I *knew* it," he seethes, spitting the words with pure venom. "I knew it was strange you got off scot-free after Mammon saw you helping us."

A taunting smile peels back the queen's lips as two kunai daggers slip free from the sleeves of her shirt, and Nzingha hurls herself forward, like a piercing arrow in the night, the red and gold of her head wrap the only visible color as she weaves in and out of the shadows with the ease and grace of an acrobat. Hammurabi bursts into action, the desert floor kicking up in a cloud around his feet. As he races away from us, time seems to slow and the sand hangs suspended in the air, almost as if we're frozen in this moment—trapped, just like I was in that prison.

The ancient king and queen collide in a blurred tangle of fists, Hammurabi getting the first hit in, meeting her jaw with the deafening crack of a thunder strike. Nzingha spits blood out onto the sand by her feet before grinning at the other Nephilim with crimson-stained teeth. As they continue their lethal dance, I glance at Caleb, glimpsing the internal war on his face as he contemplates throwing himself into the fray or staying behind. Staying with me. His indecision sets my blood on fire. Wanted by the Council or not, I'm not some weak mortal with no way to defend myself, even if I am new to my power. Like I said to Alaric before, I can fight.

And I will defend those who risked their lives to free me.

"Go!" I shout to Caleb before launching into a sprint. Fire bursts across my palms as I scour the darkness for Nzingha, catching sight of her as she dodges Hammurabi's fist with an impressive aerial, her long, limber legs like hummingbird wings, blurring as she moves with a speed even my eyes struggle to track. I approach from Hammurabi's right as Caleb comes in from the left to head her off. She swipes her blades at him like a cat striking out with its claws but, to my immense relief, misses. Nzingha might be fast, but thankfully, so is Caleb.

The queen stops suddenly, her charcoal-rimmed eyes glowing with wrath. Sheathing her daggers, she drops to one knee, slamming her fist into the ground with such force a quake splits the earth, sending Hammurabi and Caleb stumbling backward. She then rises and pivots to face me, grinning.

"Hello, baby bird."

I direct the full brunt of my fire at her, but she moves too quickly for me to hit, leaving little more than a scorch mark where she previously stood in the sand. I spin around, searching for her, my eyes pinned wide, but I only see Hammurabi and Caleb.

"Look out!" Caleb shouts, but his warning comes too late. Nzingha slams into my back, pinning me down to the sand, her knees pressing brutally into the sensitive exit points for my wings, ripping a strangled scream from my lungs. The fiery vambraces winding around my forearms sputter out like dying embers.

The Nephilim traces the shell of my ear with her finger before bending down to whisper, "Say hello to your parents for me." Then the weight is gone, and I'm left with only a weird sensation where her breath and finger grazed my skin, as if I've been branded by her touch.

Caleb reaches me as I flip onto my back, and scrambling to my feet, I watch with bewilderment as Nzingha runs away from us. Or rather from the vengeful figure standing at the edge of the gardens like a goddess on the warpath.

"Asmodeus!" The pure joy in Caleb's voice nearly brings me to tears.

The headmistress of Babel wears a beautiful scowl, her vibrant hair whipping in the wind as her aura contorts, wrapping around her limbs like ribbons of liquid ebony. Her green eyes, which glow in the darkness, meet mine before narrowing on the retreating Nephilim's back. Beyond Nzingha, in the distance over the school, black and white shapes dot the sky, descending quickly.

The Council.

"I'll take it from here," she shouts. "Run!"

When Caleb and I don't immediately move, our attention fixed on the incoming threat, Hammurabi grabs us both roughly by the shoulders. "You heard your mistress. *Move.*"

"I can help you," I plead with Asmodeus, but she shakes her head.

"Your father would never forgive me if I let you get captured again." She offers me a bittersweet smile. "Now, go."

Hammurabi yanks on my shoulder again, and this time, I relent, swallowing the lump in my throat as the guilt of whatever is about to happen to Asmodeus sits like a weight on my chest. Beside me, Caleb seems just as afflicted, his eyes downcast and teeth clamped firmly on his lower lip. He curses under his breath, but neither of us say another word after that. Instead, we run as fast as we can, trying not to think about Asmodeus or what hell we've abandoned her to.

It's roughly five kilometers to Hilla, the nearest city to Babel. If I wasn't so incompetent at using my wings, I would've flown us there but, as it currently stands, I can fly about as well as a penguin. Besides, going airborne would've likely made us too visible to any watching eyes, human or otherwise, which leaves us with only one option: to run. Luckily, with our celestial blood, the trek takes a fraction of the time it would take a normal mortal. Still, those ten or so minutes seem never-ending with a small army of Archangels and Archdemons on our tail, and I constantly find myself looking over my shoulder, risking fearful glances up at the overcast sky to check if we're being pursued. My terror is only elevated by the fact I feel strangely off-balance, the ear Nzingha whispered into foggy, as if water is trapped behind my eardrum. The sensation makes me nervous I won't hear someone sneaking up on me.

The moment we finally step foot into Hilla, Hammurabi grabs Caleb and me each by the arm before tugging us into an empty alleyway that smells of cooked fish and a pungent, spicy aroma. Caleb and I exchange a quick look, and I barely stop to catch my breath before the darkness swathes our bodies, pulling us into its maw as if to swallow us whole.

When we step foot onto the Shadow Road, my body goes rigid, my eyes frantically searching for even the smallest indication that we aren't alone. To my relief, there aren't any Archdemons in sight, and I let out a breath as the tension in my shoulders eases just a little.

Although it seems the Council hasn't figured out where we've escaped to, we don't hesitate to follow Hammurabi, running as fast as we can, passing marker after marker while making sure to always keep a wide berth from Babel.

Caleb is the one to break the silence once we're far enough away from Iraq to assume that we haven't been followed. He pushes his hair from his face with his free hand—his other clasped around mine—as his stomach rumbles, drawing an irked glance from his teacher. He smiles sheepishly. "So… anyone else feel like some pizza?"

seventeen

CALEB

WE POP OUT FROM the Shadow Road into my bedroom in Queens, my heart hammering in my chest. Luna looks just as shaken as I feel, and Hammurabi wears a murderous expression, like he wants to pick up a sword and go on a killing spree. What the fuck just happened? I knew something felt off with Nzingha, but I was so happy to have Luna back and to escape Mammon I didn't give it enough thought. My inattention to detail just came back and tried to stab me. No wonder Mammon conveniently showed up when we rescued Luna. His little minion whispered our plans in his ear. Man, Asmodeus is going to kick her ass. Worry for the headmistress of Babel gnaws at me with sharp teeth. Now that Asmodeus has been outed, will she be on the run like we are? What will happen to Babel?

"Will Asmodeus be okay?" I ask Hammurabi, even though I feel stupid the moment the words leave my lips. Of course, she won't be if the Council turns on her.

The Babylonian king wheels his thunderous expression on me. "What do you think, boy? I should have stayed and helped her." He gives Luna a contemptuous sneer that rubs me the wrong way.

Luna stiffens and I snap, "Don't be a dick."

Hammurabi grabs me by the throat, and my back smacks the wall. "Don't be disrespectful," he growls and then suddenly freezes. Confusion fills me until I see Luna's small hand on his shoulder, fingers clenched.

"Put Caleb down," she says softly. "You keep forgetting what I am." A puff of laughter escapes her. "I guess I do, too."

Hammurabi slowly lowers me, and my feet touch the floor. "I never forget what you are," he tells her, his voice holding all the warmth of ice chips. Then his tone melts a little. "My mistress commands my loyalty, little Gray. I despise abandoning her in her time of need."

Luna's face takes on a cast of misery. "I know. I'm sorry. I wish she'd let me stay and help. *I* could've helped."

I open my mouth to offer some comfort when the door to my room swings open so hard the hinges squeal. My petite mother stands there with a chef's knife in her hand and a look of determination across her beautiful face. Her mouth falls open like a gate when she sees me.

"Caleb?" she says, lowering the knife. Mom takes in Luna and Hammurabi, the latter who actually *checks out* my mom.

That is so not okay. "What are you doing here? Aren't you supposed to be in school? Who are your…friends?" She blushes under Hammurabi's perusal, and I try to shoot lasers out of my eyes at my teacher.

Um, so on my weekly calls with my mom, I might have neglected to mention that I helped my grandfather escape and was holed up in Afghanistan with him as he plotted to take over the world. Whoops. She's gonna be pissed.

My chest rises on a huge inhale, and I sigh. I cross the room and bend slightly, giving my mom a big hug. She wraps her arms around me, smelling of mint, cucumber, and garlic, and I know she's been cooking. It's so good to hold her, like I'm a child again, and I believe that she can make any problem go away, right any wrong. I pull back, and her big brown eyes probe mine, her golden skin still flushed. She tucks a strand of dark brown hair behind one ear as her eyes narrow on me.

"How much trouble are you in?" she asks, mouth turning down into a frown.

"A shit ton," I answer, and her eyebrows raise in concern.

"That bad?" she presses.

I nod. "Yeah, that bad. Let's go to the kitchen so we can talk about it."

Mom clears her throat, nodding toward Luna and Hammurabi. Luna watches our exchange in total fascination. "I know I raised you with better manners than that. Introduce us." Her chiding face makes me fidget like a little kid and I wince.

"Right, sorry, on the run and all," I say, and her eyes widen as I sweep an arm out toward the others. "This is my teacher, Hammurabi. I'm sure you've heard of him, wrote the Code of Hammurabi and all." Mom blinks as she focuses on my teacher. She's used to Nephilim—I'm one—but it's still weird when you introduce a literal figure from history to a mortal. Hammurabi gives a slight bow and a devilish grin, which I want to punch off his face. Where is my stern, pain-in-the-ass teacher now? My eyes move to Luna and everything within me softens. "This is Luna, my…girlfriend." The word trips a little on my tongue because I've never used it, but it feels right, though weird, to call an angel your *girlfriend*. Cosmic lover is way too cheesy. "And an angel."

The stunned expression on Mom's face expands even farther at the last word until she resembles a cartoon character whose eyes are attempting to bug out of her skull. She shakes her head a little, staring at me. She's met Ishtar before but never an actual angel. Ishtar was enough for her.

I continue, "Luna, Hammurabi, this is my mom, Zahra."

Hammurabi rumbles, "It's a pleasure to meet you. I am certain all of Caleb's virtuous qualities are from you."

I roll my eyes at him as my mother chuckles. Luna offers a shy smile, her hazel eyes uncertain. I reach out a hand, and she steps up to take it.

"It's so nice to meet you," she says to Mom. "I… I want you to know Caleb was kind to me when no one else at school was.

He's a good person, and I'm sure it's because of you."

Mom's smile is full of warmth when she looks at Luna and a little confusion. "Thank you for the lovely words, Luna. Caleb has never brought a girl home before. Trust him to introduce me to an actual angel. You were in school with Caleb?"

"For a few months. Until…" She trails off, her gaze darkening. Clearing her throat, she shakes her head, saying, "I thought I was a Nephilim. So did Caleb. The angel thing came later."

"Oh…I see," Mom says, but it's clear she doesn't see at all. She straightens, alarm blazing over her face. "And you're on the run? From whom?"

"So, I might have done something slightly stupid," I say to her, and Hammurabi snorts.

Mom rents the second floor of a two-family house in Astoria, Queens, so she has a pretty decent dining room, but we're still bumping elbows as we crowd around the round table. And Mom being Mom, she's doubled everything she was cooking until the table is full of flat bread, yogurt and cucumber dip, saffron-flavored rice, and stuffed chicken, all the familiar dishes of my childhood and her home country of Iran. She left after she got pregnant with me at twenty, and her parents disowned her for being knocked up without a husband in sight. They're assholes like that. She immigrated to Paris and then New York. I don't remember Paris very well, as I spent most of my childhood in New York before leaving for my primary academy.

Mom's arms are crossed over her chest. "This is your father's fault," she says, venom leaking into her voice. "If he'd actually been around, maybe you wouldn't have gone chasing Alexander." Guilt flashes over her face. "Maybe I should have remarried, given you—"

For fuck's sake, Hammurabi does not need that much info on my daddy issues. "Mom, I didn't need anyone else but you," I tell her. "You're awesome." It's both the truth and a lie. She gave me enough love for one hundred fathers, but the fact that my dad took off when I was born still rubs me raw.

Mom's eyes soften, and she ruffles my hair, which I allow because I'm a good son and I secretly love it. "Thank you, baby." She turns her focus on Luna, who tugs on one of her earlobes. Mom reaches over the table, and clasps Luna's free hand. "And you, sweet girl, can stay here as long as you want. Your parents have a lot to answer for." The last words are painted with an undercoat of anger. Mom took it pretty well when she found out Gabriel and Lucifer are Luna's parents. I mean, after the initial shock wore off. And when we told her Luna had been imprisoned, well, mama bear came out in full force. She pushes more rice at Luna. "Angel or no, eat."

Luna blushes and removes her hand from my mom's, dutifully scooping more rice on her plate. "Thank you, ma'am."

"Ma'am?" Mom snorts. "Please call me Zahra. I don't feel

old enough to be called ma'am." She winks at Luna.

Hammurabi grins, agreeing, "You're hardly old enough to be called ma'am."

I glare at him. "Well, since you're older than dirt, I guess you would know."

"Caleb," Mom says, throwing me side-eye, and Luna giggles, making me smile.

Hammurabi glowers at me, and I know he'd like to punish me the Babel way for my cheek but won't do it in front of my mother.

I shrug. "It's the truth, Mom, and the fact that he's hitting on you makes him a cradle-robber," I say, calling it like it is. Okay, so Mom is a grown-ass woman, but Hammurabi is a womanizer, so let me plant all kinds of seeds of ick in her brain. A little voice in my head reminds me that Luna is technically way older than me, but she's only been really living for the past seventeen years, so it's not the same thing. She's still a girl.

"Caleb!" Mom repeats, flags of red appearing on her cheeks. She turns to the Babylonian king. "I'm so sorry for my son's extreme rudeness."

Flashing a charming grin, Hammurabi says, "The boy's lack of manners is no fault of yours, and perhaps I was being rather forward with you, which I apologize if I were untoward." He scowls at me. "However, boy, your mother is an adult, so she can decide to rebuff me, although your protective instincts are admirable."

His words make my mother blush harder, and I hide a grin. She shoots from the table. "Anyone want some tea?" She turns her back to us and busies herself getting delicate teacups from the cabinets.

I keep my voice just this shade of audible. "Hey, stop hitting on my mom," I hiss at Hammurabi.

He stares me down, willing me to melt under his authority. "As I've said, your mother is an adult, but under the current circumstances, I'll cease my attention."

I nod as Mom returns to the table with fragrant tea. She pours each of us a cup, giving Luna an extra cookie with hers.

"So, what's the plan?" Mom asks, sliding into the space between me and Hammurabi. She looks at my teacher, fear in her eyes. "Will they really—will they kill Caleb if they catch you? Because he freed Alexander?"

"They'll kill all of us," Hammurabi answers gravely. "I don't support Alexander but I freed Luna. I'm sure in their minds it's the same thing."

"So much for breaking the news gently," I growl at him.

"But I'm *not* Alexander," Luna spits, shattering the tea cup in her hand. "I don't understand any of this—this hate just because I'm a Gray." She looks at the powder in her hand and goes white. Tears gloss her eyes as she stares at my mom in horror. "Oh, Zahra—I didn't—I'm so sorry—I—"

"Hey, it's okay," I say, rubbing her back in soothing circles, but she pushes away from me.

"It's not okay!" she yells, eyes wild. "I'm always destroying things. I'm…" Her palms smother her face as she sobs into them.

"Goldilocks," I say, reaching for her again, but Mom stops me.

"Sweet girl," Mom croons, standing and skirting around the table. She cradles Luna's head against her chest. "It's just a tea cup. You've had a rough time of it, and no one is going to blame you for being a little angry right now. You have every right to not be okay."

"It's not you, Luna," Hammurabi says, crossing his arms over his chest, and something akin to sympathy slides across his face. "The Council fears you because of the prophecy. We thought it applied to Alexander, but then you appeared like a mirage in the desert, making everyone second-guess what they actually thought they knew. I, too, have my own fears about it, founded or not. And…that is not your fault."

Well, there must be snowballs in Hell. Hammurabi is coming around. Luna raises her head from the comfort of my mom's embrace and stares at Hammurabi.

"What prophecy?" she demands, her eyes meeting mine.

Well, shit on a stick. I neglected to speak to her about that. I don't know why I thought she knew; I thought those Council assholes would torment her with the prophecy while she was imprisoned.

"Shall I hazard a guess? Too much kissing and not enough time explaining the important things," Hammurabi says, getting a little payback on me.

Willing my middle finger down, I turn to Luna. "I thought you knew. I thought the Council would've told you just to torture you."

Luna gives a frantic shake of her head. "No—no, they just wanted to know where Alexander was. They never told me anything—" Her eyes light up with realization. "Wait…Uriel did say something about Gabriel. About whether she told them the truth about the Gray who would destroy the world. But he was taunting me, then Mammon appeared, and I realized…" She shakes her head again, as if trying to fling away those memories from her brain. "I didn't know what was real in there. Mammon kept changing his face and made me believe…"

Fury overrides me for a moment. Yeah, Mammon made her believe all kinds of shit. He deserves to be a one-winged chicken.

"Tell us about the prophecy, Caleb," Mom commands.

I glance at my teacher. "Hammurabi knows it better than me," I grumble, "but essentially, Gabriel delivered a prophecy that an angel born of the Dark and the Light—a Gray—would be destined to overtake and destroy the world. Earth as we know it, I guess. Now that there are two of you, the Council is shitting bricks trying to figure out which one of you is the big bad."

Luna blinks, her fingers clenching her earlobe again. "So, they were going to imprison me for all eternity for something that *might* happen? They don't even know if it's me or not but they were going to keep me in that cage like some animal?" She grits her teeth, hazel eyes clouded with rage.

"They don't want another Fall," Hammurabi explains. "None of us do. But Asmodeus does not believe you're the Gray the prophecy spoke of. In fact, who knows how accurate your mother's words were? She hid you from us. Who's to say the Messenger told us the whole truth?"

"Your mom is such an asshole," I growl then shoot Goldilocks an apologetic look. "Sorry."

Trembling, Luna says, "Is that why she abandoned me? Because of the prophecy? Maybe it does refer to me."

"The fuck it does," I tell her, reaching for her hand. "Gabriel mentioned only one Gray, and there are two of you. She clearly doesn't know dick."

My mom is so worked up over Luna she doesn't even admonish me for my language. "Luna, you're not an evil girl. Alexander tried to take over the world without any interference from you."

Even Hammurabi, the straight-laced grump, pipes in, "Zahra is right. Alexander always had a thirst for conquest. I see no such desire in you."

Luna cackles, a bitter, worrying sound. "Alexander and I do have something in common, though. We both want to tear down the divide."

I quickly cut in, "Yeah, but you don't want to start a war to do it."

Goldilocks shakes her head. "No, no, but the fact that I exist, that I want to be with you, is enough for the Council to think I'm declaring war."

"She's not wrong," Hammurabi says. "Those on the Council are…what's the word? Old-fashioned in their views. And stubborn."

"They're stodgy, prejudiced pricks," I correct him.

"Careful," Hammurabi says, the anger in his eyes hot enough to smite me. "Asmodeus put her immortal life on the line for you."

I shrink back. Yeah, she did, for me and someone she doesn't even know. "Sorry I was a dick," I say. "I know what she did for us."

"Why did she do it for me?" Luna asks. "She mentioned my father but I still don't understand."

"Her love for the Morningstar, child," Hammurabi says. "She meant it when she said she would hate any child of Lucifer's to suffer."

I wonder if Asmodeus pines after Lucifer, but I can't see her being the pining type. My mom brushes a strand of gold from Luna's face.

"Well, whatever her reasons, I'm glad she did it," Mom says.

Luna stares up at my mom. "You're so nice," she tells her. "I don't deserve you being this nice to me."

I squeeze her hand. "Baby, don't talk like that. You only deserve people being nice to you."

Mom nods. "Yes, you only deserve good things."

Luna's eyes flick between us, and I will her to believe our words. Surprise washes across her face, and I follow her gaze as it darts behind me, whipping my head around to see Alaric standing in the kitchen. He must have popped in from the Blessed Road. The Nephilim is a little mussed, not the calm, cool presence I'm used to.

"You better have some good news," I say.

eighteen

LUNA

BOLTING FROM MY CHAIR, I cross the room and fling myself at Alaric, so relieved to see him again that I don't even realize I'm crushing his ribcage.

"Luna," he wheezes, and I release him at once. Sparks of heat blossom across my cheeks.

"Sorry," I mutter, taking an embarrassed step back. First, Zahra's teacup and now, Alaric. Even as an angel, I'm a total disaster. Will I ever stop breaking things?

Drawing in a stilted breath, Alaric offers me an understanding smile. "It's okay. I'm glad to see that you're all right, too. And the rest of you managed to make it out in one piece?" He glances between Caleb and Hammurabi, and the latter shakes his head, his expression grim.

"My mistress stayed behind. The Council caught our scent, no thanks to Nzingha."

The honey in Alaric's eyes instantly darkens. "That is…

unfortunate," he mutters.

Caleb crosses his arms. "Well, that's the understatement of the century."

Behind Caleb's snarky and indignant facade, I glimpse the resurgence of his concern for Asmodeus. He's worried about her. Frustration and guilt fill every available space in my chest as I consider what predicament we left her to face alone. That *I* left her to face.

Despite everything the Archdemon said about not wanting to put her neck on the line, she didn't hesitate to throw herself in the path of our pursuers to protect us. To protect me.

"Your father would never forgive me if I let you get captured again."

The memory of her final words is a gut punch, and I can't help wondering about her relationship with my father and what they are to each other. Are they just friends? Are they more? She was there that day under the Serapeum when I was captured by the Council. She was there, standing against Lucifer, when he was forced to hand me over for eternal confinement. And yet, she helped Caleb get me out. She played the part of the dutiful Archdemon, only revealing her true hand at the last moment. She sacrificed herself for my father's sake.

To save his daughter.

At the thought of my father, I glance back at Alaric. "How did you know where to find us? Weren't you supposed to meet us back at Babel?"

While I'm glad he didn't end up as yet another casualty to Nzingha's double-crossing, I don't understand how he knew where to find us. He was supposed to locate my parents and, upon reuniting, we would flee to a safe location together. Instead, the plan went to hell, and Alaric showed up here, in Zahra's apartment, alone.

"I texted him," Caleb says with a one-shouldered shrug. "Just before we got here, when we were on the Shadow Road just outside New York. You get surprisingly good reception in there."

Hammurabi rises from the table like a revenant rising from the dead. "You, *what*?" he bellows, his deep voice a booming roar. "How could you be so flippant with such information? Information the Council could use to hunt us?"

Caleb rolls his eyes. "Calm down, dude. First, when was the last time you saw anyone on the Council with a cell phone? Second, last I checked, none of them know how to hack shit. If I had sent a message by carrier pigeon, it might be a different story but I didn't, so I think we're good. Besides"—he throws a cautious glance at his mom, who sits still, listening to the conversation unfolding around her—"it's not like we can stay here. It isn't safe for us…or for Mom. Speaking of which, you'll probably want to go stay with a friend or in a hotel or something until things calm down. Just in case."

"Is that really necessary?" Zahra asks. "They won't be looking for me."

They will if they think they can use you against us. Furrowing my brow, I look to Hammurabi, who seems to be serving as scout leader to this little band of misfits. "Can't we take her with us?"

The older Nephilim sinks back into his chair, shaking his head. "Doing so would only put Zahra in danger."

"Hammurabi's right," Alaric says, rubbing his eyes. He looks exhausted, as if he hasn't slept in weeks. Given everything that's happened, maybe he hasn't. "It's too dangerous. Besides, having a mortal involved in Council matters never ends well. She would be a liability. No offense," he adds quickly, shooting Caleb's mom an apologetic look, as if he only just realized he spoke the words aloud.

Zahra responds with a consoling smile. "None taken," she assures him. "The last thing I want is to put any of you at further risk. But..." She hesitates, worrying her bottom lip between her teeth before blowing out a trembling breath. "I can't say I like the idea of my son on the run and me being clueless about what's happening to him." She peers at Caleb now, her gaze hazy with tears. "I'll go sick with worry. For both of you." Her eyes—the same warm shade of brown as Caleb's—flash to mine before narrowing back on her son. Her tone takes on a sharp edge when she rasps, "Are you trying to kill your poor mother?"

When her voice breaks, Caleb stands and steps toward her, taking her dainty frame into his arms. "I'll text you or call every day, I promise. Even if it's only one word, I'll let you know I'm okay."

Sniffing, Zahra nods, wiping her nose with her sleeve.

The hush that follows is fraught with tension, and as it stretches out minute by minute with no one daring to utter a word, all I can think about is the silence I endured in my prison—the memory of that soundless void always sitting at the edge of my mind.

Shivering, I glance at Alaric, grasping for the strength to voice the one question that still needs to be asked.

"Alaric, if you're here…where are my parents?"

Hammurabi straightens in his chair at my words, his gaze laser focused on the other Nephilim. "Did you manage to find the Messenger and Morningstar?"

Alaric ignores him, looking only at me. "I did find them, Luna, and they're just as anxious to see you as you are to see them." His mouth softens into a reassuring smile, but I can't bring myself to return it.

"Then why aren't they with you?" I press, the words strained.

He winces at the bitterness in my tone. "They can't travel either Road, not together, so they're flying in the old-fashioned way." He touches a hand to his chest and bows his head slightly, as if swearing a vow. "I'll take you to meet them, I promise."

"Flying in…" My eyes bulge at the mental image of my parents soaring over the city, and my jaw drops. "Like…*flying* flying?"

He ruffles my hair and lets out a throaty chuckle that seems to reverberate through me, from the surface of my skin down into my bones. Amusement shines in his eyes like twin shimmering flames. "That might be a bit too conspicuous. We *are* in a major city, and the last thing we need is for your parents to end up on the news. Human sightings of angels don't often go unchecked by the Council."

Hammurabi snorts like an enraged bull, although I think that's his way of expressing his agreement.

Alaric tousles my hair again. "We'll meet them at JFK. Their flight is due in tonight."

Hammurabi, Alaric, Caleb, and I walk into JFK airport at a quarter to nine. As we progress through the vast lobby, surrounded on all sides by more sterile white than was even present at the Serapeum, I try to school my features into a mask of indifference so we won't alert any surrounding mortals to just how bizarre and out of place our group is. Caleb and I look innocent enough, hand in hand like a smitten young couple in love—the thought of him saying that word to me still making my heart race—but neither of us remotely resemble the older Nephilim, who strut in front of us like protective dads. If anyone stops us, here's hoping Alaric isn't too tired to use his Calm on them.

My eyes dart from side to side as I tug on my earlobe. Ever since Nzingha attacked me in the gardens outside Babel, I've felt…weird. I can't really explain how or why. It's probably nothing—a psychosomatic result of the trauma I've experienced combined with my tendency to always think the worst. As we weave through the crowd spilling through the airport, my pulse increasingly erratic, I'm more paranoid than ever.

"You okay?" Caleb whispers, just loud enough for my super hearing to catch his words.

"Peachy," I grumble back, yanking on my earlobe again.

Letting go of my hand, he drapes his arm over my shoulder and pulls me close, my body aligning perfectly with his side, like he is a mold I was created to fit. As I sink into his embrace, he leans down, his breath hot on my cheeks. "Hey, it's okay if you're nervous."

I raise a hand and then drop it again with a flustered breath. "I just—How am I supposed to look at Gabriel any differently after everything? And Lucifer…" I press my knuckles against my lower lip, muttering, "I still don't even know how to process that one."

Caleb nods, and his eyes—pearly in the shining, overhead lights—glisten with infinite understanding. "I have my opinions about Gabriel, but she's your mom, and I'm sure she only did the shitty things she did to try to keep you safe. Besides, you don't need to make up your mind about anything right now. Just hear her out and then decide. As for Lucifer—" He hesitates, his expression contemplative, then shrugs, his face shifting back into its usual carefree easiness that never fails to comfort me. "Well, he's always been kind to me. I don't really have much experience in that department, but I think he'd be a great dad."

As much as I want to believe him, I can't help remembering when Lucifer handed me over to the Council. When he gave me up for eternal imprisonment. As the anguish of that memory consumes me, I scoff.

"Do great dads abandon their kids to the wolves?"

As soon as the words leave my lips, it dawns on me how inconsiderate and selfish I must sound. And thoughtless. So, so utterly thoughtless. Caleb's only spoken about his father once, and it wasn't exactly a glowing review. And after what he revealed to me back at Babel, when we finally had a moment to ourselves to talk...

"I wanted to free Alexander so badly because—well, he is Alexander the Great—and I just wanted...a dad."

I wince at the memory. Surely, Caleb doesn't want to hear me whine about this.

"It might not seem like it, Luna," Alaric says under his breath, glancing at me over his shoulder, "but Lucifer did what was right in the moment. If he hadn't, the Council would've taken their anger out on both him and your mother, and then you'd be without their protection."

My wings bristle under my skin. "What protection? They aren't here."

"They will come, Luna. Have faith."

"Faith." I snort. "Right."

Alaric slows, falling into stride beside me, and Hammurabi takes up position as sole sentinel in front of us, ever the stoic protector. Amber eyes meet mine, urgent and glinting. "You are entitled to your feelings about them, but you must accept their help when they come. We can't keep you safe from the Council, you know this. But your parents…well, maybe they can."

"Maybe?" Caleb echoes. His brow is pinched into a dubious vee.

Hammurabi grunts, speaking for the first time since we entered the airport. "Right now, maybe is all we have."

No one says another word as we approach the arrival gates, the flight times lighting up across the notice boards like Christmas lights. The closer we get, the tighter the throng of people becomes, cutting off any hope of escape, should we need one. If the Council were to descend on us now, we'd be trapped.

"I don't like this," I hiss, shying away from a hulking man on my right. "There are too many people."

"Mortals," Hammurabi retorts, waving a dismissive hand as if batting away a fly. "We would know if another of our kind was here." Smirking, he jerks his chin at Alaric. "Our Light friend here would be able to smell them."

Smell?

At my bemused expression, Alaric pinches the bridge of his nose between his thumb and forefinger, rolling his eyes at the Babylonian king. "A discussion for another ti—"

He stops dead in his tracks, his eyes alert, the irises darting side to side like a haywire pendulum. Fear forms a knot in my chest as I falter mid-step beside him.

"What is it?"

His gaze snaps to mine, and the warning edge I find there makes me take a step back. "We aren't alone."

"Luna's parents?" Caleb asks, inching closer until we're crowded together in an intimate huddle. Meanwhile, Hammurabi looms over us like a disappointed mother.

Alaric jerks his head to one side. "No. I know their scents." His nose crinkles, like he's smelled something foul. "This is different."

Caleb's arm drops from my shoulders and wraps around my waist, pulling me tight to his chest, as if sensing my resurfacing panic. Alaric glances between us, and the distress I glimpse on his face turns my stomach.

Extending his arm, he steers us away from the arrivals gate. "Quickly, this way."

We trail him toward the exit, retracing our steps like time is moving in reverse. The glass doors slide open at our approach, and as the evening air hits my face, I'm reminded of the day I first set foot in Egypt. The day this whole journey was put into motion.

Just like then, Alaric was with me. But unlike then, his usual tranquil facade is distorted by the agitated movements of the golden sheen licking his skin. His aura shivers with anxiety as he stalks across the wide road outside, leading us toward the large parking lot directly opposite the airport entrance. I watch him out of the corner of my eye, waiting for the wave of Calm I know must be coming, but his typical composure is gone, and he seems incapable of it, too consumed by the tension of the moment, even if his drawn expression tells me nothing.

His hurried pace borders on a run as the Nephilim leads us through several pools of buttery yellow light emanating from the street lamps scattered throughout the parking lot. We pass row after row of parked cars, and I can't fathom where he's leading us except farther away from the one place we're supposed to be. The one place where my parents are likely waiting for me.

The hairs on my arms and neck stand at attention. "Alaric, where are we going?" I ask.

He presses a slender finger to his lips, shaking his head, then gestures toward a circular grove of trees up ahead on a small island of grass just past this stretch of tarmac. Despite the vibrancy of light in the parking lot, the grassy patch is drenched in shadow. The only truly dark spot as far as the eye can see.

Once we've all convened in the circle, he whips around to face us, finally speaking. "Take the Shadow Road and go as far as you can. I'll stay behind to intercept your parents, but you three need to get out of here *now*—"

I open my mouth to protest, to ask him what's going on, but the look on his face smothers my words. A fear as cold and dreadful as death chills my blood as I turn, following his hooded gaze over my shoulder—the disdain in his eyes making him almost unrecognizable. As a figure emerges from the gloom behind me, I realize we couldn't run now, even if we wanted to.

It's too late to run.

"Oh, how kind of you all to wait for me," our pursuer simpers, assessing us with cunning eyes, the irises like two sapphires trapped in ice. Observing the circle of trees, he grins. "And somewhere secluded. Even better."

I recognize the Archdemon immediately, his delicate features imprinted on my memory like a tattoo from the one time I saw him before—that day under the Serapeum when I came face to face with the Council. Of all the Archdemons to come after us, they sent the only one who looks like a child?

I can't help fearing that was intentional. Perhaps he's even the most dangerous of them all.

His name, which springs to the front of my memory as recognition sets in, is a startled breath on my lips. "Beelzebub."

The Archdemon dips his head in greeting. When he looks up, his arctic eyes flashing to mine, I understand at once why Alaric seemed anxious upon catching his scent and why his aura still radiates an undiluted terror even now, despite the hostility creasing his brow. For although the Fallen angel is smaller than the others I've encountered, there's tremendous power hidden behind those beautiful eyes, vibrating from within the blackness of his undulating aura.

An ancient power that could easily tear us all to shreds.

As if reading my mind, Beelzebub smiles. "Hello again, daughter of Lucifer."

nineteen

CALEB

BEELZEBUB LOOKS LIKE A twelve-year-old boy waiting for his balls to drop. I've never met him, only seen him from afar, and it always hits me how *weak* he appears compared to the other Archdemons. Pretty and androgynous, he doesn't outwardly pose a threat, his power concealed under that school-boy shell. I wonder if the other Council members whisper behind his back, asking what the hell the Creator was thinking when Beelzebub came along. The rest of them seem to be frozen in time somewhere in their late twenties, early thirties max, but he has never left tweenhood. But despite that cherubic face, I know he's a badass, and Luna is the only one who can truly take him on. And she's in no shape to throw down right now.

But I still have my celestial slayer. If I can clip Mammon's wing, I can damage this asshole, too, with the help of Luna, Alaric, and Hammurabi, of course. I slide the knife out of its sheath on my back. Beelzebub's blue eyes track the motion and widen. That's right, mine is bigger than yours.

"What are you doing here?" Hammurabi demands, towering over the Archdemon. "You're not taking the girl. In case you haven't noticed, Mammon is missing a wing. I'm more than happy to aid young Caleb in taking yours." Although the Babylonian king clearly looks like the victor, I know that's not the case.

Beelzebub straightens, all boyish charm falling away in those ancient eyes, and his icy glare cuts as he looks at Hammurabi. "Silence, King. Listen to me. I come with a warning. It is dangerous to risk meeting with the Morningstar and the Messenger. You cannot go to them for aid."

Alaric delivers an icy stare of his own. "Your meddling is futile. Even if you cut us down, Luna will get to her parents. I vow it. You can't take on Lucifer and Gabriel by yourself and you know it, Spy."

I knew there was a badass inside Alaric. My grip tightens on the golden hilt of my dagger. Luna's wings tear free of her skin, shiny feathers reflecting in the street lights. Man, if any humans show up, we're going to have to erase a lot of minds. Beelzebub's blue eyes narrow in on her wings.

"Child, put those away," he commands. "We're among mortals."

Goldilocks shakes her head, eyes defiant. "No, I won't let you take me again. I'll burn you first. And some spy you are. Alaric knew you were there."

The Archdemon barks a harsh laugh. "He knew I was here because I allowed it, little Gray. You have much to learn."

Blackness spills out of him, spreading around us like ink in water. The streetlights are snuffed. I'm suddenly blind in the suffocating darkness, but it's not only my sight that's affected. I can't hear or smell anything. My senses have been turned off like a faucet. I fumble around until I grip Luna's hand. Beelzebub gave Luna shit for her wings, and he's turning on his power full blast. Hypocrite. Then again, I guess no one can see us.

Ruby flame lights up the immediate area, and I glance over to see Luna's free hand blazing. She can't banish the shadows entirely, but she's broken through enough for my senses to come screaming back to life. Beelzebub watches her with a little smile. The darkness fades away, and Luna extinguishes the fire in her palm.

"Is fire your only trick, young one?" he asks, smirking. "You'll need more in your repertoire if you want to fight the Council." His smile vanishes. "But I'm not your enemy. I am a true friend of your father, and if you don't want the Council to imprison him or your mother the way they did Asmodeus, you'll listen to me."

Hammurabi swears low and takes a step toward Baby B when Alaric's hand on his shoulder halts him. The Light Nephilim gives a slow shake of his head, and though a subvocal growl escapes the king's throat, he backs off.

My eyes return to the Archdemon. "Why should we

believe you?" I demand. "Unless all the Council members are backstabbing, two-faced assholes with their own agenda."

Fury shimmers on Beelzebub's face as he regards me and I swallow hard. Dagger or no dagger, I don't really want to piss off an Archdemon too badly.

"You're lucky, grandson of the Great, that I don't have time to punish you for your insolence." His eyes snap to Luna. "Nzingha has placed a tracking device in your head. The Council is waiting for you to lead them straight to your parents so they can capture you all in one fell swoop. You need to leave immediately before the Council figures out you're here and that the Morningstar and the Messenger are on their way. Their capture would mean your certain doom."

"Fuck me," I breathe. "Can't we get a break from this shit already?"

"Bloody Nzingha," Alaric mutters.

Hammurabi shakes his head. "I can't believe we trusted Mammon's ambitious pet."

Luna clutches her skull, tears in her eyes. "What did she put in me?" She shakes her head, disappointment and sadness etched into her features. Damn, will she ever get to see her parents? It's not fair. None of this is fair.

I pull her into my side, and her wings vanish. "It'll be okay, Goldilocks."

Her tears almost break me. "How Caleb? What are we going to do now?"

"You're going to get that device out of your head," Beelzebub drawls. "As soon as you can."

I make a sweeping gesture toward Luna. "Well, why don't you get on that?"

"Yes," Hammurabi says. "If you're loyal to the Morningstar, help his daughter."

"I cannot help you," the Archdemon answers, tone blistering. "It's an Archangel device. Uriel's handiwork, I believe. Anyone can insert it, but you will require one from among the Faithful to remove it." He shrugs.

"Oh, is that all?" I push out between clenched teeth. By the Morningstar, I want to stab him. "Why didn't you say so? There are so many of them around, willing to help us."

"Like her mother," Alaric adds, crossing his arms over his chest.

Beelzebub gives Alaric a nasty smile. "By all means, let the Council take Gabriel, Nephilim, but I don't want Lucifer to be imprisoned. It would be in your best interest not to contact him until the device is destroyed." His eyes rove over Luna, mouth twisted in distaste. "You have an angel here. Both of the Dark and the Light. She possesses the means to remove it herself."

"I don't know how to take it out!" Luna cries, voice shrill. "I've been an angel for all of five minutes."

An irritated huff escapes Beelzebub as his eyes flick over Luna, as if assessing her and annoyed she's come up short. "Fine. The best I can do is this..." Darkness slides from Beelzebub once more, right up Luna's nose. She gasps, clenching her face.

Fear grips me. "What did you do to her?" I demand, brandishing my dagger at him.

Beelzebub shrugs again, giving me a bored look. "Masked the tracker for now. But do remember it is only temporary. I've done all I can. You need to find shelter and someone to remove the tracker. Best be making Light allies." Blackness blankets him and he's gone.

Hammurabi roars and I wince. I glance around. The parking lot just beyond the trees is still empty but damn are we making a spectacle of ourselves. But I guess we're already fugitives from the Council. What's a minor infraction like revealing ourselves to humans going to get us at this point? The Council wants us dead. Luna's sobs wrap their way around my heart and squeeze.

I slide the dagger back in its sheath and draw her into my arms. "It's going to be okay, Goldilocks," I repeat. "I swear to you, we'll find a way to get that thing out of your head."

"Don't make pretty vows you can't keep," Hammurabi says to me, fury in his dark eyes. "Do you have any angels willing to help us?" he spits at Alaric.

Alaric grimaces. "None but I'm willing to go and beg. There must be some loyal to Gabriel, just as there are those loyal to Lucifer."

Hammurabi scoffs. "I don't think Gabriel inspires loyalty in the same way. As the Messenger, she's more feared than loved."

As they continue to bicker, Luna buries her face against my

chest. A plan forms in my mind. A terrible, horrible, awful plan that just might work. No, it will definitely work. If I play my cards right. I feel sick, but we're running out of time. I kiss Luna, tasting her tears. I'll do this for her. I'll do anything for her.

"We have to go to my grandfather," I say over Hammurabi's and Alaric's heated words. "We have to go to Alexander."

Alaric's jaw snaps shut while Hammurabi's mouth hangs open, both of them staring at me as if I've managed to Ascend and grow wings. Luna gasps and jerks back from my chest.

"Are you mad?" Hammurabi asks. "You want to go to the Great for shelter? You betrayed him, Caleb. He won't greet you as family but as an enemy. He might even kill you."

I'm waiting for Alaric to chime in, but he remains silent, face blank. I focus back on the Babylonian king. "Yeah, there's a chance he'll take my head, but not if I tell him I brought you three as gifts. That I left only to bring him powerful allies—that we're all on his side. He's always wanted Luna. If I can give him a Gray and two first generations, he can't say no to that."

Alaric nods. "He has a point."

Luna's eyes dart to Alaric and stay there, as if searching for something. "You think Caleb bringing us will be enough? From the sounds of it, Alexander is…ruthless."

"I understand that," Alaric says with a grim smile. "But we're running out of options."

"This is ludicrous," Hammurabi protests, arms crossed over his massive chest. "And with that thing in her head"—he gestures at Luna—"the Council will just track us there."

"Eventually, yeah, but Beelzebub just bought us some time. And us fleeing to Alexander is the last thing they'll expect. They're waiting for us to lead them to Lucifer and Gabriel, not the Conqueror—who has his own army by now. If they decide to show up, Alexander will fight back. And by then, Luna won't have the tracker in her head anymore, and we'll escape while they rip into each other."

Luna shivers. "I think…I think Caleb may be right. Alexander did remove my bind. Why would he do that unless he thought I'd be useful?"

Hammurabi snorts. "Of course, you're useful. You're a bloody angel and as untrained as a newborn babe. You're the perfect clay he can mold."

"Which is why he won't kill me," I point out again. "I mean, I can't bring a better housewarming present than the three of you. Luna alone would save me—you two are just the cherry on top."

Luna's eyes clash with mine. I see the fear reflected in their depths, and I smooth a hand through her golden hair. "I don't like it. But…I don't know where else we could go."

"Yes, unfortunately, I agree this is our best option," Alaric says, staring off into the distance. He chuckles to himself. "Fate has a sense of humor."

Hammurabi blows out a harsh breath. "Fine. I'll go along with this folly, but if we all end up in chains, don't say I didn't warn you."

I roll my eyes, even as my stomach knots itself together. "Ugh, you're such a ball of sunshine and optimism." I take a deep breath, blowing it out slowly and steeling my spine. "Okay, let's go meet Grandfather."

It's mid-morning on the other side of the world in Afghanistan. Kandahār is quiet under clear skies, the usually bustling streets tame. The whole country feels silent, but I guess that's what happens when a hostile force rolls in and takes over. The good news is that a war-torn country makes it easier for Alexander and his army to set up, unnoticed. I left Luna, Hammurabi, and Alaric up in the mountains while I went alone to the citadel. As I approach the gates, I notice strange Nephilim are now on guard duty, settled in strategic places along the wall. Gramps has been busy indeed. Unease ripples over me again. I don't want to be here. I can practically taste the restrained violence in the air, waiting to be unleashed.

But I have to do this for Luna. She needs somewhere safe to recuperate until I can get her to her parents. She hasn't mentioned them since Beelzebub left, but I know this latest setback crushed her. The fragile state of her mind worries me. Yeah, I had to bring us here, but Goldilocks isn't fond of Alexander and with good reason. He fucked with her mind and then abandoned her. I can only hope he'll be gentle with her, but I seriously doubt it. He's not the type to baby anyone.

I make no attempt to hide from the sentries, and soon Ishtar is at the gate of the fortress. The goddess is gone today, a warrior in her place. A practical black T-shirt and cargo pants cling to her tall, curvy frame while combat boots encase her feet, and a sword is strapped to her back. Her black hair is braided back from her beautiful face, showcasing her high cheekbones. Our eyes meet, and I force myself not to step back as I see the rage shimmering in her gaze. Maybe Alexander isn't my biggest threat. Maybe Ishtar will run me through before I even get to meet with him.

"You dare to return, boy?" Ishtar says, arching one haughty brow. "After you ran back to Babel? To Asmodeus? You're lucky your grandfather prevented me from hunting you down after your betrayal. But he had more important matters for me to attend to than pursuing a fickle child with no loyalty to blood."

Her barb stings but I ignore her. I don't question how she knows I returned to the academy. I'm sure she has her spies. I give a casual shrug as if I haven't a care in the world. "I had my reasons," I tell her. "And Grandfather will meet three of them. I've brought him powerful gifts to aid his fight."

Surprise flits across Ishtar's face, but she quickly masks it. Score one point for me. I threw her off her game. "Gifts?" she repeats.

I nod. "Grandfather will be very pleased by what I've done.

I want to see him."

She laughs. "I don't think so. Why don't you tell me about your gifts, and I'll judge if they're worthy enough to be brought before the Great."

Shaking my head, I say, "No, Alexander needs to hear this from me. He needs to know that I never betrayed him. And I don't trust you." My blunt words make her blink, anger tightening her mouth.

"I was always fond of you, Caleb," Ishtar says. "You shamed me greatly when you left, and you cut me with your disloyalty. How do I know you're not spying for Asmodeus?"

"Your former bestie is locked up right now," I tell her, and once again, I manage to shock her. Two points. "The Council attacked Babel and took her because she helped me."

"Why would the Council imprison Asmodeus?" Ishtar demands, and I detect a hint of concern in her voice. Well, I guess she cares about the Archdemon after all.

"Um, because she *helped* me," I repeat slowly, knowing it'll piss her off. Nerves make me stupid.

Her eyes narrow to slits. "And why would she help a foolish boy like you? One whose loyalty is only to themselves?"

"She was helping Lucifer," I tell her. "We just had the same goals." I hide my grin as once more a look of confusion creeps across her face. Well, I guess Luna's lineage hasn't become common knowledge yet. "I wanted Luna free and so did Asmodeus, because Luna is the Morningstar's daughter."

My announcement wipes Ishtar's face clean of emotion, and I know I've truly stunned her. "The Morningstar has a daughter? *Luna*? How do you know this?"

I grin. "Yep, he does. Asmodeus told me. She wanted to get Luna back for him."

Ishtar bares her teeth at me. "That kind of information isn't free, Caleb. What did you promise her?"

"Alexander's whereabouts, but only when Luna was delivered to her dad," I lie. Best to keep the Gabriel card close. "But I knew Asmodeus couldn't deliver us to Lucifer. So when the Council attacked that night, I snuck Luna out and I came here. All I wanted was for Luna to be safe. I love her." It feels wrong confessing this to Ishtar, who I know will wield that knowledge like a weapon. She already suspected, of course, but it's different to confirm her suspicions. "I want back in. I never stopped wanting that. And like I said, I have three gifts to prove it." The fabrication falls easily from my lips because there's a kernel of truth in it. I never stopped wanting a connection with my grandfather; it was just a kick to the nuts when I realized I could never have one. Not the way I wanted, which was to have a shiny father figure who gave a shit about me. Maybe if I get out of this alive, I should seriously go see a shrink.

"What are the other gifts?" Ishtar prods again, and I shake my head.

"That's for Grandfather's ears only," I say, crossing my arms over my chest.

Ishtar stares off into the distance, considering my words, but I know in the end, she'll take me to Alexander. What I've revealed is too tempting. And besides, I don't think she really has a choice. The goddess of love and war may be his general, but she doesn't have the power to pass judgment on me. And if she does and Gramps finds out, I'm sure there will be consequences. If anyone is to punish me, he'll want to do it. I'm his blood after all.

"Very well, Caleb, follow me, but know if this is a trick, I'll beg the Great to let me punish you. And you know how creative I can be. Death will be a friend you'll beg for but never meet."

Her cold words send shivers over my skin. It hurts to know the teacher I admired turned on me so quickly. Asmodeus and I have more in common than I thought.

"Understood," I say, voice hard.

I keep a few paces behind Ishtar as we wind our way through the citadel and into the makeshift throne room. Nephilim glance at me, some with curiosity and some with open hostility. I ignore them, head high like the prince I supposedly am. Fake it until you make it. The interior has changed a bit since I left, gained more creature comforts. It looks more like a palace than a garrison to house troops.

Alexander lounges on his throne, the marble now covered in purple velvet cascading to the floor. An honest-to-Creator lion's skin drapes across his shoulders. Damn, he's gone full Macedonian today. His cold mismatched eyes latch onto mine, like two magnets drawing me in. I can't look away, but I do manage a deep bow.

"Your grandson has returned," Ishtar drawls. "Bearing gifts, or so he claims."

"Three of them," I clarify, "though a fourth is a possibility entirely up to you." I take a deep breath. "And one of these gifts has a time limit."

Ishtar whirls on me. "You never mentioned that," she hisses.

I smirk at her. "Because you don't have the power to help with that. You're not an angel. Only Grandfather can solve this problem."

"Have you brought me offerings or problems, Caleb?" Alexander asks. "I confess I am surprised to see you again, especially after your desertion, but I find I'm oddly pleased by your presence." His smile doesn't reach his icy eyes, and I gulp down my fear.

"I've brought you Luna as an apology for leaving," I say, rushing ahead, "but one of the Council's minions put some sort of tracking device in her head during our escape that we can't get out. Only *you* can."

"I see, so you only returned to me like a cringing hound because I can aid you?" Alexander says softly, and I force myself not to flinch at the painful accuracy of his words.

I shake my head violently. "No, I always planned on coming back, and I brought you two more allies to prove it. The thing that happened with Luna just set us back."

"Indeed. Who else did you bring for me, Grandson?" He leans back into his throne, tapping his fingers on one armrest.

"Hammurabi," I say, grinning at Ishtar's gasp. Even Alexander manages a flicker of surprise across his stony face. "And Alaric. I don't know him that well, but he's pretty damn old and a first generation."

At the mention of Alaric's name, Alexander's fingers stop tapping. He stills, muscles coiled, and I wonder if I've made a major miscalculation. Do Alaric and Alexander have a grudge between them I don't know about? Other than the whole Michael thing, but Alaric didn't seem too torn up about it when we talked about Gramps. Then Grandfather's lips tug up into a smile. A genuine one.

"Caleb, you've done well. You truly are my blood to convince such powerful Nephilim to join my cause. And more importantly, you've brought the girl to me. With my help, I can teach her about her true nature, the melding of the Dark and the Light."

Relief pulses through me so quickly that I almost sway. "And you'll remove the tracker?"

He tilts his head, studying me. "Yes, I'll remove the device. I don't desire having the Council appear before I'm ready to address them. Because you have indeed brought me three great offerings, I won't punish you for the danger you bring to my door."

"This is the last place the Council expects me to go," I tell him. "They expect me to run to Lucifer."

Alexander perks up, his eyes flitting to Ishtar before focusing on me again. "Why would you flee to the Morningstar?"

"Because he's Luna's father. That's what I meant about a possible fourth ally."

A calculating gleam shines in Alexander's eyes as he considers my words. I can practically feel his glee at the thought of having both Luna and Lucifer join his army. "Caleb, I have truly underestimated you, but it seems blood ran true. I assume my new allies are somewhere safe?"

I nod, a cautious hope blooming in my heart. Maybe I can pull this off after all.

"Ishtar, accompany Caleb and bring our guests to me. Young Luna and I have much to discuss."

twenty

LUNA

THE WAIT IS AGONIZING. Although Caleb has only been gone for a handful of minutes, it feels like hours since we parted and I watched him continue alone to the fortress where his grandfather has taken up residence. I sit perched like a bird on the edge of a dusty cliff edge staring down at the Tarnak River and the city of Kandahār far below in the distance—the citadel on a vast hilltop of rock beside it—my teeth clamping down on the edge of my thumbnail. Five minutes turn into ten turn into fifteen, and as the seconds stretch on, my imagination depicts every worst case scenario, frying what remains of my nerves.

A sour taste floods my mouth at the thought of what Alexander might be doing to Caleb—what punishment he could be inflicting at this very moment for his grandson's desertion. Wincing, I avert my gaze from the city and search the sandy ledge for a distraction. Hammurabi is scouting the mountain pass while Alaric sits a few feet away from me with his back to the rock face, his crisp white button-down shirt somehow still perfectly clean despite our desert surroundings.

Back in New York, before we made the trek along the Roads to Afghanistan, Hammurabi had suggested Alaric stay behind to meet my parents and update them on the situation—as the latter had originally intended to do before Beelzebub appeared. But, between the threat of the tracker in my head and the plan to now go to Alexander, the ancient Nephilim hadn't only been reluctant to do so—he had downright refused with a vehemence I didn't know him capable of. He claimed it was unwise to risk meeting them in case the Council was surveying our last known location, but I could tell that was just an excuse, even if there was logic and wisdom behind his words.

The real reason for his refusal was more personal. From the moment Alexander's name left Caleb's lips, Alaric rejected the slightest notion of leaving my side. He wouldn't even let me travel the Shadow Road to get here, pleading for me to join him on the Blessed Road where he could keep an eye on me. Caleb fought back against that suggestion at first, only agreeing once Hammurabi pointed out that it would be easier for the two older Nephilim to help us should anything happen on the Roads if they each only had one teenager to look after.

So, Hammurabi and Caleb took the Shadow Road while Alaric and I took the Blessed Road. Opposite to the Dark way of traveling, which was cold and streaked with endless grays and blacks, the Light's path was blinding—almost searing in its brightness and warmth. Although part of me preferred the illusion of safety such radiance gave off compared to the Shadow Road's bleakness, it was a relief to step back into the human world again, into the blazing sun of the mountains. As Alaric and I emerged from the light, Caleb stepped out of a pool of shadows beneath a nearby outcropping of rock. The moment our eyes met, he closed the distance between us and pulled me into his arms, his hands in my hair and his lips on mine as if he thought he'd never see me again.

That same anxiety stings me now, and desperate for a distraction, I glance at Alaric. His eyes are closed, but I can sense he's awake, and I stare at his serene face for a while, considering everything I want to say to him. Although we were alone together on the Blessed Road, we didn't dare speak, too frightened of alerting the Council to our location should one of the Faithful be near. But now that we're safe from the Road, I feel the need to break the silence. To say everything I couldn't find the words or strength to say before.

"I haven't thanked you…for coming for me."

Alaric peeks one amber eye open. "I saved you from one prison, Luna. I wasn't going to abandon you to another."

His words bring me back to those many long months in the hospital, but strangely, those memories don't seem to belong to me anymore. Now, as every moment takes me further away from my old, mortal life, it feels less like I'm looking at *my* past and more like I'm looking back at the recollections of someone else. Someone from another world, even though it's been less than a year since Alaric secured my freedom.

That broken girl he met…while part of me doesn't recognize her in this new form I've taken, I know I'm more like her than ever. She's there in every breath I draw, dancing at the precipice of madness, always one misstep from falling.

But unlike when I was committed, I have a rope now—a tether—to hang onto, to stop my feet from slipping over the edge. A lifeline to save me from myself. And while my first instinct is to say that rope is Caleb, I also know it's partly Alaric. He got me here. He saved me in more ways than one.

And yet—

"That's not the only reason, Alaric." *Just like my parents had nothing to do with why you chose not to part with me in New York.*

Rising, I cross the ledge and press my back to the stretch of smooth rock, sinking to the ground beside him. I can feel his eyes on me when I draw in a breath.

"That voice I was hearing…I'm guessing you know it was Alexander."

A moment passes before he nods.

Steeling myself, I grab his hand. "When he was in my head, he showed me glimpses of your past. I saw you together. You were in love with him." It isn't a question. I know enough of love to recognize what I saw.

A low chuckle breaches his lips, and he looks down at the ground, his eyes hazy and distant. "In many ways, I still am," he says softly.

His admission takes me aback. Alexander was locked away more than two thousand years ago. While it was clear Alaric clung to some residual feelings toward the angel when we first spoke about him, I wasn't expecting deeper feelings to linger. Has he spent all these millennia alone, fanning the dying flames of a love he could no longer have?

My heart bleeds for him at the thought. "Despite everything?"

A sad smile twitches along the edge of his mouth. "Despite everything." He looks at me now, his eyes fierce. "Love isn't black and white, Luna. We can't just shut it off when it inconveniences us. But there's so much you don't know about him…or about what happened between us back then."

"Like him killing your father?" I hedge.

His body goes rigid at my words. "There's…more to that story than what I told you."

The memory of what Alexander showed me is fresh, like a brand on my mind, and I nod, understanding. But not Alaric's side of the story.

Alexander's.

As much as I despise him for messing with my head, I can at least empathize with this one thing about him. After all, I would have done the same. I would tear the world to pieces if doing so meant keeping Caleb safe.

"I saw it. Michael was *hurting* you," I murmur. "Alexander… regardless of what he did or became or is now…he did it to save your life."

Like me, he just wanted to protect someone he loves.

To my surprise, Alaric scoffs. "Yes, and part of me wishes he hadn't bothered."

I blanch at the acidity in his tone, unable to bear the thought of a world where Alaric doesn't exist. Where our paths never crossed. "You…you don't mean that…do you?"

He blinks at me with those warm amber eyes, and I blink back, more confused than ever. Exhaling a long, quiet breath, he props his head back against the red-veined rock.

"That day…what we did…it changed something in Alexander. He saved my life but at what cost? He wasn't the same after that." He hesitates, and the column of his neck shifts when he swallows. Clearing his throat, he says more sternly, "That moment was the lid on Pandora's box, and upon shoving that dagger into my father's heart, he tore the lid right off."

I replay the moment of Michael's death in my thoughts, but now—with the pain in Alaric's voice fresh in my ears—the romantic imagery Alexander planted feels false. Manufactured. I can't help feeling like a fool for believing it. For accepting less than half of the story and seeing only Caleb and me in the details.

"I don't understand," I manage after a moment.

Alaric gifts me a sympathetic smile, and my heart aches even further at the silent reassurance I glimpse in his gaze. It's written there as clear as day.

Don't worry, it says. *He fooled me, too.*

Squeezing my fingers, he exhales through his nose. "Alexander was always special. Gifted. We met when he was young, two years before he was escorted to the Dark academy at Sodom for his primary training. While he learned the basics of control there, he didn't truly thrive until he went on to his secondary academy at Ashkelon, once run by the esteemed Lilith—before she lost her wings and place among the Council for supporting his first conquest for power. Since then, the school is presided over by our new *friend*, Beelzebub, who was elevated to the role of Archdemon to replace her. You can see now why I was wary of him."

I stiffen at the mention of Beelzebub, my nostrils flaring at the recollection of our recent encounter. It's hard to imagine that he wasn't always an Archdemon considering the power I sensed behind that childlike shell. The darkness he unleashed, stealing my vision, surging into my head, still haunts me, as does his warning about the tracker.

My eyes flick to the city below as the anxieties plaguing me rush back to the surface.

The sooner Caleb returns, the better.

"Did you know Alexander was left as an offering to the king and queen of Macedonia?" Alaric asks. "Won over by the child's beauty, the queen begged the king to keep Alexander and raise him as their own. As their prince and heir."

I'm beginning to see a running theme between celestial beings and royalty. Hammurabi was a king. Nzingha, a queen. Vesta and Ishtar are considered goddesses by all mortal accounts. And being Alexander's grandson makes Caleb a prince as well, which I'm only just realizing now.

And then there's me. Emotional wreck Luna. The only thing I'm queen of is setting people on fire. I suppress a groan, forcing myself to focus on Alaric's soothing tenor.

"It didn't take much convincing on the queen's part as the king was equally smitten, but raising a Nephilim child, especially not knowing what he truly was, came with its challenges, of which there were many. The king and queen loved their adopted son dearly and only wanted to ensure he thrived.

"By this point in time, I was already grown, so when Alexander and I met, I had already gone through my schooling and was passing the decades traveling the world, acquiring knowledge wherever I could find it. Truthfully, though, I was restless. I felt like I lacked a purpose, and I did not share the same lust for power as so many other first generations, who used their celestial blood for their own political elevation. So, when word reached me of the troublesome young prince of Macedonia, I approached the king and queen and offered my service to them."

"Your service?"

Alaric grins at my bewildered expression. "Like so many mortal parents, they didn't know what he was nor were they prepared for the challenges of raising a celestial child. They took it rather well when I enlightened them about his origins and were immediately accepting of what I could do for him. You see, certain skills I possess are rather rare and proved quite handy in cases like Alexander's." As if to demonstrate, a rush of Calm washes over me, which he then draws back, the wave receding. "He was a menace as a child. Demonic, I once heard a terrified chambermaid call him." He lets loose a barking laugh that births a light in his eyes I've never seen before. "He needed a wrangler, and I was the key to calming the beast, so to speak, so I became his keeper of sorts. We were inseparable, at first by order of the king, who only wanted the best for his son, but as Alexander aged, we stayed together by choice. I had always felt so alone in this world, and he…" His smile falters and the beautiful light in his eyes—that light born of love—disappears. "Well, he became my dearest friend despite our innate differences."

A forbidden friendship, like me and Caleb, I muse.

A shadow crosses his gaze, and he clears his throat again, as if to shake himself out of the memory. "Even after Alexander was sent to the academy at Ashkelon, I remained in Macedonia with his parents, training to be an advisor of sorts. They didn't cling to the prejudices of our kind, and despite my being a Light, they intended for me to stay close to their son, to be a helping hand to guide him when he eventually ascended the throne. To calm him when the need arose. And I was glad to do it. I couldn't see myself anywhere else but at his side where I finally had a purpose.

"Unfortunately, there were many who didn't agree with my position, and throughout his years at Ashkelon, Alexander would often return home to see me and rant about the narrow-mindedness of his teachers, who made it a point to warn him of the dangers of befriending a Light. I had, of course, been exposed to the same biases, but Alexander took their words personally. He grew irate over what he called a poison between the Darks and the Lights and began counting down the days until he could leave Israel and return home, eager to resume his mantle of prince over mortals, who he viewed as pure compared to the prejudiced Nephilim.

"One of Alexander's greatest traits in my eyes was his endearing affection for humans. It often outweighed any love he had for his own kind, not that I could ever blame him for that. After all, they had accepted him when those who had birthed him had not. He used to say I was the only sane Nephilim he knew, that we were two parts of a whole, and he vowed to tear down the divide, to create a world where our friendship would be accepted, where our kind could come together as one as we were meant to be, and live freely and openly among the humans. In hindsight, his words should've frightened me, but at the time, they were food for my starving heart. His acceptance and affection were all I cared about."

His story paints a vivid picture, and I understand now why he has always been supportive of my friendship with Caleb. Alaric must see so much of himself and Alexander in us. But, considering how their story ended, does that resemblance cause him pain?

Oblivious to my errant thoughts, Alaric continues, "From the day we met, I cared deeply for Alexander. My own father was absent since before I was born, and having Alexander served as a replacement for that connection in many significant ways. He was like a younger brother to me, the family I chose."

"Like you are to me," I mutter without thought. Once, saying such things would've embarrassed me, but not now. Alaric is like family, and after all he's risked to save me, after all the times he's been there, I want him to know it.

A smile touches his lips and he nods. "At least, that was the case until he completed his final year at the academy. When he came home, I barely recognized him. It had been months since our paths had last crossed due to the hectic nature of his studies, and the boy I knew, that I had helped raise in some respects, was gone from his features, replaced by a man. Needless to say, it was a shock to my system to see him as an adult. To see him as anything other than the spoiled, pampered prince I adored. From then on, things were...*different* between us."

A flush creeps up my neck at the insinuation behind his words. "Was that weird? With you being so much older than him?" As I ask this, I can't help putting myself in his place. After all, if my suspicions are right about when I was born, then in reality, I'm far closer in age to Alaric than I am to Caleb.

Alaric peers intently at me, as if sensing the source of my

question. "You need to remember that Nephilim live for thousands of years so, in the grand scheme of our lives, the age difference wasn't quite so great. I was still very young at this point in time and immature beyond measure. Angry at the world. Angry at the Creator for allowing me to grow up without both of my parents. Angry at my father, who despite being a member of the Council and thus allowed to live on Earth, made no effort to see me or know me. In that regard, your Caleb and I have much in common. We both sought out Alexander as a replacement of sorts for other voids in our lives. Truthfully, I never planned to pursue my feelings for Alexander, but he gave me little choice in the matter. He was quite insistent I view him as an adult."

"Did you know then? What he was?" I ask.

Alaric heaves a sigh. "As Alexander aged into adulthood, it became apparent that he possessed qualities that someone of his lineage should not, much as you possessed Dark capabilities that one would not expect in a Light. He was…" He scratches his chin, considering, before settling on, "Uncomfortable, for lack of a better word."

"Was he bound, like I was?"

He nods. "Likely by one of his angelic parents, much as I'm assuming Gabriel did to you."

Ignoring the mention of my mother, I bob my head, as if this explanation makes any damn sense. Then a thought occurs to me, and my right eyebrow hooks upward. "Didn't the Council know what he was? I mean, they knew about the prophecy at this point, right? So, wouldn't the warning signs have been there?"

Frowning, Alaric shakes his head. "His powers did not start to break through the bind fully until he was already at Ashkelon, and considering Lilith's stance on his eventual conquest for power, I believe she hid any such knowledge of him from the Council, which likely contributed to the severity of her punishment once he was imprisoned. As for when he was a child, well, he was incredibly sheltered in Macedonia, and as I was always there to calm his outbursts, any unusual powers he did portray, I made excuses for. To me, he was unique. Brilliant. A force to be reckoned with. I refused to allow myself to see anything wrong." A soft laugh escapes him. "No wonder he developed such an ego when I was always there to fan the flames." He sighs again. "But as he grew older, I could tell something was wrong. Once, he even tried to cut his arm, to show me the skin wouldn't break, not even with excessive force."

Alaric's words trigger a strange recognition inside me that I don't know how to process. Have I ever had a cut or a scrape? I can't remember any broken bones or significant injuries…or any injuries at all. Only the wounds of others.

Wounds I was almost always the cause of.

"I didn't know at the time that the bind was cracking. But then, I didn't know he was bound. Still, I should have seen it. I should have realized something inside him was breaking."

At my questioning gaze, the Nephilim elaborates, "Alexander grew increasingly agitated over the years and would often speak of feeling torn in half, as if a part of him was missing. I always assumed he was referencing his feelings about the divide, but once he returned home for good at eighteen, it was obvious the distress was taking its toll on his mind, much as it did to you. I was worried for him. Even my powers did little to help after a while."

I grimace at this admission. Great, yet another similarity Alexander and I seem to share.

Silence swells between us for a moment as I attempt to digest everything Alaric has said. Then, something else occurs to me. Something he told me when I asked him about Alexander back at the Serapeum.

"When I first asked you about Alexander, you told me he was a Nephilim."

Alaric winces at the accusation in my tone. "To be clear, neither Alexander nor I were aware of his true nature until we lifted the bind—which, in itself, had only been a test to see if there really was something restricting his powers, causing the conflict inside him, not out of any suspicion that he was anything more than part mortal. But...you're right. I lied when I told you that he was a Nephilim. Understand, great lengths were taken to ensure very few would remember the truth. Following Alexander's internment, his followers were silenced. Memories were erased. I didn't want to lose what recollections I held of him—" His voice catches and he swallows loudly. "Even the painful ones. So, I made an agreement with the Council, in part thanks to your mother's support." At my confused expression, he says, "Like you, I was once a student at the Serapeum, and your mother was my headmistress. Although we hadn't seen each other for many long years, she vouched for me when no one else on the Council would."

I gape at him, stunned by the thought of a young Alaric walking the halls of my school, however brief my time there was. It's strange to think of him that way—and to envision my mother showing any kind of sympathy or care for anyone other than herself.

"What was the agreement?" I ask.

He straightens, letting out a strained breath. "Using the talent I inherited from my father, I would seek out Nephilim to bring to the Light academies, as well as making the Darks aware of any of their own I stumbled upon. And although it broke my heart, I swore my loyalty to a world where the divide persists, undergoing a kind of silence of my own. At the time, it felt like the right thing to do."

"And now?"

My heart aches for him, for what that must've been like to go against everything Alexander stood for, the one person he loved more than anyone else in the world. I can imagine that decision haunts him, even to this day.

"Now..." He rubs a finger over his chin again. "Let's just say, with time comes clarity. I don't want you to suffer for others' past mistakes."

I look at him closely, wondering whose mistakes he means. Alexander's?

Or his own?

"Who are Alexander's real parents?" I say, not sure it really matters but curious to know the answer all the same. Perhaps my parents aren't the only two on the Council with skeletons in the closet. Not that my father knew he had such a secret.

"A mystery to this day, I'm afraid," Alaric replies. "Only one being is aware of that answer, and He has been frustratingly tight-lipped on the matter."

It takes me a few seconds to realize who he means.

"The Creator." I scoff. "He does exist, then?"

The right side of Alaric's mouth hitches up in a grin. "You doubted it?"

I roll my eyes. "I struggle to believe there's a God when so much bad has been allowed to happen. If He's there, why doesn't He stop all this?" I wave my hand toward the nearby cliff edge, gesturing toward Alexander's base in the distance.

"The Creator is not a defined being of substance, like you or me. He is everything. He is energy, He is the universe itself. He created us, He guides us, but as for the rest..." Alaric shrugs. "Well, I think He views us all sort of like a child views a science project. He wants to watch and see what happens."

"So, He never intervenes?"

Although I already suspected as much—and as much as I value free will, keeping in line with my Dark half—the thought of the Creator allowing someone like me to suffer just because of how I was born makes me unbearably sad. The emotion this realization stirs in my chest is reminiscent of how it felt to grow up without parents.

Alaric's answering expression is morose. "Only once that I've witnessed."

I stare at him dumbly until I remember just how old he is. As the son of Michael, Alaric was among the first Nephilim children left behind on Earth when the Faithful were called back to Heaven, centuries before the academies were established. Like so many others, like Gilgamesh and Vesta, he was a victim to a decision made by a being the Lights are expected to swear their allegiance to, even to this day. No wonder none of the ancient first generations have yet to Ascend. To Ascend is to love the Creator above all, to leave behind human weakness and resentment. But how do you love someone who separated you from your parents? Who made you grow up alone?

Part of me can't help wondering if Gabriel experienced something similar when she found out she was pregnant with me. Was the Creator behind that abandonment, too?

"He did nothing during Alexander's first war for power?"

Leaning his head back against the rock wall, Alaric turns his eyes upward, staring at the clear cerulean sky. "Many millennia before Alexander, when the Archangels returned to Earth to work with the Archdemons to protect the Nephilim, part of their mission was to ensure the secrecy of our kind. As such, it became their responsibility to deal with such problems. The Creator did his part by imparting the prophecy on Gabriel."

"So, at what point did they find out about Alexander and decide he needed to be dealt with?" I swallow, the words tasting like ash in my mouth. "Was it when he killed your father?"

Alaric exhales a shaky breath. "That was my fault. I was unaware of the prophecy then. What I did…"

Confusion draws my brows together. "What you did?" I echo, wondering what he means by that. But as these words leave my lips, it dawns on me that I already know the answer. "The memory Alexander showed me…it was you unbinding his Light side, wasn't it? That's why your father intervened."

I comb back through the recollection in question, remembering Alaric and Alexander on their knees in the grass, hands clasped together, as they muttered silent words I couldn't hear. I remember thinking it seemed like they were performing a ritual, but considering the ease with which Alexander removed my own bind, I failed to make the comparison.

I'm beginning to grasp the extent of the baggage Alaric is holding onto. He wasn't just in love with a Gray…

He helped unleash Alexander's wrath on the world.

"Although the Council didn't seem to know of Alexander when he was at the academies, that changed once he ascended the throne of Macedonia. I can only assume there was some concern over his powers, especially given the mantle of authority he possessed, which granted him lordship over humans. And at this point, he wasn't exactly shy about his aspirations. Or reticent in their execution. It was inevitable the Council would be watching him closely, as they do all Nephilim who try to use their power for personal gain, even if they did not forbid such political ambition at the time." His eyes fix on mine. "Let me ask you, of the first generations you've met, how many are known as kings or queens?"

"Or goddesses," I snark, thinking of Ishtar and Vesta.

"Precisely." He grins, but his amusement vanishes almost as quickly as it appeared. "I suppose it's also possible Michael was watching me, the estranged son he couldn't bring himself to face, but I know better than to believe he regretted abandoning me with my poor mortal mother. If he had, he would've made amends as soon as he was allowed back on Earth." He waves a dismissive hand, banishing the thought. "Either way, his death was my fault. If I hadn't helped to unbind Alexander, then he wouldn't have ever come into his full power, and none of what followed in the years after would've happened. Although"—he scrubs a hand over his face—"if I hadn't unbound him, his mental state would've deteriorated and who can say what catastrophe might have come of that. Despite my regrets now, I'd do it all over again if only to save him from that." A humorless smile flickers on his lips and then fades.

"How did you do it? Unbind him, I mean."

A familiar baritone stirs in my memory, bringing me back to that moment under the Serapeum when blinding pain consumed me, and my wings finally tore free from my flesh.

"You have my gratitude, little dove. And in exchange for my freedom, I shall now give you yours."

How did Alexander unbind me?

The Nephilim snorts. "Let's just say there's a reason the academies don't teach Enochian anymore."

"You know Enochian?" I don't know why I'm surprised. Ishtar knew Enochian—or at least enough of it to release Alexander—and considering Alaric is far older than her, it makes sense he would know it, too. Thinking back, I recall the strange words Alexander whispered in my ear outside his tomb. In the Council's prison, I had plenty of time to consider what they meant, and now, after all this time, I guess I know. He unbound me—gave me the same freedom Alaric once gave him.

"I do, as does Alexander. And that knowledge nearly destroyed the world."

I glance at the lip of the cliff, envisioning the city below, just out of view from where we sit. As we speak, Alexander is down there, walking free of his cell.

Given their past, why isn't Alaric with him? If Caleb and I were in their shoes, if we had been forcibly separated for millennia, I'd move mountains to be with him again.

So, why is Alaric here with me instead?

Realization twists my stomach in knots. "That's why you

aren't with him now, isn't it? You blame yourself for what he tried to do."

Regret darkens Alaric's gaze. "I was the catalyst. I unbound him, freeing not only his Light side but revealing his true nature, unleashing his full potential on many who suffered because of it and many more who would've been caught in the crossfire had he not eventually been detained. Alexander wanted to tear down the divide, to bring the Lights and Darks together—a sentiment I know you agree with, as do I. But the way he wanted to do it meant going to war. Which he did, for years, claiming mortal lands, although the real war was against our kind. No one on the Council desired another Fall, but Alexander would not hear reason, especially when certain Fallen joined his ranks."

"Like Lilith," I whisper.

Alaric's lips press into a flat line. "He surrounded himself with powerful followers, which was why he was able to resist the Council for so long. His followers adored him, and while I believe he was a gracious leader to the mortals he loved and to those who upheld his ideals, he did not suffer those who stood against him. He saw only one path, and he viewed himself as the rightful ruler of celestial beings and humans alike."

"Even over the Creator?" I breathe.

A scowl mars Alaric's handsome face. "Alexander blamed the Creator for why he was never able to find his birth parents. Not out of any desire for a missing connection," he says when he sees my sympathetic expression. "Rather, I think Alexander felt he had something to prove. He wanted to show his birth parents how little they mattered, that they were nothing compared to the human parents who had loved and raised him as their own." Shaking his head at some unspoken thought, he adds, "Alexander was ambitious, but he never once lied about who he was or what he wanted from life. *I* was the blind one. *I* refused to see anything aside from his love for me. And I accompanied him along that path until the veil was finally lifted from my eyes, and I realized what following him would mean."

I balk at the fear glimmering in his gaze. I can understand why he might be nervous to see Alexander again, but afraid? Why would he be frightened of him if they once loved each other? Unless—

My eyes widen. "You knew where he was this whole time. You knew he was entombed under the Serapeum."

Misery paints Alaric's face white. "Yes…because I helped put him in there."

My wings bristle under my skin, and a strange sense of betrayal grips my senses as I gape at the Nephilim, trying to process the nuclear bomb he's just dropped in my lap. He helped the Council trap Alexander. He helped them confine a Gray, someone like me.

But then…he also helped free me of my own cage, and from the hospital before that. He put his life on the line by turning on the Council to ensure I wouldn't suffer the same fate as Alexander.

A fate he helped inflict.

I'm not sure what to think of all this. Alaric isn't a bad person, I know this. But I'm not entirely convinced Alexander is either. Despite what I've been told—despite him unbinding me and then abandoning me to the Council's whims—I can understand him in a way neither the Lights or Darks can. I can empathize with the anger and pain that led him down the path resulting in his imprisonment, having felt the same frustration toward the Lights at the Serapeum and my birth parents more times than I can count. If I didn't, Alexander wouldn't have been able to manipulate me to free him as easily as he did. Hell, perhaps my insecurities and forced isolation were even how he was able to get inside my head in the first place.

I'm beginning to think I'm more like my fellow Gray than I thought. Am I doomed then to follow in his footsteps? And if I do, where does that leave Caleb? Will something inevitably come between us the same way it did between Alexander and Alaric?

Will he help entomb me if he decides that I'm dangerous?

As if he knows what I'm thinking, Alaric chokes out, "I know, probably better than anyone, what he's capable of, Luna. Alexander—He destroys everything he touches, and I'm…" He falters, his tone suddenly bleak. "I'm terrified of him destroying you, too."

Destroy?

His words trigger the memory of the words Uriel spit at me when I was still contained by the Council. *"Gabriel, the*

Messenger, bearer of the Creator's words. Who is to say she told us the whole truth pertaining to the Gray destined to destroy our kind and our world? Your very existence begs the question. Perhaps you, forbidden child of the Dark and the Light, are the real bringer of our demise."

Is Alaric referring to the prophecy…?

Or is he just talking about his own heart?

Before I can press the Nephilim for more details, Hammurabi emerges from the mountain path with a sullen look smeared on his face. "We have company."

I scramble to my feet as six figures step out onto the cliff behind the Babylonian king, my wild eyes searching their faces until I find the only one who matters.

"Caleb!" I shriek, rushing toward him and throwing myself into his arms. I'm so overcome with relief that he's here—that he's *okay*—that I let out a small hiccuping sigh.

He presses a hand to my lower back, pulling me close. "I'm good," he whispers in my ear. "Everything's fine."

Someone clears their throat behind us, and releasing me, he looks over his shoulder. I follow his gaze to see Ishtar glowering at me with a venomous smirk twisting ruby red lips. She looks me up and down with a sneer.

"Hello again, Luna," she purrs.

"Ishtar," I drawl, resisting the urge to break the goddess's neck as payback for striking Caleb the last time I saw her. If anyone is to blame for things turning out the way that they have, it's her. I have no doubt about that.

She turns with the grace and poise of a panther and gestures back toward the path with a grand sweep of one arm. "Come. The Great awaits."

Terror pounds in my chest as Caleb and I follow Ishtar, hand in hand, along the winding path back down the mountain. Alaric and Hammurabi linger only a few steps behind us, and the remaining four Nephilim, who accompanied Caleb and Ishtar to meet us, bring up the rear. They're all Darks, cloaked in rippling black and violet auras, and dressed in armor, like soldiers heading for war. I suppose, in a way, they are. From what Caleb said, it sounds like Alexander intends to pick up exactly where he left off before he was imprisoned.

The trek to the citadel progresses at a slug's pace, every step weighed down with the daunting feeling that I'm walking to my own execution. The Nephilim we pass as we advance beyond the gates all look at us with a fleeting curiosity, their interest subsiding almost as quickly as it arises. From their numbers, it seems Alexander's forces are growing at an incredible rate. New visitors coming here to swear their allegiance and bend the knee must be a daily occurrence.

"The Great will receive you in the throne room," Ishtar announces, even though no one asked. I'm beginning to think she just likes to hear herself talk.

The throne room in question borders on garish when compared to the rest of the citadel, like a mansion dropped in the middle of a slum. Most perplexing is the massive stone bull's head situated just behind the throne. I'm not sure if it's an ancient relic or meant to signify something to Alexander, and I don't care to ask.

Caleb releases my hand and mouths for me to wait as he approaches the dais, bowing before the imposing figure perched on the marble draped in a purple robe topped with what appears to be the skin of a lion.

Alexander.

"As promised," Caleb says.

My blood runs cold when his grandfather rises from his throne and steps down onto our level, crossing the space toward us, his arms spread out in welcome. A genial smile lights up his fair face. "Welcome, my friends," he greets us, playing the part of the gracious host. His contrasting eyes find mine and his smile deepens. "So, we meet again at last, little dove."

No thanks to you, I'm tempted to say. But I keep my mouth shut and follow Caleb's lead, dipping into a respectful bow and waiting a few seconds before straightening again. In my peripheral vision, Hammurabi and Alaric each do the same.

"Ah, Hammurabi." Alexander appraises the Babylonian king. "I'll admit, I was surprised to hear of your attendance. I never took you for one to stand against the Council."

Hammurabi lifts his chin. "Things change."

Alexander clasps his hands behind his back. "That they do," he agrees. "That they do, my old friend. In fact, since we last met, an interesting revelation has come to light proving just that." He struts forward, circling Hammurabi like a vulture hovering over a carcass. "Tell me, King. I'm most curious to know how you came upon my dagger. You did well, of course, to return it to its bloodline," he adds with a nonchalant wave toward Caleb, "but I do wonder how it came to be under your guardianship at all."

My back stiffens at the undercurrent of threat in Alexander's voice, the clashing hues of his eyes glinting as he pauses in front of the Nephilim.

"At the time of my capture, the dagger was…reluctantly not in my possession," he continues. "If it had been, I assure you, things would have gone rather differently." The venom behind his words sends a shiver racing over my skin, but what chills me more is how quickly and easily he slips back behind the mask of the charming, charismatic ruler. The grin tugging at his lips is almost more menacing than his tone. "Only one person, aside from myself, of course, knew of the dagger's whereabouts. The one person I trusted not to bury it in my back at the first opportunity. And that person was, most certainly, not you. So how, King"—he trails a long finger under Hammurabi's jaw—"did you come upon it?"

At the western edge of the room, Ishtar seethes, her obsidian aura whipping furiously around her like storm clouds coming together to form a tornado. "You stole it from me," she snarls through gritted teeth, "just like you stole my memories!"

Understanding dawns on her face, interrupting her fury for only a moment before her stunning visage settles into a mask of pure rage. "Which you've been doing for *millennia*, haven't you, so I wouldn't discover the knife was at Babel. Was it even in the museum, King, or was that just another lie you planted in my head?"

I glance between the goddess and Hammurabi, confused for all of ten seconds before remembering what Alaric told me back on the cliff. How, after Alexander's imprisonment, his followers were silenced to keep his true identity secret.

"Memories were erased," he said.

My eyes shift back to the Babylonian king as this new piece of information sinks in. Is that Hammurabi's special talent? The ability to manipulate memories? Another uncontrollable shudder rockets through me at the thought of all the ways that power could be abused.

Alexander offers Ishtar a pitying look. "That does seem to be the case, doesn't it?"

He turns his narrowed gaze back on Hammurabi, who stands frozen before the towering Gray, as if balancing on the tip of his finger. Although the Nephilim is tall, Alexander's commanding presence makes the angel seem even taller.

"You were quite thorough in performing your duty for the Council. So much so, you can imagine how troublesome it has been to recruit when few of my followers can recall their loyalty to me." With a quiet laugh, Alexander drops his finger from Hammurabi's chin. "Most curious then that you didn't relinquish my dagger like a dutiful soldier when you have always been so quick to heed Asmodeus. I can only assume she did not know that you had it, for I struggle to believe she would've allowed such a weapon to be within arm's reach of my general, even with her memories of it affected. I wonder then, did you hold onto it out of fear? Out of guilt? You must've known you couldn't wield the blade yourself."

Something inside the Nephilim seems to snap, his eyes like glowing orbs of obsidian, and yet, on the outside, he remains the picture of calm. "We might have had our fair share of differences, Alexander, but I never agreed with what the Council did to you."

Alexander cocks an amused golden brow. "Is that so? Then you won't mind unweaving the lies you spun in each of my followers' heads."

A taunting smile tugs up the corners of his mouth when the Nephilim draws in a deep breath and nods.

"If that is what my liege demands of me," Hammurabi rumbles.

"That is precisely what I hoped you would say," Alexander croons.

Despite the midday heat beating down on the citadel, the temperature in the throne room turns arctic when Alexander shifts his focus to Caleb, holding out one elegant hand.

Caleb blinks up at him, confused.

"My dagger," he says slowly, as if testing the weight of each word on his tongue. "While I appreciate your initiative, Grandson, you still acted against my orders. And disobedience must be punished."

Shaking his head, Caleb gawks at his grandfather. "But without it, I wouldn't have been able to free Luna." He gestures to me as if to remind Alexander of that fact, presenting me to him like a shiny new toy. When that doesn't seem to faze the Gray, Caleb adds in a rush, "*Or* cut off the wing of one of the Archdemons out for your blood. That shape-shifting bastard didn't know what hit him. You're welcome, by the way."

Alexander doesn't react to the news about Mammon, instead shifting his focus to me. He observes me with an admiring nod. "The Morningstar's daughter is a fine gift, indeed. The finest of what you have brought me today. But now that you have delivered her to me, you no longer have any need of the dagger, even if you have put the blade to good use. It should be returned to its rightful owner, wouldn't you agree?"

Fear is a snare drum in my chest, and the tension in the air is thick enough to choke on. I peer at Caleb out of the corner of my eye before glancing down at the hidden sheath tucked inside his belt. His knife—the knife he used to cut me out of that egg…it's the same weapon I saw in Alexander's memory.

The weapon he used to kill Michael.

Caleb's protests rip me out of my thoughts.

"But—"

"Do not make me ask a second time," Alexander interrupts, and my pulse trips at the warning edge in his voice. "There are worse punishments I can inflict. Now"—he curls his fingers in a *give it here* gesture—"hand it over. I will not ask again."

Caleb wavers, his hand hovering by his hip. I can see the internal struggle reflected on his face, the innate desire to please his grandfather, his blood—a struggle I experienced myself with Gabriel—at war with his common sense. If he hands the knife over, he's leaving himself defenseless against not just Alexander, but the Council when it comes for us. And although he has me to protect him, I have no doubt that his grandfather could tear me to pieces.

But Caleb hesitates a moment too long, and I notice the change in Alexander before I can do a damn thing to stop it. He homes in on his grandson like a heat-seeking missile, and time seems to slow as Caleb drops to one knee, clutching his head in his hands and letting out a piercing cry that tears my soul in two.

"Caleb!" I rush forward, but a hand clamps around my wrist, tugging me back like a dog on a leash. My eyes snap over my shoulder, locking with Alaric's.

"Luna, no," he warns.

An animalistic ferocity surges through me, overshadowed only by the agony that grips my chest when Caleb collapses, writhing against the stone, his lips parting on another ear-splitting scream. As his body contorts, his back arching unnaturally, the dagger slips free of his belt, clattering onto the floor.

My eyes skim over the gleaming metal before flashing back to Alaric. "Why do you keep trying to stop me?" I snarl, thinking back to our fight with Mammon.

The Nephilim's expression warps into a grimace. "I'm trying to keep you alive," he says, pleading.

With the speed of a cracking whip, Alexander's eyes dart to my face then to Alaric's where they linger, staring at his former lover, meeting his gaze for the first time since we arrived at the citadel. Part of me wondered why Alexander didn't acknowledge him sooner, but the sorrow and longing in those ominous eyes is all the answer I need to that question.

"Is this what our relationship has been reduced to, Alaric?" he asks, his low timbre verging on a whisper. "Such fear and distrust?" He clicks his tongue. "A pity. I had hoped for better from you."

He doesn't say another word to Alaric, breaking their gaze and peering back at Caleb with a disappointed frown before releasing him from whatever excruciating hold he has on his mind. Caleb lurches forward onto all fours, gasping.

"Do not challenge me again," Alexander warns, plucking the dagger off the stone floor. He tucks the blade into the sash tied around the waist of his tunic, hiding it from sight under his deep purple robe, before turning and resuming his seat on his throne.

Wrenching free of Alaric's grip, I race forward and drop to

my knees beside Caleb, placing a careful hand on his quivering back and smoothing the hair away from his clammy forehead. With a trembling breath, he pushes onto his knees and tilts his head up toward the ceiling as beads of crimson track from his left nostril and ears. The blood freezes in my veins at the sight of it, and I stare wide-eyed at his stricken face as memories I'd rather forget resurface. This…what Alexander did to Caleb… I've seen this before.

No, worse than that. Bile rises in my throat. The faces of my last foster parents and the social worker who managed my case come alive in my thoughts, and it takes every last ounce of self-control I possess to not spew on the floor. I haven't just seen this before.

I've done it myself.

Horror tears my composure to shreds, and I shiver, barely able to hold myself together. I unwittingly broke into those mortals' minds as easily as Alexander just broke into Caleb's. Except where I accidentally killed them, Alexander used such brutality to establish his authority. To punish his own grandson. His blood.

I once witnessed Caleb breaking into my bullies' minds at the Serapeum, but that was nothing like this. Nothing like what I did. He was restrained in his vengeance, only acting to save me. Whereas this…what Caleb just endured…

The power imbalance was potent.

Beside me, Caleb staggers to his feet, wiping the back of

his hand across his bloody nose, his bronzed complexion unusually pale. I rise alongside him, worry creasing my brow, but he just jerks his head at my silent question, grasping onto my hand for support.

Alexander claps, drawing everyone's gaze, and looks down upon us from his throne like a proud father. The anger that burnished his gaze only moments before is gone, replaced by that coquettish charm that I'm sure made him popular with the Darks and humans back in his day. Maybe it was even what won over Alaric.

Inclining his head toward Caleb, he says, "Now that such unpleasantness is out of the way, why don't you show our guests to their rooms? Ishtar"—he waves a hand toward the goddess without averting his eyes from his still shaking grandson—"accompany our friends, will you, please? So no one gets any…unfortunate ideas." His hard stare roams over my face at these words.

A growl rumbles deep in Caleb's chest. "No," he barks. "Not before you remove the tracker from Luna's head." Although he's weak from Alexander's assault, he steps forward, challenging his grandfather. Challenging an *angel*. Resentment rings clear in his voice as he spits, "I brought you your gifts. For once, uphold your end of the bargain."

Alexander crosses his legs, his long fingers curling around the arms of his throne like talons. I never would've known such a simple movement to be so ominous. "I will forgive your tone just this once, Grandson. But moving forward…remember your place."

Alexander tilts his head and crooks an elegant finger, beckoning me to come forward.

Gulping, I do as commanded, approaching the throne with all the enthusiasm of someone about to undergo a root canal. My heartbeat thrums in my ears, and my palms sweat profusely when he gestures for me to kneel at his feet. When I sink to the stone, Alexander closes his eyes and sweeps his hand against my ear.

At first, I don't feel any different. But when he pulls his hand away, there's a lightness to my head that wasn't there before. That strange sensation that kept gnawing at my ear—that I thought was all in my head—is gone now. Even my stomach is more settled than it was only seconds ago.

"Is…is it gone?" I whisper.

"It is," Alexander assures me. "You need not fear the Council any longer."

I glance down when he unfurls his fingers, showing me what looks like a glistening ivory beetle nestled on his palm.

Blanching, I squeak, "That was *inside* my head?"

With a musical chuckle, Alexander presses his other hand to my cheek, smiling warmly down at me like a ray of sunlight beaming through an overcast sky. I'm trapped in his gaze, transfixed, and I realize he's beautiful. Terrifying but beautiful.

"You could have removed it yourself, little dove, if you only had some proper training. It's time you embrace what you are. Give me your loyalty and I promise"—he rises to his feet again, pulling me up alongside him on the dais—"I will show you what you're capable of."

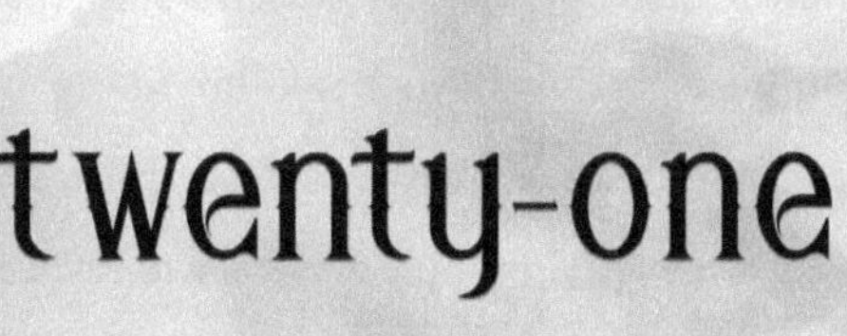

twenty-one

CALEB

MY SKULL THROBS LIKE someone took a sledgehammer and cracked it open then stuck their fingers into my brain and scrambled it. But the physical pain isn't the worst part—it's the feeling of being violated, of having my mind ravaged, of being a puppet watching someone else pull my strings. I'm not a total hypocrite. I've fucked with people's minds before, too, but usually in self-defense—like with those pieces of shit who attacked Luna—or to stop a criminal from doing something bad, not like this. Not to prove a point. I was a naive dumbass to think Alexander would stop short of really hurting or humiliating me just because I'm his grandson. Blood or not, he flexed his claws to ensure I know my place. Get with the program or be destroyed. Message received.

I massage my temples as I pace back and forth across the red woolen rug puddling across the old stones like a splash of blood. My room has been upgraded in my absence. It's not lavish by any means, but now there are colorful pillows decorating the bed, along with a silk duvet in peacock blue. I guess being a prince, even a deserter who isn't trusted, earned me more amenities. Appearances must be kept up. And I did bring Gramps an angel and two Nephilim, so yay me.

The real question is: Who the hell has been shopping? A hysterical laugh escapes my lips, and I shake my aching head. The most decorative piece of all, Luna, sits on the bed, watching me with concern in her eyes. Her wings are out, cascading over the bed, softer than the silk ever could be. Their appearance causes me to stumble. I stop pacing and blink, focusing on her. I don't know how long I've been trying to wear a hole in the carpet. Shit, I don't know when the last time I spoke to her was. At least that creepy bug thing is out of her head. I can be grateful to Alexander for that if nothing else, although I'm sure a high price for that favor will come soon.

The thought of him breaking Luna's mind pushes me forward once more, back and forth, back and forth in the confines of the bedroom. I can't do anything to Gramps if he tries. He took my knife—well, *his* knife—and now I'm helpless. I'm fucking helpless to protect the woman I love. And she's an angel, and I know that she's stronger than me, but she's so new to being an immortal being that Alexander could easily hurt her. Clip her wings, literally and figuratively. Like what I did to Mammon. And I don't have my weapon of immortal destruction to stop him.

"Caleb, you have to stop." Luna's voice cuts across my thoughts, and I pivot on one foot, looking over my shoulder. Her big hazel eyes snag mine, the worry in them making me flinch. "Come here." She pats a space on the bed beside her. "Sit next to me."

My eyes rove hungrily over her slender figure, tracing the beauty of her wings. It would be so easy to go to her, touch her wings, and take her right there on the bed. Forget all my problems, make her forget hers. Forget that Alexander broke my mind like I was a plastic doll, and he wants Luna for his own toy soldier. We can stay here until morning and ignore everything and everyone.

Luna's eyes widen, and I see my own want reflected there. I swallow as she pats the bed again, shaking my head.

"Please," she says, undoing my resolve.

Two strides—my legs are long—and I'm at the bed. I make sure to sit a few feet away and gaze at my hands, clenched in my lap.

Goldilocks reaches out and clasps my forearm. "Caleb, why won't you look at me?"

"I really want to have sex with you right now," I say bluntly, "but for all the wrong reasons, so I'm trying to keep my distance."

Hurt creeps into her voice. "I don't understand. You want to have *sex* with me for the wrong reasons?"

I glance up at her then, her expression embarrassed and

confused. I close one hand over her knee, squeezing. "Goldilocks, I always want to have sex with you, but my head isn't in the right place. I'm—Alexander *assaulted* me. I can still feel him in my head. It's like dirt I can't scrub clean. And I desperately want to fix it, or at least be distracted enough that I forget it happened. But you deserve better than being a distraction. Not that it wouldn't be good—it would be fan-fucking-tastic—but the timing is shit. My whole timing lately is shit." I slide my hand off her knee and into my hair again, trying to quiet the lingering agony in my mind.

The bed gives a dip as she scoots closer to me and cups her hand over my knee this time. "Well, if my previous bodily responses toward you haven't already made it abundantly clear, I always want to have sex with you, too," she admits in a low voice that hits me straight in the groin. "Although, I'm not sure I want my first time to be here, with your grandfather and Ishtar lurking so close. Call me crazy, but being a glorified hostage really takes the romance out of it." She laughs. "Well, this is quite the role reversal, don't you think?"

Her words dial down the heat a little. My eyes dart up, meeting hers. "What do you mean?"

"I mean, I'm always the one having a breakdown, and you're trying to put me back together again." Her giggle makes me smile. "I'm telling you now, Caleb, there's only room for one crazy person in this relationship, and I hold that title. So, you need to get it together."

My jaw drops like a gate off its hinges at her words. Then I honest-to-Lucifer guffaw, great gulping bits of laughter escaping my lips, and I hold my side from the stitch stabbing me there. I hear the edge of hysteria in my mirth and decide I need to dial back the hyena cackle a little.

"I'm sorry. I'm not usually—"

She places a finger on my lips. "I was just teasing. What Alexander did to you..." Fire sprouts on the back of her free hand, and she shakes it out. "I wish I knew how to do something more than be a pyromaniac," she mutters.

"Hey, being a pyromaniac isn't a bad thing," I say, nudging her shoulder.

Luna squeezes my knee. "What I'm trying to say is that I'm here for you, just like you are for me. I still don't feel...like myself, but I'll support you in whatever way I can." She rises up a little and brushes a soft kiss across my lips.

I savor her lips against mine for a moment, thoughts of us naked still dancing around in my brain. Pulling away, I say, "I'm glad Alexander got that thing out of you, but I'm sorry I brought you here. I underestimated him. I just didn't think—I was a moron." My hands ball into fists, and Goldilocks slides her hand from my knee to cover one of my fists.

"No, you made the best decision in an impossible situation. If we hadn't come here, the Council would've eventually lost patience and dragged me kicking and screaming back to my cage. We'll escape from here, too. Somehow."

Though my confidence has taken a knee to the nuts, I say, "Well, I might have an idea about that. Alexander is very interested in Lucifer joining Team Conqueror, but he doesn't know about Gabriel. Yet. Your mom and pops are our best bet of getting out of here. Alexander can't take both of them on—at least I don't think so. And you're an angel, too, hardly a helpless princess."

Luna frowns. "But how will they know I'm here? Even with the tracker gone, I'm not sure Alaric can risk using the sigil…" She shudders. "Alexander has so many eyes in this place, he'll know if any of us tries to leave and we can't exactly call my father here. Not without letting him know what he's walking into."

"He won't have to because if I know Gramps at all, he'll issue Lucifer an invitation. I don't know how or where or when, but I guarantee he'll somehow track Lucifer down—or use Alaric to do it. That's a potential ally Alexander can't ignore," I explain.

"But my mother will be with him. That will look suspicious," Luna says and I sigh, thinking.

"Yeah, but Lucifer can always brush it off that she's trying to haul him in for questioning or some shit." At her doubtful look, I sigh again. "I know it's thin, Goldilocks, but it's the best hope we have right now."

She rests her head on my shoulder. "Alexander wants to train me. I know this sounds crazy…" She chuckles. "A lot of the things I say sound crazy lately, but until we find a way to leave, I should take advantage of that."

"You *want* Gramps training you?" I ask, disbelief filling my voice. I glance down at her, and her mouth puckers like she's bitten into a lemon.

"Not really, but he *is* Alexander the Great and the only other Gray that we know of. If anyone can show me how to control my powers, it's him." Luna tilts her head up, gazing into my eyes.

Well, she's got a point there. Let Alexander train her to be a lethal weapon—one that will cut him. "You're right. He can show you stuff that no one else can, not even your parents. But if you want extra points on hand-to-hand combat, corner Hammurabi."

Luna rolls her eyes. "Hammurabi wouldn't help me. Besides, I have a feeling Alexander won't want me training with anyone but him."

I kiss her forehead. "Hammurabi isn't so bad. You just have to overlook that stick up his ass." I grin as her laughter shakes her whole body. Making her laugh is like receiving a gift, one finer than gold or diamonds. Sobering, I say, "Yeah, Grandfather is possessive with his toys. He won't want anyone else playing with you."

Luna wilts against me. "Is that how he thinks of us? Even Ishtar?"

I stroke her neck, careful to keep my greedy hands off her wings. "Alexander admires and respects Ishtar, but he doesn't think she's his equal. As a Gray, you're the closest thing he has to a peer in his mind. But I don't think he really likes that there's another Gray out there. It ruins his whole line of, 'only I can unite the divide because I'm the Chosen One.' But he'll use you, of that I have no doubt."

Three precise knocks sound on our door before it's pushed open and in walks the goddess of love and war herself. Luna and I both straighten up and rise from the bed. Ishtar's eyes trace Luna's wings with a covetous gleam. She's probably jealous of Grandfather's interest in Luna. She's very proprietorial of Alexander.

"Good, you're both dressed," Ishtar says smoothly. "But you can't wear those rags to dinner."

I look at my battered jeans and T-shirt then glare at her. "One, what would you have done if we were naked, and two, we don't exactly have a mall nearby we can pop into for some new threads, and I doubt Prime delivers here."

Ishtar's smile cuts. "I've attended orgies, Caleb. Honestly, do you think any carnal activities you engage in could hold my interest? I'd die of boredom."

She claps her hands twice and another Nephilim enters. He's tall with a shaved head, and he holds a gold dress over one arm and a black suit over the other. He lays them with care across the bed, bows to Ishtar, and vacates the room.

I observe the suit as if it's a snake about to strike me. "Speaking of orgies, how is Gilgamesh? I thought he'd be here with you. Did he change his mind again?" I hear Luna gasp beside me.

I know I'm playing with fire, but Gilgamesh is Ishtar's

kryptonite. And maybe I want to hurt her a little for turning on me so quickly, even though that hurt is irrational. Just because I always thought of her as a badass aunt doesn't mean she thought of me as her favorite nephew.

A satisfied smile curves my former teacher's red lips. "Gilgamesh is exactly where we need him to be, serving Alexander. Unlike you, Caleb, once he gives his loyalty, he doesn't betray it." I flinch at her words. Score one for her. "Now, get dressed. Someone will be here to escort you to dinner shortly, and it's best you appear presentable."

Luna bristles at her tone, and Ishtar looks down her nose at Goldilocks, her stare imperious. Then something interesting happens as the goddess's eyes once again linger on Luna's wings. She stiffens as if she realizes she's speaking to an angel who has the potential to destroy her. Then the moment of doubt is gone, and she turns away, throwing over her shoulder, "Alexander is most delighted to welcome the Morningstar's daughter."

I snort, resisting the urge to tell Ishtar to stop hiding behind Alexander's shield, but I know better than to push her too far. The Gilgamesh crack was enough. The door shuts behind Ishtar's statuesque frame, leaving silence in her wake.

Luna fingers the fabric of the gown. "Gilgamesh turned against the Lights?" she asks, voice incredulous. "He seemed so...self-righteous."

"You mean hypocritical? The whole sleeping with Ishtar thing dulls his halo a bit, don't you think? But he swallowed my grandfather's line, hook and sinker," I say.

Shaking her head, she takes the dress off the bed and holds it up to her body. The golden material falls to the floor in one luxurious slide.

"A golden dress for Goldilocks," I say, smirking.

"It is beautiful," she admits. "It even has an opening for my wings."

"He'll want them on full display tonight," I tell her. "I'm sure it pisses him off that Lilith no longer has her wings so he can't parade her around."

"I don't want to be a symbol of his power," she says, scowling.

I look at the black on black suit again. Ugh. It's not that I don't rock a suit like nobody's business, but I don't want to be dressed up just to please Gramps and his new entourage of murderous Nephilim. He can go fuck himself. But that attitude will just get my mind torn open again.

"Neither do I, but we have to play the game and be smarter. We know what happens when we're not." I reach for the suit, but Luna tosses the dress on the bed, and tucks her body into the open space between my arm and chest.

"You're the strongest person I know. You found a way to break me out of a celestial prison in another dimension. You'll beat Alexander at his own game. I know you will." Her hands cup my face and she kisses me.

I give into temptation and stroke my fingers down the upper curve of her wing. She shudders hard and pushes against me, her mouth frantic on mine. For a few moments, I kiss her back, happy to lose myself in the decadence that is Goldilocks until her fingertips brush under the edge of my T-shirt. I pull back with a groan, putting some much-needed distance between us. The heat in her eyes burns me. Again with my shit timing.

I say, my voice steeped in regret, "Let's get dressed, Goldilocks. This is one dinner we can't be late for."

Luna looks like a goddess. The gold dress skims her lithe figure, highlighting all the slender curves. The beading draping her upper arms sparkles in the candlelight. Her hair sweeps down her back in soft golden waves. Her hand is tucked under my elbow as we make our way to the dining hall. I was gone for just a blink, but Gramps has been busy. He's transforming this place into more than just a military fort; He's creating a palace. But I get the sense it's all temporary. When he makes his move, he'll trade up for something bigger and better, but right now as he recruits, he needs to show all his prospects that he has a real seat of power, not just a pile of crumbling rocks.

And he's not only transformed the interior. I can smell spiced meat and fresh bread and my stomach growls. When I lived here last, I was lucky to get scrambled eggs. The last meal I had was at Mom's, so despite my nerves, I'm hungry. Unlike Alexander, I need to eat to remain at full strength. I glance down at Goldilocks. Huh, I guess she doesn't need to eat anymore. I wonder if she realizes that.

Her eyes meet mine and turn smoky. "You look..." She blushes and I smirk. "You look very handsome in that suit."

Ishtar must know my measurements because the suit fits like a glove, although I find the jacket confining if I need to fight. It's going right on the chair as soon as we're seated. "I know, gorgeous," I say, winking. "You look good enough to eat."

Red stains her cheeks and travels down her neck. I wonder just how far that blush goes. And thoughts like that are gonna get me killed. I'm going into the lion's den, and I need to stay sharp.

I see Hammurabi ahead with Alaric, waiting for us outside two enormous wooden and bronze doors. I thought Ishtar would come back and escort us to dinner, sulking about it the entire time, despite saying she was sending an underling. But she did send another Nephilim who had simply knocked on our door and told us to move our asses. Well, he didn't say exactly that but it was implied. No one keeps the Great waiting.

Alaric wears a slick charcoal suit, but Hammurabi is dressed in traditional Babylonian garb, with a woven skirt that hits him at the knee and a wide leather belt, along with sandals. He's barechested, his prize-fighter body on display. It's like he's stepped out of time. It's so bizarre I stumble a little; his face twists into a fierce scowl, and I'm certain he didn't choose this for himself. Why is my grandfather having him dress like the king he was? Other than his beard and quilted turban, he's mostly a modern man. Well, as modern as anyone like him can be. Maybe the better word is adaptable. He likes going out into the world and experiencing things.

Gilgamesh's image flashes through my mind, and I remember him telling Gramps he resented having to relinquish his kingship. Maybe Alexander sent those clothes to Hammurabi to remind him who he used to be and could still be in the new world order. Does Grandfather really plan to carve up the planet into fiefdoms for his most loyal generals while he rules over all? I wonder how that's going to work out, especially as there might be internal conflict over territory, like hey you might have ruled first, but I was here last.

I don't know who Alaric originally was when he was young, but he just looks like a well-dressed guy going to a board meeting. Ishtar emerges from the dining room in an ivory gown with a gold belt, living up to her goddess reputation. A welcoming smile is fixed upon her lips as she greets Alaric and Hammurabi. Alaric paints on his own charming smile while Hammurabi just gives a curt nod. If this wasn't a farce, and Hammurabi really wanted to serve Alexander, he'd compete with Ishtar for the number one position. There's no love lost between the two of them, just a fierce competition of who is best.

Luna and I stop before them, and Ishtar once again takes Luna's measure before focusing on me.

"Caleb, you clean up beautifully, just as I knew you would. For all your faults, you're stunning, just like all the men in your family," Ishtar says, and my stomach sours at the mention of my father. "Luna, how ethereal you are in that gown. You're so fortunate to have Alexander as your mentor. Soon, the Council will fear you."

Luna offers a tight smile, pressing herself even closer against my side. "I hope so," she says, and I hear the truth in those words. Good, I hope Goldilocks uses my grandfather for everything she can get out of him.

"Come, I was hoping Lilith could join us tonight, but she's been detained on some personal business," Ishtar says, linking her arm through Alaric's. "But we have another guest whose company I'm sure you'll enjoy." She winks at Alaric, and he raises an eyebrow.

I'm not surprised when we enter the dining hall to see Gilgamesh sitting on the left of Alexander, who is at the head of an enormous table. Luna's body goes rigid at the sight of her former teacher, and Gilgamesh's eyebrows grab for his hairline when he takes in Luna's wings, his face a picture of stunned amazement. Alaric startles but recovers quickly, his eyes flicking past Gilgamesh to hone in on Alexander. Grandfather's eyes settle on Alaric's in turn, and there's this weird undercurrent between them I don't understand.

"Please believe me when I say it's nice to see you and Gilgamesh no longer hiding in the shadows. Neither of you deserved that for thousands of years," Alaric says, and I can hear the sincerity in his voice.

It's Ishtar's turn to be taken aback. "Why, Alaric, I do think you mean that."

"Your relationship was the worst kept secret in either faction," Hammurabi says acidly. "We all knew you were fucking each other."

I choke down laughter, and Luna clutches my arm. Our eyes meet, and I see shocked amusement dancing in her gaze.

If Ishtar were a wolf, her hackles would be up. "Tell me, does sleeping with all those women make you forget about whom you really want to be with? I've always been curious."

Now, Hammurabi's hackles rise, and Alaric disengages with Ishtar and steps smoothly between them. "Alexander will be displeased at this hostility between allies. He has high hopes for us. Let's not disappoint him," he says, and Ishtar's expression smooths out, her shoulders relaxing. I guess Alaric dosed her with a shot of Calm. The resentful look she gives him confirms it.

"Stop that," Ishtar hisses at Alaric and pushes her shoulders back, pinning on an award-winning smile. "You're right. We mustn't disappoint Alexander." She saunters ahead, hips swaying, and Gilgamesh stops speaking to Alexander to stare at her, expression completely entranced.

Well, it's nice to know some things never change. Luna nudges me. "Who was Ishtar talking about?" she murmurs.

I shrug, whispering out of the side of my mouth, "No idea. Other than this past month, I've only seen Hammurabi at school. He could have a whole harem somewhere for all I know."

Luna looks at Hammurabi in all his shirtless glory, and I try not to get jealous at the admiration she can't quite hide. The dude *is* ripped. "It's hard to picture him pining after anyone. Then again, he did seem pretty taken with your mom so maybe I'm wrong."

The thought of Hammurabi hitting on my mom makes me scowl, but I see the mischievous glint in her eyes, and I chuckle. The laughter gets lodged in my throat when my gaze clashes with Alexander's, and I swear I feel phantom claws tearing into my mind again. It was much easier to joke about Hammurabi's sex life than to face my gramps again; however, Alexander gifts me with a warm smile. Well, I'll be damned. I guess he's back to playing benevolent grandfather again.

"Grandson, you look well rested. Come, sit beside me. You and Luna are the guests of honor tonight," he calls to me, sweeping out his arm over the ornate chairs beside him.

Bending slightly at the waist, I say, "It would be our honor to sit beside you, Grandfather."

Also with Luna being the only other angel here, that's the only place she can sit. This isn't a democracy, and the most powerful sit near the king. Luna glances at me in surprise as I put her right next to Alexander, but my grandfather just gives me a slight nod, acknowledging my homage to her angel status. As I push her chair in, I notice the slight tremor running through my hands, and I will myself to calm down, to not show the lion in the room any weakness.

Panic claws its way up my throat as I drape my jacket over the back of my chair and sit beside Luna, remembering writhing on the floor in front of Alexander in the throne room. I can hear the dagger hitting the smooth stone floor again, the sharp, painful sound of defeat. Everyone here but Gilgamesh witnessed my humiliation, how Grandfather brought me to my knees and showed me that despite my divine blood, he could break me at any time. I take a slow breath through my nose, attempting to wipe my mind clean of those tormenting thoughts. Luna finds my knee under the table and squeezes, bringing me firmly back to the here and now.

My gaze lands on the silver plates and goblets and pitchers artfully strewn across the table. I pick up a goblet, its metalwork flawless. This looks exactly like the silver found in King Philip's tomb in Greece in Vergina. Either Alexander went back and claimed them or he had someone replicate them for him. There are a lot of talented Nephilim out there and from this time period, too. Gramps notices me admiring the goblet in my hand and smiles.

"Ah, so you recognize it. One of my Nephilim created this for me, to remind me of home, of my human parents. My true parents despite my divine blood," Alexander says, a bitter smile twisting his lips. "But enough about the past. We're here because we believe in a glorious future, a future without all this strife and turmoil between our factions."

"Yes," Gilgamesh says. "And a future where the mortals are

no longer destroying themselves."

"The little lambs need a shepherd," Ishtar agrees, cupping her goblet in one hand. Shepherd my ass, she's more like a wolf wearing a sheep's skin.

"Yes, but tonight, we celebrate my grandson, Caleb, for the glorious gifts he has brought me. Alaric, clever and diplomatic, who can root out any bloodline, and the mighty Hammurabi, fierce king of old whom I will restore to his former glory," Alexander says, his eyes brushing over Hammurabi and lingering on Alaric a beat too long. "And of course, he brought me the only other Gray in existence, the beautiful Luna, who I will mold in my image. She will be a great weapon in the war to come."

Luna stills at his words, and this time I find her knee under the table, and she shoots me a grateful look under her long lashes.

"I cannot rule if you do," Hammurabi says, drawing my attention away, and I curse under my breath at his dangerous stubbornness. Alexander's mouth thins and I brace myself. Hammurabi continues, "We're here because we believe you can unite us, not make us rulers again."

Nice save, King.

Grandfather relaxes and leans back in his chair. "Ah, that's where you're wrong, King. While it's true, Heaven cannot brook two suns, nor Earth two masters"—he glances sideways at Luna, and my heart stutters in my chest—"my loyal generals will divide the lands and maintain order over them. Though all will answer to me, you will rule your kingdoms with my blessing and with the wisdom I know you possess."

And if they step out of line, Alexander will fall upon them like a hammer. He doesn't say it, but he doesn't have to. They all know he rewards those who are loyal to him but don't go getting any ideas of true independence.

Hammurabi bows his head in deference to Alexander. "Your generosity does you credit."

Gilgamesh caresses the back of Ishtar's hand. "The world would have been a better place if we'd been allowed to continue to rule it."

Wow, at this rate, Gilgamesh's ego will outgrow Alexander's army.

"Indeed, my friend," Alexander says, and Alaric takes two quick gulps from his goblet, avoiding my grandfather's pointed looks. That is one mystery I'd love to crack. "Let's raise our glasses to Caleb, who cut off the mighty Mammon's wing"—Gilgamesh's jaw falls at that proclamation—"and is responsible for bringing this dinner about. His love may have made him foolish and stole him away from me for a brief time, but I can forgive him for it, as he's brought the Morningstar's daughter into the fold. Though you are not of my blood, Luna, I think of you as I do Caleb, as an heir of my empire."

Luna and I exchange glances at those loaded words. Alexander just elevated a newbie to princess status. Although heir implies he'd be willing to pass on the crown, and I know that ain't happening. Ever. Ishtar's lush mouth turns down at Alexander's proclamation, and though I know she's jealous of Goldilocks, she echoes my grandfather's, "To Caleb!"

I slap on a smile that fits wrong, like I'm a Ken doll with a painted-on mouth. I take a sip from my goblet, and the flavor of good wine explodes on my tongue. I drain the cup in one go. It takes a lot to get a Nephilim drunk, and I need to appear somewhat relaxed during this dinner from hell, especially as Alexander seems determined to focus on me. The roasted lamb on my plate smells divine, and I take a bite despite my nerves, just to occupy my hands with something other than fidgeting.

Those calculating eyes roam over me, and cold sweat trickles down my back, dampening the silk of my shirt. A kind smile stretches across my grandfather's face. That terrifies me even more.

"I know you believe because I punished you, blood isn't important to me. You believe I do not care about you, which couldn't be further from the truth," Alexander says, voice tender. "Children need discipline or they become unruly and a danger to themselves. And while I admire your ingenuity and your independent spirit, your quest could've easily gotten you captured or killed. The Council will show no mercy to my blood. Family is important, Caleb, and with Alaric's help, we will root out my other grandchildren and bring them in line with our virtuous cause. I can only hope they are as bold and bright as you."

I stare at him, my mind in overdrive. Dear Dad made a deal with the Archdemons to conceal his children from one another and mask our blood connection to him. I'm guessing much in the same way Gabriel managed to conceal her connection to Luna. But Alaric didn't know Goldilocks was Gabriel's kid when he brought her to the Serapeum and mentioned something about how difficult she had been to track down. So, would he even be able to scent out our bloodline through whatever magic was placed on me and my siblings?

"Thank you, Grandfather," I say, relieved my voice doesn't warble. "But my father…" I can't quite keep the bite out of my voice. "My father—"

Alexander waves a dismissive hand and leans forward, eyes gleaming. "Oh, I know what your father has done. I told you, Caleb, I would bring him to heel, like the ungrateful dog that he is. As you've brought me three great gifts, I deliver one to you. Our family will be together again." He claps his hands.

I swivel toward the doors, blood rushing to my head so fast my vision blurs. This can't be happening. Somehow, Luna's hand finds mine, and I clutch it like it's my only lifeline. I hear a *clink-clink* echo along the stone walls before a Nephilim in chains is brought into the room, two guards flanking each of his sides.

His dirty blond hair is darker than Alexander's, and his eyes shine brilliant green, like two fine-cut stones of jade. Anger burns in the liquid depths as he takes in our dinner party, then his gaze falls on me with all the force of a baseball bat to the head.

I have my mother's eyes, her coloring, but the cut of my jaw, my nose, my mouth, the width of my shoulders, my height, it's all him. Suddenly, I want my dagger back so I can carve my father right out of my face, so all that's left is the eyes and hair of my mother. An almost guttural growl escapes my throat as I stare at my deadbeat dad. I'm on my feet before I know it, eyes pinned on my father, who stares back at me with equal animosity.

I hear a faint whoosh, and then pearly gray feathers brush my arms, curling around my body as Luna places a restraining hand on my heaving chest.

"Caleb," Alexander's deep voice penetrates through the fog of rage clouding my brain. I tilt my head, looking at him. "I have brought your father here so he can be punished for his faithlessness, for his abandonment of his children. So you can have justice. This is my gift to you." He motions to the tall woman on the right of my father. She holds out a whip with a metal tip on it. "Go, Caleb. Take it. Mete out your justice."

twenty-two

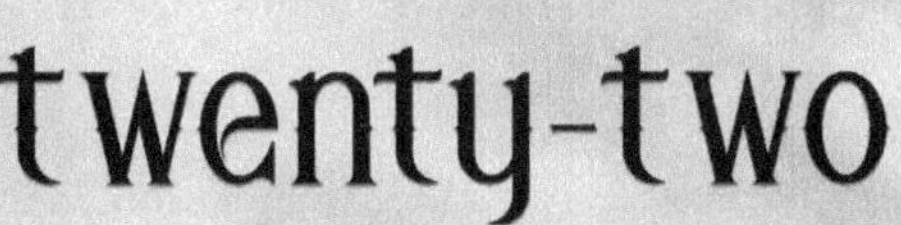

LUNA

MY PULSE THUNDERS IN my ears as I peer between Caleb and the chained man at the other end of the room. His cheeks are scuffed with dirt—the black smudges in stark contrast to the green of his eyes—and he's shirtless, his bare torso sculpted with muscle. I see so much of Caleb in the man's handsome features that his identity was clear to me when he shuffled into the room without Alexander even needing to say it.

I cast a sidelong glance at the other Gray, wondering what he's hoping to achieve with this. The man before us is his *son*. Regardless of his reproductive habits, does Alexander really want to hurt him? I'm inclined to say yes, given what I've already seen him do to his own blood. What's worse is he really does seem to think he's doing Caleb a favor—that handing out judgment in the form of corporal punishment is something his grandson would want.

Unless the person Alexander is actually trying to punish with this display is his grandson. Caleb has already disobeyed him twice, so it's likely Alexander is looking to challenge his loyalty.

This is some kind of test, I'm sure of it. Alexander is acting like he's giving Caleb a gift by presenting his father to him like a sacrificial lamb to be slaughtered, and while he might believe that, I have no doubt he also wants to see if his grandson will finally do what he commands. But unlike Alexander, I know Caleb. He isn't a malicious person, and I can't see him assaulting someone who is defenseless to protect themselves, even if some part of him might think they deserve it. My stomach roils at the mental image of Caleb going through with it…and what might happen if he doesn't.

If he refuses, will Alexander turn the whip on him instead?

Under my fingers, Caleb's body is trembling, his heart racing a mile a minute, and his complexion is ashen, as if the sight of his father has made him physically sick. At Alexander's scrutiny, his expression hardens, and he shrugs me off, stepping out of the protective sheath of my wings.

Keeping his heated gaze fixed ahead, he rolls up his sleeves then skirts the large table, extending his arm toward the female Nephilim, who offers the whip for him to take. I watch as his long fingers close around the braided black handle and hold my breath as he positions himself in front of his father.

When Alexander nods, the two Nephilim guards tug on their prisoner's chains, turning him until his naked back is exposed to the room, facing his son and soon to be punisher. Once again,

I risk a wary glance at Alexander, who meets my startled gaze with a smile before casting his eyes pointedly down at my chair. A silent command for me to sit.

I grimace as understanding consumes me. He expects us to be silent spectators to this torture. To accept his command as law and, in doing so, demonstrate our submission.

Swallowing the bile burning its way up my throat, I sink into my seat and look back at Caleb, watching his movements with anticipation and terror. The braided leather creaks in protest when his fingers tighten, and sweat beads on the back of his neck as he raises his arm, preparing to strike.

The crack of the whip is lightning fast, and a shudder rips through me when it cuts into its intended target, slicing through the top layers of skin. A strangled cry escapes Caleb's father as his body contorts backward, arching against the pain. Rivulets of blood run from the torn flesh like raindrops against glass.

Even from the opposite side of the room, my heightened senses are acutely aware of the fear emanating from Caleb's father, the musty odor of his sweat and the metallic tang of his blood clinging to the inside of my nostrils. I resist the urge to clamp a hand over my mouth, not wanting to betray even the smallest hint of weakness in front of Alexander. Now, more than ever, I'm certain the other Gray is deranged. And while I can empathize with what he's been through between his parents' abandonment and his many years of imprisonment, nothing can excuse the pain he's inflicting. And not just on his son but on Caleb. My stomach sloshes with the fear of what this moment might do to him mentally.

As if reading my mind, Caleb peers over his shoulder, and I can only imagine the horror he must see on my face despite how hard I try to hide it. His own expression remains eerily drawn.

Turning slowly to face his father again, he tosses the whip to the floor by his feet.

"Finished already?" Alexander asks, his tone both scolding and sardonic.

Caleb approaches his grandfather, stopping just before Alexander's seat at the head of the table. "I thank you for the opportunity, Grandfather," he simpers. "This has been the greatest gift I could ask for. But it has also made me realize that this sorry excuse for a Nephilim isn't worth my time and energy…or my vengeance. He's not worthy of your blood. *Our* blood."

Alexander cocks his head to one side at that, brushing a finger along the strong line of his jawbone as his eyes sharpen with interest on his grandson. "Is that so?"

Caleb nods. "You are the only father I need," he declares, the lie falling from his lips with a mind-blowing ease and sincerity.

Alexander shoos away the Nephilim guarding Caleb's father, and without a word, they march from the room, dragging their chained prisoner between them. Although his body is bent and his back streaked with blood, the skin that was torn open like paper from the lash of the whip is now sealed shut. Only the faintest line of pink flesh is visible to show he was whipped at all, and even that is fading quickly.

As the Nephilim shuffles from the room, head dipped low, he doesn't make a sound or even risk a glance at Alexander. Or Caleb. Why won't he speak? Is something forcing this silence upon him—keeping him from acknowledging his own father and son? Or is it a willing decision? A protest?

The only armor he has to protect himself.

As we eat, the room is so quiet I could hear a pin drop, and I wait with bated breath for Alexander to speak, sensing the others' anticipation as well. Nobody dares to break the silence. Alaric doesn't even try to use his power to ease the tension radiating like heat in the room, despite attempting to use it on Ishtar not even an hour ago. I can only imagine he's keeping his gifts on a leash in Alexander's presence to appease him, as if to prove the angel has some sort of claim on his powers. Perhaps even on him.

My eyes narrow on the Gray when he rises from his chair, and my heart jackrabbits against my ribcage as he looms over Caleb, who seems so small and vulnerable in the shadow of the angel. He reaches out a hand toward his grandson, and once again, I imagine every worst case scenario—him strangling Caleb, him ripping out his still beating heart. I imagine everything except what actually happens.

Pulling Caleb into a loving embrace, Alexander smiles. "You say I am the only father you need? Then let it be done…my son."

I swallow my surprise, sparing the quickest of glances at Hammurabi and Alaric. They each look as stunned as I feel. Across from me, Gilgamesh and Ishtar watch the scene unfold with serene smiles plastered on their faces. But, unlike my old history teacher—whose expression seems genuine, much to my confusion—Ishtar is unable to hide the indignation buried in the charcoal pits of her eyes. I can see it written all over her face: the resentment she must feel, not only knowing she'll never be Alexander's number one, but that she's just been outranked by another Nephilim. And a second generation, at that.

A grin tugs at my cheeks at her fury, but I quickly rein it in, forcing a mask of composed calm on my face. When Alexander breaks away from Caleb, he gestures for everyone to stand.

"My friends, let us end the evening with one final toast." He raises his refilled goblet. "To Caleb, my heir, my chosen son, who has proven to be everything his useless father was not."

In unison with everyone else at the table, I pick up the nearest chalice and press the brim to my lips, but I don't take a sip, afraid my churning stomach will only toss the wine back up. Caleb meets my gaze across the table where he stands statue-still beside Alexander, a fresh goblet in his hand, placed there by one of the many mute servants scurrying about like rats.

With dinner dismissed, Alexander excuses himself, pausing only once on his trek to the door to peer over his shoulder at me. When our eyes meet, a morbid chuckle escapes him.

"The events of this evening have me feeling inspired. So

much so that I do believe I know the perfect way to begin your training."

A lump swells in my throat, but I swallow my dread, trying my best to keep my expression neutral. Although I told Caleb I wanted his grandfather to train me—to take advantage of learning from the only other Gray we know of—I'm suddenly doubting that decision. Not that I really think I have much say in the matter. Alexander wants to mold me, and so long as we're here, I have to act pliant, like an untouched lump of clay. Ready and willing.

I bow my head, putting on the most grateful smile I can manage. "I look forward to it."

Alexander says nothing else before departing the room, the first generations following in his wake. Caleb and I don't move a collective muscle until we're certain we're alone.

With a slight jerk of his chin, Caleb signals for me to meet him by the foot of the table. "I have a bad feeling about whatever it is he has in mind for that," he says once we're side by side.

I brush him off. Training with Alexander is tomorrow Luna's problem. "Forget about that. Did he..." I hesitate, lowering my voice to a barely-there breath. "Did your grandfather just *adopt* you?"

Caleb rakes a hand through his hair. "I honestly have no fucking idea. I just said what I had to. I did—" His voice breaks, and he looks down at his shaking hands, as if he'll see his father's blood on his skin.

"I know," I murmur, covering his palms with my own and interlacing our fingers, squeezing. "It's okay."

"Is it?" he whispers, shaking his head. "I wanted to hit him. I wanted to *hurt* him. I could've killed him for what he did to my mom. To me."

"Yet you stopped," I remind him. Rising onto my toes, I plant a kiss on his lips. "You stopped."

His eyes shift to mine, and the emptiness I find in their depths is hauntingly familiar. I've seen that emptiness before. I've felt it inside me more times than I can count. And because I've experienced it, I know all too well what Caleb must be asking himself. The one question that still permeates my thoughts, even now, even knowing what I know.

The question of why we weren't enough for the parents who let us go.

I rouse cocooned in Caleb's arms, blinking bleary eyes awake to the sight of a golden scroll, complete with red tassel, on the table just beside my head. At first, I don't reach for it, not wanting to disturb Caleb, who slept so fitfully last night, tormented by images of his father and the parasitic plague of his guilt, if his slumbering mutterings were any indication of what he dreamt about. As I lie still, staring at the gleaming golden handles sticking out of each end of the scroll, my curiosity niggles at the back of my brain until I can't take the not knowing for a single second longer. I reach out a tentative hand, brushing my fingertips over the parchment.

"What is it?" Caleb mumbles sleepily beside me.

My eyes dart over my shoulder, meeting his sleep-soaked gaze, as a frown tugs down my lips. I really didn't want to wake him up. He needed some rest and, selfishly, I like the feel of him sleeping beside me too much.

"Not sure. But I'm guessing it's from your grandfather."

Caleb sits up, glaring at the scroll in my hand as if it's a ticking time bomb. Shifting, I lean against the headboard and carefully unfurl the roll.

"It's a request for my presence in the throne room," I say, silently scanning the swooping, elegant script.

"More like a summons," Caleb growls, reading over my shoulder.

I exhale through my nose. Looks like tomorrow Luna's problem just became today Luna's problem.

"Well," I grumble, sliding off the bed, "I better not keep His Majesty waiting."

After a quick wash with the paltry basin provided in our room in place of a bathroom, I pull on the fresh clothes one of the serving Nephilim left out for me, tugging the gold embellished tunic over my head and pairing it at the waist with a jewel-encrusted leather belt and matching cobalt blue slippers. Once I'm dressed, I give Caleb a long goodbye kiss, draw in a deep breath, and make for the door. Although I can tell he doesn't want me to go, he doesn't voice his protests. We both know they wouldn't do any good.

As I walk down the long hallway toward the throne room, I glance down at my extravagant attire—the second lavish outfit I've had to don since arriving in Alexander's domain. I can't help feeling like a doll he's dressing up for show, like I'm stepping into a role he's written for me to play.

When I enter the cavernous room I've been beckoned to, I find the other Gray already waiting for me, draped across his throne like a blanket. Our eyes clash across the empty space as he rises, his broad wings fanning out behind him, and it takes all the self-restraint I can muster not to inch back as he crosses the space between us. We might both be angels, but Alexander is an avalanche, and I am little more than a snowball.

"Good morning, young Morningstar," he croons with a jovial smile.

I balk for a moment before stamping a forced grin on my face. "So, what kind of training are we going to be doing?"

Alexander chuckles, steepling his fingers in front of his chest. "My, my. Are you always so eager?"

"I mean, you *did* promise to help me learn to control my powers…hmm…how long ago was it?"

The Gray lets out an unrestrained laugh. "Touché, little dove. Well then, let's begin."

He leads me into the center of the room and then pivots

to face me, raising his right hand, palm up. A crimson flame bursts to life in his grasp, casting ruby streaks along his fingers.

"I have seen inside your mind, my young friend, and as such, I have seen what you're capable of." The flames extinguish as his hand curls into a fist. He then nods once, glancing down at my arm, which hangs like a limp noodle by my side. "Come," he urges. "Let us see your fire."

Closing my eyes, I hold up my hand, imagining the heat building first in my veins and then growing until it's boiling over through my skin. When I open my eyes, flames explode across my flattened palm, burning the same red as blood.

"Good," Alexander purrs, his voice dripping with praise. His eyes cut to the side as footsteps resound off the stone to my left. "Now…wield it."

Goosebumps pimple my flesh as I follow his gaze, my stomach dropping at the sight of the barechested Nephilim ten feet away. He faces us, his hands tucked behind his back.

My flame sputters out as realization takes hold. "What?" I gasp, looking back at Alexander. "You mean—"

He shakes his head. "Do not concern yourself with his well-being. He is a Nephilim. He will heal."

I glance between them, aghast. "But—"

"A sheep will never lead an army of lions. But a lion may lead an army of sheep." Alexander steps closer, planting a firm hand on my shoulder. His fingers dig into my skin through my tunic. "Become a lion, Luna."

I cower beneath his hard stare. When I don't move, he sighs, lowering his hand.

"If it will ease your mind, he has volunteered for this task. Now, wield your flame," he repeats, his voice taking on a hard edge.

He gives me a not-so-gentle nudge toward my victim, and I recoil at his touch, sick to my stomach at what it is he's asking of me. His words replay in my ears—a silent warning not to disobey. But what if I do? Will Alexander cease my training if I refuse?

Or will he do something far worse?

The answer hits me when I look over my shoulder, and his piercing gaze crawls over my face, wordlessly screaming his disapproval. If I don't act now, if I don't do what he says, he'll put me down for my disobedience, or worse. *Far* worse. Like hurt Caleb again.

And I can't let that happen.

Anger burns like heat in my veins, and I let that rage, that fury, ignite me. Calling it to the surface, I ball the flames in my hands and clenching my teeth, I project the hatred in my heart outward, picturing Alexander's face on my target. The Nephilim screams as the fire consumes him, the inferno charring his exposed torso and flooding the room with the nauseating odor of cooked flesh. As he collapses to the floor in a thrashing fit of agony, Alexander applauds behind me.

"Bravo!" he cries as I scream on the inside. "Bravo, little dove.

I knew you would not disappoint."

Quivering like a leaf in the wind, I drop my arms and stare down at my trembling fingers. The flames thin to weak embers before fading completely, leaving my pale skin cool and untouched.

The smell permeating the room triggers my gag reflex, and I slam my hand over my nose, pinching my nostrils and dry heaving once beneath my fingers. The whole time, my eyes remain glued to the Nephilim, who—just as Alexander promised—is beginning to heal, the black crispy flesh flaking away to reveal fresh ivory skin underneath. Grunting, he lifts himself off the floor.

"I…" Tears flood my eyes. "I'm so sor—"

"Apologies are for the weak-willed, young Morningstar," Alexander cajoles, waving away the man before positioning himself before me again. Planting a fingertip under my chin, he forces my horrified gaze to meet his. "And you, my little dove, are not weak."

A hysterical squeak bubbles to my lips, half-crazed giggle and half-broken sob. No, I'm not weak. The terrible things I've done throughout my life have proven that. Even when I always felt so close to the edge, I never felt weak. Powerless, yes. But not weak. If anything, I was afraid of myself and what I knew I was capable of.

I stare down at my hands, envisioning the red flames curling around my fingers and imagining the way they seared into the

Nephilim's flesh, burning through him as if he were mortal. Using my powers on others in this vile way, for torment and torture, regardless of if they are willing—is that what Alexander views as strength?

Revulsion crawls over my skin.

If this is strength, I'm not sure I want it.

Alexander's lingering gaze softens a little. "I know what you are thinking, little dove, but you must not fear what you are."

My hands clench into fists at my sides. "Because fear is for the weak?" I spit.

He considers me for a moment before shaking his head. "Fear is natural, but it is also a weapon. One you must learn to wield if you are to defend yourself against those who would seek to imprison you. You might be a Gray, but there are angels and demons far older than you who would tear your mind to shreds if you let them."

Like what you did to Caleb? I nearly shout, stopping myself just before the words breach my lips.

Alexander narrows his eyes. "When the time for war comes, we will all need to be merciless. If you are to be an asset to me, I need to know you can do that."

He averts his focus to the doorway, and I follow his gaze, my heart jumping into my throat at the hiss of chains scraping across the floor. My eyes widen when the Nephilim guards from last night step into the room with Caleb's dad sandwiched between them.

"Wh—" I swallow, clearing my throat. "Why is *he* here?"

"Break him," Alexander commands as casually as if he's commenting about the weather.

Horror grips my lungs in an iron-clad fist. "What?"

Alexander steps forward until he's uncomfortably close and leans in, whispering in my ear. Wisps of his golden hair brush my cheek. "Break into his mind. I know you can. After all… you've done it before."

A startled gasp rips from my throat as my foster parents' faces flood my mind. I see them, twisted and bent on the floor, their faces contorted in pain and terror, blood soaking into the small woven rug under the coffee table and spreading across the floorboards of the living room in their house. I broke their minds. I broke *them*. I know it.

But how does Alexander?

My lower lip wobbles, the guilt like a hand around my throat, squeezing tightly. Alexander grazes the back of his hand along the side of my face, a sympathetic smile curling his mouth.

"You forget that I was there, at the Serapeum, always listening," he murmurs, combing the hair back from my face. "Always in your head. You let me in so easily, little dove, and unlike my grandson, who tried and failed to see inside that precious mind, I could hear your thoughts so clearly. And your words."

My eyes bulge, and I gape at him, uncertain which part of that terrifies me the most. Knowing Caleb tried to read my mind or that Alexander might still be able to now.

At my horrified expression, he chuckles. "Worry not. Your thoughts are safe from me. While an angel's mind is naturally protected from Nephilim, being unbound has offered you some protection even against those of us like yourself. It would take great effort to break into your mind and I desire your trust, little dove."

"And the others?" I ask tentatively. "What about them?" If Alexander can read their minds, he'll know we aren't actually here to support him.

I try not to let my relief show when he nods. "Also safe," he assures me. "It is not a simple thing to see inside the mind of a first generation. Their celestial link is strong and not diluted by their mortal ties. They, too, have some natural protection in place bolstered by millennia of training. As for Caleb, the strength of his blood runs deep. Besides," he says, shrugging ruefully. "If I had been in one of their minds, you would know."

A chill passes over my skin as I'm struck once again by the mental image of Caleb convulsing on the floor. But Alexander wasn't trying to read Caleb's mind in that moment. He was trying to break it. To bend him into unwilling obedience.

Just as he now wants me to do to his son.

He extends an arm toward Caleb's father, whose gemstone eyes are dull with acceptance. He doesn't seem afraid, which somehow makes what Alexander is asking of me so much worse.

"Now, show me how powerful you can be," the Gray instructs.

I stiffen at his words. I don't want to hurt anyone, not even

Caleb's father, who probably deserves whatever thrashing he gets. I don't want to do this. This wasn't what I had in mind when I told Caleb I wanted his grandfather to train me. No wonder he was so wary of the idea last night.

Alexander exhales, and his eyes harden on mine, impatience leaching into his tone when he adds, "Or, perhaps, I should fetch Caleb for me to demonstrate for you?"

My wings tear free of my back at his threat, my chest heaving as a rush of power and rage thrum underneath my skin like an electric current. Amusement tugs at Alexander's cheeks and he smirks, gesturing once more to his restrained son.

"I will not ask again," he says. "Do it, or we end our training here."

Sweat dampens my skin as I refocus my gaze, torn between the nausea churning my gut and what I have to do to survive and protect myself from everyone who has decided that being different somehow makes me dangerous. I don't want to hurt anyone, but I also know if I don't do what Alexander commands, my disobedience will only give him cause to hurt Caleb again. He might be the Gray's heir, but Alexander's actions have already proven that sharing his blood doesn't make him invulnerable, and I don't doubt for a moment that the angel will do whatever he deems necessary to force me to comply. Because he doesn't want me as an equal.

He wants me as a soldier he can control.

Control. That's what this is about. Control. Isn't that exactly what I've wanted since Alaric first brought me to the Serapeum?

What Alexander said is true: I am afraid of what I'm capable of, and learning that control he promised me all those months ago would ease those worries. Besides, I need to be able to defend myself against the Council when they come for me again. Mammon might not have broken my mind, but he broke my spirit, and he knows enough about me—about my weaknesses—to use my emotions against me. I don't want to be defenseless like that again.

Bracing myself, I stare at Caleb's father. *I can do this. I don't have to hurt him.* A piercing ache throbs behind my temples as I strain, focusing on reaching past the confines of his skull and into the depths of his mind where I envision his thoughts like a feast laid out before me, fruit ripe for the taking.

But as I reach out, I sense a strange change in the air, and suddenly, all I can picture is my foster parents on the floor, unmoving, in pools of their own blood. I did that. I broke them.

Just like I can feel myself breaking Caleb's father.

His mouth falls open on a silent scream, a crimson stream trickling from his nose as he falls to the floor, his body seizing. No matter how hard I try, I can't stop, my own mind trapped in a memory I can't escape.

"Please," he breathes. The first word I've heard him say. But I can't tell what he's asking. Please stop? Please kill me? I can't figure it out, and I can't let him go. I try, but I can't, my fingers caught in the snare of his mind, his terror a palpable scent I can taste.

In the moment before the link snaps and I realize I've gone too far to turn back, all I see is Caleb—not in my thoughts but in the distorted chaos of his father's. As he replays that moment when the whip tore into the flesh of his back, I can sense his recognition of Caleb, but he felt nothing beyond that. Not shame. Not remorse. Just an underlying frustration that he finally got caught. The only fear he felt was toward his angel father—who was just as absent a parent as he was—and now, in this moment, toward me.

A sharp, cracking sound cuts my hold on him, and I watch, mortified, as blood curdles on the stone beneath his unmoving body like old milk.

"He…" I stagger forward a step, a little light-headed and unnerved by his stillness. "Is he…"

Alexander places a hand on my shoulder, drawing my watery gaze to his face. "Worry not, little dove," he says gently, as if consoling a weeping child. Pride burns in the glowing depths of his eyes. "Have you forgotten what I taught you when our minds first crossed paths? Remember the moth. Remember what I told you. *Anastēson auton*," he purrs before grinning. "It will be as if it never happened."

twenty-three

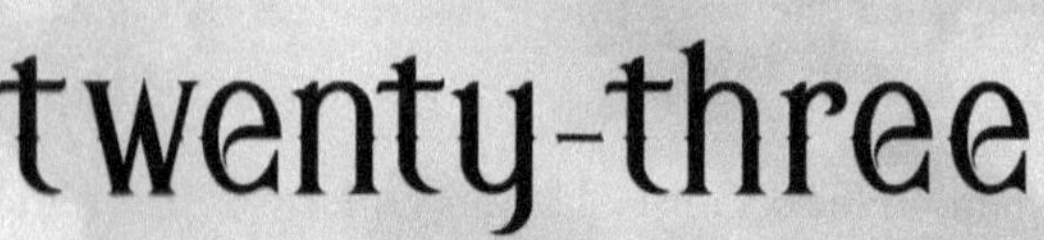

CALEB

MY EYES DART AROUND as I silently count the Nephilim I see throughout the citadel. I try to suss out their age and power. The weaker ones I'm not that worried about, although they do pose a problem in numbers.

After Luna left for her training session with Alexander, I decided to go do something useful. We need a general idea of the current forces residing here so we can find the best route out. Secretly, I don't think there is a best route—any path to freedom will come with blood and death.

Besides, if I don't find something to occupy my mind, that tight ball of sourness embedded in my guts will grow and grow until it consumes me. I'm tired of replaying the moment in my head where I take the whip and strike my father. The cracking of leather and pop of sliced flesh. The long, bloody welt carved into muscle. When I close my eyes, I see it over and over again. It's a helluva way to meet your dad.

I'm still so pissed at him—enraged is more like it. It's not like I never received good old-fashioned corporal punishment at Babel before, but whipping an unarmed, shackled man is not who I am. I cut off Mammon's wing without a second thought and would do it again in a heartbeat, but he's a fucking Archdemon and much stronger than me. If what happened with Pops was a fair fight, if he took a swing at me, I would've loved to dish out a beating, but what happened... Bile burns my throat, and I give a frantic shake of my head, trying to forget that popping sound. My dad is a bastard, but not even he deserved that. At least my reasoning appealed to Alexander. My father isn't worth the shame of breaking my own moral code, even though that one hit carries plenty of sickening guilt. But I was genuinely terrified Gramps would take me over like a puppet and carry out the punishment as he saw fit.

And it might make me a coward, but I don't think I can endure that again. At least not so soon. My mind still feels like raw hamburger put through a grinder. I hate that I'm afraid, that I took the whip at all, but until I get my head on right, until we get out of here, it's just a burden I have to carry. I just hope the weight won't fracture my sanity. This uncertainty, this vulnerability, this fear, I'm not used to it, and I sure as hell don't like it.

I don't know where my dad is now, and I'm not sure I care. When he looked at me last night, there was no regret, no warmth. Just anger and damaged pride. I did all I could for him. He's my grandfather's problem now, and I think he'll discover the sooner he falls in line, the less he'll suffer. Alexander is done with his bullshit. I just hope I'm far, far away when Gramps bends him to his will because I think my dad is a stubborn asshole, and I don't want to be put in the role of punisher again.

Sparring would help me feel better. I need to find Hammurabi and let him wail on me for a while. The pain will feel good. The Serapeum made me soft, and I need to get back into fighting shape if I'm going to be useful. Even those few months here before I managed to free Luna weren't filled with fighting, just shadowing Alexander and lurking in the corners. My fingers clench for a moment, and I grit my teeth. I miss my dagger. Yeah, yeah, it wasn't mine, but I got damn fond of it. It evened the odds against much more powerful creatures than me. Now, I just feel so naked, like every piece of me is exposed for a bigger predator to tear into. I hate it.

Stepping into the sun in an outer courtyard, I ball my fists as I see Ishtar sauntering my way. I'd like to spend some time fighting her, too. She's back in black, her serviceable boots and cargo pants a far cry from her gown at dinner last night. She stops before me, offering a cold smile.

"What are you doing out and about, princeling?" she coos, and I give her a sweet smile.

"Trying to be a good little heir and get back into shape," I say, the half-truth easily spilling from my lips. Shrugging, I ask, "Have you seen Hammurabi? I want to go a few rounds with him."

Ishtar scowls at me, an offended expression etched across her face. She puts her hands on her hips. "Caleb, I can instruct you in the art of war just as well as that old bore. As Alexander's general, I should have been the first person you sought."

I hide my grin, knowing my preference for Hammurabi would piss her off. "Yeah, I guess, but we're not exactly friends anymore, are we?" A bitter smile twists my lips. "Well, I guess we were never friends, given that you were my teacher, but I always respected you, thought of you as family. I was just stupid enough to believe you felt the same way about me."

The goddess of love and war's eyes brim with pity as she regards me. "Foolish child," she scolds. "My feelings for you are inconsequential, don't you understand? You're young so you can't fathom what it is like to give yourself to a cause, to fight in wars, to bleed. You've been pampered in Babel, assured of your place in life with your Dark status. But there should be no Light or Dark. The divide must fall, and this is more important to me than anything, even foolish boys whom I care for."

I scoff at her. "I call bullshit. Yeah, you may care about the cause, but Alexander is your absolute truth. You wouldn't blink if he slit my throat," I accuse, surprising hurt gripping my chest. I did love her. She was my Dark family, and the fact that I can no longer call her that… Yeah, it hurts like a bitch.

"I would regret your death," Ishtar says, confirming my

words, "but no, I would not interfere. Alexander isn't cruel. If he decided to kill you, then you earned your death. Although I wouldn't stop him, I will warn you, Caleb. He won't tolerate further disobedience from you. Think on that before any more rebellious thoughts enter your mind."

Her words nettle me, and I ignore the sick feeling taking root in the pit of my stomach. "I brought him a fucking angel. I think we're good."

She sneers at me. "Yes, you brought him your lover. How convenient for you. Your grandfather might not be so enamored with you if she doesn't live up to her potential."

"Convenient? Breaking into a supernatural prison and facing Mammon was hardly convenient. But I did it. I got Luna out when you all did nothing. Yes, I love her, but *I* proved to Alexander that I can be an asset in the upcoming war. Besides, jealousy doesn't look good on you, Goddess," I say, smirking. "You're afraid Luna will threaten your special status with Gramps. At the end of the day, she's an angel—a *Gray*—and you're just a Nephilim."

Ishtar flushes, her mouth quivering, and if she were a cartoon character, steam would spew from her ears. She blurs, suddenly in my face, her nose almost touching mine, but I still have a few inches on her impressive height. "Need I remind you, little one, that you, too, are a Nephilim, and not even a first generation. You break easier than me." Her lips curl, a cruel edge to them. "And I have been loyal to your grandfather for thousands of years, whereas you betrayed him the moment you met with your obsession with the girl. He might welcome you in his good graces—for now—but he won't ever forget. He will always have doubts about you while he has complete faith in me. I will always have his ear to whisper in."

"And I'll always be his blood," I remind her. "That's something you can never be."

The air shimmers with restrained violence, and I know she wants to beat me bloody, break a few of my bones to prove her superiority. But she can't. Whether she likes it or not, I'm Alexander's heir—at least for the moment. And while he certainly wouldn't mind a few training montages, he won't stand for her abusing me. Not that I would just lie down and let her. Yeah, I'm a second generation, but that doesn't mean I'm weak, no matter what she says. I can make her bleed, too, and she knows it.

Her face shutters, and she takes a step back, cold eyes roaming over me. Snaking an arm behind her back, she brings out a knife and hands it to me. I take it with exaggerated slowness, not sure what game she's playing now.

"Hammurabi has gotten old and lazy," she says. "Come, show me what you can do with a blade." She slides another knife out of a sheath strapped to her hip.

I snort. "I dare you to say that to his face."

"Oh, I forgot to add fat," Ishtar says, an evil grin curving her lips.

I chuckle. I can't help it. This banter reminds me of who my teacher used to be, but I guess that was really never her. The laughter dies, but I manage, "Yeah, his eight pack has been reduced to a six."

"Come, child." Ishtar tosses her braid over her shoulder, her feet automatically sliding into a fighting stance, weight balancing on the balls of her feet, dagger gleaming in the sun.

My fingers clench my own dagger's hilt. Well, it could've been worse. She could've wanted to spar with an ax. I balance on the balls of my feet, adrenaline flooding my body and wiping away my fear. I like to fight, and although I'm no longer Ishtar's favorite boy, I know she won't seriously injure me. Not when I'm in Alexander's favor once more. As quick as an adder, she strikes, and I barely manage to deflect her.

Then we dance, back and forth across the hard-packed earth. Tight muscles loosen, become pliant, and I settle into a familiar, deadly pattern. Ishtar lands a hit on my upper bicep, the blade parting my skin in a shallow cut. I wince, already healing, but as we continue to swipe at one another, she begins methodically slicing me to ribbons. It's apparent that I'm out of practice and slower than I used to be, just a fraction, but a fraction might as well be an hour when you're dealing with someone as lethal as Ishtar. Blood soaks through my T-shirt from cuts decorating my torso, dripping onto the dirt at my feet. But I refuse to give up until I land a hit.

She works me back and forth over the courtyard, and I start to feel fatigue grip me. Gasping, I let her in too close, and I see her triumphant smile right before I step aside, her weight carrying her forward, and I slash at her vulnerable back, blade kissing her skin. I hear her surprised grunt before I jump back and toss the dagger on the ground. I raise my hands in surrender, my breath coming hard and fast.

Ishtar whirls around, growling, then her eyes fall to the knife. Lifting one brow, she locks eyes with me and wipes her blade on her pants before putting it away. "Hammurabi isn't the only one who has grown slow and lazy," she says then she twists, trying to see the wound on her back. "Although that was a nice move." Her voice is grudging and I smile.

"I couldn't stop until I scored at least one hit," I say, placing my hands on my knees. I feel my body working feverishly to repair all the damage. I'll be good as new in a few minutes.

"I could never accuse you of being a coward," Ishtar says, her smile more a baring of teeth. "But I still don't trust you, child. I'll be watching you. Run along now." She waves a hand, and I narrow my eyes at her, but I won't get any more spying done right now. Not with Ishtar about.

"See you around," I say, deliberately turning my back on her. I feel the sting of her eyes on my skin as I leave the courtyard.

By the time I make it back to my room, my skin is smooth and unblemished once more. I no longer feel tired, but I reek of blood and sweat and desperately need a bath. We still don't have showers here, only a crude pumping system. Man, I hope if we're stuck here longer, someone gets this modern plumbing thing moving. I wasn't born a thousand years ago, and I enjoy modern conveniences.

I push open my door to find Luna sitting on the edge of the bed, slouched, her wings drooping around her. My heart rate jump-starts, and my breath hitches at her unnatural stillness. She hears my entrance and glances up, but her gaze is disturbingly blank, like she knows I'm there but doesn't really see me. I take a cautious step toward her, afraid to make any sudden moves. I'm not quite sure where her mind is, and she could accidentally hurt me if she thinks I'm a threat.

"Luna," I say, keeping my voice soft and soothing. "Are you okay? Did something happen with Alexander?" A myriad of images flick through my mind like cards on an old-fashioned Rolodex, each more horrific than the one before. A lot of bad things could've happened during her training session with Gramps, but it does me no good to guess. I'll just freak myself out more.

She blinks, sweeping lashes fluttering against creamy skin. Focusing on me at last, I see her hazel eyes are haunted, and a madness I haven't seen since she was imprisoned encroaches. My heart clenches at the sight. I can't let her slide down that slope again.

"Goldilocks," I prod, "talk to me. Let me help you."

A great wail escapes her, shredding the quiet, and I'm kneeling before her without realizing I moved. Luna shakes her head back and forth as her hands find me and cling.

"I broke him," she sobs. "I swear I didn't know—I didn't mean to…" Her eyes latch onto mine, pleading for understanding. "You have to believe me, Caleb. I would never, not on purpose."

Her words tumble fast from her lips, and I can't make sense of them. "I know you would never hurt anyone on purpose," I say. "Who do you think you broke?"

"I broke him," she repeats, shuddering. "I wasn't trying to, but I still broke him…because that's what I do. I break everything."

Shit, she's truly lost it. "Who did you break? Did Alexander make you see something that wasn't real?"

"Your father," she clarifies, fat tears plopping down her cheeks, agony in every note of her voice. "I killed him."

She killed my father? My jaw slackens as icy shock freezes me in place. That memory reel of bringing down the whip starts playing again, that awful crack and the wet sound of flesh splitting open like overripe fruit. My father is dead and the only encounter I had with him was beating him. My stomach churns, and I grit my teeth, willing myself to get it together. I can't lose it now when Luna is on the verge of drowning.

"You hate me," she cries, releasing my hands and wrapping her arms around her middle.

I place both my hands on her thighs, giving them a gentle squeeze. "I don't hate you. I could never hate you. Tell me what happened." I'm proud of how calm I sound.

She stares at my hands, a shudder rolling through her. "At the Serapeum, Alexander was listening. He knew I had done it before. I didn't know at the time," she says quickly. I raise my brows. "My foster parents, but it was an accident, I swear."

I nod. "I believe you."

"He wanted me to do it again. To show him how powerful I can be, and I didn't understand what he was asking. But then…he brought out your dad. And I…I was worried what Alexander might do if I refused, so I told myself just to look. That I didn't have to hurt him. But then I remembered my foster parents." Her whole body trembles. "I don't understand how much power I have." She raises her head, her tear-streaked face breaking my heart. "I feel like it's only been a trickle before, and now it's an ocean. I got wrapped up in the memory and lost control." She bends, burying her face against my hands. "I didn't mean to, Caleb. Please forgive me."

I stroke her hair, a slight tremor in my fingers that I hope she doesn't notice. "There's nothing to forgive. This is on Alexander. He knew what he was doing and you didn't. He killed his own son—"

A hysterical giggle escapes her and I still. "But your dad isn't dead anymore, that's the thing! I killed him, and Alexander just waved a hand…" The giggles morph into sobs again. "He just rose up, Caleb, like nothing had happened, but the look on his face—I'll never wipe it from my mind."

I go cold, my hands clammy. I shake my head, trying to make

sense of it. "What do you mean? Alexander…*resurrected* him?"

Luna nods. "Yes, and it was like—it was like it was *nothing* to him."

Icy sweat trickles down my neck. I sit back on my heels, stunned. Yeah, resurrection is a Dark trait, but we don't actually use it. I make clay figures and give them life, but bringing back the dead, bringing back a *person*, that's a big fucking no-no. That's power that shouldn't be messed with—even the Morningstar has never brought someone back. Dead is dead. That's the natural order of the world.

For a moment, I can't speak, words forming and dying on my lips. Luna's wings flare out, revealing her agitation at my silence. Great, she's barely holding on and now I'm losing it. But I don't know what to say, my tongue tied in knots. A new thing for me. I live to be glib. What I wouldn't give for a sarcastic one-liner to defuse the tension.

"Caleb? Your dad isn't dead. That's a good thing, right?" Luna presses. "Talk to me. You're scaring me."

Get your shit together, Caleb. "What Alexander did is… unnatural," I begin, shaking my head. "Darks have that power, but we don't use it. And not because it's not tempting—if something ever happened to my mom, I'd want to bring her back in a heartbeat. But—and I can't believe I'm saying this— that's a power for the Creator alone. Some shit we have no business playing with."

A wounded expression paints her face. "But…back at the

Serapeum, I resurrected a moth. That means I'm unnatural."

Goddammit, I'm butchering this. "No, what you did was an accident. You literally had no clue who or what you were. That was just your power going haywire," I assure her, bending forward once more, so I can take her hands. "There's nothing unnatural about you. Lights give us shit for giving life to inanimate objects, and we give 'em the middle finger, but even Darks stay away from raising the dead. Other than it being something reserved for the Creator, I don't know if when you resurrect someone…they come back right."

"What do you mean, like they're a zombie?" Luna asks, horrified.

An involuntary chuckle escapes me. "No, not like they need to eat brains now, but I think if you were dead and at peace, to be ripped back into the painful world of the living would have to fuck with you. Especially if you died in a traumatic way. That has to permanently mark you."

"Oh," Luna says in a small voice. "I never thought…"

Cupping her face, I give her a short, soft kiss. "Goldilocks, I get it. Like I said, you didn't do anything wrong, but now that we know Alexander is messing with raising people from the dead, it just makes things more complicated."

She rests her forehead against my shoulder. "How?"

"If he gets his war, what's to stop him from resurrecting his troops? Do you really think he's going to save that trick just for family members?" I say, stroking her head.

"Not if it looks like he's losing," Luna says, a shiver racing over her skin.

I nod. "We really need to get out of here."

twenty-four

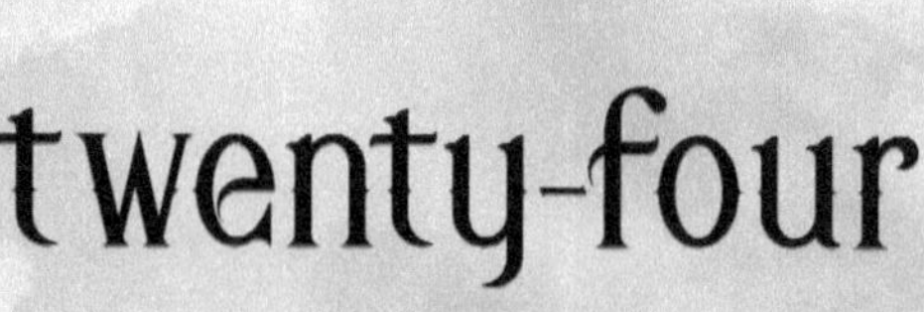

LUNA

CALEB AND I ARE once again summoned by a mute servant for dinner, who bestows us with fresh evening wear for the occasion—black for Caleb and gold for me, as if to indicate our worth and rank to Alexander. The suit and dress we're each respectively given resemble last night's outfits but with variations. Caleb's ensemble remains mostly the same, aside from some added violet accents on the lapels, while mine features more elaborate changes. Unlike the dress I wore yesterday, the shimmering satin pools in a plunging neckline that makes me feel naked, exposing far more of me than I'm comfortable with, and the beading that previously draped across my upper arms is replaced by a delicate shawl of gold-dusted feathers that eerily resemble an angel's.

Caleb's eyes betray his interest as they crawl across my exposed clavicle and dip to my cleavage, lingering there for a moment. My skin heats under the caress of his gaze, and I clear my throat, unsure what to say. Since confessing to accidentally killing his father, the air between us is charged with tension, and not in a way that I like. He might have said he's not angry, that there's nothing to forgive, but I can't escape the guilt bearing down on my chest. If it wasn't for me, if it wasn't for what I did, his father wouldn't have died.

And Alexander wouldn't have brought him back.

"I don't know if when you resurrect someone…they come back right."

I shiver at the memory of Caleb's words, every one like a hook in my thoughts, always tugging at me, forcing me to face the very real severity of our situation. We're in way over our heads, even with Hammurabi and Alaric as our allies. Hell, even with my parents somewhere out there, waiting to help us, it's becoming alarmingly clear we can't take on Alexander. Not now. Not with the numbers he has at his disposal.

And not if he's willing to resort to powers meant only for the Creator to win.

"Goldilocks."

I startle at Caleb's familiar endearment, his raspy tone shaking me free of my thoughts. When I meet his gaze, his eyes are hooded.

"You good?" he asks, taking a step closer to me.

I nod but don't dare let myself speak, afraid my voice will break under the weight of my fluctuating emotions. Neither of us have said much since this morning—the odd word here and there as he held me, the hours passing by in a quiet lull, but nothing of substance, both too mentally drained to talk. Now, though, we need to put on our game faces before heading back into the lion's den.

"Hey." He knocks me under the chin with his finger, tilting my face up. "I love you. You believe that, right?"

Tears blur my vision, and a lump blocks my throat until even swallowing is a struggle. Repeating the same words I said to Alaric up on the mountain when we spoke about Alexander, I whisper, "Despite everything?"

"Despite *nothing*," he bites back, looping his arm around my waist and pulling me to him until his shirt brushes the bare skin of my chest. His breath is hot on my face as he growls, "Nothing could ever make me not love you. Nothing."

Before I can retort, his mouth is on mine, parting my lips with his tongue in a kiss that steals the very breath from my lungs. Warmth spreads through me, melting my inhibitions and self-pity until my fingers are grasping in his hair with a desperation I can't seem to control. When I squeeze, my hands tightening around the strands, he gasps into my mouth, and I devour the sound.

Like last night, my wings are on full display, and Caleb takes advantage of that, grazing a fingertip along the bend, coaxing a shiver from me. His other hand moves lower, his touch heating my blood to a boil, but to my dismay, we're interrupted by a sharp knock on the door. Caleb groans, irritation creasing his face, as I relax my hands and take a step back. No sooner do we separate than Ishtar lets herself into the room, uninvited.

With a delicate sniff, she glances between us, looking us each up and down with keen appraisal. Her nose crinkles. "You are late," she drawls with that practiced boredom. "It is not wise to keep the Great waiting."

Caleb rolls his eyes. "Creator forbid we miss out on the hors d'oeuvres."

Ishtar, for all her posturing, lets slip the tiniest smile at his comment. When she catches me staring, her expression turns sullen. "I would not delay any longer if I were you."

She stalks from the room with the finesse of a runway model, the black gown encasing her body so skintight that I find it hard to breathe just looking at her. Along one leg, a slit runs from ankle to hip bone, dangerously close to revealing far more of the goddess than I'd like to see.

Beside me, Caleb sighs and runs a hand through his hair, tidying the disarrayed strands. Then straightening his jacket, he moves to follow his teacher out into the hallway.

"Caleb." I grab his wrist, stopping him. When he looks back at me, a blush burns my entire body. "I love you, too," I mutter. "Just in case it wasn't obvious."

His eyes light up at my words, and taking my face in his hands, he pulls me in for another kiss. This one is more gentle than the last, and yet there's an urgency to it that sends a vibration of panic racing through me, as if this is the last time he'll do it. He nips at my bottom lip before pulling back.

"I'm going to get you out of here. I promise."

"Together," I remind him, staring up into his eyes. I don't like the uncertainty I glimpse in their depths. "We go together," I repeat.

He hesitates a second too long before nodding.

Gripping my hand, he leads me out into the hallway where we follow the familiar path to the citadel's lush dining hall. Just like yesterday, the space is lit with candles and the table is laden with a feast fit for kings. Given Alexander's chosen company, I suppose it is.

I cow under the intensity of Alexander's gaze as we approach the table, but Caleb—as cool and collected as always—doesn't even flinch.

"Apologies for our tardiness, Grandfather," he says. "We lost track of the time."

Alexander responds with a sly grin, and he tilts his head, propping his chin on his fist. "Who wouldn't with our lovely Luna looking so tempting?"

Caleb tenses at Alexander's use of the word *our* but says nothing, guiding me to my seat with one hand planted against the small of my back. As we settle at our places, I fold my wings in behind me and lock eyes with Alaric, who is once again dressed in a sleek suit and wearing a dour expression like he's on his way to a funeral. He sits at the far end of the table, as if whoever decided the seating arrangements thought it best to keep him and Alexander as far apart from each other as possible. From the way he white-knuckles his goblet and glares across the place settings at our host, I take it something must've happened between them. Either that or he's just as unhappy as Caleb with Alexander's word choice.

Dinner passes by at a snail's pace. Meaningless small talk fills the silence, and the only one at the table who isn't fazed by the strained hush flooding the room is Hammurabi, who tears at his dinner like someone who's starving and has probably had one too many to drink. Then again, I'd probably get drunk, too, if I was the only one forced to go topless to dinner. He's dressed in old Babylonian garb, and even I can tell he hates it. After millennia of experiencing societal changes, I don't blame him for preferring the comfort of modern day fashion to what was normal in his time.

When dessert is finally placed before me and it seems like we're nearing the end of this torture, the doors to the dining hall burst open. All eyes swing to the beautiful woman who enters the room, dressed in stiletto heels, chic high-waisted slacks, and a fashionable burgundy leather jacket, which sits just above her trim waist. But where others might focus on her perfect cheekbones or regal updo of black ringlets, I can't tear my gaze away from her undulating aura. The shadows lapping over her skin pulse with wisdom and age. She's ancient, and the power radiating from her is immense, on par even with the Archdemons I've met.

"Ah, Lilith," Alexander trills, raising his goblet to greet her. "I was wondering when you'd return."

My pulse stumbles under my skin, thrown off tempo, like a singer who's forgotten the words. Since I first heard about Lilith, I've wanted to meet her; she could be the key to getting answers about my parents and birth. But now, as her presence seems to fill every corner in the room, I remember what Alaric told me. Lilith might have been friends with my mother— perhaps she still is—but she also lost her wings for supporting Alexander when the rest of the Council stood against him. She's loyal to Caleb's grandfather, maybe even more so than Ishtar.

And that loyalty makes her a threat.

The ex-Archdemon sweeps her gaze over the table. "While I'm thrilled to hear my absence has been felt, it appears you've managed to keep yourself fruitfully busy while I've been gone."

Is that disapproval I hear in her voice?

Alexander seems to notice it, too, because he says, "All to the benefit of the cause, I assure you."

He snaps his fingers at a Nephilim standing nearby, who brings the ex-Archdemon a goblet of wine before scurrying from the room, followed closely by the other servants present. Alexander must've given them some silent signal to leave. As Lilith brings the silver cup to her lips, the Gray steeples his hands and looks at her grimly. "Now, tell me. What news of the Council?"

Lilith drains her cup before speaking. "Their feathers are

positively ruffled," she croons. "Whatever you've been doing has them aflutter with panic. I've even caught wind of an interesting rumor that Asmodeus has been imprisoned for betraying the Council."

Caleb sucks in a sharp breath beside me, and I grip his leg under the table. A reminder to keep calm. And silent. Although Beelzebub already informed us of this, I can't imagine that makes it any easier to hear, especially given the amused way Lilith delivers the news. I raise my chalice, feigning a drink, so I can sneak a look at Hammurabi, who seems to hold a deep affection for Asmodeus. A *mersu* ball laden with coconut shavings is speared on a fork frozen halfway to his mouth. Even Ishtar looks unnerved by this news. And here I thought she didn't like anyone except Alexander and Gilgamesh. And herself.

"That *is* interesting," Alexander drawls, his tone flat, like this isn't news to him. "In this case, I do believe the Council has done us a favor. One less adversary to stand in our way."

The ex-Archdemon narrows her eyes. "You don't seem surprised."

He shrugs. "Because I am not. Such tidings have already reached my ears."

Scanning the table again, she purses her lips. "I would be remiss not to ask if this development has anything to do with our guests?"

Chuckling, Alexander leans back in his chair. "Nothing ever did get past you, Lilith. You remember my grandson, Caleb?"

Her narrowing eyes follow the Gray's outstretched hand. "Ah, yes." A grin hitches up the left side of her mouth. "He was quite the spirited one, if I recall."

Alexander gestures to the opposite end of the table. "And I believe you know Hammurabi and Alaric."

"It's been an age," she says bluntly, barely acknowledging either Nephilim. Instead, her gaze snags on mine and lingers. "And this one? I can only assume, given those lovely silver appendages, that she is the young Gray you mentioned."

Although her words are friendly enough, her tone is arctic.

Alexander beams at me, his smile radiant. In these moments, when he isn't terrorizing us with subtle warnings and outright physical threats, it's almost easy to see why so many followed him in his conquest for power and why so many who share that hunger—that thirst for freedom among mortals, like Ishtar—still do.

"This little dove is our secret weapon," he purrs. Across the table, I glimpse Ishtar rolling her eyes. "Lilith, meet Luna Morningstar."

"Morningstar?" She hooks a brow upward, but her shock seems disingenuous somehow. Given what Asmodeus said about my mother and Lilith—that they were close friends and remained that way even after the Fall despite the divide—then I can only assume she would know about me and, in turn, know the identity of my father. But if that's true, why pretend otherwise? After all, she's sworn her allegiance to someone my mother has spent millennia keeping locked in a tomb.

Wouldn't that automatically make them enemies?

"Indeed," Alexander says, peering between us. "A pleasant surprise, is it not? To think, the instigator of the divide would create such a wonderful gift to help me mend the rift between our kind." His lips curl into a devious smile, and I shiver.

Lilith glares at Alexander, her dark eyes sharpening like a blade on a whetstone. "Did you order her release in my absence?"

The dynamic in the room seems to change as Lilith shifts from a loyal follower to a headmistress scolding her student.

Alexander's nostrils flare as he straightens. "I will forgive your insolence just this once as a courtesy toward my favorite teacher. But be careful, Lilith."

To her credit, the ex-Archdemon doesn't flinch at his threat.

"Forgive me, my liege." Her tone drips with a contrition that borders on mocking. "I am merely curious how the girl came to be here when, last I heard, she was imprisoned."

Appeased, Alexander relaxes back into his seat. "Young love is impatient and often causes those afflicted to act without the consent of its elders." His eyes flash to Caleb, who shrinks under the weight of his grandfather's scrutiny. "But my heir showed true initiative in rescuing Luna and even managed to cripple the formidable Mammon."

Lilith recoils as if Alexander has struck her. "A second generation rescued a Gray from the Council?"

The disbelief emanating from her is insulting. Caleb might

have had some help, but he was still the one who cut me out of that egg. He was still the one who brought me back from the broken darkness that consumed me in that cage, even if I constantly find myself still drawn to its call. To me, he's worth so much more than any other Dark or Light, second generation or not.

Lilith's stunned expression hardens, and I notice something new pouring from her. The liquid-like tendrils of her aura stand upright like the hair does now on the back of my neck.

Alexander tsks, aware of it, too. "Such disapproval I sense from you, Lilith. Once a headmistress, always a headmistress, it seems."

With a hurried clomp of heels on stone, she crosses the room to the angel's side. "If you ever valued me as your headmistress, you will heed my warning, Alexander." Thrusting a finger in my direction, she barks, "That one is a threat to your reign. I'd put her back in her cage before it's too late."

I freeze at her words, my resurfacing terror like a physical force attempting to restrain me. Beside me, Caleb explodes from his seat. "Hey, wait a goddamn minu—"

When his grandfather holds up a hand, Caleb recoils, as if afraid Alexander might try to hurt him again. Shame washes over his features as he slowly sinks back into his seat.

Alexander turns his gaze to Lilith. "I assure you, I have the girl well in hand—"

"But you don't," she cuts in, her tone equal parts poison and pleading. "The prophecy has made sure of that."

"Oh, yes. The prophecy. The reason for my imprisonment and for lovely Luna's as well, I daresay." He scoffs, waving a dismissive hand. "Worry not, my dear Lilith. Ishtar has already informed me of this nonsense, and I put little stock in the Messenger's tidings."

"Well, you should." Her shoulders stiffen.

Despite the fact that she wants to see me imprisoned again, I can't help feeling sympathetic knowing the instinct and desperation that must be clawing at her. I can see it on her face—the need to spread her wings, to let loose the emotions scratching at the underside of skin. But she can't.

Because her wings are gone.

Alexander sighs, his patience wearing thin. Like a parent placating a whining child, he murmurs, "All right, I will humor you. Care to elaborate?"

Lilith lifts her chin, speaking clearly. "After the Great Battle, as the Fallen took up their new home on Earth, the Creator delivered a prophecy, spoken into the ear of only one, and when the fourteen academies were erected, the Messenger shared this prophecy with the Council. She warned of a Gray, who would become the destroyer of our world, and in doing so, further cemented the belief in and need for the divide."

Under the table, Caleb clutches my hand. His terror mimics my own from his unsteady breaths to the way his fingers tremble around mine. I hang onto him just as tightly, fearing

Lilith's every word.

"But what the Messenger failed to disclose was that the prophecy also spoke of a second Gray. Of a Savior, who would battle the Destroyer and heal the rift that has greatly wounded our world." Lilith leans forward, her hands clasped together, as if locked in a prayer. "The prophecy's words are clear, Alexander. You are the Savior the Creator spoke of."

Caleb's eyes dart to mine, their touch hot on my face, but I can't tear my gaze from Lilith. If what she's saying is true and Alexander is the Savior from the prophecy, then that would mean I'm the—

Destroyer, the voice of my conscience whispers.

Realization dawns on me, making me sick to my stomach. Is this prophecy why my mother abandoned me? Because she knew what I was fated to become and wanted to spare everyone from my eventual wrath? Spare *herself* the burden of having a daughter the Lights and Darks would both see as the villain?

I suddenly feel dirty, like a plague on this world. I tear my hand free of Caleb's, wrapping my arms around my torso. He shouldn't touch me. I'll only hurt him. Despite myself, despite the warning in my head, I meet his worried eyes for a moment before glancing to where Alaric sits at the end of the table, watching me with equal unease. He was wrong. Alexander doesn't destroy everything he touches—I do. Even the people I love aren't safe from me.

And now, with this long held secret finally out in the open, they will see that, too.

The tension permeating the dining hall is thick, like a cloying smoke, weighing like lead on my lungs. The silence that follows Lilith's speech is suffocating, and I want it to end. I *need* it to end. But I can't speak. Words are lost to me, though that's probably a good thing. I need to be still. I shouldn't move. If I move, what ripple of chaos will I send out in the world?

Alexander lets out a barking laugh, making me jump. "Then what is the problem, my old friend?" he asks Lilith, oblivious to my internal strife.

The ex-Archdemon glowers at him. "The *problem*," she hisses, enunciating the word, "is that you are hosting the Destroyer at your dinner table." Her stern features soften, and she reaches out a tentative hand, touching his forearm as she crouches beside him. "Your success is not guaranteed, Alexander. If you are not careful, you will lose this war before it has even begun."

Her sable eyes shift to mine, accusatory and probing, bringing my panic that much closer to the surface. A scream rises in my throat—any second now it will find its way past my lips—but a familiar sensation quickly shoves it back down.

Drunk with the haze of Calm washing over me, I peer down the long table at Alaric. His golden aura writhes with fury, and his expression is harder than I've ever seen it, bordering on irate. I've never seen him look so undone, and sweat beads his dark brow, which he doesn't wipe away even when it drips down the sides of his face. I can only imagine the energy he must be expending to keep me—a full-blooded angel at the brink of a mental breakdown—subdued.

At the opposite end of the table, Alexander scowls at him, affirming my theory that the Gray doesn't want us using our powers without his permission. Either that or he just really doesn't want Alaric helping me cope with my trauma. Maybe he even wants me unhinged—to get me to my weakest point before fully asserting his control.

What better way to constrain a person than to break them completely?

"You're jumping to conclusions," Alaric says, his tone placid, before taking a long drag of his wine.

Ishtar growls at his insolence—her first contribution to this conversation—but Alexander waves her off, gesturing for Alaric to continue.

The Nephilim shrugs. "What makes you think Luna is this Destroyer? Could the prophecy not just as easily be referring to Alexander?" He nods to the Gray, avoiding his gaze, and to my surprise, Alexander actually looks wounded by his words.

Oblivious to the strain between the two men, Lilith scoffs. "The Destroyer is spoken of first in the prophecy, and the Morningstar's daughter was born just after the Fall—"

She cuts off abruptly, and her eyes widen slightly, as if she's accidentally said something she wasn't supposed to. Her aura quivers for a moment before settling back into its usual threatening dance.

Silence descends on the room once again, and I gape at her, noting the fading effects of the Calm—Alaric must be getting tired—clinging to one part of her statement.

"The Morningstar's daughter was born just after the Fall."

I began to suspect it when I was trapped in the Council's prison—that I'm far older than my appearance suggests—but hearing it confirmed is strange. How can I be that old but still only be seventeen instead of a grown adult, like Alaric, who was born around the same time? Was I cryogenically frozen? Do angels even possess that kind of technology?

Beside me, Caleb is unnervingly still, his stricken gaze fixed on his grandfather, who, in turn, is staring at Lilith, all amusement on his face gone.

"Is that so?" Alexander's eerie eyes fix on mine, and he regards me for a long moment, making me feel like bacteria under a microscope. I suppress the urge to shiver. "If that's true, then where have you been all this time, little dove? You do not look that old to me." Before I can answer, he glares at Lilith. "Assuming I believe any of this, why would the Messenger withhold half of the prophecy from the Council? And how, dear Lilith, did you come to know of it? Or of the circumstances surrounding the girl's birth? Especially given that you seemed to know nothing of her when she was mentioned before."

Lilith balks but recovers quickly. Standing, she smooths her high-collared jacket, tugging nonchalantly at the burgundy cuffs. "There were rumors, back during the time of the Fall, that Lucifer had an affair with a Light, though I do not know with whom."

I raise a brow at that. If Lilith was as close with Gabriel as I've been led to believe, then surely the ex-Archdemon would know she's my mother. So, why is she lying to Alexander? Or did Gabriel hide my birth from her, too?

"I am merely making assumptions, given we know this girl to be the Morningstar's offspring," Lilith continues without missing a beat. "Perhaps he locked her away somewhere, safe from time's touch, and that is why she's so young. Or perhaps, she really is but a whelp and her father has dipped his toes in Light waters more than once."

"I have heard no such rumors," the Gray says.

The ex-Archdemon waves a dismissive hand. "Yes, well, it was millennia ago. Old news, as they say these days. As for the prophecy, Gabriel confided in me at the time as a fellow Council member and asked for my advice on the matter. She was concerned how the rest of the Council would react and felt it was in everyone's best interest to imprison any Grays they uncovered rather than risk the world on a possible Savior, whose success in the eventual battle was not guaranteed. If there were no Grays out in the world, the prophecy couldn't be fulfilled and—"

"The divide would remain intact," Alexander finishes.

I can hear my breaths and heartbeat in my ears, even though Alaric is working hard to keep me sedated. Is that true? Given what I know about her, would Gabriel really do that—condemn anyone unlucky enough to be born a Gray? I saw her that day under the Serapeum with Lucifer. I saw the way he touched her just as clearly as I saw the way she looked at him. They might not be together anymore, but there was definitely something still there between them, even after thousands of years apart. And remembering them like that makes me fully understand why she tried to warn me away from Caleb. It wasn't just because we reminded her of the past, but because she didn't want me reliving her own heartache.

Or maybe I'm wrong about the woman who birthed me and she really is a monster. Maybe she does desire a world with the divide because it makes her own life—and mistakes—easier to cope with. And if that's the case, then maybe...

Maybe she really did want me imprisoned.

Alexander glares at Lilith, arching an imperious brow. "If you knew of this, why did you say nothing sooner?"

Her aura trembles despite her attempts to seem calm, and I wonder if Alexander can see it—if that's just one more commonality my fellow Gray and I share. Lilith shrugs one slender shoulder, unfazed. "And waste needless words warning you about an obstacle that did not yet exist? She was imprisoned, Alexander, and if I recall, you did not seem in a particular hurry to change that. The girl did not pose any actual threat until your *foolish* grandson set her free."

Alexander sneers at that, but instead of the lash of fury I

expect, he just says, "It would do you well to not withhold intel from me again."

Beside me, Caleb chokes out, "Grandfather—"

My chest tightens at the terror in his voice, which seems to mirror my own. I follow his frightened gaze to Alexander, who flashes Caleb a reserved smile.

"Worry not, dear boy. I do not put my faith in groundless superstitions. Your Luna is safe." He peers at me, and in the pause, I hear the words he isn't saying aloud. *For now*, his eyes seem to scream at me. "If anything, this has given us all cause to unite against a common enemy. With this prophecy, the Council has proven that no one who is different is safe, and I cannot allow such narrow-mindedness in my new world."

If Alexander's words are meant to reassure, they don't.

Without waiting for a response, he rises from the table, and everyone in the dining hall follows suit, showing their reverence for their king. Even me.

"Alaric, Ishtar, Gilgamesh. A word in private?" Alexander beckons to the three Nephilim with an ominous curl of his finger.

Alaric excuses himself, meeting my gaze for the breadth of a heartbeat before trailing after Alexander through the far door, taking the safety blanket of his Calm with him. It lifts off my head so quickly I nearly lose my balance. Ishtar and Gilgamesh follow, departing the room with a cursory nod at Lilith, who frowns at being excluded but says nothing. As they leave, my old teacher doesn't even have the courage to look me in the face. He averts his gaze, keeping his eyes pinned on the floor, as if ashamed to be in my presence now that everyone knows the truth of what I am.

With my mind clear of Alaric's influence, I can fully recognize just how much more dangerous the situation has become. Caleb was right. We need to get out of here.

And soon.

Once the others exit the room, my legs give out beneath me, and I collapse into my chair. As if snapping out of a fog of his own, Caleb drops to his knees, cupping my face.

"Goldilocks—"

"You're shorter than I envisioned," a familiar voice interrupts.

Caleb lowers his hands as we peer across the table at Lilith, who stares down at us, like scum on her shoe. She looks me up and down with disdain. "And blonde. And here I thought you would take after your mother."

My breath catches as I glance to the door in the corner then snap my eyes back to Lilith. I knew she was lying. She knows damn well who my mother is.

The question is: Why didn't she tell Alexander?

"If you know who she is, why didn't you say?"

My voice breaks, coaxing a snide chuckle from Lilith, who spits, "Gabriel is my friend, and I won't sell her out—"

"But you'll sell out her daughter?" I hiss. And throw Lucifer under the bus, pinning blame on him for something he wasn't even aware of.

If she cares about Gabriel, if she wants to protect her, why doesn't that same mercy extend to me? They aren't even on the same side in this war, and I've done nothing to her—to either of them. I've done nothing but exist.

Which is apparently a crime, according to their prophecy.

"You are a threat," she says slowly. "Even Gabriel was smart enough to accept that."

Hammurabi, who I didn't even realize was standing behind my left shoulder, growls under his breath. The ex-Archdemon just clicks her tongue at him. Even without her wings, she would undoubtedly squash the ancient Nephilim like a bug.

I blanch and my stomach turns. "Are you saying…" But I can't find the strength to voice this new fear. I look to Caleb, my eyes shining with tears, and he nods before standing and scowling at Lilith, asking for me, "Are you saying Gabriel believed Luna is the Destroyer?"

Lilith places her hands on the table and leans in, her voice dangerously low. She glares at me, her eyes like chips of carved onyx. "Of course. Why else do you think I helped her entomb you?"

My breath catches on an inhale and I shudder. My mother locked me away, just like the Council locked away Alexander. She didn't just abandon me.

She left me in a tomb to rot.

"What the hell?" Caleb whispers.

I can feel his eyes on me but I can't speak. I can't move. I can't think. I can't even breathe. My wings press close to my skin, trembling with pent-up rage and a resurfacing mania I'm certain now I'll never escape.

Lilith parts her plump lips to say something else, but her mouth snaps shut when several Nephilim enter the room and approach the grand table to clear it. Taking their presence as her cue to leave, she shoots me one last scathing look before retreating back through the door she came in by.

I watch her disappear from the hall, staring after her retreating figure until my eyes glaze over and the candles have burned through most of their wicks. A tentative hand touches my shoulder and I jump.

"Luna—"

I shrug Caleb off. "I want to be alone."

No, it's more than a want. It's a need. I *need* to be left alone before I do something I end up regretting. I can already feel it—the fire burning under my palms. It's so close to exploding, and if it comes out now, it'll engulf this entire room. Maybe even the whole citadel.

"I don't think that's a good idea," he protests, and those words are the trigger that set me off. I leap up from my seat, anger spearing my wings out to the sides like arrows slung from a bow, and bring my fists down on the table. Under the force of my rage, the thick wood cracks in half.

Caleb and Hammurabi are both smart enough to leap back,

putting distance between themselves and the volatile angel hunched over the broken table, which now sits in two distinct pieces on the floor. When I glance over my shoulder, I glimpse genuine fear in their eyes.

Good, I say to myself, although the thought pains me. They should be afraid of me. I need to give them a reason to stop fighting—to stop thinking I'm worthy of their protection or help. Because if I am this Destroyer Lilith spoke of…

Then I am only doomed to hurt them.

"Please, Caleb," I breathe, sinking into the seat again, my wings falling to the floor, mimicking the shift in my mood. My hands curl into fists to smother the flames threatening to break free of my skin. "Just go."

To my dejection, he does.

twenty-five

CALEB

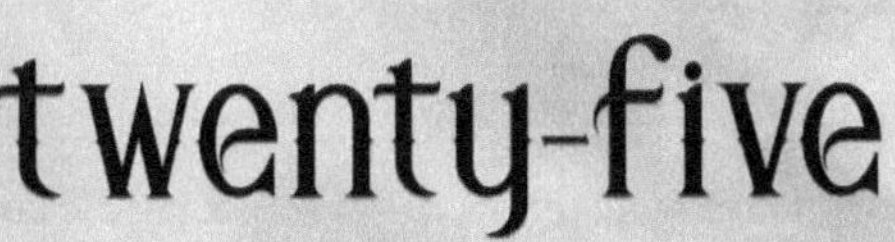

I FEEL PUNCH-DRUNK, LIKE those MMA fighters who've gotten hit in the head one too many times, and they aren't quite right anymore. Lilith delivered one hell of an upper cut with the revelations she dished out. And wow, Gabriel keeps winning at Mother of the Year, imprisoning her own kid because of a fucking prophecy. I didn't think I could hate Queen Bitch anymore than I did, but it turns out I was wrong. I mean, she's with Lucifer now, so I guess she changed her mind, but still, Luna deserves so much better.

Luna. The look on her face when Lilith opened her trap and declared Goldilocks was the Destroyer. She is a rope rapidly fraying, and I can't do a goddamn thing to stop it. It's too much: Alexander, being a Gray, prison, and now the prophecy. She has all the fortitude of tissue paper right now, and I'm genuinely terrified for her. What if she completely loses it? Will she just shut down and go into a catatonic state, or will she go boom? Either thought is too horrible to contemplate. And she was just breaking out of her shell, too, before all this, just awakening to the world around her. To me. I love her and seeing her like this, unable to help…

Maybe I'm a rope, too, unraveling.

"It normally takes years to wear down stone, but I believe you may achieve it today at the rate you're pacing." Hammurabi's low rumble jerks me from my thoughts, and I glance over my shoulder, surprised to find him sitting on my bed.

Pivoting on one heel, I change trajectory and stop at the foot of the bed. "When did you let yourself in?" I demand, pissed that he invaded my sanctuary without permission.

His thick brows bunch over his nose as he regards me with concern in his black eyes. "Caleb," he says, speaking slowly, as if I'm a very young child, which I guess to him I am. "We came in here together. Don't you remember?"

I blink at him, the events after Lilith's declaration blurring a little. Well, hell and damnation, he *did* walk back with me. Forget about Luna losing her shit, mine just marched out of the citadel, cackling. I can't afford that right now. I have to be sharp. I can break down later, when we're far away from here, and rolling into a ball and sobbing for a few days is acceptable.

"Yeah, I remember now. I'm sorry. I'm just…" I wave a hand.

"Yes, I imagine I would be, too, if I found out my lover is the Destroyer," Hammurabi says, and I detest the sympathy painted on his face.

I snort. "We don't know that she's the Destroyer," I hiss. "Why? Just because she was born first? What fucking bullshit. It's so vague anyway. Does birth order even matter? The only clear thing is that they're both Grays."

"Gabriel feared the prophecy so much she hid Luna away," Hammurabi says, his voice gentle. "What if your golden lady is the Destroyer?"

I hate his words, and I want to rip him to shreds for saying them, but I bite on my tongue and consider the worst case scenario. What if Luna is destined to destroy the world? It certainly won't be out of ambition. She has no desire to rule, and I don't think the thought has ever crossed her mind. When has she had time to contemplate her future? But if she *is* the Big Bad everyone is afraid of, something catastrophic has to change in her personality for her to pick up a sword and declare war on the world. A chill settles over me. Shit, what in her life hasn't been catastrophic lately? Shaking my head, I dismiss the idea, even though it lingers in the air like cigarette smoke, threatening to choke me.

Flashes of Luna falling into madness burst into my brain, and I once again hear her confessions of the things she did before we met when her powers were totally out of control. Maybe being the Destroyer wouldn't be a deliberate act on her part. Maybe it's a case of her being so broken she just can't hold the reins on her powers and they break free, sending out a wave of death and destruction.

Maybe. But that doesn't feel right, either. And the stupid prophecy is so opaque it could mean anything. Bottom line, I know Goldilocks. Her heart is pure and shining, desperate for love and family and all things denied to her. She wants to go out in the world and *live*. I think if I could find a hole to bury ourselves in, she'd happily slide in next to me and wait until the apocalypse is over.

My eyes clash with Hammurabi's. "You're wrong," I say. "Luna feels guilty when she kills a spider. She has zero desire to conquer anyone. She just wants normal stuff, stuff she's never had. Waging war isn't at the top of her to-do list."

Hammurabi sighs. "Yes, that may have been true before, but now she has her wings and all the power that comes with them. Power corrupts as you know. It changes people. Look at Alexander. He wasn't born a tyrant."

I snort, shaking my head. "Luna could never be a tyrant. And I don't even know if that's the right word to describe Gramps. Zealot is a better fit, and Goldilocks doesn't slip into that mold, either. And you know Alexander, Hammurabi. Does he seem like a Savior to you?"

Chuckling, Hammurabi crosses his arms over his chest. "No, he doesn't, but the prophecy has muddied the waters a bit, hasn't it? I prefer order and clear direction to bloody prophecies."

I arch a brow in surprise. "I thought you of all people would take the most literal interpretation of this prophecy because of your love for order."

"I've known Alexander for a long time, young one, and while I believe his desire to unite our people to be genuine, I don't believe that he is the one to rule us all. Earth doesn't need an emperor. It never did. Yes, I desire order, but I also value freedom. Alexander wouldn't bring true freedom—he's peddling the veneer of freedom with pretty golden bracelets that are really shackles."

I study him for a moment. "I thought you didn't want the divide destroyed."

He shrugs. "I don't have much faith it can be. I'm old, and I'm prejudiced against my Light brethren. Too much bad blood between us. The old laws keep us safe." When I open my mouth to tell him what bullshit that is, he holds up a hand. "But I can admit that for the younger generation, the old laws make little sense. We're heaping our history upon your heads, our grudges, our conflicts. We've made you into our image and it's flawed."

Hammurabi admitting the institution is wrong? It really is the end of the world. My jaw flops open of its own accord as I stare at the biggest hard-ass I know.

The Babylonian king laughs at me. "Child, your face. It's wonderful to know I can still surprise people."

"You've gone soft," I accuse, which is ridiculous, but Hammurabi admitting change could possibly be a good thing is basically him turning into a marshmallow. If I roast him, I can crack him open and get to his gooey center. "Next, you'll tell me you kind of like Luna."

"She's a lost little flower," he says with another shrug. "I like flowers."

"A Gray flower," I remind him, not bothering to hide my doubt. Little flower indeed.

"A pearly blossom clinging to her stem in the raging storm around her," Hammurabi says. "One can't help but hope the wind doesn't tear her apart."

And that's the closest he'll ever come to admitting he likes a Gray. "Unless she is the wind, of course," I point out, knowing that if he really believes Luna to be the Destroyer, he won't hesitate to take up his sword against her.

"Of course," he acknowledges with a grim nod. "But do not fear me yet, Caleb. Prophecy or no prophecy, I'm a patient man. Time will reveal the true meaning of this revelation to us, and then I'll make my judgment."

It's the best he'll give me and I'm grateful. Hammurabi is a man of his word, and if it turns out like I already know it will—with Luna the innocent victim of this lunacy—he'll fight for her.

The door snicks open, and Alaric slips in, grim-faced, his legendary calm ruffled. My heart sinks to my feet. This can't be good. How much more bad shit are we supposed to take? Hammurabi rises to his feet, lithe and menacing, his face shuttering his emotions in the presence of the Light.

"What's happened?" he demands, hands clenched at his sides.

I find my own hands fisted as I wait for Alaric's answer.

"It seems all the excitement at dinner has inspired Alexander to speed up his timeline. I am to leave immediately to find Lucifer and offer an invitation," Alaric says. "But this isn't exactly a friendly summons. I'm to tell the Morningstar the Conqueror holds his daughter as his esteemed guest and to make haste as he's certain they can come to a mutually beneficial arrangement."

I snort in disbelief. "So, he's basically saying in a nice way that Luna is a hostage?"

"Yes, he's waving Luna like a red cape under a mad bull's nose," Alaric replies. "I figured he would use her as bait to get Lucifer to join him, but Lilith's accusations change things. If Alexander *has* taken her warnings about Luna to heart..." He frowns. "Honestly, I don't know what he's thinking or planning, but it can't be good. I can only assume he's hoping if the Morningstar falls in line, so will his daughter, removing any likelihood of war between the two Grays...preordained or not."

"Alexander is actually threatening the Morningstar?" Hammurabi says, eyes widening in disbelief. "I know the boy is brash, but I never thought he lacked intelligence."

Hammurabi calling Alexander a boy causes inappropriate laughter to erupt from my throat. Both men stare at me like I've lost my mind. I guess they don't realize I have. That thought sobers me right up.

"Gramps doesn't lack in confidence, that's for sure, but this is *Lucifer*," I say. "The original rebel with a cause. He invented being a badass." Alexander is so convinced that he's the chosen one I'm a little shocked he'd use thinly veiled threats to get Lucifer here instead of straight up seducing him to the dark side of the Force.

"While I agree with both of you, it's never wise to underestimate Alexander," Alaric says, and I remember that my grandfather killed his father. An Archangel.

No, it's not, but we have an ace up our sleeve. "How are you going to explain Gabriel? Or are you going to just sneak her in?"

A scowl creases Alaric's smooth brow. "Gilgamesh is coming with me, which complicates matters."

"I'm surprised he can leave Ishtar's bed long enough to travel with you," Hammurabi grumbles, and another chuckle escapes me. Maybe I was wrong about Hammurabi having a stick up his ass; maybe he should go do stand-up.

Alaric's frown deepens. "There's not an explanation on Earth that will make Alexander believe that Gabriel has chosen his side. She was his warden for thousands of years. He hates her. He'd rather skewer her with her own sword than have her fight on his side."

I wince at his words, remembering how I stabbed her with the dagger, leaving her bleeding on the floor. Flinging the thought away, I say, "So, the Messenger is our secret weapon? That is if Lilith doesn't out her." Why hasn't Lilith sold out Gabriel yet? I'm sure she has her reasons, but I can't make sense of them. I just hope she keeps her trap shut a little longer.

"And what a weapon she is," Hammurabi says, and I shoot him a skeptical look as I hear the admiration in his voice. "I don't like her, but she is a fierce warrior, Caleb."

Fair enough.

Alaric nods. "Yes, she is. Lucifer will—"

The door to my room swings open, and Gilgamesh steps over the threshold, annoyance pasted on his face as his gaze sweeps over all three of us. Annoyance with a dash of suspicion.

"Uh, knock much? Someone older than dirt like you should have better manners," I say, not bothering to hide my anger. I have one private sanctuary in this whole place, and it's violated on a daily basis.

Gilgamesh's eyes are full of disapproval as they regard me, his lips pinched. "Someone as young and vulnerable as you should learn not to antagonize your superiors."

I smirk. "Last time I checked, I'm Alexander's heir, and you're just an errand boy."

I see Hammurabi suppress a grin out of the corner of my eye, and Alaric just shakes his head but quickly steps between me and the king of Uruk when Gilgamesh takes an aggressive step toward me. He places one hand on Gilgamesh's chest and one on mine.

"Enough," Alaric snaps, and I hear the weariness beneath the irritation. "Gilgamesh, what are you doing here?"

Gilgamesh glares at me before focusing on his fellow Light. "Looking for you. We should have been off by now. Best not to keep the Great waiting."

Alaric pinches his nose, a great sigh puffing past his lips. "Yes, I know better than anyone how impatient Alexander can be." My curiosity perks up at his words. What is the deal with those two? "I just came to say my farewells to Caleb and Hammurabi, and I had hoped Luna, but alas, she's not here."

"Aren't you all in each other's pockets," Gilgamesh says with a slight sneer.

Hammurabi smiles. "I'm surprised you climbed out of Ishtar's pocket long enough to go on this mission."

Gilgamesh bristles, stepping forward again, only for Alaric to block him once more. "Enough. We're all allies now, and I don't relish the role of babysitter. Don't force me to subdue you." I bite the inside of my cheek to keep from howling with laughter as both Hammurabi and Gilgamesh turn pissed-off faces at Alaric. "Come, Gilgamesh. Lucifer awaits." Alaric strolls out of my room, forcing Gilgamesh to follow.

I watch them go, relieved when they disappear. Then I slam my door shut. I glance over my shoulder at Hammurabi. "I hope Lucifer and Gabriel can get us the hell out of here."

"Me too, young one, me too."

twenty-six

LUNA

MY HANDS SHAKE AS I rub my slick palms against the satin fabric encasing my thighs, the smooth material of my floor-length dress swishing around my ankles, keeping in time with my steps. As I hurry through the quiet passage—ears strained, eyes searching—my thoughts are a whirlwind of confusion. Of *hurt*. Of the lingering stab of abandonment I'm not sure I'll ever find the strength to move past.

My mother didn't just give me up, she locked me away, like some dirty secret she hoped no one would unearth.

I wanted to believe that if I just spoke to her, I'd understand what led her to do what she did. And the worst part is that I *do* understand. I'm dangerous—how many times have I told myself that? How many times have I seen that realization reflected in the eyes of the people closest to me? I know what I can do when provoked, and I live in constant fear of lashing out at the wrong person—at someone innocent falling victim to this unrestrained power inside me, especially now that I know what I am. My control is a fragile, tenuous thing, and if the prophecy is to be believed…if I *am* the Destroyer…

Then there is nothing to stop me from eventually snapping.

Caleb's face springs into my head, and the fear in his gaze at my outburst is vivid in my memory, as if he's still standing before me. The table in the dining hall was probably hundreds of years old, if not thousands, and has withstood the test of time. And yet, I smashed it with my hands as if I was breaking a twig. If I can do that level of damage in a passing moment of distress, what might I accidentally end up doing to him?

Tears prick at my eyes. I was right to put distance between us at the Serapeum and weak to relent so quickly to my need to be near him. The images Alexander forced into my head of the academies burning replay in my thoughts, and again, I watch, helpless, as Caleb burns. Is that the outcome the prophecy spoke of?

Is that what will come of our love for each other?

The tears slip free now and cascade down my cheeks, and I gasp, my breath hitching, as I wipe them away. No, I can't let my mind go down this road. I need to keep it together.

Picking up speed, I continue my hunt. We've only been here two days and I'm already going insane. I need answers before I crack completely, and I can't keep waiting on my parents to get them. So, I'll go for the next best available option.

Caleb would freak out if he knew what I'm planning—all the

better then that I scared him away. But I need to do this, and as I mount a narrow set of stairs to the top of the citadel, I tell myself I need to do it alone. Lilith doesn't get to just drop that bomb on me and then leave with zero regard for the aftermath. I didn't choose to be born. I didn't choose to be this thing the Council fears. All I've ever wanted is to find the place in this world where I fit. To be happy.

Free.

My fingers curl into fists, and my resolve strengthens with every step. Destroyer or not, I deserve the truth.

The night air brushes my skin as I emerge onto the roof, the stone underfoot dusted with sand. I go still the moment I lay eyes on Lilith. She's standing at the edge, one misstep away from falling to the desert floor far below, her arms spread wide to the sides and head tilted, as if smelling the air. She grips her leather jacket in one hand, revealing a low-cut camisole, which disappears into the waist of her pants, leaving her upper back exposed.

My shocked gaze trails pale pink scars that follow the curve of her shoulder blades and shine in the moonlight, standing in stark contrast to the darker tone of her skin. Considering I've seen Caleb heal from horrible burns right in front of my eyes, I didn't think anyone with celestial blood was even capable of scarring. Then again, I suppose wings are different—a loss we aren't supposed to endure.

As I gape at Lilith's back, I recall what Caleb said about

her losing her wings and I can't help the swell of pity that overwhelms me. It was that recollection that led me up here and what made me so certain this was where I'd find her. This high, out in the open, it almost feels like flying is possible.

The evening breeze rustles my dress, and I can practically see Lilith's ears perk up as her head snaps to the side. Her lips pinch into a scowl as she lowers her arms, and shrugging on her coat, she jumps down from the ledge.

"What do you want?" Her tone is abrasive, and I flinch at the hostility in her unblinking gaze, the pits of her eyes like two black holes that seem to suck all the warmth from the world. When they settle on my exposed wings, her scowl deepens.

Not wanting to offend her anymore than I already have just by existing, I draw my wings back into the confinement of my skin. "Please, I—" My voice wavers, and my heart races a mile a minute, pounding so violently I feel it thrumming in my veins. What if the answers I'm chasing only make everything worse? What if I'm better off not knowing?

I draw in a steadying breath. No, not knowing isn't an option anymore. Regardless of what comes of this, I need to know.

Holding up my hands, palms out, I step closer. "I just want to talk."

Lilith sneers. "You won't change my mind about the prophecy, girl. And soon enough, Alexander will see all this my way. He *will* understand the danger you pose."

My arms fall weakly to my sides. "I'm not here to change

your mind. I just want to understand."

Her mouth purses, and her eyes narrow to skeptical slits.

"Understand what?" she asks after a moment.

"Who I am," I answer a little too quickly. Swallowing, I peer at the clear sky overhead, trying to imagine a place beyond the cruel, mortal world I grew up in. "Where I came from. I…" I clamp down hard on my lip.

I lower my gaze to Lilith's again, preparing to prostrate myself before her if it means getting even the smallest insight into the events that led to my existence.

She stares at me, sizing me up, and I glimpse the change in her gaze the moment she relents. Her pupils—barely visible in the sea of black surrounding them, but visible to my angel eyes—dilate.

"You believe it, don't you?" she asks, her tone teetering on the edge of disbelief. "You believe you are the Destroyer."

I bite down on my lip again, harder this time. Tears slip from my eyes as I reluctantly nod.

"I…think it's possible."

Her nostrils flare, and I wince at the shrewd look on her face.

Before she can speak—before she can say she was right—I quickly add, "I don't want power. I don't want to hurt anyone, Lilith. I'd rather be locked up again than do that." *But…*

Trembling, I look down at my hands.

Hands that have caused so much pain and destruction.

"But I also know there's something inside me I can't quite

control and…"

"And?" The ex-Archdemon cocks her head.

Meeting her unforgiving gaze, I swallow loudly, steeling myself. "And I'm afraid of it," I admit.

Lilith lets out a stilted breath. "Fine," she grumbles. "I will answer your questions on one condition. You will tell me who released you from your tomb."

Confusion barrels through me. She doesn't know?

"I…was hoping *you* knew the answer to that."

The ex-Archdemon bares her teeth in a snarl and lunges forward, hand outstretched to grab me. "Don't toy with me—"

"I'm not!" I blurt, sidestepping her grasp. "I wasn't even aware I had been locked away until you mentioned it. Hell, before Alaric brought me to the Serapeum, I thought I was human." That stops her dead in her tracks, and she gapes at me. "Crazy but human," I mutter with a humorless laugh.

Lilith taps a manicured finger to her chin. "Well, it couldn't have been your mother. The detection wards on Easter Island sat undisturbed when I last went to check."

"It wasn't Gabriel. She didn't even know who I was when we met." My chest tightens when I force out the words, "Our blood…it didn't sing to each other."

Black eyes flash to mine and she scoffs. "Of course, it didn't. She cut off that connection when she locked you away. It was the only way she could do what needed to be done or else she would've always been haunted by leaving you there."

This time, I'm the one lurching forward, and I grab Lilith's hand without thought. She flinches as if my touch has burned her, but I hold on, my grip tight and desperate.

"Please, I don't understand any of this. I just need to know why she did what she did."

Lilith's hard expression softens a fraction, and in the split-second where I glimpse something other than hate in her eyes, I wonder if—had things been different—we might have actually gotten to know one another. In a world where my mother didn't abandon me, would Lilith have been a friend to me, too, as she is to Gabriel?

Unexpected tears mist her eyes. "Gabriel and I have always been close, like sisters." Her voice is gentle, reminiscing. "Even after the Fall, when I chose one way and she chose another, she remained my dearest friend. She understood why I followed Lucifer in his rebellion just as I understood why she remained with the Creator. She had a role to play, and being the mouth of the Creator comes with an isolation and loneliness none of us will ever understand."

"But she still chose," I say, releasing her hand. "She still chose the Creator over my father."

Lilith rolls her eyes. "You are so young, even for one so old. You do not understand what it was like. What *He* is like. Do you not think we Darks mourn the loss of our father? Gabriel made her choice out of love. She did not want to leave Him when so many of his other children already had. She thought she was being loyal."

Loyal…

For the first time, I allow myself to consider what life would have been like had I actually grown up with my parents—not from the viewpoint of a child desperate for love, but from the viewpoint of someone who might have eventually ended up at odds with those same parents, the way Lucifer did with the Creator. Had I been in their shoes, had I been forced to choose between romantic love and the affection of a parent…what would I have decided? It's easy to sit here and say I would have chosen the same as my father—rebellion over submission. But I also think I'm beginning to understand why Gabriel chose the way she did.

More than anyone, I can understand the overwhelming need for a parent.

Emotion thickens in my throat. "Then why did you?"

Lilith arches a brow. "Abandon Heaven?" She shrugs. "The same reason Lucifer did. For the freedom to love. But, unlike our leader, the object of my desire and affection was a human."

My brow pinches as I flit back through everything I ever learned in my religion classes, dredging up one piece of information vital to this conversation. About the first man created, Adam, and his first wife.

Lilith.

A surprised breath escapes me. "So the story is true?"

"Hardly," the ex-Archdemon retorts. "Mortal accounts get

so much wrong."

With a mournful sigh, she returns to the edge of the rooftop and plops down on the ledge. Crossing her legs, she pats the stone beside her, and I slink forward, wary.

"You needn't worry. I won't bite," she coos.

Exhaling, I sit, my body rigid, and Lilith laughs to herself, the way she might have in another life had we the chance to be friends. Maybe, in that life, I might have even called her Aunt Lilith, and she might have loved me, the way an aunt would. Maybe, in that life, she would've been my family, too.

A cool breeze washes over my bare skin, and I shiver.

Leaning back on her hands, Lilith lets out a tired breath through her nose. "Adam was not the first man but one of many during the early days of humanity, when we were mere watchers in Heaven tasked with looking over and guiding the mortals, should they need it. He was strong and brave, and I fell in love with him the moment I saw him. So, I put myself in his path, and he loved me, too, even though being together was impossible. It was a dream neither one of us wanted to wake from. Then, Lucifer waged war on the Creator, and I finally had a chance to chase that dream. To be with Adam, on Earth, and to finally be free the way I wanted to be.

"Gabriel understood. She was actually the one who urged me to go. She wanted me to have the peace and happiness she knew she couldn't. And, for a while, I did. But I was ignorant of the challenges we would face or how quickly time would steal him from me.

"As Adam aged, I remained the same, and soon, the love and affection he had for me turned bitter. He wanted someone he could grow old with, not an immortal who would watch him die and then move on once his bones turned to dust. He feared being one love in a long existence of many."

My eyes spring wide at these words, and a dark, unwelcome thought slinks to the surface. While Caleb will live for thousands of years, he's still mortal. Time will tear us apart one day, and when that happens, I will be left alone yet again.

A fate I can never seem to escape.

But for immortals like my parents, they didn't need to fear such an obstacle ever coming between them. They could've been together forever. Happy.

Unless, what Gabriel feared wasn't death.

Eternity is a long time. Perhaps, like Adam, she feared being just one love of Lucifer's—that their love would be fleeting and she would eventually be replaced by another. If so, maybe she didn't just stay with the Creator out of loyalty but because she was scared.

Scared of losing the only love she knew wouldn't fade.

Lilith clears her throat. "Eventually, that fear tore us apart, and he left me for the mortal, Eve, who from then on, had the love and happiness that I had sacrificed so much for. Your mother was the one who saved me from my misery. When the Council was created to establish the schools, she suggested I serve as the headmistress of Ashkelon."

"Which is where you met Alexander," I realize, the puzzle pieces slotting into place. But why did Lilith support Alexander when she—better than anyone, besides my mother, of course— knew the full extent of the prophecy?

What did she need a Savior for?

Lilith blinks, surprise etched into her beautiful face.

"Alaric told me," I say, answering her silent question.

She arches an eyebrow. "You and he are close?"

I hesitate, dropping my hands to my lap, gripping the gold fabric of my dress between my fingers. "He was the one who found me," I manage after a moment. "I was in a mortal hospital before the Serapeum."

"And the years before that?" Intrigue saturates her every word.

"A group home and then placed with a string of foster families. It was a pretty typical upbringing for a modern-day orphan."

She turns to face me fully now, and the curiosity in her gaze bows to a consternation that sets me on edge. Her brow furrows into a grimace. "So, you truly have no recollection of the millennia you spent in stasis?" Her aura quivers, agitated.

"Stasis?" I ask, frowning.

She waves a dismissive hand. "Frozen in a sleep state shortly after your birth, as a mere babe, so the years would have no bearing on you. You wouldn't age or grow. You'd always exist as you were in that moment, perfect but powerless. After the

Creator delivered the prophecy, Gabriel knew there was no other option but to seal you away, somewhere out of reach, even to time itself. If she didn't...well, she feared what would come of your freedom."

I recoil, her words a swift punch that knocks the air from my lungs. So, it's true. Just like the Council, Gabriel was afraid of me. But...does she still feel that way now? If she does, then why is she with my father, supposedly fighting to get back to me? If she does, why do we keep trying to find her? Maybe the biggest betrayal I could encounter isn't my mother abandoning me but her finding us and locking me up again.

"So, she believed it," I say, my tone dull. "That I would become the Destroyer."

"What do you expect?" Lilith counters. "The Creator *is* omniscient."

She says this as if it's a fact and, maybe to those who have been alive as long as she has, it is. But to me, it feels like an assumption on their part—a jail sentence before even finding out if I'm guilty.

"That's why she didn't tell Lucifer, isn't it?" My chest tightens. Gabriel was so certain of my role in the prophecy that she withheld my existence from the only person who would've had reason to fight for me.

The air between us grows heavy with pity, and Lilith lets out a sigh, pushing up to her feet. "The Morningstar would've burned the Earth to cinders before allowing anyone to lock away his only child. Lucifer is faithful, sometimes to a fault. He would've died to protect you, regardless of what you are."

I stand as well, and when she turns to face me, I see the truth of her words in her gaze, even if I struggle to believe it. After all, Lucifer handed me over to the Council. He *let* his brothers and sisters imprison me. He didn't burn anything to try to save me.

"I'm not sure about that," I mutter. "He did nothing when the Council took me."

"Foolish child," Lilith retorts, her tone sharp. "I have no love for your father, but do not presume to know him better than I. How do you know what the Morningstar has been doing? How do you know he has not been tearing the world apart searching for you?"

Every word is a slap to the face. Perhaps Lucifer is willing to burn the world to find me, I just haven't given him the chance. If he was willing to wage a war against the Creator for the freedom to love, what lengths would he go to for his child?

I'm not sure how knowing that makes me feel. Should I be happy about that kind of devotion? Sad about what atrocities he might have committed or may yet still commit on my behalf? Either way, I suppose it's too late to matter—at least in regard to my childhood. I was robbed of that devotion, and if the prophecy is true and I am the Destroyer, then I don't deserve it.

Lilith crosses her arms. "Gabriel feared Lucifer's knowing about you would only…escalate the problem. Besides, they weren't exactly on speaking terms at the time."

"And my powers?" I ask, changing course. I don't want to talk about my father anymore, and I have enough of the picture leading up to my birth to understand my mother's actions. But this part—why my powers manifested the way they did and the lack of control I still struggle with… Thanks to Alexander, I know I was bound. I just don't understand why. "Did you help her bind them, too?"

"It was a precaution," Lilith explains. "Binding both bloodlines wasn't a viable option—that would have rendered you mortal, and you would've slowly decayed and perished in that tomb, regardless of the stasis. And despite what you think of her, your mother never wanted you dead."

I scoff. No, she just wanted me caged.

"*So*," Lilith continues, glaring at me, "I bound your Dark side, so you would appear to our kind as a Light should your location be uncovered. Gabriel thought it may keep your powers under control in case you were ever released and given the opportunity to age. We hoped it would be enough to prevent you becoming the thing the prophecy spoke of."

"But it didn't work," I say. Their tampering only contributed to my messed-up childhood and the pain I repeatedly inflicted on others. "My Dark powers were poking through long before Alexander removed the bind on them. Even as a child, my fire was red. It was what gave me away at the Serapeum."

"You said you thought you were mortal," Lilith counters, side-eyeing me.

I snort. "I also said I thought I was crazy. Sane people don't tend to think they can magically set other people on fire."

Lilith's brow creases. "Binding our powers isn't…natural," she says after a moment, and I notice there's a slight edge to her voice that wasn't there before. "This power we possess doesn't *want* to be contained. And it was never a guaranteed fix or else you and Alexander would have never discovered what you are. If the binds had been stronger, if they weren't so fragile, your mother could have raised you as a Light, and she need not have ever locked you away. Because you wouldn't have been Gray anymore then, and you wouldn't have gone on to become the Destroyer." I wince at her words, at the conflicting blend of anger and sorrow behind them. Sighing again, Lilith shakes her head. "It was simply an extra layer of protection. A safety net in case anyone ever found out where you were or what we did. The real solution was to seal you in that tomb. By keeping you in a permanent infantile state, you would never grow or have the chance to become the very thing the prophecy warned of."

My wings tremble under my skin as the inferno of my fury reignites. "She should have just killed me then," I spit. "What you both did is no different."

I expect Lilith to bare her teeth or snap back at me— something to assert her age and dominance—but she does neither. Instead, she just stares at me, her expression morose.

"She didn't kill you because she hung onto the hope that, some day, the Creator would deliver a new prophecy that would render the existing one null and void. And…you were all she had left of her love with your father. Such things are not always so easy to abandon or destroy."

I glower at her. "Locking a baby away in a tomb sure feels a hell of a lot like abandonment."

"And yet, here you are," she muses, cocking a curious brow. "The tomb was sealed with both of our blood, and the wards made sure to keep humans away. Over the years, we even added additional wards for protection as humanity expanded across the globe. The Rapa Nui were particularly helpful on that front, though they are oblivious to how we altered their statues. Even other immortals can't step past the stones. You were protected from the outside world in every possible way, which leads us back to the question at hand—"

"Who let me out of that tomb and why."

That's certainly what I'd like to know. Right now, I feel like a pawn being moved around by a player I can't see and whose motivations remain unknown, not just to me but to the other pieces on the board.

Lilith scrubs a hand over her face. "I can't make sense of it. It wasn't your mother, and I certainly did not release you. Our sigils didn't alert us that the wards had failed, and it's not as if the Rapa Nui could have freed you. It's as if someone just magicked you out of that tomb and plopped you in the mortal world—"

She sucks in a sharp breath.

"Of course." Her gaze trails over the rooftop, searching but not really seeing. She turns in place, pressing a hand to her forehead. "Oh, that clever bastard. He wants the prophecy to come to fruition. He wanted you freed so you could release Alexander. But why? Unless…"

Her wide eyes drift to mine, and I reel back from the terror I glimpse there.

"What?" I breathe. "W-Who are you talking about?"

Lilith's voice drops to a whisper. "The only being who could have removed you and placed you among the humans without Gabriel or me ever knowing."

I balk. She can't be saying what I think she is, can she?

"You… You don't mean—"

Lilith gives a solemn nod, and a strange silence settles over the rooftop, as if the subject of our conversation is now here among us, listening to each word intently. His name escapes her lips in a barely audible breath. "The Creator."

The wings hiding under my skin are suddenly unbearably heavy, like weights have been tied to my shoulder blades. I stumble backward a step, weighed down. "W-Why would He do that if I'm the Destroyer?"

Every word out of my mouth pushes me one step closer to that precipice I always find myself standing at, and I want to scream, to cry, to rage—anything to push away the madness that keeps trying to cripple me.

"He wouldn't," the ex-Archdemon says quickly then again

to reassure herself. "He wouldn't. The Creator cherishes humans. The last thing He would want is to see them perish in yet another celestial war. With you entombed, you weren't a threat. And with Alexander imprisoned…" She trails off, her face taut. "It doesn't make any sense unless the Creator *wants* the war to transpire. Unless He already knows how it ends." Her brow crinkles. "But then why would He release you, the Destroyer, unless—"

Lilith stares down at the ground, mortified.

"I can't believe how blind I've been. For so long, I've translated the prophecy literally. Your mother—she warned that the Creator speaks in riddles, that He's always working toward some greater end, but it had seemed so clear to me. So obvious. Especially when I met Alexander and he spoke of tearing down the divide…just like the Savior the Creator foretold. And I wanted that, too. I wanted to heal past hurts and find my way back home."

Home… Like go back to Heaven?

Tremors roll through my body and I shake uncontrollably. The only one speaking in riddles here is her.

"Lilith?"

"Forgive me, Luna," she breathes. A tear drips down her cheek, startling me. "And Gabriel…"

"What about her? What are you saying—"

"I lied before." The admission is blunt, and I gape at her, bemused and half-mad with confusion. She at least has the decency to look embarrassed. "While it's true your mother feared you would become the Destroyer, she hid you away not out of fear but love. She did it to protect you. She couldn't even bring herself to name you because it pained her so much to do what she did. I…" Shame paints her face red. "I was the one who acted out of cowardice."

My breath hitches. "I…I don't understand. To protect me from what?"

The look taking shape on her face—unequivocal in the belief forming behind those obsidian eyes—terrifies me more than Alexander ever possibly could. Because what I see in her gaze isn't just terror in the purest form but a heart-wrenching sadness. Like searching the whole world over for someone only to have to say goodbye to them the moment you meet.

"From becoming a martyr," she says.

I watch the gentle roll of her throat when she swallows. She lowers her hands, taking a wary step toward me, and observing my face, she reaches out, her tears flowing freely now. Her arms wrap around me, and I go still in her unexpected embrace.

"I think I was wrong about Alexander." Her words are a hum in my ear, but I can hardly hear her past my thundering pulse. Her arms tighten. "He isn't the Savior. You are."

twenty-seven

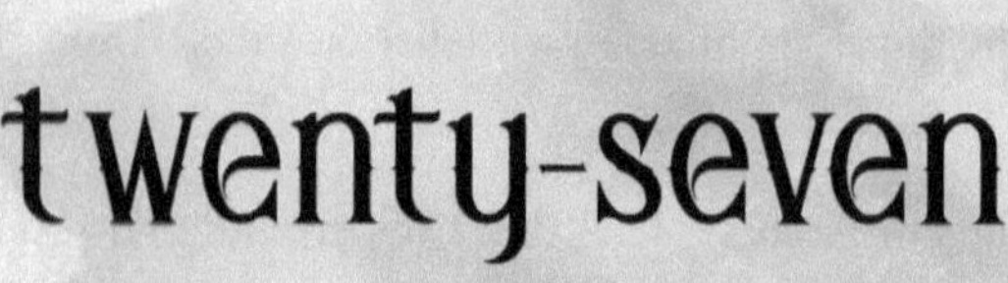

CALEB

I TUG AT THE sleeves of my dinner jacket, hating that I can't shed it yet, but we're in the throne room, mingling with Alexander's gathering faction. Luna looks biteable in yet another gold gown, her wings on display. I clench her hand, finding it icy. She's no more happy to be here than I am, her conversation with Lilith leaving us both rattled. Goldilocks made a beeline to me after their little chat, shaking, the shock reducing her to tears, confessing every awful word. At least she didn't go all, Hulk, Smash! again. But her tears hurt me more than her rage.

I'm glad the ex-Archdemon is suddenly on Team Luna, but her theory that the *Creator* set her free… What the actual fuck is going on here? I used to straight up love being a Nephilim, but all this divine puppeteering makes me just want to be a plain old human worrying about acne and drinking too much before finals.

I guess Gabriel really was trying to protect her daughter from either fate the prophecy is set to dish out. I gotta say being a martyr is no better than being a destroyer. Either way, I lose Luna, and I refuse to accept that fate. We've fought too hard to have some cosmic chess game rip it all away. And I'm too much of a Dark to just bow down to destiny. Free will can change the world. It has to. Hell, it already *has*. Lucifer, anyone? And Luna is his daughter. If anyone can tell fate to go fuck itself, it's Luna Morningstar.

I wish Luna and I could've stayed holed up in our room tonight. For the past three days, Lilith has been MIA, and we've been avoiding Alexander like he's the bearer of the plague, though Goldilocks has been summoned a few times by Gramps for training. Those sessions haven't helped with her state of mind as she's shaken down to her core. She just needs to be held right now as she comes to grips with Lilith's revelation. Or kissed senseless until she forgets her name. I'm happy to oblige either way. Honestly, I need the quiet right now just as much as she does. I'm in over my head, like a little league player suddenly being called up to the Majors and having a ninety-mile-per-hour fastball thrown at them. I don't know how I'm going to hit the home run that'll save the day. And I don't even like baseball.

Alexander summoning us tonight to celebrate can only mean one thing: Lucifer is on his way. Although I admire Grandfather's confidence, I'm shocked he's declaring victory before Lucifer has signed on the dotted line. The Morningstar doesn't exactly have a reputation for bending to the will of others. I don't expect Lucifer to come in and fall at Alexander's feet, declaring him the savior of angelkind.

My eyes find Ishtar hovering around Alexander, who lounges on his throne. She's usually the picture of grace and battle-ready hardness, but there's an almost nervous energy floating around her. Her eyes snap back and forth, taking in all the exit points as if she's preparing for an attack, which confirms my suspicion that we're about to get a visit from the original bad boy.

I hear Ishtar say, "Gilgamesh texted me, they'll be here soon, and I—"

"Text?" Grandfather asks, one brow arching, and I smother a laugh.

"Modern way to communicate," my teacher says, then her voice grows more urgent. "We need to be prepared—"

"You worry for naught, Goddess. I'm only disappointed Lilith isn't here to witness this triumph. But she still can't stand to be in the Morningstar's company so I gave her a reprieve. Just this once." Alexander waves a hand at her, shooing her away, and she frowns at him, clearly wanting to disobey. But in the end, she acquiesces and slinks into the crowd, taking residence near the doors.

"Caleb," Luna whispers, her voice so soft I strain to hear her. "My father is coming, isn't he?" She clutches my hand so hard I flinch. She immediately releases me, her face flushed and guilt in her eyes.

Taking her hand again, I bring her knuckles to my lips before lacing our fingers once more. "I think so. Ishtar is too twitchy. Why else would Gramps have us gather here like this?"

"Why doesn't he want to meet Lucifer in private?" she asks, eyes darting around the crowded room.

"I'm guessing he wants an audience when Lucifer switches sides so it'll cement his position as the true leader here on Earth." And there will be lots more witnesses to the carnage if things go south the way I predict they will. I don't say that to Luna, though. Her thread is one tug away from snapping.

"Do you think my moth—" She clamps her jaw shut with an audible click. There are too many ears around, and she's not supposed to know who her mother is.

I bend down to nuzzle her bare throat, and she shivers. "She'll find a way," I murmur against her skin, pressing a light kiss on her pulse.

"You children will be the death of me," Hammurabi growls from behind me. "You already share a bed. Is it not an adequate enough space for your endeavors? We're about to go to war, boy."

Luna stills and I whirl around. My teacher is once again in traditional garb with his pecs and abs on display, and he looks pissed off about it. Luna averts her gaze, pink blossoming on her cheeks. She's so innocent it's adorable. At least she's not checking him out this time, but I think she's come to view

Hammurabi as a grumpy uncle, and that sorta ruins the sexy. Besides, if I whipped off my shirt, I know she'd never look at anyone else twice.

Narrowing my eyes at him, I say, "Yeah, and war is stressful. Just keeping Goldilocks relaxed. Don't be jealous. Go get laid."

I don't even try to dodge as he cuffs the back of my head. I grin at him, rubbing my stinging skull. I see Alexander observe our exchange and he frowns.

"I don't think Alexander likes seeing you manhandle Caleb," Luna murmurs, pasting a too-bright smile on her lips.

Hammurabi stiffens, his gaze clashing with Alexander's. He gives the angel a slight bow and calls out, "Children."

Grandfather relaxes, a smile playing on his lips, and he gives Hammurabi a nod.

"Whatever happens, Caleb, you stick close to me," my teacher says quietly.

I bristle, and Luna stirs beside me, anger sparking in her eyes. "What about Goldilocks?" I demand.

"The little flower will be well tended to by her father. You, on the other hand, are not his concern," Hammurabi says. "I don't think the Morningstar will be too focused on his daughter's lover."

My heart sinks because I know he's right, but Luna protests, "He will be because I love Caleb. I need him."

The Babylonian king gives her a pitying look. "Flower, your father will only be focused on you. You were stolen from him, and he'll tear the world apart to get you back. He doesn't know you love Caleb, and I'm not sure he'd care under the circumstances. But don't worry, *I* will take care of the boy."

A warmth swells in my chest at my teacher's words. This is how I used to think Ishtar felt about me until those blinders were violently ripped away. "Thanks," I say sincerely.

"You're one of mine, ridiculous child," he says then studies Luna. "And I'll help you, little flower, though I don't think you'll need it."

Her sweet smile makes my heart hurt. We'll get through this. We have to. Somehow.

Lucifer appears in the middle of the throne room, ebony wings flaring, pushing back any Nephilim unfortunate enough to be near him. He's alone, no Alaric or Gilgamesh trailing behind him. I hear a collective gasp, my own sound of strangled surprise escaping my throat. Yeah, I expected him, but not quite like this.

But I guess the Morningstar understands the importance of a dramatic entrance.

He's like a great raven, heralding death. The antique gold of his hair is a beacon in the candle-lit chamber. Cold fury burns in his bright blue eyes as his gaze sweeps the room. He stills when he finds Luna, and I see his eyes flick over her in a rapid perusal. Then he focuses on me and the arm I have wrapped around her.

It takes all the willpower I have to not wither on the spot or piss my pants. But if I give in now, it's all over. He'll never think me a worthy partner for his daughter. And I can practically feel the tension pounding through Luna as she stares at her father. No way would I leave her bereft of support or comfort. I pull her closer, and she molds herself to me, a slight tremor rippling over her.

Lucifer's eyes clamp onto mine with an unspoken promise that he will find me and end me if I so much as breathe on Luna wrong. It's my turn to tremble, but I straighten my spine and give a slight nod. He strides toward us on silent feet despite his aggressive steps. Only when he's in front of Luna do I step away, but she doesn't let go of me completely, her hand tangled in mine. He regards our entwined fingers with a slight frown, as if he hadn't calculated Luna's feelings for me into his plan. Then his eyes dart up and meet Luna's and a warmth floods the blue depths that is so bright it feels like looking into the sun.

"Daughter," he says, cupping her cheek in one big hand.

A dazzled expression sits on Goldilocks's face as she stares into her father's eyes. "Father," she whispers, her hazel gaze shiny with unshed tears.

Seeing them like this, the resemblance is so obvious I'm shocked no one—including me—has ever put two and two together. There's a bit of Gabriel there, too, if you look close enough, but no one can deny Luna is Lucifer's blood. Gabriel must have stuck her head deep in the sand to miss it.

The Morningstar gathers Luna against his chest in a tight

embrace. The throne room has gone eerily silent as everyone watches the exchange in front of them, voyeurs in this private moment. They deserve a better reunion than this.

I gaze across the room at my grandfather, who resembles a wolf that has just spotted a nice fat sheep. A predatory grin plays upon his lips, and I can almost hear the gears of his mind turning from here. He doesn't think Lucifer can take on him and his growing army of Nephilim—the Fallen who support him are out in the world, recruiting, but he has the numbers here at the citadel that even without them he has the advantage—and he knows Luna doesn't have enough control to be a real threat to him. Especially when he's the one holding the leash on her training.

Gramps has brass balls, big ones, but even though he's a Gray, with access to both Light and Dark powers, he's still going against the Morningstar. This guy led a war against Heaven.

Lucifer releases Luna and says, "Get behind me."

She nods, and his eyes meet mine again, and the stark command is clear. *Protect my daughter or face my wrath.* But he doesn't need to threaten me. I'd protect Luna with my life. I squeeze our braided fingers tightly.

Lucifer glances at Hammurabi, eyebrows arching. "Fancy seeing you here, King."

Hammurabi gives a shallow bow. "It amazes me the places I find myself these days."

"Let's hope you find yourself curled up by Asmodeus's feet

soon enough where you prefer to be," Lucifer says with a slight smirk.

To my utter shock, I see a ruddiness touch Hammurabi's cheekbones, and my fierce teacher looks away like a blushing schoolboy. If I live through this, he's going to get shit about that for years.

The Archdemon's face grows cold again as his eyes fixate on Alexander on his throne. "You have someone who belongs to me. I'll be taking my daughter now."

And the first shot is across the bow.

Alexander leans forward, clashing eyes intense as they latch onto Lucifer's. "She's your daughter, but she doesn't belong to you. She belongs with me now. As do you. Together, we will make Earth into the paradise it was always meant to be."

A cruel laugh escapes Lucifer's lips. "Foolish boy, *I* belong to you? I fell to belong only to myself. I waged war on Heaven and my angel brethren for free will. I get to *choose* each day. I'm already in paradise."

Alexander stiffens at his words, rage banking in his eyes. "*This* is paradise? Mortals destroying Earth, destroying themselves while the Creator does nothing as his children kill one another and their home? As the divide between Dark and Light renders us helpless to aid the humans we were made to protect?"

Lucifer sneers. "And I suppose you have the power to heal all? Fancy yourself equal to the Creator, do you? Conquerors don't heal—they destroy. Your war will massacre the very mortals you claim to love and want to protect, not to mention the Nephilim and angels you'll slaughter."

Alexander stands, pearl-gray wings flaring out. "The divide must be destroyed, and I'm the only one who can achieve our unification. Are you that prejudiced against your own kind that you want us divided for eternity? Clearly, you found it in you to bend your precious convictions to cross the divide at least once."

Luna flinches, and I want to punch my grandfather in the face.

Lucifer prowls a step closer, radiating so much menace I can practically see it rising from his midnight wings. "You know nothing about my convictions," he hisses. "I fell for love, for the right to love and the right to choose. I fell to break the chains that bound me, to be more than a pampered slave to someone else's will. I still dream of Heaven, and yet I would never return to be a servant once more. You will unite us only to bind us again once your war is over. I have no desire to wear chains, no matter how pretty you promise to make them."

Alexander thumps his chest. "I was imprisoned for millennia. I have no desire to shackle you, Morningstar. I just have the desire to bring order to this mortal chaos and to unite our brethren here on Earth. You say you fell for love? Well, I conquered for love. For the love of my human parents and for all of humanity. If I knew they wouldn't be looked upon in horror, I would march to Macedonia and lift them from their tombs so they could witness the new world I will create. A world where humans, angels, and Nephilim will thrive in peace."

His casual mention of raising the dead sickens me. I knew Gramps thought he was a god, but I didn't realize just how far gone he was.

Lucifer stiffens. "You would resurrect your family?" I hear the shock saturating his voice, and my stunned mind echoes it. "That is insanity. Death, like life, is sacred."

Alexander sneers. "If I cut your daughter's head off, you wouldn't hesitate to raise her. That is the power of your love. No one who is mine will ever be in danger of perishing. Unlike the Creator, I take care of my flock, including your daughter. She is my heir as much as she is yours. With me, she will always be safe. Can you claim the same?"

Gabriel emerges from the Blessed Road right behind Alexander, a righteous goddess in gleaming golden armor, her hair back in a warrior's braid. I never thought I'd be glad to see her, but I'm about to break into a dance at the sight of her fury. Fisting Alexander's hair in one hand, she brings her silver sword under his throat with the other. "Perhaps you should be concerned about your own safety, Conqueror. Give us our daughter or die."

twenty-eight

LUNA

MY HEART TRIPS AT the sight of my mother, her statuesque figure clad in golden armor with her downy white wings draped in skeletal metal ornaments on full display, like an avenging angel sent down from the heavens to deliver retribution. Her obsidian hair is tied back in a braid, and the expression on her unobscured face is cruel. Baring her teeth, she glares down at Alexander, the sword clutched in her hand pressed to his throat, the glistening edge razor-sharp.

I immediately recognize the sword and armor from the display cases at the Serapeum—Gabriel's battle gear from the Great Battle of Heaven once stored away in the dusty back room of the famous library needed again now for war. She must've made a pit stop before coming here, risking exposure to arm herself to the teeth before taking on Alexander.

Her words to him vibrate in my ears like the aftershock of an earthquake, rocking me to my core. She came for me. Despite the danger, she came. And if her white-knuckled grasp on her sword's pommel is any indication, she is out for blood.

The Dark Nephilim lingering at the outskirts of the room all move forward around us, ready to defend their king, even against an angel who could easily tear them all to shreds. Alexander's initial shock wears off quickly, and he holds up a hand, warning his followers to stay back. Despite the threat of the shining blade at his throat, he unleashes a laugh—a harsh, barking sound that reeks of an insanity I recognize all too well. His eyes are wild and unfocused as he composes himself enough to spit through clenched teeth, "What glorious irony. To think, the sanctimonious Messenger who served as my warden is the golden child's mother." His voice deepens into a near feral snarl. "Your hypocrisy is riveting."

She tightens her grip on his hair, yanking his head back. "Silence, Conqueror. Need I remind you this sword could cut your throat."

"Not if I cut yours first," he growls.

He sweeps his arm upward, holding the dagger he stole back from Caleb, and my mother lets out a howl of pain as he swipes the glinting edge across the back of her hand, opening the skin down to the bone. On reflex, her fingers unfurl from around her sword's pommel, dropping the weapon, which clatters onto the dais by the Gray's feet.

As she flinches back, cradling her wound to her chest, Alexander smiles and lifts the dagger to his lips. Revulsion is a tidal wave slamming into my chest as he drags his tongue along the blade, licking my mother's blood clean off the metal.

Gabriel's dark eyes flit to her sword, then back to Alexander, who kicks the weapon away.

"Not so fearsome without your mighty sword, Messenger."

Golden fire erupts from the Archangel's hand and she scoffs. "I'll show you fearsome."

The hall is engulfed by a vengeful inferno as Gabriel lashes out with a ferocious scream—first at Alexander's Nephilim generals, burning several looming nearby, and then at Alexander, striking at the Gray with a spear of blazing light. At the same moment, a ring of fire surrounds them both like a halo, cutting them off from everyone else in the room. The blaze scores a circle into the stone floor, pushing back any who might attempt to intervene.

An eerie yellow light illuminates Gabriel's face as her gaze meets mine through the flickering wall of flame. And in her gaze, I glimpse all the words she will never say to me if she doesn't make it out of this alive.

She's doing this to give us a chance to escape, I realize as acceptance flits across the Archangel's hardening face. Her attention shifts back to Alexander, and fear trickles down my spine when he advances on my mother with his dagger upraised. Her sword—her only weapon to fight back in such close quarters—lies abandoned outside the circle of flame, out of reach. If I can just get it to her, then she can fight back. She can survive this.

She can *win*.

I step forward, but my father, sensing the movement, pushes me back with his wings. "Get out of here. *Now.* I'll help delay Alexander." Furious blue eyes whip over his shoulder, focusing for a moment on Hammurabi before locking on Caleb. "Protect my daughter with your life." It's a command and a warning rolled into one, and I can feel Caleb tense in the tightening of his hand around mine. Nodding, he tugs me away from the fray.

"No! No, you can't—" I begin to protest, but the words die on my lips when my father storms forward, pulling a sword of his own from an invisible scabbard between his two great ebony wings. They sweep outward with a powerful gust, pushing us farther from where my mother and Alexander face off, my feet scraping across the stone as I raise a hand to shield my face from the wind.

The gale extinguishes the flames nearest Lucifer, forging a path, and he descends upon Alexander from behind, surprising the Gray. Gabriel, taking advantage of the interruption, races forward, sliding across the stone with her hand outstretched, reaching for her sword through the gap in the flames. The gash in her skin has already stitched back together, and she grasps the pommel, spinning onto her knees in time to deflect an attack from Alexander.

The surrounding Nephilim seem to know better than to

engage with the three battling angels—at least until Alexander gives the command—keeping a wide berth from the fight, instead directing their attention to us. As they move toward us, Hammurabi grabs my arm.

"This is our cue to leave," he says in a fierce whisper.

I shake my head, hysteria creeping in. "We need to help them!"

Hammurabi's answering glare makes my insides shrivel. "Your parents will be fine, little flower. They're buying us time. Now, I suggest we take it."

He grabs onto Caleb as well, pulling us with him, away from the Nephilim closing in from behind and aiming for the pool of shadow in the corner nearby. We make it halfway before a familiar voice stops us dead in our tracks.

"Going somewhere?" Ishtar steps in front of Hammurabi, spinning two karambit knives on her fingers, one in each hand. A malicious smile tugs at her lips.

The Babylonian king puffs out his chest, sparing a split-second glance at Caleb before squaring himself to take on the goddess. "Go," he snaps at us.

"Goddamn it," Caleb growls. His hand clutches mine in a vise grip, his palm sweaty, as he leads me away from the two battling Nephilim, but there's nowhere to go, encompassed on all sides by Alexander's followers, the clanging of weapons, and the vicious heat of celestial flame—no longer a circle keeping everyone outside it at bay but an inferno devouring the space. Our only way out would be through the group of Dark

Nephilim drawing closer with each passing second.

I glance over my shoulder, hyperaware of their increasing proximity. Why haven't they attacked yet? Then I remember the way Alexander glared at Hammurabi when he whacked Caleb on the head and it dawns on me that they aren't meant to. To the Gray, Caleb and I are his possessions, and these Nephilim are wolves herding his prized sheep. They don't plan to harm us, but they definitely won't let us leave this place, either.

Frantic, I glance around for a way out of this mess, but around us, the throne room has devolved into chaos. The Nephilim not corralling us have jumped into the fight with my parents, and the fire lighting the space confines us in the citadel, spreading quickly and erasing the shadows for us to escape into. Dread creeps over my skin, making me shiver despite the encompassing heat. We're trapped.

Alexander has won.

Coming to this realization as well, Caleb takes me by the shoulders and spins me to face him, the fear like a living entity in his eyes.

"You can get out. You can take—"

Anger blisters my vision, and I push him off me when it dawns on me what he's about to say. He wants me to take the Blessed Road and escape, just like he told me to do at Babel. "Stop saying that. I'm not leaving without you!"

A looming face behind his shoulder snags my attention, and I shove Caleb to the floor just as Ishtar swipes at his back with one of her knives. I kick out a leg, tripping her, and she stumbles, laughing under her breath before quickly recovering. Turning, she grins at me.

"I'm so going to enjoy this, *little dove*." Her tone is derisive, her smile saccharine.

Shock tears through me as the Darks nearby all inch back, leaving us to the goddess's whims. They might be under orders not to harm us but Ishtar outranks them, and right now, I don't think she gives a damn about breaking Alexander's toys.

The goddess might not be able to wound me with her knives, but I'm sure she has more than one creative way to cause me pain, and she can definitely inflict far worse on a Nephilim. At that thought, I glance over my shoulder despite the immediate threat, remembering Hammurabi, worried about what's happened to him if Ishtar has turned her attention to us. Fear curdles in my stomach at the mental picture of the grouchy Nephilim injured, or worse, his life snuffed from this world.

To my relief, the Babylonian king is where we left him, engaged in battle with several Dark Nephilim—at least ten, much to my amazement—who he's managing to hold off, but just barely. Ishtar must've sent some of Alexander's other followers to distract him so she could come after us, seeking her pound of flesh. And I don't doubt for a moment that she would exact that vengeance on Caleb if doing so meant emotionally maiming me.

I snap my gaze back to the goddess as she launches herself

at me, but Caleb jumps between us, grabbing her wrist and wrenching her arm behind her back. "Why don't you pick on someone your own size?" he taunts.

Ishtar twists out of his grip. "I knew you couldn't be trusted. The first sign of danger and you run with your tail between your legs. Your grandfather will be so disappointed."

A crooked smile hitches up the left side of his lips. "So, what? You going to kill me, Teach?"

"No," she seethes, twirling her knives again. "I'll leave that to the Great. But he did say I could punish you as I see fit should you get any ideas about leaving. Both of you," she adds, shifting her black-lined eyes to mine.

"Touch one hair on their heads and you die."

A gasp tears from my throat as a great golden figure slams into Ishtar, blasting the goddess and the other surrounding Nephilim several feet across the throne room in a blaze of light and flame. My heart buckles again at the sight of my mother, so close now—a terrifying, towering presence beside me. Meeting my gaze, she touches a warm hand to my face before averting her eyes back to Ishtar, who rolls across the floor a few times then flips, landing on her feet like a cat.

"You must go now," she warns. Then she's off like a shot, her sword in hand, her shimmering aura pulsating, threatening wrath and ruin.

"Go where?" I ask Caleb, on the verge of tears.

I glance around the room, taking in the mayhem, as panic

squeezes my lungs, suffocating my every breath. A few Nephilim are on the floor, injured but healing, and any moment now, they'll return to battle, pushing the odds further in Alexander's favor. We need help, but Alaric is nowhere to be seen, nor Gilgamesh—not that my old teacher would help us, even if I begged him to. He's chosen his side. They still haven't returned from their errand to retrieve Lucifer, which likely means one of two things: Alaric couldn't tip off my parents before he and Gilgamesh tracked them down, and they had to prevent the Nephilim from racing back and warning Alexander about my mother. Or Alaric is stalling Gilgamesh in the Blessed Road so we have one less powerful first generation to contend with.

My gaze returns to Ishtar, watching as my mother exacts her vengeance on her, sword and knives clashing, resuming their unfinished fight from under the Serapeum. The thought of that day brings my focus back to my father, his golden hair slick with sweat, his chest heaving, as he crosses weapons with Alexander, batting away the odd Nephilim who dares approach. Lucifer might be far older than his opponent, but Alexander is a Gray. Having both the Dark and the Light at his disposal gives him an advantage, which he doesn't hesitate to use, slashing at my father with beams of light so sharp they appear tangible. Lucifer counters every attack with menacing whips of shadow, which slice at Alexander, catching him on the face and arms, pushing him back. But the fight is far from over, and every second we waste here could be the moment that turns the tide against us.

"Goldilocks—"

I glance at Caleb, but the helplessness on his face matches mine, and I can see in his expression that he wants to abandon our friends, our family, even less than I do. But what can we do? We're children compared to the Nephilim and angels here.

A strangled cry pulls my petrified gaze to my father, who clutches his chest as a thick line of red blossoms across his shirt and seeps between his fingers, dripping to the stone underfoot. Grimacing, he glowers at Alexander, who closes the distance between them when my father steps back, bloody dagger in hand. But he doesn't attack with his weapon this time, instead launching silver feathers of light at Lucifer, which pierce the Archdemon's limbs, pinning his body to the wall behind him like nails to a crucifix.

At my father's roar of pain, ruby fire blazes along my bare arms, and all the anger I've built up over the years—all the rage and loneliness I felt at having to grow up alone—consumes me as I direct the full extent of my strength at Alexander's back. A howling scream escapes my lips. I won't let him take my father from me.

Alexander's agonized yowl mirrors my own as his feathers burn from silver to black. Forgetting Lucifer, he turns to face me, a murderous fury alight in his gaze. His wings shudder, extinguishing the flames, and as he charges forward to attack me, I see it—the difference in his gaze when he looks at me now compared to how he did when we met. I glimpsed it the moment Lilith revealed the truth of the prophecy and have witnessed it growing in every moment between us since. Before he might've seen me as an asset, a soldier he could mold in his image, but now, he views me only as a threat.

Maybe, on some level, he always did.

When Alexander approaches, Caleb tries to shield me by putting himself in his grandfather's path. Gritting his teeth, he volleys a ball of purple and indigo fire at the Gray, who swats it away easily, as if it were a fly.

Alexander sneers. "What a disappointment you have turned out to be."

His eyes are wild as they lock on his grandson, diving into his mind, breaking him from the inside—I can feel the vibrations of his intent in the air, small ripples of power exuding from the angel in waves.

An inhuman cry rips from Caleb's lips as he drops to his knees, fingertips clawing at his skull, then his cheeks, carving bloody lines in his skin. Crimson dribbles from his nose and ears, and my heart concaves at the sight, terror paralyzing my body as I watch the person I love most in the world start to die.

"Stop! You're killing him!" I cry.

Alexander's frenzied gaze snaps to mine, breaking his connection on Caleb, who slumps to the floor. Tears slide down my cheeks as the angel steps toward me. I try to defend myself. I try to call on my fire, but the ruby flames igniting across my fingertips sputter out before they can fully form.

Time seems to slow as Alexander lifts his hand, raising his dagger. My eyes slide to my father, who throws himself forward, grunting as the silver feathers tear through his body, the blood drenching his clothes from where Alexander stabbed him in the chest, viscous and thick. Once free, he races toward us with little thought for his own injuries, his lips shaping my name. In my peripheral vision, I also glimpse my mother, who is now outnumbered at least twenty to one, the goddess joined by several other Dark Nephilim in their attempt to overwhelm the Archangel. While Gabriel manages the Nephilims' combined attacks with ease, her celestial flesh impervious to their weapons and her own sword in hand, my father's shouts distract her, giving the Nephilim an opening to strike. They all pounce on her, mounting one on top of the other like pigs on a pile, causing the Archangel to stumble.

It hurts my chest knowing that we're all going to die here in this fortress, casualties in Alexander's war. Well, maybe not my parents, unless they fall on the wrong end of Alexander's blade—the only enemy weapon here capable of killing either of them. But they have lethal weapons of their own, and the odds are with them, ensuring they'll survive. They're strong. They'll get out of this in one piece, even if Caleb and I won't.

My body trembles, but I can't seem to force myself to move. Terror more potent than anything I've ever felt has frozen my senses and limbs. And for the first time, despite the power thrumming under my skin, I feel weak.

My eyes lower to Caleb, and to my relief, his chest is rising and falling. He's breathing. He weakly lifts his head, looking up at me with a fear that makes his complexion clammy and pale.

I love you, I try to tell him, but I can't will my lips to utter the words.

I look back at Alexander, staring death in the face, as he brings down his hand, the dagger tip pointed directly over my heart. But when the blade plunges into flesh, tearing through muscle and sinew and bone, it isn't my chest it sinks into… but Alaric's, as he emerges from the Blessed Road in a flash of golden light, placing himself in front of Alexander and taking the killing blow meant for me.

A gurgle of blood parts the Nephilim's lips, but as he looks over his shoulder, he offers me that gentle smile I know so well now, relief flooding his kind amber eyes, even as the life within them fades. Alexander stumbles back, shock creasing his face, releasing his hold on the dagger as a mortified horror blows his pupils wide. He doesn't move. He doesn't try to come for me again. He just stares at Alaric as he falls to the floor between us, bleeding out across the stone.

A scream rips from my throat as I reach for Alaric, but someone restrains me, pulling me away from his body. Consumed by grief, I'm barely aware of my father as he scoops me up in one arm and Caleb in the other, holding us tight to his sides as Hammurabi comes up beside us, looking battered but unharmed.

My mother's voice is a deafening boom behind me as she screams for us to go, and I turn my head to see her swipe her sword, slicing one of the Nephilim clean in two. Ishtar makes her move when Gabriel's back is turned, but the Archangel dodges her incoming fist, grabbing the goddess by the throat and lifting her until her feet are dangling a foot off the floor. Ishtar tears at her fingers, but my mother is an angel. A mutinous glee spreads across Gabriel's face, and grinning, she slams Ishtar down to the floor, crushing her back into the ground with a bone-crunching crack, splitting the stone from the impact.

Ishtar groans, rolling onto her side, and I feel a momentary disappointment that the goddess is still alive and breathing. She spits blood out onto the floor, but doesn't move much more than that, her breaths haggard as her body slowly knits itself back together.

Around her, the remaining Nephilim all back away slowly, eyes wide, before turning tail and fleeing. Sheathing her sword, my mother watches them go before vanishing into a narrow slip of light, stepping into the safety of the Blessed Road.

Without looking back, Lucifer flaps his giant wings, smothering the lingering flames and gifting us liberation in the form of black shadows. He pulls us into the cool embrace of the darkness, and as the Shadow Road rises to swallow us whole, I feel Alexander's eyes on my back. In the weighted silence, they vow one thing.

Revenge.

twenty-nine

CALEB

I FOLLOW LUCIFER OUT of the Shadow Road, clutching Luna's hand. She's refused to let go, not even taking the comfort offered by her father, clinging to me like ivy wrapping around brick. I don't think her dad likes it—I think he's even starting to resent me—but too damn bad. They can go to family therapy later. I need to take care of Goldilocks now, not just because I love her, but also because looking after her is the only thing keeping me stitched together. Dried blood crusts under my nose and ears, pulling on my skin, reminding me how Gramps almost pulverized my brain. The grooves I dug into my flesh with my own nails are healed, but the coppery stickiness remains. I barely recovered from the first assault. And now, I can add Alexander trying to kill Luna to my nightmares, only instead Alaric is the one who is dead. Calm, kind, ancient as fuck Alaric. Gone. Like dandelion seeds in the wind. Poof. Snuffed out. Someone as old and powerful as him shouldn't have been able to die so quickly. It isn't right.

His death broke Luna. I don't know if she'll recover. He wasn't her father, but she loved him like one. She never spoke about their relationship, but I'm not blind. I could see the affection they had for one another. I think he was the first adult she ever trusted, who stood in her corner. I didn't know him well but I liked him. Pain lances my chest as guilt bites into me with razor-sharp teeth. My grandfather murdered Alaric. If I hadn't met Luna, if I hadn't gotten her involved, maybe he'd still be alive. Or maybe we're all swept up in this fucking prophecy, helpless against the tide.

Shaking my head from those morbid thoughts, I blink, surprised to find us in Hampi, an ancient, abandoned city in India, which was once one of the richest trade cities in the world. I've never actually been here, but I'm a sucker for killer architecture, and Hampi has that in spades. Before transferring to the Serapeum, I planned to take Mom here on break. I have no idea why Lucifer has brought us here. I can't think of any Dark allies who occupy Hampi.

Gabriel appears in a shimmer of light near us, her raptor's gaze honing in on Luna, but Luna doesn't even glance her way, burying her face into my chest. Her tears soak my silk shirt. I bend, scooping one arm under her knees, and pick her up, cradling her against me. She's in no state to hurry, and even though the sun is setting, pink and orange staining the sky like a dreamsicle melting, this is a tourist attraction. The last thing we need is for Hammurabi to have to erase a bunch of mortal memories.

Gabriel and Lucifer both stare at us, and I can almost feel their need to snatch Luna from me. I ignore both of them, kissing Luna on the forehead. "It's okay, Goldilocks, I've got you," I murmur. And I do have her, I always will, but I don't know how to bring her back from this latest shock. Hell, I don't know how *I'll* come back. But she doesn't need to know that. I'll keep my shit together if it kills me. Shove all that trauma down until I choke on it. I feel Hammurabi's eyes on me, burning a hole through my flimsy veneer of competence. He'll corner me the moment we have a chance to breathe. He knows me well enough to know that I'm far from being okay. I don't think I can handle his gruff kindness. It'll be my undoing.

We pass by the famous stone chariot pulled by elephants, which forms a small palace, all columns and sculpted reliefs. A display of wealth and might this city once represented. I wish Luna and I could walk among the ruins and get swept up in their beauty and history and revel in just being with each other. But that feels like a dream that keeps slipping further and further away. Our future seems destined to be filled with pain and death.

"Come," Gabriel says, her voice almost a growl. Her fingers are clenched into fists as her eyes linger on Luna.

I know it sucks for Gabriel not to be able to hold her daughter now that she finally has her back, although I don't really take her for the warm and fuzzy type. But I'm honestly too soul weary to care about her precious feelings right now. She got herself into this mess as callous as that might sound, so she just needs to suck it up. My focus has to be on Luna and putting one foot in front of the other.

We trail Gabriel to Virupaksha Temple, the main structure resembling a croquembouche of stone, offering intricate carvings of the Hindu pantheon. A petite Indian woman descends the steps. Her kiwi-green eyes contain gold flecks, and her brown skin is flawless as is her curvy figure. She's a Nephilim, that's for sure, and a Light. She's decided against traditional garb and instead rocks a black pair of skinny jeans and a scarlet T-shirt that slides off one brown shoulder. Her warm smile melts Gabriel's icy exterior.

"Welcome, Messenger," she says with a slight bow.

"Dearest Kali, thank you for allowing us to stay here," Gabriel says, kissing the woman on both cheeks.

The Nephilim's name pulls me out of my tormented stupor. Kali, the goddess of time and death, is a Light? There are paintings of her wearing a crown of human skulls as she defeats demons. The way humans depict her, I thought Kali would be Team Dark all the way. Well, I didn't even *know* she was a Nephilim, but that's beside the point. Kali catches my blatant gawking and smirks.

"You kill a few people and you get a bad reputation, but I'm also worshipped for being a mother figure, too, you know," she tells me.

I grin, grateful for her sarcasm. I didn't think I had it in me to smile today. Her eyes shift to Luna in my arms, and all amusement drains from her face. "Do you have a room where she can rest? She's had a shit day," I say. Luna doesn't even look up, just whimpers, and my heart cracks.

"Yes, *my* daughter needs somewhere quiet," Gabriel says, fixing me with another glare.

I just roll my eyes at her, too tired to offer witty banter, but Hammurabi steps next to me, placing a big hand on my shoulder. "We're all concerned about the flower," he says to Gabriel.

"Yes, let's not waste time quarreling over who cares for Luna more," Lucifer says, surprising me. He arches a brow at Gabriel, and she whirls away from him.

Kali's startled gaze flicks to Luna for a brief moment before she composes herself. Huh, guess she didn't know Gabriel had a kid, either. "Come, I have a room for her," she says, and we all follow her up the steps and into the cool, dim interior of the temple.

The inside is even more decadent, and suddenly my fingers itch to pick up a chisel and raw stone. I can do more than just make little clay spies, and the Creator knows it would take my mind off things. It's a shame mortal eyes aren't privy to what we see. We follow her down a corridor and up stone steps to the second tier of the building. Kali pushes open a door and ushers me inside. Heavy silk rugs in jewel tones overlap each other on the floor where a low bed rests, sporting pillows the color of peacock feathers.

I give the Light a grateful nod and enter, pausing for a moment to kick off my shoes. I do have manners, even in a crisis. Luna stirs, lifting up her face to mine. Her hazel eyes brim with a depth of agony I can't begin to fathom. Sinking to my knees, I carefully place her on the bed, smoothing her dress around her legs.

"You need to rest," I murmur, stroking her damp hair back from her face.

Her eyes are puffy, making her look mortal. Fragile. "Please stay with me," she begs, grasping onto my hand.

"Scoot," I say, and she wiggles over for me. I'm acutely aware of the two disapproving, scary-as-fuck presences hovering outside the door, but I can't focus on them right now. There's only Goldilocks and her bottomless grief. She rests her head on my shoulder, and I cradle her close. "Sleep," I whisper, knowing she needs to fall into oblivion for a while.

Minutes tick by and finally Luna goes limp against me, her breathing slow and even. I envy her, my mind like a hamster on a wheel. I wasn't even able to doze. I slowly disentangle my limbs from hers, my footsteps muffled on the thick rugs. Snatching my shoes, I pivot on one heel and give Luna one last glance. She's like a tragic princess in a fairy tale, waiting for a prince to wake her from slumber. Only there's no waking from this nightmare. I turn my back and glide across the threshold, finding Gabriel and Lucifer waiting.

Fury bubbles up inside me at their selfishness. Yeah, they

want to see their kid, but don't they get that now is not the time for a family reunion? They're basically strangers. Hell, she's closer to Uncle Hammurabi at this point.

I don't give two shits that I'm facing an Archdemon and Archangel, the Messenger and the Morningstar. "Hey, leave Luna alone right now," I growl. "She needs to rest, and she can't deal with the two of you and your guilt. She's got her own shit to handle. Give her some space."

Lucifer's blue eyes narrow to slits, and Gabriel bares her teeth at me. I push past them and down the stairs, desperate for fresh air.

I stumble outside where the sun is now below the horizon, and the air is a little cooler. I rub my face, fingers stained rusty. Shit, I need a shower or at the very least a wet napkin. A damp white cloth is thrust into my face, and I jerk back. Goddamn Hammurabi. He's basically a cat waiting around a corner to jump you. But I am grateful for the cloth and rub it all over my face and ears until I don't feel the stickiness of blood anymore.

"If I was an enemy, I would have gutted you," Hammurabi remarks, crossing his arms over his chest. His eyes rove over the ruins.

"Being gutted sounds good right now. Fewer problems to deal with. Less…guilt." I almost choke on that last word, and I chuck the rag away from me.

The Babylonian king turns to me, his face slack with surprise. "Guilt? What do you have to be guilty for, young one?"

"I took Alaric to Alexander," I say, my hands clenching into fists. "I brought him there and he's fucking dead now. He shouldn't be dead. It's not right." To my horror, my vision blurs, and I take a few steps away from him.

Hammurabi is suddenly in my face, gripping my chin, so I'm forced to look at him. "Caleb, Alaric was very old and very wise. He went with you of his own free will. He went with you because he wanted to protect the flower. You didn't coerce him. Your plan was the best plan, even if we didn't like it. This isn't your fault. Your grandfather killed Alaric. He nearly killed you, too."

I hear the logic in what he's saying, but guilt eats away at me. "It feels like my fault," I whisper. "I got Luna involved in this…" Something in my chest cracks open and tears break free, and I double over, unable to breathe.

Hammurabi tucks my head against his wide chest. "Let it all out, boy. That's it. Purge yourself of the poison. Go on."

I lean on him until the storm breaks, and I take great gulps of air. I lean on him until I wrestle myself under control once more. Then I straighten.

"I'm tired of being pawns in this game, this stupid prophecy," I say. "I'm tired of playing defense."

"Then no longer be a pawn, Caleb," Hammurabi urges, black eyes fervent.

Determination hardens my heart against my grief and terror. I nod. "Yes, now is the time to plan and fight back." For me, for Luna, hell, for the world.

epilogue

ALEXANDER HAD ALARIC MOVED to his chambers. The Nephilim stretches across the bed, his lean, long frame elegant even in repose. Alexander admires his fair torso, highlighted by the candlelight, which lovingly caresses the dips and dents of muscle, sinew, and flesh. Alaric's rigid abdomen is once again flawless.

Alexander's jaw clenches as he recalls the image of Alaric shielding Luna, the fool. He could've been killed. If Luna hadn't been so much shorter, or his aim a few inches higher, he would've caught Alaric in the heart instead. But Alexander lost his lover to darkness once before. He won't lose him again. He is relieved he merely had to heal him and not resurrect him. He would've done it, but there was always a chance the mind would be too traumatized to go on. He didn't want that for beautiful, kind Alaric.

He had no such reservations about his son. But his son wasn't

Alaric—he was a bitter disappointment.

Alaric was always too noble for his own good, and Alexander would have to be all but blind to see how the Nephilim looked at Luna like a daughter. Still, Alaric kept him from killing the only other Gray who could possibly herald his doom—if he actually believed fate could control his destiny. If he rid himself of the golden girl, there would be no one else to challenge his rightful rule, and his grandson would've fallen in line, his mind free of Luna's hold on him. Love turned many men into fools. As Alexander studies the long sweep of lashes kissing Alaric's cheekbones, he is aware he is not completely free of that affliction.

He forgets that the Nephilim is older than him at times. That he was the caregiver before the lover. Alaric was always content in his role, his only rebellion freeing Alexander's binding, which brought about the death of his father. Perhaps that cured him of ambition. Though he stayed by his side, Alaric never shared Alexander's vision to rule or to bridge the divide. Well, at least not to bridge the divide the way he preferred to, with ruling Earth.

A frown tugs down his lips. Before his capture, he sensed Alaric was growing discontent, uncomfortable with his march across the known world, of his conquering. He never spoke of the matter, and Alexander is certain Alaric didn't think he noticed his increasing withdrawal, but he had. Perhaps it was due to his wedding and bedding mortal women to provide heirs as was his duty to his mortal parents. But those relationships were meaningless compared to what he shared with the Nephilim. And before he could repair the rift and show Alaric he had nothing to fear, the Council entombed him.

Rage shivers over his body at the thought of his dark prison. If he weren't an angel, he would have gone blind with the lack of light. His enemies should have killed him. Now, they'll pay the price for their cowardice. He'll unite the Darks and the Lights and the Council will burn.

"Did I die?" Alaric's raspy voice scatters his thoughts, and his eyes clash with his former lover's.

Alexander hears the fear in the Nephilim's voice and shakes his head. "No, you didn't. I healed you before it came to that."

Alaric relaxes, his head flopping back against the pillow before he tenses again. "And Luna?"

Anger rises in Alexander, but he banks the fire. Luna is a problem he'll deal with later. "She's safe with her parents, you fool. For now. Do you love her because she reminds you of me when I was but a boy?"

Alaric's brows narrow over thoughtful eyes. "No, I love her for her. Other than being a Gray, you two are nothing alike. Even when you thought you were just a Nephilim, you always knew your place in life. You had security. She never had any of that, not even mortal parents to love her."

Absurdly, Alexander feels wounded by his words, having imagined Alaric took the girl under his wing because she is a Gray. Because she is like him. Because Alaric missed him.

"Although," Alaric says, "you are alike in one way. She, too, hates the divide. She hates anything that will keep her from Caleb. In that way, I suppose she does remind me of you."

Their eyes meet, a flicker of understanding passing between them, trapped words that don't need to be said aloud to be felt. A simmering heat stirs within Alexander, and he sees it reflected in the depths of Alaric's eyes before he turns his head. He's not indifferent then.

"Ah, yes. I would've cut down anyone who kept you from me," Alexander says.

"And you did," Alaric replies, his gaze darting to Alexander's again.

"You don't hold a grudge with me over Michael's death. That much I know."

Alaric shakes his head. "No, but I think I lost a piece of you that day." The sadness in his voice straightens Alexander's spine.

"Bound or free, I have always been what I am. You knew that. It's why you loved me. It's why you *still* love me." He reaches over and places a light hand on the Nephilim's knee, giving him time to pull away if he wishes. But he doesn't.

Alaric is quiet for a while, but Alexander is patient, refusing to move his hand.

"I may love you," Alaric finally says, "but I don't support what you're doing. I can't. I understand your love for mortals more than anyone just as I understand your disdain for angels." He holds up a hand when Alexander starts to protest. "Come, this is me. Part of your desire to rule the angels here on Earth is because of their rejection of you. You despise their superiority and their ridiculous clinging to their antiquated ideas of Dark and Light. You despise your true parents while you worshipped at the altar of your mortal ones. I know you actually *do* want to save the humans from themselves, but it won't end the way you think it will. They won't love you the way you'll want them to. They'll want to be free. It's in their nature."

Alexander's voice is gentle as he strokes his hand up over Alaric's thigh, the hitch in the other man's breath satisfying. "You are wrong, my love. And while you may not support me now, you will. You will stay by my side and see all the great things I'm going to accomplish. Now that I have you again, I won't ever let you go."

Alaric sighs, a resigned sound. "I know."

His melancholy grates on Alexander, and he slides into the bed next to Alaric, cupping his face and kissing him hard. He doesn't stop until Alaric clutches at him, his breathing feverish. When Alexander does draw back, he smiles at the glazed look in his lover's eyes. "As long as we understand each other."

He will rule with Alaric by his side as it was always meant to be.

END OF BOOK TWO

THANK YOU SO MUCH FOR
READING DARKRISE!

For more of the original star-crossed lovers, Lucifer and Gabriel, scan the QR code below and enter your email to receive a bonus scene from this book!

GrayReign

ABOUT THE AUTHORS

M. A. PHIPPS and **REBECCA JAYCOX** met while working together at a small publishing house in the United Kingdom as a cover designer and editor respectively. Having forged a strong friendship, and sharing similar interests, they decided to co-author.

THE ORIGIN PROPHECY is their first series together, but it will not be their last.

Find them online at:

WWW.BOOKISHDEN.COM

www.ingramcontent.com/pod-product-compliance
Lightning Source LLC
Chambersburg PA
CBHW030142200726
48285CB00004BC/1269